Remembering Jamie

Brotherhood of the Black Tartan Book 5

Nichole Van

Fiorenza Publishing

Remembering Jamie © 2021 by Nichole Van Valkenburgh
Cover design © Nichole Van Valkenburgh
Interior design © Nichole Van Valkenburgh

Published by Fiorenza Publishing
Print Edition v1.0

ISBN: 978-1-949863-12-3

Remembering Jamie is a work of fiction. Names, characters, places and incidents are the products of the author's imagination or are used fictitiously. Any resemblance to actual events, locales or persons, living or dead, is entirely coincidental.

All rights reserved. No part of this publication may be reproduced, stored or transmitted in any form or by any means without the prior written permission of the author.

To Ray and Karen,
For showing us all what true enduring love looks like.
The brightness of you both lives on in all of us.

To Dave,
For being my own bright light.

Old Kilmeny Castle
Aberdeenshire, Scotland
May 10, 1822

Miss Eilidh Fyffe was rather a connoisseur of despair.

She instantly recognized the flavor of it—

The dip of dread in her stomach.

The desolation that bleached color from the world.

The hopelessness of staring up from a deep pit, wondering *how* she was going to get herself out of this quandary.

Case in point . . .

Eilidh watched from her bedroom window as Reverend Gillespie and his wife rushed from the castle door to the waiting coach.

The early hour, the trunks strapped to the carriage boot, and the way the reverend kept glancing back at the castle—as if expecting Eilidh to race out and demand answers—had been all the confirmation she needed of their intent.

The Gillespies *meant* to leave her, to abandon her to an uncertain fate.

Eilidh swallowed.

After everything that had transpired. After her own tireless care and dedication.

They would simply . . . walk away.

Or, in this case, ride off in style in a wealthy man's carriage.

Of a certainty, there would be some logical explanation for their hasty departure, something to justify (from Eilidh's point of view) their heartless betrayal of her trust. Briefly, she imagined Reverend Gillespie explaining in his deep baritone.

"Eilidh," he would say on a sigh, his voice dragging her name out—AY-lee, *"it is sorrowful that we must now say farewell, but the Lord has called us to forge onward in our missionary efforts. Remember,* Eilidh *rhymes with* gaily, *Miss Fyffe, and therefore, you will find reasons to be happy, even though we are parting . . ."*

But of course, in reality, the Gillespies had said nothing.

The reverend had never been one for long goodbyes. Even easier to avoid the tears and recriminations altogether and scuttle off at dawn.

Or was it rather that Eilidh herself was not worthy of the courtesy of a goodbye? Reverend Gillespie insisted God had forgiven her sins, but the man sometimes did not behave as if he *himself* did.

Despair tasted acidic and bitter in her throat.

How was she to get home now? Had they even left her funds for the stagecoach?

And how was she to explain the situation to the owner of this castle, whomever he or she might be?

This trip to Scotland with the Gillespies was meant to be a visit to Mrs. Gillespie's elderly cousin, Mrs. Campbell. But was even that truth?

They had arrived the evening before, passing a gleaming modern estate before stopping in front of an ancient castle perched on a cliff high above the North Sea. The sun glittered low on the horizon, but as they were so far north and so close to June, the hour was well past supper.

A kindly housekeeper had shown them to their rooms, explaining that, due to the late hour, Mrs. Campbell would see them in the morning.

It had been odd for the cousin not to greet them personally, but as Eilidh was merely a lady's companion to Mrs. Gillespie, she had said nothing. She had tended to Mrs. Gillespie next door and then retired to her own well-appointed bedchamber.

Eilidh had found the bedroom itself to be encouraging. One could learn much about a hostess based on how she treated those she perceived as beneath them. In this case, the soft down of the bed tick and luxury of the brocade curtains had lifted Eilidh's spirits. Her room was that of an honored guest, not a servant. She had eaten dinner from a tray before a cheery fire and had promptly fallen asleep.

Hours later, she had awakened to the sound of horse tackle outside her narrow window and whispered voices in the hall.

And now, Eilidh leaned forward, nearly pressing her face to the glass. Reverend Gillespie and his wife finished settling themselves into the carriage. A footman shut the door and then climbed up beside the coachman.

Eilidh watched the carriage until it disappeared down the rough lane.

So . . . now what?

She was abandoned.

In a castle.

In northern Scotland.

With no money.

And her supposed friends, some of the few she could claim, had just forsaken her.

A freezing chill—void of warmth and hope—seized her mind.

A blank nothingness.

Instead of shivering it away, Eilidh welcomed the numbness.

It was a long-time companion.

Within the frozen deadness, she did not need to feel the sting of the Gillespie's desertion. She could avoid the acidic taste of despair, and the sinking tide of hopelessness that threatened to drag her out to sea.

Instead, she could logically dissect the situation and make appropriate decisions.

She was rather a professional at starting her life anew, was she not?

Six years. She had served Mrs. Gillespie for *six* years as a lady's companion. They may not have always been kind, but the Gillespies had usually been fair. Why had they not simply informed Eilidh that her services were no longer needed? Why not leave her with Simon in Yorkshire? Why bring her all this way just to sneak off at the break of dawn?

It seemed needlessly cruel.

But then life since her father's death had been peppered with cruelty.

Simon was the only bright spot—a miraculous, solitary touch of grace that God had granted her. She could almost hear his soothing voice in her ear, telling her that she was safe, that all would be well. That if she needed a place to fall, he would catch her.

She simply needed to return to him.

After six years of suffering the repercussions of actions she could not remember, she was ready to move on. To finally progress beyond her guilt and anger and horror. To take Simon's steady hand in hers and race into their bright future together, arms wide.

Eilidh hugged her elbows, the chill in her chest spreading, causing her fingers to tingle and buzz.

She might be experienced when it came to dealing with desertion, but that didn't mean she found the experience pleasant.

Once more, she would cast herself upon the kindness of strangers.

And if they turned out not to be kind . . .

Well . . . that did not bear thinking upon.

AN HOUR LATER, Eilidh had summoned the courage to face her fate.

After all, the occupants of the castle would soon learn—if they did not already know—that the Gillespies had departed. How long would they allow Eilidh to stay?

Perhaps this Mrs. Campbell would be understanding and motherly and even feed her breakfast before casting her out. Most importantly, perhaps the lady would lend her the money to return to Yorkshire and Simon.

Eilidh dressed, proud that her hands only shook slightly. Her wardrobe consisted entirely of Mrs. Gillespie's cast-offs, and so the fabric of her gowns had been turned and re-sewn many times over. The muslin was so worn at the seams, she pulled cautiously as she did her buttons, pleading with the cloth not to tear altogether.

Once safely dressed, she tamed her thick curls into a tight bun at the nape of her neck and wrapped a woolen shawl tight around her shoulders. All in an attempt to prevent the damp of the castle from colliding with the chill lodged in her chest.

She surveyed herself in the small mirror over the fireplace, rising on tiptoe to see her entire face. Wary eyes peered out—more greenish today than gray, thanks to the faded blue-green muslin of her gown.

She looked like the poor companion she was—short, impoverished, and easily overlooked.

"You were born a lady," she told herself. "Do not forget it, no matter the troubles you encounter today."

It was something her mother, the granddaughter of a squire, had always said—*Circumstances do not determine a lady's behavior. Innate character does. Be a lady, even if the way is not easy.*

Eilidh packed the remainder of her meager belongings into her small travel case. If she had to leave quickly, she wished to be ready.

Swallowing, she unlatched her bedroom door and peered out. Her bedchamber was one of two off a small hallway. She walked to the narrow spiral staircase at one end, a window there lighting her way. A glance out of the wavy glass showed only the vast expanse of the North Sea.

Like most Scottish castles, this one appeared to be a rabbit warren of tight passages and even tighter staircases. The bottom of the staircase ended in a hallway, likely the largest in the castle. Even then, it was only wide enough for two people to pass one another. At the far end, she could see another staircase descending—the main steps that led to the front door.

She saw no one. The castle appeared empty.

Surely, that wasn't the case. Someone had to be here.

Clenching her fists into her shawl, she continued forward. A heavy oak door stood open to her right. She glimpsed a high ceiling decorated with filigreed plasterwork.

The great hall, then?

Smells reached her. Bacon. Potato scones. Tea.

The scents of comfort and warmth.

Her stomach growled.

Someone was in residence.

Please, Lord, let me at least have breakfast before being cast out.

She could face just about anything, as long as she had a full stomach.

Taking a deep breath, she walked through the door and into the great hall. A carved wooden screen separated the bulk of the room from prying eyes.

Cautiously, Eilidh peered around the screen.

It felt a bit like that first glimpse of one's cards while playing Brag (Mrs. Gillespie's favorite pastime).

She wasn't sure what she expected to see.

An empty room?

A regal, elderly lady eating breakfast?

Predictable cards, in other words.

But that was *not* what greeted her.

Instead, her eyes met the gaze of a handsome man sitting at a table in the center of the room.

He looked entirely too much like the Knave of Spades.

Eilidh froze, her heart speeding up.

In the game of Brag, the Knave of Spades never boded well.

The rest of the setting came at her in pieces.

An enormous fireplace to the right stretched from floor to ceiling, flames licking upward in the hearth. The large table sat before it, blackened with the heft of hundreds of years of wear.

To the left, a trio of modern, arched windows cut through the thick stone blocks. Swords, claymores, shields, and spears covered the walls, as if the centuries of Scotland's wars with England had disgorged themselves into the room.

The man faced the door, his chair placed between the fireplace and table. His posture was relaxed, one arm resting on the tabletop, his feet stretched out and crossed at the ankle.

She knew this man.

Or, perhaps more accurately, she knew *of* him.

A knowledge that sent her heart thumping and her hands shaking. A tight knot of emotion built in her chest.

Knave of Spades, indeed.

"Ye are finally awake," he smiled, pushing to his feet and greeting her with a short bow. "Please. Have a seat."

He waved a hand toward the chair opposite him on the table.

She finally noted the repast that had been laid there—soft-boiled eggs, thick slices of black pudding, and bacon. A plate of potato scones sat nearby. A teapot steamed beside a dainty teacup and saucer.

More to the point, there were no other people present.

She pulled her shawl tighter, her eyes returning to him.

Though he had stood to greet her, he hadn't introduced himself as propriety would demand. But then, this man had never been much of a gentleman.

"I know you," she said.

"Aye, lass. That ye do." So calm. Confident.

"You are Master Kieran MacTavish."

"Aye." He nodded again. His eyes never left her face. "I am."

"You were my father's—Captain Charles Fyffe's—protégé. He trusted you." She had seen Master MacTavish once or twice from afar, speaking with her father.

"He did."

"My father was a fool to do so." Eilidh breathed in a slow breath. "You showed your true colors in the end."

If her words stung, Master MacTavish didn't show it.

A log settled in the enormous hearth, sending flames up the chimney.

He clasped his hands behind his back, weight shifting to his right leg, all of him appearing at ease. But his pale eyes held a nearly feverish light, drilling into her with unnerving intensity.

Why was *he* here, of all people? What did he want with her?

She had seen him only once—that she remembered—in nearly a decade. Master MacTavish had visited Yorkshire in December last, appearing outside the house Reverend Gillespie had let. They had spoken for only a minute before the roil of anxiety he evoked got the better of her and she had run away.

Master MacTavish had done wrong by her father—a slight Eilidh found hard to forgive.

From what she knew, Kieran MacTavish had been orphaned as a boy. Her father, Captain Charles Fyffe, had taken the child under his wing, hiring him as a cabin boy before Eilidh was out of leading strings.

However, her father had always kept the lad separate from his family, leaving him aboard ship when they returned to Dumbarton. MacTavish was of a lower social class and, to quote her father, 'a wee bit feral.' Not the sort of person her father wanted associating with his gently-born wife and daughter.

And true to his nature, MacTavish had grown up to be a Don Juan like that of Lord Byron's namesake poem.

Whenever her father returned home from a voyage, they all heard tale of Master MacTavish's exploits. Oh, the lad was a hard worker and a sharp seaman and made grand promises to repay Captain Fyffe's kindnesses one day. But MacTavish liked whisky and he liked the lasses. He had run amok through more than one port.

Because of this, Eilidh had never been properly introduced to MacTavish. She only had a handful of memories of seeing him from afar—enough to recognize the man but no more.

That said, she clearly remembered the months leading up to Captain Fyffe's death. The pleading letters her father sent, begging for Master MacTavish's assistance in their hour of need—to fulfill his promise to repay her father's years of care and friendship.

Master MacTavish's silence had been as deafening as it was cruel.

She stared at the man now, so at ease before her.

Her eyes darted to the breakfast laid on the table and then slid back to him.

Loyalty to her father trumped her present need for food and security.

"I do not understand this situation. Why are *you* here?" She scanned the room, ascertaining that they were, indeed, alone. "Are there no others? Where is the Gillespie's cousin?" She looked back at him. "Or is this Mrs. Campbell, like the purpose of my trip here, merely a convenient fiction?"

"There is a Mrs. Campbell, though ye are correct, she is no relation to the Gillespies." His smooth baritone rumbled through the room. "But be comforted. Ye are among friends."

"Friends?" Her tone held a note of scorn. "*You* have not been a friend to myself. More to the point . . . I don't like you." She *had* to say it. To voice the emotions banding her chest.

They felt too huge to be anything other than dislike—fear, anger, remorse, and the strangest urge to . . . to *weep*.

Her throat ached with it.

If she thought he would react to her statement, she was mistaken.

He didn't so much as blink.

He appeared as immovable as the medieval oak table beside him—formidable and rooted in place.

He nodded his head. "I cannae say I return the sentiment."

Eilidh paused, a frown denting her forehead.

What did *that* mean?

"Ye are an honored guest of Violet Campbell, Countess of Kildrum," he continued. "Her ladyship occasionally goes by Mrs. Campbell when circumstances require it."

His accent thrummed with the singsong lilt of the Firth of Clyde, west of Glasgow.

He sounded like home.

She didn't trust it for a second.

"The honored guest of a countess?!" Eilidh huffed a laugh, pulling her shawl tighter. "Now I know you are spouting falsehoods. I've never met this countess."

But she paused at that.

Had she met this countess? Eilidh had been born a lady; her extended family perhaps had such connections. Was meeting this countess one more thing she could not recollect?

"You're correct. Ye havenae met her ladyship. Please. Come." He beckoned with his hand. "Sit. Eat. Ye must be hungry. Allow me tae explain to ye."

Warily, she inched toward the table, her shawl still clasped tightly in her fists, as if the wool could stand as a barrier between them.

He watched her with those intense eyes, waiting for her to sit before retaking his own seat.

Eilidh averted her gaze and studiously piled food on her plate.

She *did* dislike him.

She disliked the handsome angle of his jawline. The leashed power in the breadth of his shoulders. The faint lines beside his eyes, as if he had spent too many years laughing, perhaps some of them at her family's expense.

She disliked that he appeared well-off, dressed in an expensively tailored coat and blue satin waistcoat with silver buttons. Where had that money been when she and her family were in need?

She disliked that after everything she knew—and many things she suspected but did not remember—she felt a tug of attraction toward the man.

That would not do.

She reached again for the blank numbness, sinking deeper into it.

Nothing this man would do or say could hurt her.

She refused to care.

She had Simon and Yorkshire. She had a plan and a future waiting for her.

She simply needed food in her stomach and a way home.

"Actually, I have changed my mind," she said between bites of smoky bacon. "I cannot imagine anything you have to tell me about this castle or its inhabitants applies to myself. The Gillespies have finally washed their hands of me, that much is obvious." Her voice hitched at the sting of that betrayal. *Just ask for money and return to Yorkshire.* "I have no intention of imposing on your hospitality, or this Mrs. Campbell . . . ehr, Lady Kildrum . . . whomever. If you would be willing to lend me enough money for the stagecoach back to Yorkshire, I will be off as soon as I am finished eating. If you give me your direction, I will repay the loan as soon as I am able, upon my honor."

He sighed, clasping his hands on the table.

"Jamie . . ." he began.

Those two syllables slammed into her chest, a battering ram against the numbness that protected her, that held the blind panic at bay.

Her fingers spasmed around her fork.

"Jamie is dead," she managed to whisper past the aching lump in her throat. "My brother is dead."

"Aye, but ye took his place, lass. *You* are Jamie now—"

"No!" She slapped her fork down, her head snapping upright.

"I ken that ye dinnae remember—"

"I am Eilidh." She dragged out her name—*AYYY-leeee*—extending the long-A and landing hard on the long-E and sounding as censorious as Reverend Gillespie in the process. "Miss Eilidh Fyffe. James was my younger brother. He died—" She swallowed, taking in a deep breath, allowing the sludge of feeling to flow in and then out again. "—he died in July of 1815."

"Aye. It's coming up on seven years since your brother's and father's deaths."

"If you know all this, then where were you in 1815 when we sorely needed you?"

Master MacTavish sat back in his chair. "Jamie—"

"*Miss Fyffe,* if you please." The riot of her emotions punched a hole in her numbness, bitter questions tumbling out. "Where were you then? Where were you when Jamie died? And then my father not even a day later?"

He scrubbed a hand over his face, shook his head, and then pinned her again with his pale eyes.

His gaze stirred something in her chest . . . some faint memory.

He had eyes like the horizon on an icy winter's day—the lightest shade of blue—chilly and cold and entirely unnerving.

His knee bounced as he sat in the chair, evidence that he was not perhaps as composed as he appeared.

She looked away, picking her fork up. She had no intention of allowing good food to go to waste. Who knew when her next meal would be?

She certainly would *not* be remaining in this castle with this man.

"I failed ye. I did." He nodded, knee still bouncing. "I didnae know your father was so ill. He didnae confide in me, initially. And then I was out of reach of his letters. I would have been there, had I known. I am here for ye now."

"It does little good, nearly seven years on." Eilidh snorted and then instantly regretted the inelegance of it. She was a lady; she would behave as one. "You promised my father. You promised you would watch after myself and Jamie once he was gone."

"And I did. I did care for ye—"

"How dare you!" Eilidh's temper snapped. Her fork clattered onto her plate. "How dare you say you cared! Jamie died and then my father died and I was left alone. I had nothing! I was all but turned out into the street by my father's creditors. I faced a choice of the workhouse or . . . or *worse*—"

Eilidh broke off, looking away and pinching her lips shut . . . terrified by all she could *not* remember. Fearing that she had actually chosen the 'worse' option. That in her youth and desperation and stupidity, she had compromised every moral, ladylike stricture under which she had been raised.

For not the first time in the past six years, she was glad her family was dead and gone. That her parents would never suffer the shame of her dishonor. That she, herself, did not remember the specifics of it all.

"Aye. You faced terrible choices, lass. Ye did. But what happened next? After your father and Jamie died, when ye faced the prospect of penury, what did ye do?" Master MacTavish's eyes glowed with an intense light. As if her answer were of consummate importance. As if he were eager for her to admit her foolishness.

Eilidh faltered.

She could not answer his question, not truthfully at least. She suspected she knew the answer. Surely, it was embedded deep in the murky recesses of her mind.

But suspecting was not the same as *knowing*.

Worse, Master MacTavish seemed to know exactly what happened to her.

She didn't want to know.

She *never* wanted to know.

The anger and indignation that had fueled her words evaporated, draining off like sea water through a scupper.

Heart-pounding fear and confusion washed in behind.

She wanted safety. She wanted to go home. To hear Simon's soothing baritone reading to her from *The Times* over tea. To walk in the warm light of English sun in a place where dark memories remained buried and gone.

Where she could leave the past . . . truly in the past.

Had she not already suffered enough for her sins? For the reckless behavior that had shattered her life? Why must she revisit it now, seven years on?

Master MacTavish continued to regard her.

"What happened then?" he repeated, softer now, coaxing, encouraging. "What did ye do?"

"Why are you forcing me to say this?" Eilidh resisted the urge to bury her face in her hands. "So you can deride me? Judge my choices once again?"

"I will never judge ye, lass." His tone was low and earnest. "I didnae then, and I willnae start now. I'm here tae help."

Eilidh snorted again. Five minutes in this reprobate's company and her manners were already in shambles.

She said nothing for a long moment. Instead, she dragged the tines of her fork across her plate, studying the zigzagging lines it created.

Finally, she said the only thing she could:

"I don't know what happened after that, not for sure." She lifted her eyes to his. "I don't remember. With very few exceptions, the entire year after my father and Jamie's death is a black void."

2

Kieran stared at Miss Eilidh Fyffe . . . at this beautiful woman who did not remember that she was his wife.

His wife!

Seeing her like this—after assuming her dead for six years—was a hellish sort of pain. His interaction with her in December had been so impossibly brief.

And now . . . after plotting and planning for months to bring her back to him . . . to have her here . . .

He wasn't sure if he wanted to sing hymns of praise or collapse into weeping.

She looked so much the same—pocket-sized with a heart-shaped face, broad forehead, and pointed chin. A smattering of freckles dusted her nose and cheeks. Her eyes were the same soft silvery green-gray, fringed with dark lashes.

And yet . . . she was utterly altered.

She wore a dress rather than trousers, for one thing. Kieran had rarely seen her in a gown, the most memorable occasion being their wedding day. Her dark, unruly hair was long now and severely styled, pulled against her skull with militant ruthlessness.

Even her accent had changed, no longer the cultured Scottish lilt of her upbringing or the guttural brogue she had adopted after her father's death. She sounded more English, traces of Scotland only occasionally rising in her vowels.

Most significantly, there was a wariness to her, a quiet hesitance that had never been there before.

Ah, my love. What horrors have ye suffered?

Part of him had hoped . . .

That if they could only speak to one another, that she would . . .

She would . . . remember him.

How could she have forgotten all that they were to one another? How could that knowledge simply have been . . . erased?

The worst of it?

He would not be telling Miss Eilidh Fyffe she was his wife. At least, not anytime soon.

"Overwhelming her with information will likely do more harm than good," his friend, Dr. Alex Whitaker, Lord Lockheade, had said just yesterday evening. *"Ye mustn't push, Kieran, no matter how much you're tempted. We must simply give her time and provide opportunities for her memory to return naturally."*

Kieran had agreed.

But now, with Jamie before him, achingly beloved and yet hauntingly different, he wasn't sure he could withhold everything in his heart.

It was a hellish sort of pain to pretend not to love her.

As if sensing the weight of his affection, she looked away again, her eyes fixed on her breakfast.

"Allow me to tell you what ye did after your father and James died," Kieran said.

"Master MacTavish, I do not wish to have my youthful stupidity recounted—"

"Nae. Please hear me out. This is helpful, I promise ye."

She relapsed into sullen silence, the stubborn set of her jaw abruptly so familiar that he had to stifle a smile.

Here was the woman he knew—obstinate, fiery, resolute.

She was not entirely gone, his Jamie. Sparkling flashes of her did surface.

He continued on, "Ye buried your father and brother and sold what ye could of your father's effects and paid his debts. But after that, ye were impoverished without a way to provide for yourself. Ye had few choices."

"Women rarely do," she said, brows drawing down. "I remember bits and bobs of this. I certainly remember the grimness of the choices I faced. My memory is not entirely derelict." She all but rolled her eyes.

"Aye." Though if she had forgotten Kieran, then her memory was more damaged than she yet realized. "I had sent a letter to your father a few months before his death, promising that I would give Jamie a position aboard ship. Your brother was handy with a chisel and lathe—or so your father said—so I offered him employment as carpenter's mate aboard *The Minerva,* an apprenticed position where he would learn the trade."

She reached for the teapot and poured herself some more tea. The slight tremor of her hand, however, betrayed her.

Ah, my love.

She was not as unaffected as she appeared.

She didn't raise her head to look at him, preferring instead to appear engrossed in stirring sugar into her tea.

"Knowing this," he continued, "ye took Jamie's letter of commendation, cut your hair, put on your brother's clothing, and came aboard *The Minerva*, no one the wiser. Certainly not myself. I had scarcely seen ye before ye landed aboard ship, so it was weeks before I realized what had happened." He clenched his hand. The shock of *that* discovery still haunted his dreams.

She swallowed and raised her head, looking away from him.

"Do ye remember at least that much?" he asked.

She did not reply.

Silence hung in the air between them.

Kieran waited.

Finally, she brought her eyes back to his.

"I remember . . . very little," she admitted, the words reluctant. "I remember the moment of Jamie's death. The horror of it. And then my father dying the next day. I remember feeling panicked, knowing that I had no living family to turn to for help. I sold the tester bed and my father's worn clothing—anything to bring in a few coins. I remember the despair and terror of having no good choices for my own future. Everything beyond that is mostly blank until . . ."

The silence returned.

Kieran's right leg bounced, the jittery state of his nerves demanding an outlet.

"Until?" he prompted.

She sucked in a slow, deep breath. "Until I awoke in a hut on the island of New Caledonia in the South Pacific. Mrs. Gillespie and the Reverend were at my side. I had received a rather severe head injury. Somehow . . . a whole year had passed that I had very little recollection of. I dimly remembered that I had been aboard a ship called *The Minerva.* I had a memory of Dr. Alex Whitaker, as he was kind to me, along with a vague recollection of native villagers pulling me from the ocean and rowing me on an outrigger. Reverend Gillespie says they brought me to him because I appeared pale, like the European missionaries."

She continued to avoid looking at Kieran, her words wooden, her tone subdued.

Again, words and behavior he would never have associated with his wife.

Jamie was vibrance and color. A flamingo feather on white sand. A crimson hibiscus flower against lush greenery. Not some drab, faded woman in another's cast-offs, frayed and worn.

The thought hurt.

It made him want to snatch one of the claymores from the wall and battle something mythological and dangerous.

But like such monsters, the battle he fought here was intangible.

She needed to remember.

She *had* to remember.

So many questions scalded the back of his throat.

Things she had to know but would not say.

Namely, that Jamie had been *increasing* when last he saw her. What happened to their child? Kieran thought he knew, but he wanted to hear it from Jamie herself.

It was the one question Alex specifically ordered him not to ask.

"No matter what happens, bite your tongue, Kieran," Alex had said. *"Give her time to volunteer the information. Your only goal should be to re-earn her trust."*

So instead, Kieran offered simpler information.

"Allow me to fill in a few gaps for ye, then. Aboard ship, ye formed a friendship with myself and four other men—Andrew, Rafe, Alex, and Ewan"—he named them, ticking off on his fingers—"and we called ourselves the Brotherhood of the Tartan, as we were all Scottish. The Brotherhood was marooned in the New Hebrides; *The Minerva* sailed off without us. Only yourself remained aboard ship from our wee band. It was supposed that *The Minerva* wrecked on a reef soon after. We assumed for years that her entire crew perished, yourself included. But a wee while back, we discovered that Captain Martin Cuthie, and his first mate, Mr. Robert Massey, survived. Significantly, both men claim that an explosion destroyed *The Minerva.* Last autumn, we learned that ye had survived as well, though ye suffered from an alarming loss of memory."

Jamie paused, her jaw tightening. "Yes, I have been told much of this. But as I have no recollection of any of these events, I fail to see why I am here now." She sipped her tea before raising her eyes to his. "What is the point of this, besides poking a stick at the hornet's nest of my memory? Some things are best left alone or one is liable to be stung."

Kieran swallowed back the jolt of anguish her words caused. The point of all this was to remember *him*, to remember their love—

She will need time, Alex's voice rang in Kieran's ears, his doctor's voice calm and steady. *Be patient. Do not press her too hard.*

Easy for Alex to say.

Significantly harder for Kieran to do.

Six years.

Six years of not knowing what had happened to her, believing her dead, trying to convince his heart that she couldn't possibly be alive.

And yet his heart had insisted. Somehow, he had known that she was out there. Waiting to be found.

He wanted her back. He wanted his wife, Jamie, who laughed and cajoled and loved him with bright ferocity.

He wanted to know each thought in her head, the details of every day that had transpired without him at her side.

And he wanted it all now, now, now.

He was so damn tired of waiting.

"Why am I an *honored* guest, as you say, of the Countess of Kildrum?" she asked.

He clasped his hands on the table and forced his restless muscles to relax. "As I said earlier, ye are among friends. Ewan Campbell, who was the artist aboard ship, married the Countess of Kildrum two years ago. Her ladyship has kindly housed ye here in Old Kilmeny Castle. Kilmeny Hall, the grand estate ye passed along the lane to the castle, is her ladyship's abode. The other members of the Brotherhood are here, too, but they are staying in the Hall."

He didn't add that they were all similarly anxious and hopeful, wanting Jamie to remember their shared history and friendship.

She sipped her tea, absorbing this information. "You are *still* dancing around the point, Master MacTavish. I fail to see what all this has to do with me, specifically. You have clearly plotted with the Gillespies to essentially abduct me for no true reason that I can discern—"

"Like myself and the others, the Gillespies *do* care about ye, lass."

"Forgive me for not believing you." Jamie winced and shook her head, that lovely jaw of hers clenching again. "Tell me why I should remain another hour in this place?"

Kieran hated the insecurity rolling off her, the wee tremor in her fingers as she held her teacup.

"Ye are here because questions about *The Minerva*'s true fate continue to be raised," he replied. "A procurator fiscal in Aberdeen—Mr. Patterson—lost a cousin aboard the ship. Given this, Mr. Patterson has convinced the Judge Admiral in Aberdeen to open yet another formal inquiry."

"An inquest?"

"Well, *inquest* is a rather English word for it. Mr. Patterson will conduct what he has been calling a 'fact-finding inquiry' tomorrow at Kilmeny Hall. Your presence, as well as mine, has been commanded."

Her nostrils flared. "Why? I cannot remember anything useful."

"Aye, and the procurator fiscal has been repeatedly told this. Mr. Patterson's reply is, 'I shall be the judge of that.' We were told tae deliver you ourselves, or Mr. Patterson would have ye summoned. As your friends, we decided ye would prefer to travel here in a fine carriage, as opposed to a prison wagon."

"I see." She paused. "But . . . but why involve the Gillespie's in this at all? Why not simply tell me the truth? I would have come."

Kieran stared at her. "Would ye, though?"

A pause.

Finally, she sighed. "Well . . . I would *likely* have come."

"Precisely."

Another pause.

"Was . . . was Gillespie paid off?" she asked, her voice faint.

"In a sense." Though he said the words gently, there was no way to spare her this additional hurt. "A donation was made to his next trip to New Caledonia in the South Pacific."

"How much?"

Silence.

Her eyes narrowed. "How *much*, Master MacTavish?"

He was going to have to tell her. Damn Gillespie and his greedy heart.

He wiped a hand down his face. "Two thousand pounds."

"Two *thousand* pounds?!" She hissed at the sum. "That's . . . that's staggering! Why wasn't *I* offered that money? I would have happily walked here for two thousand pounds!"

"Is that all it would have taken?" Kieran raised an eyebrow. "I shall have tae remember that in the future."

Her eyes narrowed, not appreciating his attempt at humor. "So Gillespie makes off with a King's ransom for luring me to you, while I receive nothing?"

"Oh, I didnae say that." Kieran wanted to list outright everything he would give her—his beating heart, his endless devotion, every last shilling to his name. Instead, he went with, "Mr. Patterson would like tae speak with ye tomorrow—"

"So you've said."

"—and ye must look the part of a proper lady." He turned to consult the long clock standing in the corner. "I do believe Lady Kildrum's fine dressmaker from Aberdeen shall be arriving within the hour to see ye outfitted with a new wardrobe."

Silence.

Jamie blinked, as if struggling to process what he had just said.

"Gillespie gets money. And I receive . . . *dresses*?" She imbued the word with acidic disdain.

"I do believe most women find dresses to be desirable things," he smiled wanly. "I suspect that there will likely be shoes and a bonnet or two thrown in for good measure."

"And if I want money, as well?"

He studied her. Perhaps he had been wrong earlier. Perhaps she did know that he would give her everything.

Every last cent to his name. The very breath in his lungs.

"I will deny ye nothing," he whispered. "Tell me what ye want, and I will see it done."

She didn't hesitate. "I want to go home."

"Home? To Dumbarton?" He named the town near Glasgow where the Fyffe family had lived.

"No. To Yorkshire. *That* is home now."

Kieran forced himself not to react.

Time.

She needed time.

Time to adjust.

Time to trust him again.

Time to remember.

But how was she to do those things if she left him?

"Tomorrow, after this meeting with the procurator fiscal, will you give me the funds to return home?" she asked.

No! was the only answer that rang through his head.

Kieran ran a hand over his face.

"Or do ye think because ye paid Reverend Gillespie two thousand pounds to deliver me here," she continued, the sharp bitterness of her tone cutting him, "that ye are now *owed* something? That because of my behavior aboard *The Minerva*, I am a woman of loose morals who can be purchased?"

Kieran flinched. "I will never take anything from yourself that is not willingly offered."

She snorted, folding her arms. "So you will give me your word that I will be allowed to return home?"

"You're not a prisoner here."

"Without ready funds, I might as well be."

She stared at him with those silvery eyes of hers, cold and flinty.

He rubbed his breastbone, trying to loosen the knot there—the place where, in his memory, she looked at him with adoration or love or frustration or *something* other than brute indifference.

How could he promise to let her go when he had only just secured her presence?

"Let us see what the procurator fiscal has tae say," Kieran finally replied. "I willnae make a promise I cannae keep."

"Cannot?" Her chin notched higher. "Or will not?"

"Please dinnae push me, Jamie."

She recoiled at the name.

"I am Miss Eilidh Fyffe. You would do well to remember that." She pushed back her chair. "Jamie is dead."

Kieran swallowed, unable to form a reply.

Because as she whisked out of the room, he abruptly feared she spoke truth.

August 1815
Nearly seven years earlier

How is the new lad coming along?" Kieran asked Mr. Chen, the ship's carpenter.

"He is a fast learner, that one. Very quick." Mr. Chen smiled, his teeth flashing in his sun-browned skin.

"Good." Kieran looked across the deck to where James Fyffe worked on a replacement block for the mizzen mast. The boy was small for his fifteen years but wiry and capable, easily using a handful of horsetail to smooth splinters out of the wood.

"I thank ye for taking him on as an apprentice," Kieran continued, turning back to Mr. Chen. "I owe the lad's father an enormous debt. This is one small way to repay it."

More to the point, Kieran could think of no one better suited to help Captain Fyffe's son navigate these first months at sea than Mr. Chen.

Kieran might be young in body—only twenty-six the summer past—but he had been at sea for nearly two decades. Sometimes, he forgot how hard adapting to ship life had been. But Mr. Chen had a way of seeing the bigger picture of things.

"I am glad of the help." Chen stretched, arching his back. "Sometimes, I fear I am too old for a life at sea. But how could I give it up?"

Kieran knew Chen's history—their years of serving together had led to more than one lengthy chat. Originally from China, Chen had left Shanghai aboard an English merchant ship nearly thirty years before.

"I prefer to look outward toward the world," he said. *"Not inward like many of my countrymen,"* referring to China's preference to avoid entangling themselves with other nations.

For his part, Kieran appreciated Chen's skill as a carpenter. He brought innovation and a different way of viewing problems.

"When she's not trying to kill us, the sea can be a charming mistress," Kieran chuckled. "I love nothing more than an expanse of ocean before me."

"True. And this voyage promises to be a memorable—"

"Oy! Chen!" Captain Cuthie's voice rang across the deck.

Both Kieran and Chen turned toward the sound.

Cuthie scowled down at them from the forecastle. "I'm not paying ye two to chat like debutantes at their first ball. Save your blethering for the lasses when we dock in Plymouth. Chen, I've a problem up here I need your eyes upon."

Chen looked at Kieran—giving the barest of eyerolls to express his opinion of Cuthie's often heavy-handed leadership—before walking off to speak with the captain.

Just beyond Chen, Mr. Andrew Mackenzie and Lord Rafe Gilbert stepped onto the deck. The two men saluted Kieran and then wandered over to speak with Dr. Alex Whitaker and Mr. Ewan Campbell who were standing near the main mast. The four men were the only non-crew aboard ship—the ones who directed *The Minerva* on her current expedition of biological discovery to the South Pacific.

Mr. Mackenzie, a wealthy man of business and avid naturalist, had financed this voyage with the aid of a group of aristocratic investors.

The other men had come aboard as assistants to him—Lord Rafe, as a fellow biologist and friend; Dr. Alex Whitaker, as a physician to the two men; and Mr. Ewan Campbell, as a talented artist who would draw their finds.

Kieran liked all four men, and intuition told him they would become good friends before their journey ended. They were all Scots, after all. Right now, they laughed at something Mr. Campbell was drawing, the men standing on tiptoe and leaning in, looking far too much like eager children. Kieran grinned along with them. Mr. Campbell was something of a giant, towering over everyone else. The poor man was constantly having to duck and contort himself in order to fit into the cramped quarters aboard ship.

Kieran turned his gaze back to James Fyffe. He had hardly spoken to the lad, even though they were three days out from Aberdeen harbor now. As master of *The Minerva*, Kieran was in charge of the ship's navigation, as well as ensuring she was outfitted and in ship-shape condition at all times. If Captain Cuthie was the ship's father, Master Kieran MacTavish was her mother.

Consequently, Kieran had greeted James when he came aboard, just as he did all new recruits. As ship's master, Kieran didn't wish to be seen as playing favorites. And then, he had been so busy with supply orders and assisting the crew during the first days out of harbor, he hadn't had a moment to properly speak with the lad.

Or rather, whenever Kieran *had* found time to speak with James, the boy was nowhere to be seen. It was almost as if the lad were avoiding him, but that thought was ridiculous. Why would James Fyffe be avoiding him?

Kieran owed the boy a debt of gratitude.

The boy's father, Captain Charles Fyffe, had been a father figure when Kieran had been orphaned at just nine years old. Much of the success of Kieran's career was due to Charles's insights and assistance.

"Here. This is for ye." Charles slipped a handful of banknotes into Kieran's pocket.

"I cannae accept this. You've already done too much—"

"Ye may have a new position aboard that frigate, but ye need to look the part, Kieran. Buy yourself a new coat. Ye can repay me later."

Kieran swallowed. "I can never repay ye, Charles."

"Of course, ye can," Charles chuckled, his light-gray eyes striking against the backdrop of his weathered face. "I'm almost in my dotage, and I've two children at home who may need a helping hand someday." He nodded toward the banknotes. "Consider that insurance, if ye will."

Kieran swallowed and nodded. "I will absolutely honor this debt, my friend. Thank ye."

Kieran shook off the memory.

Across the deck, James struggled to lift a coil of rope out of the way.

Kieran chuckled, his feet already moving to help. The poor lad. He was small and rather underfed. His trousers hung loosely, as if they had once belonged to a larger boy. Or, perhaps, James had recently lost weight.

"Here. Let me help ye, lad." Kieran reached down and lifted the heavy rope out of the way. "This rope is almost as large as yourself."

James lifted his head, a pair of wary, silvery eyes studying Kieran from under a thick mop of blue-black curls. Unusual eyes. The boy definitely had Charles's coloring, though not the former captain's rugged features. The lad was nearly delicate, by comparison.

Granted, it was hard to tell.

James Fyffe was utterly filthy. Grime streaked his face and his hair matted in clumps.

"We need tae get ye a bar of soap, James," Kieran smiled. "Less than a week at sea, and you're already fit for Newgate."

Kieran thought to make the boy laugh.

Instead, James flushed under the dirt. The boy looked away, but not before Kieran noted something hard and angry in the lad's gaze.

"I meant to jest," Kieran continued. "Though at some point, I'm sure the captain may request ye bathe yourself."

James nodded, still looking anywhere but at Kieran, his jaw clenched tightly and lips pressed into a thin line.

An awkward silence fell between them.

"How fares your father?" Kieran attempted to change the topic. "I know the accident that ended his naval career was a sore trial. I regret I haven't seen Charles in what? Three years, at least?"

James stilled and then slowly lifted his gaze. Again, Kieran noted the boy's unusual eyes—not quite gray, but not quite green either. Like the ocean under a cloudy sky.

"My father is dead." James spoke the words flatly. No emotion. But the turmoil in his gaze spoke of grief and anguish.

Kieran gasped, heart lurching in his chest.

"Dead? When? How?" He shook his head. "Why was I not informed—"

"Ye didnae ask now, did ye?" James interrupted, voice hard. His voice had a husky timbre and hummed with the brogue of the Firth of Clyde.

"I apologize, lad. I should have spoken with ye afore now." Kieran shook his head. James did not need his ineffectual apologies. "How did your father . . ." His voice trailed off.

"My father died last month." James blinked quickly and looked away. "He had been ill for quite some time with consumption. The accident sapped his strength and work was difficult for him. Facts ye might have known had ye bothered to write with any frequency. But I guess the *lasses* in Plymouth are more important to ye."

The scathing bitterness in the boy's tone cut deep. Yes, Kieran had once had a bit of a reputation for being wild but that had been years ago. One did not become a ship's master at such a young age without learning to modulate one's appetites.

Regardless, that did not negate the truth in James's words.

Kieran should have, at the very least, written more often. He could have even visited, he supposed. It was just . . .

Charles had always kept his family separate from his crew. After all, Captain Fyffe was of a decidedly higher station in life. It had honestly never occurred to Kieran that he would be received, were he to call upon Charles at home.

And Kieran *had* written when he was in port. When all of Charles's correspondence had finally caught up with him—his friend's pleas to find work for James aboard ship—Kieran had replied instantly with promises to help the lad.

That said, he should have realized that the accident which ended Charles's naval career would have caused a strong reversal of fortune for the family. Obviously in looking at it now, Charles had been too proud to refer to such things, and so Kieran had assumed all was well. That despite his accident, Charles as a gentleman had other sources of income.

But Kieran should have been wise enough to read what was *not* said. That Charles required assistance and financial support, along with a position for James.

Instead, Kieran had done . . . nothing.

James had every right to be bitterly angry with him.

Silence.

The ship rocked. Sails snapped. Someone called from high up the rigging.

"I'm so sorry, lad." Kieran swallowed. "You're right. I should have written more often. I should have visited."

"Then why didn't ye?" the lad bristled. "Why can I trust your words now?"

"'Tis a valid question," Kieran sighed and gave the boy the truth. "I took so long tae reply to Charles's letters because these past few years I have been sailing the South Pacific. My first employ as ship's master was on a merchant vessel bound from Sydney. Even the Royal Mail doesnae reach that far, I'm afraid. I wrote as soon as I could."

James snorted, but a wee frown dented his dirty brow, as if Kieran's words were not what he expected.

"I did wrong by your father, and yourself, by extension," Kieran continued. "Captain Fyffe was the best of men. I'm right gutted tae hear that he is gone."

"Me, too."

More silence.

"How can I help ye? Dinnae ye have an older sister at home?"

James flinched. "Eilidh? Eilidh is . . . no longer with us."

Kieran passed a hand over his face. His sister had died, too, then? How much suffering could this poor lad endure?

No wonder his clothing hung on him. The boy had likely lost weight in his grief. More to the point, James was an orphan now. Just as Kieran had been when Charles hired him.

Looking at the lad was like peering into his own past.

"Is there nothing I can do for ye?" Kieran asked again.

A long silence. James stared at the rope in his hands.

Finally, he raised those striking eyes back to Kieran.

"Ye can call me Jamie, if ye like. It's what my father and sister called me." The boy paused. "And I like the idea of keeping that wee bit . . . alive."

Kieran nodded, his throat tight. "Welcome aboard then, Jamie. I'm pleased tae know ye."

How did it go then?" Dr. Alex Whitaker, Lord Lockheade, asked. "Meeting with Jamie?"

"Not great." Kieran grimaced and picked up a rock, tossing it over the cliff's edge, watching it arc down to the sea below.

"How was it *not great*?" Andrew Langston, Lord Hadley, snorted. "Jamie is here, is she not?"

Kieran, Andrew, and Alex were walking the path that snaked along the cliffs beside Kilmeny Castle, discussing Kieran's conversation with his wife that morning.

Though it was May and the summery daylight felt never-ending, the wind was cool off the North Sea. It tugged at the stoic gorse clumped along the cliff face, ruffling the yellow flowers. Kieran's greatcoat billowed behind him, a sail catching a northerly wind.

He shook his head. "My wife's body is here, but in a sense, Jamie herself is not. Miss Eilidh Fyffe is an older version of the girl she was before *The Minerva*. A woman who never experienced the epiphanies that Jamie did aboard ship. More to the point, she dislikes me." Kieran swallowed back the sting of Jamie's words from earlier in the day—*I don't like you.* "I'm right back at the beginning with her."

"Have patience," Alex said. "She has had a tremendous shock with the Gillespie's leaving her as they did. It was cowardly of them."

Kieran didn't disagree.

He had little respect for Reverend Gillespie and his wife. The reverend had held Jamie hostage from them for months, refusing to allow the Brotherhood any contact with her and refusing to answer Kieran's questions about what had happened to Jamie's child. Gillespie implied that the child was no more but insisted Kieran would have to have the tale from Jamie herself.

Fortunately, the demands of the procurator fiscal had finally forced Gillespie's hand, compelling the man to negotiate a solution with the Brotherhood. The reverend had transported Jamie to Kilmeny under the guise of visiting an elderly relative. Kieran had been appalled when the Gillespies had immediately returned home the next morning, not even having the courtesy to bid Jamie goodbye.

His wife deserved better than to be treated like an abandoned pup.

The three men walked in silence for a bit. The sweet scent of the blooming gorse threaded in and out as the wind swirled up the ocean cliffs.

Sea birds skimmed the sea. Their calls echoed along the cliffs, winging over the lull of the waves and the never-ending rustle of wind.

Kieran supposed if any sound could define Scotland, it would be that of wind.

Endless. Constant. Blustery. Wind.

"My emotions are all *doilt* and confused," Kieran finally said. "I'm so happy to have my Jamie here. To know that she is safe and well-cared for. But at the same time . . ."

"I warned ye it would be hard." Alex paused to peer down the side of the cliff. He looked back at Kieran. "Ye will want to push, to have answers as quickly as possible, to reclaim the relationship ye once had. But ye must go slow with her. In this, the tortoise will win more handily than the hare. Jamie's memory loss is a delicate thing, as I cannae say what precisely has caused it. She experienced a significant head injury, and it could be that her memories are truly gone. Or it could be that her memory loss is more akin to what the French would call *le vent du boulet*—"

"The wind of a cannonball?" Andrew translated, pulling off his hat and running a hand through his light brown hair.

"Aye. It is used to describe the mania that grips some soldiers when they return to normal life after the horrors of war—melancholia, an aversion to loud noises, difficulty sleeping, hallucinations, or even complete memory loss of events. I often think that the conflict with Napoleon continues on in the minds of soldiers who have returned. Though our Jamie was not a soldier, she could have suffered something similar—trauma that caused memory loss. I think the reaction is the brain's way of protecting someone from the horror of difficult memories. Unfortunately, only time and patience will reveal the sort of memory loss she has experienced. I have heard anecdotal evidence from other physicians that a caring environment, patience, and time can help a patient feel ready to face harrowing memories."

The thought haunted Kieran. That they still didn't know what had happened to Jamie after she was separated from them.

Their expedition had reached Vanuatu in the New Hebrides without incident. But then Cuthie had betrayed the trust placed in him and marooned the Brotherhood on the island, sailing off in *The Minerva* with Jamie still aboard. A Portuguese whaling ship had found the Brotherhood a month later. The whaler reported sailing through the wreckage of *The Minerva*. All hands on board were assumed lost.

When the Brotherhood finally made it back to London a year later, they had reported all this in a formal inquiry to the Admiralty. The sinking of *The Minerva* was ruled a tragic accident. Everyone assumed the case was closed.

But then Captain Cuthie and his first mate, Robert Massey, had surfaced two years ago. Another inquiry had been conducted, informal this time. Nothing had come of it.

But then, when Jamie herself had appeared the previous winter, many had voiced grave doubts as to what specifically had happened aboard *The Minerva*.

All of which explained why the procurator fiscal and Judge Admiral wished to pose more questions about the ship's sinking.

"How can I best help her?" Kieran asked. "Aside from being patient, of course."

"I've worked with a few ex-soldiers who struggled with this sort of thing," Alex said. "Talking through the events seemed to ease many of the symptoms."

"But, as ye say, it may be that my wife doesnae remember the events because they were so traumatic."

"That does seem to be a wee bit of a Catherine Wheel," Andrew offered, setting his hat more firmly atop his head. "Jamie suffered a trauma that caused her to lose her memory, but in order to restore her memory, she needs to relive the trauma."

Alex nodded, expression grim. "It might help if she engaged in activities that were common aboard the ship. The familiarity of them might shake memories loose."

"The question remains, of course, if the procurator fiscal will be understanding of her injuries when we meet tomorrow?" Kieran clasped his hands behind his back, forcing himself to breathe through the worry and anxiety banding his chest.

"Aye," Andrew nodded. "Alex and I have used what influence we have to keep this matter quiet. But if legal accusations are made . . ."

Kieran swallowed.

Mutiny.

Andrew didn't say it. But it hung there, looming between them.

Kieran's behavior during those last couple hours before *The Minerva* marooned them on Vanuatu could be viewed as mutinous. If Cuthie pressed the matter, Kieran could find himself swinging from the end of a rope fairly quickly. That was always his fear, was it not? That one of these inquiries would lead to formal charges of some sort.

"Stop worrying about it," Alex muttered at his side. "It will do no good. Worry is simply borrowing tomorrow's trouble and stealing today's joy."

"Yes. But if charges are leveled against me, my time with Jamie may be cut short," Kieran said. "If she knew we were handfasted, maybe she would be less skittish and more willing to accept me."

"I disagree," Alex shook his head. "I think knowing you two were handfasted would cause her alarm and anxiety, causing her to retreat. It's been over six years since ye last saw her, Kieran. Much has changed for both of ye. You need to relearn one another. Woo your wife again."

"I like that idea," Andrew said. "I wouldn't mind wooing my Jane one more time. Lot of fun tae be had in wooing. Do ye need some suggestions?" He said the words conversationally, but there was a teasing gleam in his gaze. "Friendly advice?"

Kieran rolled his eyes. "I think I can manage the wooing on my own, thank ye."

"Are ye sure?" Andrew smoothed a hand down his waistcoat. "I'm happy tae lend ye snippets of my vast knowledge on the subject."

"I dinnae need your sorry advice, Andrew," Kieran snorted. "It's a wonder Jane tolerates your ugly mug."

"I think the same thing every day," Andrew agreed cheerfully. "I'm a fortunate man."

"Besides, the true fun begins *after* a successful wooing," Kieran continued.

"True that. But perhaps you'll see success in short order. Jane says a new wardrobe always cheers up a lass," Andrew chuckled, "so mayhap Jamie will be more amenable."

"One can hope." Kieran nodded. "She is with the dressmaker now in the great hall. They all but shooed me out the door."

The friends walked on for a few moments, the endless breeze rippling the sea grass lining the tops of the cliffs. A pair of gulls raced by, their calls soaring over the wind.

Kieran paused and surveyed the ocean undulating before them.

Alex nudged his arm. "Let Jamie ease into being here, and don't worry about the future. For now, we will simply celebrate the fact that she has returned tae us."

"Aye," Andrew agreed heartily, stopping on Kieran's other side. "There is much good tae anticipate. Ewan and Violet are expecting their first babe within the next few weeks, or so Alex tells us."

Alex nodded. "Mother and baby are doing well. The bairn could come at any time. I've spoken with the midwife who will be attending the birth, and she seems a most competent woman. Violet will be in good hands."

Kieran smiled. It was Violet's impending labor that caused them to choose Kilmeny Hall and its neighboring castle as the place to bring Jamie. Ewan, understandably, refused to travel with his wife so close to giving birth. The Brotherhood had come to him instead. Rafe, the final missing member, would arrive later tonight.

"And even though the birth is near," Alex said, "Violet is still set on hosting the countess's annual midsummer festival on the night of the summer solstice. Her twin sisters—Lady Aster and Lady Rose—are visiting friends but should return soon, so at least Violet will have help with the planning of it."

Kieran motioned for them all to continue walking. He clasped his hands behind his back.

"Along with that—" Andrew turned to Kieran. "—is now a good time tae ask if you've made a decision about my offer?"

"Offer?" Alex asked, looking at them both with a question in his eyes.

"Andrew is trying tae pilfer my good looks and endless charisma for his own gain," Kieran deadpanned.

"When ye have so much tae offer, Kieran, ye need tae share the wealth." Andrew leaned toward Alex. "Actually, I've taken pity on his ugly face and asked him to join me in business. I've bought too many ships, and I find myself in need of someone to either captain one or manage the fleet. Kieran won't make up his mind as tae which he prefers."

"I dinnae like being beholden tae ye, Andrew," Kieran said.

"Nae, you're flirting with me and dashing my hopes. Make up your mind and be done with it, aye."

"As I keep saying, I'll make no decision until Jamie is in a place tae help me make it."

Andrew heaved a mock sigh. "Well, knowing Jamie as I do, I can say that is a wise choice."

Kieran smiled and then paused, looking back at Kilmeny Castle. The building was a typical Scottish fortress—a five-story tower house with a small forecourt before the front door. No ramparts. No gatehouse. No fenestrations or moat. Not even a grand entrance. Just pure practicality.

But it was this practicality that withstood the passage of time. The simple solidity of the castle walls allowed them to outlast the battering of the ocean winds and the endless ebb and flow of the tides below the cliff.

His love for Jamie felt like this—strong, steadfast, enduring.

He would be her bulwark.

The mooring that held her fast and safe until she was ready to face the storm.

EILIDH WATCHED THE three men walk back toward the castle, her forehead pressed against the glass in the stairwell. The wind whipped their greatcoats behind them and tugged at their hats.

Master MacTavish was easy enough to distinguish, with his loose-limbed walk and innate grace.

The tall, sandy-haired gentleman beside him merely looked . . . striking and imposing. She did not know him.

But the third man—dark-haired and smartly dressed—was definitely familiar. Was he Dr. Alex Whitaker?

She had very few snippets of memory from her trip to the South Pacific. But one of the clearest was a conversation with the doctor.

"How is your hand?" Alex asked, smiling as he crouched down beside where she worked on deck.

She looked down at the bandage wrapped around her palm. "It's healing."

"Good. I'm glad of it. Keep it clean."

Eilidh looked down at her hand now, running her thumb over the thin white scar across her left palm.

How she had been injured, she couldn't say. All she had was that brief snippet of conversation.

She looked back to the men. Were they part of this 'Brotherhood' Master MacTavish had mentioned earlier?

MacTavish chuckled at something the sandy-haired man said, pointing a finger at him. If she opened the window, would she hear his laughter on the wind—

Eilidh abruptly turned away from the window, retreating the few steps to her bedchamber before her eyes could do something foolish . . . like linger on Master MacTavish.

She did not trust the man.

He had always been too attractive for his own good. A bit of a lothario, her father had always said. A little too ready to act on the appreciative looks women sent his way.

Consequently, she would be avoiding Master MacTavish as much as possible.

Fortunately, her bedchamber was a lovely retreat. Eilidh sat in one of the wingback chairs before the fireplace.

The dressmaker and her assistants had left an hour past.

She likely should have refused the gift of clothing, but poverty had a way of squeezing the pride out of a person. The clothing was worth a small fortune if sold, and she was in desperate need of funds. Master MacTavish *did* owe her family a debt. Her father, had he lived, would be glad to see it paid.

And because of that, Eilidh had not been shy when ordering. If Master MacTavish had the funds to donate a small fortune for Reverend Gillespie's return trip to the New Hebrides, he could certainly afford extra coin for her wardrobe.

And what a wardrobe it was. Three day dresses. A walking dress. A pelisse. A spencer. She even had an evening gown in the loveliest shade of purple—a *silk* evening gown. All with matching bonnets and gloves and shoes and a gloriously soft Paisley shawl of Kashmir wool.

A cream muslin dress and the pelisse would be ready for tomorrow.

What would Simon make of it when she returned to him? Would he mourn the fact that his straitened finances would have struggled to afford her such luxury? Or would he rejoice in their good fortune, as now his income did not *need* to accommodate a new wardrobe for her?

Briefly, she contemplated writing him, requesting his aid in returning home. Simon would come to her immediately. She knew this.

But she would be leaving the day after tomorrow, as soon as this business with the procurator fiscal was done. She would likely arrive before any letter reached Simon. Therefore, writing him was a moot point.

Nothing would induce her to remain here. To pick at the black scar of that missing year.

She stared into the flames flickering in the hearth.

Memory was a funny thing . . . what she did and did not remember.

She remembered her life before *The Minerva* with vivid clarity—her parents, her brother. She could easily recall their fine house, perched on a rise of land outside of Dumbarton along the Firth of Clyde. From the sitting room window, they had a view of the vast inlet with Dumbarton Castle nestled atop a mount jutting out of the water.

She and her mother would sit for days at that window—her mother embroidering while Eilidh read aloud. Every few minutes, one of them would lift her head to study the expanse of the firth, watching ships come and go, praying for Captain Fyffe's safe return.

And her father always returned unharmed, with tales of exotic lands and gifts for herself and James.

That was . . . until the fateful day when Eilidh was fifteen. On *that* day, her father's crew had carried him home on a litter. A falling mast had clipped his right side, shattering the bones in his arm and badly damaging his leg. The arm had survived, but her father had lost the use of it, and his leg healed poorly, requiring him to use a cane for the rest of his life.

Naturally, her father had been forced to retire, greatly diminishing their income. They sold their lovely house and moved to meaner quarters close to the wharf.

Eilidh's mother descended into melancholy over the change in their circumstances. She had passed away not even a year later.

Eilidh swallowed and turned away from the fire. She slid her feet from their slippers and tucked them underneath her. The sun dipped toward the horizon, sending long streaks of color across her bedchamber.

Why were these the things she could remember? The punishing blows that battered the Fyffe family?

Every last heartache crystalline in her memory.

After her mother's passing, her father developed clear signs of consumption. Eilidh took in sewing to provide extra coin. James worked odd jobs for a local stable. And for a while, it had been enough.

Her father had worried about their future—Eilidh's and Jamie's. She wrote out the letters he dictated from his sick bed, begging Master MacTavish to take on James. She had poured her own heart into her father's words, praying between sentences that MacTavish would honor her father's kindness. That he would agree to be a guide to James as Charles had been to Kieran.

It had taken seven letters and nearly two *years* for Master MacTavish to respond. With each missive sent and silence received, Eilidh had seethed in frustration. And when he finally *did* reply, it was with vague excuses about being waylaid in Sydney or some such. Eilidh had doubted the truth of it.

The Royal Mail reached Sydney.

Master MacTavish had simply not cared enough to address their needs.

Regardless, his letter promised Jamie a place aboard a ship named *The Minerva.* Her brother simply needed to present himself and the letter on the date and at the place stated, and a position would be given him.

Her father died, believing that Jamie—and by extension, Eilidh—would be cared for.

But unbeknownst to him, Jamie had died the day before, taken down by the same disease, consumption eating him from the inside out. Her father had been too comatose and senseless to realize it, and she had not wanted to burden his final hours with the grief of Jamie's death and terror for her future.

Eilidh curled her knees up to her chest and turned sideways in the chair, pushing back thoughts of Jamie's brutal final hours, of her father's slow slide into oblivion. Of the death knell of coughing, coughing, coughing echoing through the damp cold of their house. Of the clawing desperation of those final weeks . . .

Emotions clutched at her. Fear. Frustration. *Panicpanicpanic*—

She breathed in slowly, reaching for the numbing calm.

It rose up easily, an old friend, offering comfort.

She sat still for a long moment, allowing the numbness to fully engulf her.

This was the problem with her memories. They were a never-ending quagmire, lurking, patiently waiting for the right moment to pounce and pull her under.

How could she remember in frightening detail the horror of James's death when her life after devolved into only a few vague snippets of scenes?

She remembered the morning after her father's death, the terror of being so very alone in the world. No money and no respectable options.

She remembered contemplating MacTavish's letter, promising employment for Jamie—did she have the courage to take her brother's place? Poverty and desperation made one consider things previously thought impossible.

And then . . .

The sway of a hammock rocking her to sleep.

Dr. Whitaker binding her wound.

A crew member climbing the mizzenmast.

A flock of white cockatoos soaring overhead.

Hands pulling her out of the ocean, her head a blinding pulse of pain.

And then . . . waking up in the Gillespie's hut on the island of New Caledonia, so disoriented, so confused as to how she had gone from Scotland to the South Pacific in the seeming blink of an eye. An entire year lost.

The unknown horror of what she had done caused terrifying fits of panic—her hands would shake and her lungs would tighten until she feared the tremors would stop her heart.

Even now, she shrank from the memories of those first awful months with the Gillespies, the bleak darkness of that time, the empty hollow within her belly, the agony of her shame. The endless recriminations: How could she have behaved in such a fashion? How could she have tumbled so far as to find herself shipwrecked and *enceinte* on the other side of the world?

She *never* wanted to remember why she had assumed Jamie's persona. To recall in excruciating detail why she had forsaken morality—the most precious gifts of character and gentility her mother had instilled in her—only to wake up face-down in an ocean half a world away.

Retreating into numbness had been the only possible solution. The fear of her uncharted memories was too much to bear.

It was better to feel nothing at all.

Therefore, she had spent the intervening years studiously avoiding thinking about her time aboard *The Minerva.* Eilidh had waited upon Mrs. Gillespie, reading aloud as the older woman knitted stockings for the poor souls in the local workhouse. She had thrown herself into Reverend Gillespie's charitable endeavors. All the while, hoping her good works might cleanse the stains on her own soul.

"Your past decisions cannot be changed, Miss Fyffe," the reverend often said. *"But such erroneous choices need not be carried into the future. Pledge now to do better. To be better."*

Eilidh had nodded and agreed with all her heart. Her past did not need to dictate her future, no matter how much pain lurked in her chest.

She was ready for a new life—to shed the last vestiges of her former self and reclaim her reputation as a lady.

A bright future had finally—*finally!*—arrived. One where she would thread her hand through Simon's elbow and smile as he chatted with Mrs. Brown about her spaniel's stomach ailments or discussed a mathematical puzzle in *The Gentleman's Diary* with Mr. Potter. A simple, calm place where the dark tidal wave of her lost year could not reach.

Therefore, she would swallow back her anxiety, give whatever information she could to the procurator fiscal tomorrow, collect the rest of her new lavish wardrobe, and then be on her way . . .

. . . leaving Master Kieran MacTavish and everything else to do with *The Minerva* as nothing more than a shadow disintegrating in the blinding light of her vibrant future.

SEPTEMBER 1815

"You were wise to bring aboard such excellent whisky, my friend." Rafe tilted his glass toward Andrew.

"Aye." Andrew leaned back in his chair. "Nothing tastes like home quite as much as whisky—"

"Haggis," Alex interrupted. "Haggis tastes like home, too." All eyes turned to him. Alex shrugged. "I dinnae drink alcohol, so it had tae be said."

Kieran reached for his own glass, pouring another finger of the fine Scottish whisky Andrew had supplied.

"Well, we dinnae have haggis at the moment," he said, "so whisky will have tae do."

They were all seated around a table in Andrew's quarters. The cabin had become a gathering place for them all—Kieran, Andrew, Rafe, Alex, and Ewan. A space where they could all be their most Scottish selves.

As a part-owner of *The Minerva* and the gentleman financing their excursion, Andrew had been given the largest guest cabin, the one big enough for a bed, a desk, and even a wee dining table. Though tonight, poor Ewan was perched on the foot of Andrew's berth. The artist had sat too forcefully in his chair the night before and snapped a weakened leg right off. Ewan had sheepishly taken the chair to Mr. Chen for repair, blushing as he explained what had happened.

Kieran sipped at his whisky, humming appreciatively. "It will be a long time afore we see bonnie Scotland again, gentlemen. Enjoy the whisky while we have it, I say."

The remains of their dinner lay scattered atop the table—a bowl of mushy peas, the crumbs of freshly baked bread, a slab of creamy manchego cheese, the cleaned bones of a roasted chicken, and even a thick slice of boiled plum pudding gleaming with currants and plums.

As the paying, high-station passengers, Andrew and his friends dined on significantly better fare than the hardtack and salted beef provided to the rest of the crew. Though Kieran had not known the other men before this voyage, as a senior crew member, he was entreated to join them.

No one enjoyed the promise of a good meal as much as a sailor. Kieran knew this and, as ship's master, ensured the provisions aboard ship were of the highest standard. An entire menagerie of animals was lodged on the lower deck—chickens, pigs, goats, and even two cows. The animals would provide fresh milk and eggs, slowly being slaughtered for meat as their journey progressed.

"So you're in charge of the ship's navigation, not Captain Cuthie, correct?" Alex looked at Kieran and braced his elbows on the table, using a last piece of bread to mop up some peas.

"Aye. I'm the one who charts our course and makes recommendations—"

"Och, you're being a mite humble," Andrew snorted. He leaned toward Alex. "I made sure that Cuthie hired Kieran here. Every sailor in Aberdeen told me the same thing: *Hire Master MacTavish. He's the sharpest navigator in the merchant fleet.* Ye don't make recommendations, Kieran. Ye give orders and even the captain follows them."

Kieran felt his cheeks warm. Damn, he hated blushing.

"Is that so?" Alex grinned, looking at Kieran.

"I've sailed around Australia before," Kieran nodded. "It was terrifying, most of the time. But that terror compelled me to study the Southern Pacific waters thoroughly and chart a safer course. So, yes, Cuthie does listen when I speak."

"Well, I'm glad the man pays attention tae something other than his own ego." Rafe shook his head. "I cannot say I approve of our captain's leadership style."

Ewan snatched a slice of plum pudding, his long arms easily reaching the table from his seat on Andrew's bed. Kieran had realized over the past few weeks that Ewan never really stopped eating. His large body required incredible amounts of fuel.

"If you're charting our path," Ewan said around a bite of pudding, "what will our course be between now and when we reach Australia?"

"Aye," Andrew grinned. "Dazzle us with your navigatorly knowledge."

Kieran shook his head at Andrew's good-natured teasing. He picked up the cheese knife.

"Well, as youse all know, we just resupplied in the Azores." Kieran pointed to the salt cellar as if it were the islands. "We're now entering the longest stretch of the trip without land as we go through the Doldrums that straddle the equator. Hopefully, the winds will stay with us, and we willnae end up becalmed." He dragged the knife across the table, moving right to left, ending by pointing at the platter with the picked-clean chicken. "Once through the Doldrums, we'll resupply in Rio de Janeiro in Brazil and exchange our cargo. From there,"—he drew the knife back to the right—"we'll head southeast to Tristan da Cunha—"

"I find it fascinating that we go to South America before heading east again toward Africa," Alex said.

"Very navigatorly," Rafe agreed with a wink.

Kieran shook his head and huffed a laugh. "I ken it makes no sense, but it's the fastest route given ocean currents and trade winds. Now . . . where was I?"

"Tristan da Cunha," Alex prompted, pointing at the bread bowl.

"Isn't that where the government decided to exile Napoleon Bonaparte, in the end?" Rafe asked, brushing bread crumbs off his fingers.

"Nae, that's on Saint Helena. Stop trying tae distract my navigating." Kieran waved the knife at them. The men laughed. "After Tristan da Cunha, we'll enter into the Roaring Forties." He drew the knife toward himself. "That's the latitude where the ocean current moves swiftly toward the east. That will have us arriving in Sydney hopefully a week or so before Christmas." He drew a line toward the cheese board at his right and then tossed the knife onto it.

"And that's all before our expedition really begins." Andrew snatched up the discarded knife and cut a slice of manchego cheese before reaching for more bread. "We won't start our naturalist explorations in truth until we arrive in the New Hebrides."

"Aye," Kieran nodded. "If all goes well, we should arrive there by February."

Ewan shifted on the bed, tucking his long legs to one side. "That's a long time living in one another's pockets."

"Already *peely-wally* at having to look at Kieran's face, are ye?" Andrew quipped, winking.

Kieran laughed, downing the remainder of his whisky.

"Nae!" A blush climbed Ewan's cheeks. With his red hair and fair complexion, the artist's emotions tended to leak onto his skin. "I was more thinking youse lot would be tired of my muckle self." He lifted one hand, palm out and as large as a dinner plate.

"Ewan, ye are the gentlest man I've ever met." Rafe shook his head. "I don't think it possible to tire of your company."

Ewan's blush deepened. He ducked his head and went back to eating his pudding.

"Besides," Alex chimed in, "as a medical professional, I consider emotional bonds tae be a sort of preventative medicine. Those who feel part of a larger group often weather the storms of life more readily. Therefore, as Scotsmen, it would be beneficial for us all tae become close friends." He grinned. "Doctor's orders, if ye will."

"Well, there ye are." Rafe waved a hand toward Alex. "We have to remain friends—a Brotherhood of Scots. It's a medical necessity."

Andrew belched and reached for the whisky bottle. "Are we naming ourselves then? Forming a proper fraternity? Like Robin Hood and his Merry Men?"

"Aye." Rafe raised his glass.

"I would be for it," Alex agreed.

Ewan nodded, cheeks still painfully red.

All eyes turned toward Kieran.

"What does your navigatorly instinct say, Kieran?" Andrew asked.

Kieran stroked his chin, as if thinking.

But he had already landed on the perfect idea—

"The Brotherhood of the Tartan," he said, breaking into a grin. "That should be our name."

"I like it." Andrew raised his glass.

"Aye," Alex said. "And we pledge tae always stand with one another."

"And tae remain true friends throughout this voyage and beyond," Ewan added.

"Hear, hear!" Rafe smiled. "Now what will our first order—"

A knock sounded at the door.

Raising his eyebrows, Kieran leaned back in his chair and opened the door. Andrew may have the largest cabin, but that didn't mean it was, well . . . large.

Jamie Fyffe stood in the doorway, Ewan's repaired chair in his hand. He looked at the assembled men with wide eyes.

"Mr. Chen asked me tae deliver this to youse." He hefted the chair with one hand.

"Thank ye, Jamie." Andrew motioned for the lad to come in. "That's right kind of ye."

"Did ye repair it yourself?" Ewan asked, taking the chair from Jamie.

The boy nodded, dragging the dirty cuff of his coat across his equally filthy nose. Every third day or so, Jamie would splash some water on his cheeks and call himself clean, but the lad was generally appallingly dirty.

Kieran sighed. He remembered being a youth and hating to wash himself. Jamie just needed to be taken in hand. To be tutored as Charles

Fyffe had educated Kieran—a kindness that Kieran had failed to repay to Charles himself.

Guilt was a terrible bed-fellow, Kieran had decided.

But as Kieran watched the members of the newly formed Brotherhood of the Tartan ask questions of Jamie and admire the clever repair of the chair, an idea flashed through his mind.

"Jamie," Kieran said, "ye hail from Dumbarton, do ye not?"

"Aye," Jamie nodded.

"Ye seem a right proper Scotsman."

Jamie raised a dirty eyebrow, motioning a hand down his small person. "Well, I'm no' quite a Scots*man*, am I now."

That elicited a chuckle from the gentlemen.

"Right ye are," Kieran grinned. "But someday, sooner than ye ken, you'll grow tae be a *braw* man."

"And still a Scot," Rafe said.

Jamie shrugged, looking away.

Andrew smiled, looking pointedly from Jamie to Kieran. "I ken where you're going with this, Kieran. I approve."

"Aye," Alex nodded, waving a hand toward Kieran. "Carry on."

A quick glance at Rafe and Ewan showed their agreement.

Kieran turned back to Jamie.

"Are youse all having a laugh at my expense?" Jamie frowned, not missing their conspiratorial glances.

"Hah! I condone that show of Scottish cheekiness, Jamie," Kieran grinned. "We've just decided tae form ourselves into a Scottish club of sorts—the Brotherhood of the Tartan. But it turns out, we need a sixth member of our band—" This, of course, was an absolute lie. "Mr. James Fyffe, would ye like tae join our brotherhood?"

Jamie froze, looking back and forth between them all, eyes flaring wide.

"Me?" he squeaked, pointing at his chest. "Why me?"

"Why?" Ewan smiled. "Because like all of us, ye find yourself far from home."

"Aye," Andrew agreed, "and standing together makes the distance feel more bearable. Will ye join us, lad?"

Emotion banded Kieran's chest.

It was hard to determine the feeling precisely . . . some mix of pride, regret, and grief over the loss of Charles Fyffe.

A desire to offer Jamie the help and support that the lad's father had given Kieran.

A sense of hope that Kieran could atone for his sins where the Fyffe family was concerned.

"Are youse sure?" Jamie continued to stare, studying them each in turn. "Ye aren't bamming me?"

"We are in absolute earnest," Alex said.

"Aye," Kieran agreed.

Jamie turned and met his gaze.

"Then . . . aye," the lad nodded. "I would be honored tae be the sixth member of the Brotherhood of the Tartan."

6

Nervous?" Master MacTavish asked, his voice echoing in the entryway hall.

"Of course. How could I not be?" Eilidh replied, smoothing her gloved hands down the fine-spun wool of her new pelisse.

She had no regrets about its expense.

The garment was luxurious—a sky blue with smart golden military-style braiding across the bodice. It was the most fashionable thing Eilidh had ever owned, even in the days before her father's injury and the fall of their fortunes. The matching buttery-soft gloves were a cloud on her hands.

After living so many years on Mrs. Gillespie's leftovers, it was fortifying to feel like a true and proper lady again.

And given the anxiety that battered her numbness, she needed all the bolstering she could manage today.

Why she felt such anxiety was harder to pinpoint. Was it the looming questions from the procurator fiscal? Or, perhaps, the knowledge that she would soon meet men she had supposedly considered friends?

They followed the butler across the domed entrance hall. Unlike the castle, Kilmeny Hall was airy and modern, with a grand pedimented facade and symmetrically-placed, floor-to-ceiling windows.

Eilidh had never been inside so fine a house.

Master MacTavish walked beside her with what she could only assume was his typical swagger. He wore a great kilt today, a dark tartan slashed with bold stripes of red and white and gold. The hilt of a *sgian dubh* glinted from the top of his gartered stockings.

He looked like a Highland raider intent on pillage and conquest, completely at odds with the refinement of their surroundings.

Eilidh was a rather pocket-sized woman, so she was accustomed to feeling small beside men. But even so, MacTavish exuded strength and masculinity. The top of her head didn't quite reach his shoulder.

She swallowed.

"Are you going to tell me who I will meet?" she asked.

"The Brotherhood," he said.

Eilidh nearly rolled her eyes. "I understand that. But who, specifically, belongs to this Brotherhood, aside from Dr. Whitaker? You have told me nothing about them beyond their first names."

Oddly, her snippy tone brought a smile to his face. "Patience, lass. We all want tae see how much ye remember before we make introductions."

Ahead of them, the butler pushed open the door, motioning for Eilidh and Master MacTavish to enter the drawing room.

Eilidh walked into the room and paused.

It was full of people, all slowly rising to their feet, every head turned her way.

Some faces seemed familiar.

Others . . . did not.

The fluttery, panicked sensation increased, urging her to race from this place, from these people and the lurking memories they represented.

A hand touched her elbow.

Eilidh flinched away, following the outstretched palm up to Master MacTavish's pale eyes.

"My apologies," he said. "As I said, before I make introductions, we would like to see who ye recognize."

Of course.

She closed her eyes.

Think upon Simon. How he smiles attentively and never says an impolite word when Mrs. Green chatters on far too long. Recall the weight of his hand in the small of your back whenever the dark panic of your memories loom. You must go through this in order to return to him.

Taking a deep breath, Eilidh opened her eyes and dutifully studied each person in the room.

Four men. One woman.

All the men sported a length of plaid in the same tartan pattern as Master MacTavish.

Her eyes instantly went to the lithe man that she had recognized the evening before.

"Dr. Whitaker." Eilidh nodded her head and bobbed him a small curtsy.

"Miss Fyffe." He bowed, low and courtly, the tartan sash across his chest slipping slightly.

Unconsciously, she ran her gloved thumb over the scar on her palm.

"Ye look lovely," the doctor continued. "It is wonderful tae have ye with us again."

"Thank you. And you."

Eilidh said the words reflexively and then frowned. The entire exchange felt . . . odd. Stilted. As if it were the first time they had ever been so polite with one another.

She looked beyond Dr. Whitaker to the others. They all studied her with rapt attention, as if she were a unicorn who had stumbled into their midst.

It was rather unnerving.

A tall, broad-shouldered sandy-haired man leaned against the fireplace mantel, his dark great kilt a mirror of Master MacTavish's. Here was the man she saw walking with MacTavish and the doctor the evening before.

A dark-haired man stood beside him, a white scar running from his right temple down his cheek. Like Dr. Whitaker, the man wore a tartan sash atop an immaculately-cut superfine coat of deep green.

Eilidh frowned further. Neither man looked familiar, but she felt a tug of something warm when she looked at them.

It was frustrating. Memory teased at her—a toy dangled just out of reach. As if she should know the men well, and yet when she reached to recall anything tangible, she only encountered empty air.

In front of a long sofa, a kilted red-headed man stood with his arm around a woman. He was enormous, towering over them all.

But the giant ginger, at least, was . . . familiar. An image of him sketching a bird flitted through her mind.

Eilidh blinked and the memory fluttered away.

Was this Mr. Ewan Campbell then? The artist Master MacTavish had mentioned yesterday?

If so, the woman at his side would be Lady Kildrum, the countess that Eilidh had yet to meet. Tall, with chestnut hair carefully styled, her ladyship was expensively dressed. Though no gown could hide the girth of her pregnant belly. Eilidh noted the careful way Mr. Campbell held her, his large hand spanning the small of her back.

A pang of anguish sliced through her chest.

There was a babe who was clearly wanted. A child, conceived in love, who would come into this world with two doting parents—

She looked away, fingers clenching into fists, her thumbs tucked against her palms. She imagined the raised white scar on her left palm—a wound that, though healed, had forever changed the appearance of her hand.

Was her whole self—skin, limbs, emotions—now like her hand? The torment of her lost year a jagged blemish that had altered her forever?

"Perhaps ye should introduce me after all, Master MacTavish," she murmured.

The men all exchanged a look—part surprise, part concern.

"Ye dinnae recognize any of us except Alex, lass?" the red-headed giant asked.

His voice was familiar, too, and yet . . . everything about him remained tantalizingly out of reach, like grasping at fog.

Eilidh shook her head, hands fisting tighter, eyes darting again to her ladyship's pregnant belly.

Most of her longed to run—out the gilded drawing room door, down the marble steps, and onto the gorse-lined lane, her feet racing away from here.

She didn't want whatever memories these men might conjure. She had forgotten for a reason, had she not?

Frightful things happened to her aboard *The Minerva*. Her racing heart and damp palms testified to it.

"Heaven knows what you were subjected to aboard that ship," Reverend Gillespie would rant. *"Those men should pay for the hideousness of their crimes, crimes they forced you to participate in, Miss Fyffe. Such transgressions should be brought to justice before God and man."*

And yet . . .

Her eyes dipped to where Mr. Campbell's hand rested around his wife's waist.

His was the mien of a man who valued women, who would go to great lengths to protect those he loved.

Her heart continued to pound in her chest, the vibrations threatening to set her hands to shaking.

She took in a deep breath and coaxed the numbness to flood her mind. Anything to stem the maelstrom of emotion that swirled beneath her breastbone.

No matter her personal feelings, the stark truth remained—if she wished to return to Yorkshire and Simon, she needed to endure this meeting.

"Let me introduce ye, then." Master MacTavish touched her arm again, as if to lead her farther into the room.

Eilidh shied away once more.

His touch was a battering ram against her indifference.

It wasn't revulsion, precisely.

But his touch . . . hurt. It caused an upwelling of confusing sentiments that she disliked feeling, and so she shrank from the emotion as much as the weight of his warm fingers.

Master MacTavish took in a deep breath, his chest heaving, eyes meeting hers.

"Please, Miss Fyffe," he murmured. "No one here means you any harm. I wish there were a way to help ye understand that."

"Perhaps ye should have given me a choice in the matter." The snippy words tumbled out, along with the Scottish lilt of her upbringing. "Perhaps ye should have asked what *I* wished."

So much for acting like a lady.

"Aye, we likely should have," Dr. Whitaker said, drawing near with outstretched palms, as if she were a skittish fawn he feared would bolt.

It was not an inaccurate assumption.

The doctor shot a weighted look at Master MacTavish over her head. For his part, MacTavish grimaced and turned away, walking over to gaze out the window.

Eilidh followed him with her eyes, pulse clamoring in her ears.

"Come, Miss Fyffe," Dr. Whitaker said, drawing her attention. "Allow me to make the introductions." He offered her his arm.

After a pause, Eilidh nodded and threaded her hand through his elbow. Touching the doctor unearthed no sentiment, oddly enough.

Why was that? He was part of the same horrific time of her life. Why did Master MacTavish provoke a tidal wave of harrowing emotion? But Dr. Whitaker only kindled warmth and affection?

The doctor made the introductions.

The sandy-haired man before the fireplace was Andrew Langston, Lord Hadley.

"Though ye knew me as Mr. Andrew Mackenzie. My situation was elevated a few years back," he clarified. "It's good tae see ye, lass."

The darker man in the green coat—the one with a scar upon his cheek—was Sir Rafe Gordon.

"Ye knew me as Lord Rafe Gilbert. Unlike Andrew, my situation didn't so much elevate as slide sideways." Sir Rafe shot Lord Hadley a wry grin. "We are delighted to have ye among us again, Miss Fyffe."

The enormous redhead was Mr. Ewan Campbell, as Eilidh suspected. His wife, Lady Kildrum, was a countess *suo juro*—in her own right—and owned Kilmeny Hall and its lands.

Even Dr. Whitaker was no longer simply Dr. Whitaker but had somehow become the Marquess of Lockheade.

When the introductions were done, Eilidh was invited to sit on a chair across from Lady Kildrum. Master MacTavish stood beside the arm of the chair, hands clasped behind his back.

Silence hung for a moment.

Eilidh felt like an interloper, mingling with such august company. Moreover, why did these gentlemen claim Master MacTavish as a friend? Did they know of his dreadful reputation? Or, as men, did they know and simply not care?

After all, they had all been aboard *The Minerva* when she had been—

Eilidh forced her mind back from that abyss, from the urge to stare at Lady Kildrum's distended stomach and weep until her chest hitched and her lungs burned.

Numb. She would remain numb.

Dr. Whit—ehr, Lord Lockheade—checked his pocket watch.

"The procurator fiscal should be here soon," he said.

"About time," Lord Hadley snorted. "I am more than ready tae wash our hands of this once and for all."

"Aye." Sir Rafe nodded, his white scar standing out on his tanned skin.

Their eyes kept drifting to Eilidh as they spoke.

"It's a wonder tae have ye here, Miss Fyffe." Lord Lockheade smiled. "Ye have been greatly missed."

"Thank you." Eilidh nodded but said nothing more. She had no real memory of these men, so she could hardly return the compliment. "May I ask . . . why are you all wearing the same dark tartan? I don't recognize the pattern."

Lord Hadley smiled, pinching a bit of the great kilt wrapping his chest. "It's your tartan, lass."

"Mine?"

"Aye. Ye are part of our Brotherhood of the Tartan, and we all consider ye to be a true friend. So when we thought ye dead, we renamed ourselves the Brotherhood of the *Black* Tartan. To go along with the name, I commissioned this tartan in your memory. The black ground represented our grief and anger." Hadley traced a wide, cherry-red band on the tartan of his kilt. "Red for our guilt over innocent blood spilt. A little gold for hope, a wee bit of green for growth."

"We all wear it from time to time," Sir Rafe added. "It was our way of honoring your memory."

"Aye," Mr. Campbell agreed. "But today, we wear your tartan tae let ye know that we stand in solidarity with yourself. That ye are never far from our hearts."

Something tumbled in Eilidh's chest at the men's kind words, an ache that made her throat sting. She had no reason to doubt their sincerity, and yet . . .

She struggled to merge the men's words and actions with the events she knew had to have occurred aboard *The Minerva.*

It made no sense.

"Evil comes in many forms," Reverend Gillespie's voice echoed in her mind. *"Do not be deceived if, at first, it appears welcoming and enticing."*

But the Brotherhood appeared to be genuinely . . . caring. Moreover, did evil parade around in tartan colors signifying real grief and loyalty?

Eilidh rather thought not.

"Would you care for some tea, Miss Fyffe?" Lady Kildrum asked, a kindly smile on her face, her ladyship rather proving Eilidh's mental point.

"No, thank ye." Eilidh shook her head.

The agitation currently churning in her stomach rebelled at the thought of food. After so many revelations, her cherished numbness was at best a scattered wish for calm. She needed a moment to rebuild her equanimity.

Fortunately, as if sensing her need for relief, the gathered men moved on to discussing things *not* related to her.

Mr. Campbell described the painting he was working on for submission to the Royal Academy salon. Lady Kildrum had built an enormous glasshouse studio for her husband behind the west wing of the house. Mr. Campbell spent most days there painting.

Lord Lockheade spoke of changes he was making to his principal seat, Frome Abbey, in Wiltshire. Apparently his wife, Lady Lockheade, was spending time with her sister, nephew, and self-important brother-in-law in London, allowing Lockheade a chance to visit Scotland.

"Don't think ill of me," Lockheade said, a rueful smile tugging his lips. "I adore my Lottie with every piece of my soul, and I am glad she has found a measure of accord with her sister. But I am not as forgiving as my wife and, therefore, welcomed the excuse to avoid Lady Margaret and Lord Frank."

Laughter greeted his comments.

As the men talked, Eilidh's gaze kept skittering back to study Master MacTavish. There were *five* men in this room—all of them handsome—and yet her eyes only seemed to care about Master MacTavish.

Was it the fact that he was a finely-formed man? After all, with his pale eyes and dark hair, he cut a memorable figure and well he knew it.

Sir Rafe spoke of the farming he was undertaking with his small estate in Perthshire, wishing to secure the property for his children. His wife, Lady Sophie Gordon, had given birth to a healthy baby boy just four months prior.

"He's an eater, is my lad," Sir Rafe said with a smile. "He's nearly as wide as he is tall at the moment."

This led to Lord Hadley talking about his daughter, Isolde. "She discovered running about three weeks ago, and it's been a bit of a nightmare, if I'm honest. She can vanish in the blink of an eye."

"She's dauntless, that one," Mr. Campbell smiled.

"I can feel the gray hairs coming on." Lord Hadley pulled at his light brown hair. "Do ye hope for a lad or lass with this baby, Ewan?"

"My biggest wish is for Violet and the bairn tae be healthy." Ewan blushed and reached for his wife's hand. "But I adore the thought of having a daughter."

"You would," Lady Kildrum laughed, leaning her head affectionately on his shoulder.

"Well," Sir Rafe nodded, "I hope we'll be able tae greet your new babe at the midsummer festival in June."

"You will all be most welcome." Lady Kildrum rested a hand on the curve of her belly.

Eilidh swallowed, staring at her ladyship's fingers. At the tender way Lady Kildrum cradled the babe in her womb. At the gold wedding band winking in and out of the light.

Eilidh had to look away after a second, her eyes stinging, her own fingers curling inward around the scar on her palm.

Why was it some wounds never healed entirely?

The men continued to speak back and forth around her.

Of course, their superficial conversation was only a smoke screen for the true concern weighing on them all.

"What will happen with the procurator fiscal?" Eilidh finally asked, unable to stop the question from spilling forth into a lull of conversation.

"Mr. Patterson? He will merely ask questions about what ye remember, Miss Fyffe," Lockheade said, gently.

"But I don't remember anything," Eilidh protested.

"Aye, and Mr. Patterson has been told that ad nauseam," Sir Rafe sighed.

"The authorities have questioned us more than once over the years," Lord Hadley added. "But then some wee tidbit of information surfaces, and we're summoned once more."

Hadley and Sir Rafe exchanged a weighted look with Master MacTavish.

Eilidh frowned, her own eyes darting between the men. "Am I missing something here?"

"Nae. Nothing will come of it." Master MacTavish fixed the others with a stern expression.

"I hope not," Hadley said, "but with every exchange, we dance a bit closer tae the possibility."

Silence hung.

Eilidh looked back and forth between them. "I would appreciate some explanation before I am tossed into the lion's den with Mr. Patterson."

"It doesn't impact ye, lass," Master MacTavish said, jaw clenched.

"But it could," Sir Rafe said.

Mr. Campbell studied Eilidh from his seat beside his wife, his eyes kind. Eilidh sensed that this was his habitual mien. That despite the intimidating size of his enormous body, he was at his core, an astonishingly gentle soul.

But why did she feel that way? Was it simply intuition? Or did she remember this from their former deeper acquaintance?

"Miss Fyffe should be told," he said, looking at the others. When no one objected, Mr. Campbell continued, "Unlike the rest of us, yourself and Kieran were members of the ship's crew. Therefore, Kieran's actions—and by extension, your own—could be viewed as mutinous during that last night before Captain Cuthie marooned us. The captain had wrongfully imprisoned Andrew and Rafe and . . . there was a fight between yourselves and the captain and his men—"

"I fought the ship's captain?!" Eilidh reared back, horror clogging her throat. "Why would I . . . How could I . . ."

"Aye. It might seem hard tae believe without your memories, but aye, ye did fight."

"Ye were remarkably brave," Sir Rafe agreed. "Ye saved us."

Eilidh was sure her eyes were saucers. Her? A fighter?

The very idea was laughable to her current self.

But she had been a different person aboard that ship. One who had donned trousers and impersonated a brother and abandoned being a lady. So perhaps it wasn't such a stretch that she would fight, too.

But still.

"The point is," Hadley said, "that as crew members openly fighting against the ship's captain, Master MacTavish and yourself could be charged with mutiny—"

"It willnae happen," Master MacTavish bit out.

"Kieran—" Lockheade began.

"Nae. The Admiralty has had ample opportunity tae charge myself over the years, and they havenae done it. Cuthie knows that he is also guilty of crimes around those same events. Andrew was a part-owner of *The Minerva*, and technically, Cuthie's employer. And yet, Cuthie had him chained and beaten. Andrew has not levied charges of assault against Cuthie, and so, in turn, Cuthie has not pursued accusations of mutiny against myself—"

"*Are* you guilty of mutiny?" Eilidh asked.

Kieran shrugged. "I suppose it depends upon your point-of-view, but a case could be made. In order to claim I mutinied, Cuthie has tae admit his own perfidy."

"In short," Hadley said, "we exist in a sort of rapprochement with Cuthie and Massey. We stay out of one another's orbits—Cuthie and Massey have remained abroad for years now—and neither of us says a word, thereby maintaining an equilibrium. With neither side willing to make an accusation or bring corroborated evidence, the Admiralty can do nothing."

Master MacTavish turned his head toward the sound of a carriage on the front drive, his chin lifting, his attention instantly arrested.

The movement was so familiar, something aching and hot caught in Eilidh's throat.

Abruptly, she saw him in her mind's eye, that same expression on his face, only this time striding across a ship's deck, his coat flapping in the breeze, ruggedly handsome and moving with liquid ease—

She grasped at the image, but it slipped away in a wispy puff.

Was it a memory? Or just a fanciful thought?

Hadley walked over to the window, looking out to the drive.

"That will be Mr. Patterson himself. We shall resolve this simply enough, I am sure." He turned back to Eilidh, his expression unreadable. "Perhaps we can finally, once and for all, put this behind us."

Eilidh looked down at her gloved hands, her thumb running once more over the scar hidden on her palm.

Yes.

That was precisely what she wished.

She wanted to put *all* this behind her.

She wanted to leave this place—to return to Yorkshire and Simon and the cocooned life she had fought so hard to claim—and never think upon *The Minerva* or its crew again.

Her missing memory becoming like the scar on her hand—a small blemish she scarcely noticed.

SEPTEMBER 1815

Jamie was still avoiding him.

Kieran's fingers tapped out a frustrated tattoo on his upper thigh.

The lad had readily jumped into being a member of their brotherhood. A day didn't pass without Kieran seeing Jamie laughing with Andrew, or watching Ewan show him how to carve figures from wood, or helping Alex mix a tincture. Jamie had even begun learning how to fence with Rafe.

But Kieran?

Nothing.

Three weeks on and Jamie continued to give him the cold shoulder.

Every time Kieran had approached and attempted a conversation, the lad clammed up, bent his head over some bit of wood, and responded with monosyllabic grunts. As if he couldn't wait for Kieran to be gone.

But then, Kieran would find the lad studying him at odd times. Like when he stood on the forecastle, reveling in the vast expanse of the ocean. Or when, in the equatorial heat, Kieran and Rafe had stripped to the waist and fenced until they dripped with sweat. Jamie had watched with wide-eyed fascination. Kieran, mopping his brow with his shirt, had even tried to talk to Jamie afterward. But the youth had merely folded his arms and stared at his feet, his jaw mulishly clenched.

Did Jamie truly hate him so much? How could Kieran help the boy if Jamie never accepted his genuine offer of friendship?

Presently, Kieran scoured the rain-soaked deck. The crew were laughing and calling to one another, everyone in some state of undress.

Rain decorated the ocean around them with concentric rings. It was the kind of storm one occasionally experienced in the Doldrums—warm, fresh rain without high seas. Kieran had immediately ordered all empty water casks to be brought up from the hold, allowing the rain to fill what it could.

Along with that, he commanded the scuppers be stopped up, forcing the rain to pool on deck instead of running off. The crew were ordered to wash their clothing and bathe—the first proper bath in nearly a month.

Kieran had hoped Jamie Fyffe might wash himself properly for once.

But as he surveyed the deck, looking in and around the water casks, the boy was nowhere to be seen. Mr. Chen was near the forecastle, talking with their cook, Mr. Aksoy. But the carpenter's grimy mate was notably missing.

Kieran pulled on his wet—but now clean—shirt, the linen fabric sticking to him. Thankfully, they were in the tropics, so the warm air would dry everything within an hour or two of the rain letting up.

The members of the Brotherhood were laughing together near the mizzenmast, stripped to the waist and passing around a bar of soap. Jamie wasn't with them.

"Have ye seen Jamie?" Kieran asked Ewan. "I cannae find the lad, but ye be a head taller than everyone else, mayhap ye can see him?"

Ewan's eyes flashed wide. He spun in a circle, easily looking over the crowd of men. He shook his head, wiping rain out of his eyes.

"Nay. I cannae see him." Ewan looked down at Kieran. "Wee little mite, that boy, dinnae ye think? Bit scrawny, even for a lad of fifteen."

Rafe shot Ewan a hard look. Ewan shrugged.

"Agreed," Kieran frowned, too frustrated to parse the odd conversational undercurrent. "We need tae clean him up and then see that he gets more rations."

"Or ye could just let him be?" Alex offered.

Kieran shook his head. "Nae. I'm the ship's master and responsible for the hygiene aboard this vessel. Captain Cook showed the world that cleanliness goes a long way toward overall health aboard a ship. Jamie needs tae bathe."

Andrew sighed. "Kieran," he began.

"Nae." Kieran held up a hand. "I willnae hear any more arguments against it. I'll dunk and scrub the lad with my own hands if I have tae."

Kieran walked away before his friends could protest. He circled the deck one more time, just to be sure the boy truly wasn't hiding behind a barrel.

No Jamie.

Shaking his head, Kieran headed below deck. Jamie had to be on the ship somewhere. He would find the lad and drag him aboveboard, kicking and screaming, if necessary.

James Fyffe would soon realize that Kieran did, in fact, take his obligations to the boy's father seriously.

Below deck was utterly deserted, as he had expected. Pigs snuffled in their pen, while the goats *baa*-ed. Somewhere, a chicken clucked and cackled.

Kieran headed first for the carpenter's cabin. The carpenter's mate bunked with the carpenter, so it seemed logical to find Jamie there.

But pulling aside the carpenter's sliding door revealed no one. Just two neatly made beds to one side of the room and a workshop full of tools on the other.

Frowning, Kieran continued to hunt, remaining silent. He climbed down to the berth deck, again, finding no one. Just rows of empty sleeping hammocks, rocking in time with the waves.

Finally, he descended to the steerage deck where casks of supplies and crates of goods bound for Rio and Sydney rested. The bowels of the ship reeked of tar and grog.

He waited, listening as his eyes adjusted to the dim light. He heard nothing beyond the creaking of the ship. If the boy was hiding down here, Kieran would have a devil of a time finding him.

He spun in a circle, intent on calling out, when a flicker of candlelight winked from behind lashed casks of hardtack.

Found ye.

Scowling, Kieran rounded the corner, a stream of frustrated words on his tongue. But he came to an abrupt stop, the words dissolving in his mouth. All the air in his lungs left in a gut-punched *whoosh.*

It took him a moment to understand what he was seeing.

A graceful bare shoulder.

The arch of a feminine neck.

Milky skin turned golden in the candlelight.

He blinked, chest working to absorb the shock.

A woman.

This was definitely a *woman.*

A *naked* woman, sitting with her back to him, a wool blanket wrapped around her lower half.

She leaned forward, dipping a cloth into a basin of water before continuing to wipe her neck.

Kieran knew he should look away.

He should.

He *would.*

But . . .

It was just . . .

A woman!

Ship!

Here!

Naked!

Woman!!

Some sense of his own shock must have carried to her.

She froze, the cloth pressed to her neck.

She glanced over her shoulder and then shrieked. Snatching up the wool blanket, she pressed it to her front and whirled to face him.

They regarded one another for the space of three heartbeats.

Thump.

Thump.

Thump.

Kieran's blood was a pulse in his ears.

So . . . he had found Jamie.

Or . . . the *lass* pretending to be Jamie.

She stared at him in wide-eyed shock.

How had he ever thought her to be a boy?

He was such an *eejit.*

With her face clean, the elegant swoop of her jaw could only belong to a woman.

She was petite and small and devastatingly beautiful.

No wonder she remained filthy. How else was she to disguise such loveliness?

She licked her lips, chest heaving under the blanket clasped to her.

"Who are ye?" he asked. "Not James Fyffe, obviously."

"No." She shook her head.

"Ye still have the look of Charles. Are ye . . . are ye the sister then? Eilidh, was it?"

"Aye." She nodded her head. "Jamie died. I took his place."

Her hands shook where she held the blanket. Kieran's eyes dipped down to them. He swallowed.

He lifted his eyes back to hers.

She had not missed his perusal. She pulled the blanket tighter around her chest.

"Why would ye keep your true gender from me?" he asked, voice terse. "Ye should have told me immediately—"

"And then what? I know your reputation," she snapped. "Do ye think to use me now? Treat me like the poor lasses the crew visits when we anchor in port?"

Kieran flinched, the bald assumption in her accusation literally stealing his breath.

"P-pardon?!" he managed to gasp.

"I will not be forced to act like a wh—"

"No one will harm ye, lass!" He held out a staying hand. "Not while I have breath in my body!"

"For all the good that does me! *You,* with your libertine ways, pose the greatest risk of all."

Kieran's jaw all but dropped.

Bloody hell but this lass was brazen.

How had she gone to putting him on the defensive?

She was the one who had lied about her identity and stowed away on *his* ship.

"Ye dinnae know me, lass," he said, tone sharp.

"I know *of* ye, and that is sufficient, I ken."

"No. No, it isnae. Ye know only a wee part of me. Just as I, at this moment, only understand a wee part of the events that have led to a woman washing up in the hold of my ship."

She did not respond but merely clutched her blanket tighter.

Kieran shook his head. "I willnae have ye casting such unwarranted aspersions against my character. Just as I will make no assumptions as tae your own." He waved a hand, indicating her current state of undress and the absurdity of their surroundings.

"Finish bathing," he ordered. "I will await you in my cabin where we will discuss your future."

He spun on his booted heel and left.

TWENTY MINUTES LATER, a clean, bedraggled 'Jamie' hesitantly knocked on the open door to Kieran's cabin.

Even dressed in baggy trousers and an ill-fitting coat, she was so obviously, well, a *she.*

How had he ever been so blind?

"Come in," he nodded. "Please shut the door."

She froze. Her silvery eyes looked at him in alarm from under a mop of damp curls.

Kieran took in a slow breath, tamping down his frustration.

"As stated earlier, I willnae hurt ye. I give ye my solemn oath—ye will always be safe with me." He intended the words to be soothing, and yet, she continued to hover just inside the door.

He sighed, trying again. "I ken I made poor choices as a lad. I did run wild through more than one port of call. But that was when I was sixteen and seventeen . . . a mere youth. I havenae been that person in nigh upon a decade." He motioned again toward the door. "But at the moment, I dinnae want any others overhearing our conversation."

She squared her shoulders as if donning her courage, and then nodded, shutting the door.

She looked around the room.

Kieran supposed she saw quarters that were small but intensely tidy. A neatly-made bed ran along one wall. A desk was bolted to the floor against another. Maps and several charts hung on the walls. A shelf above the bed contained an astrolabe, sexton, and a collection of books. Two wooden chairs sat in the middle.

He motioned for her to sit in one chair.

She slid into it, perching on the edge.

He took the other.

"Your full name?" he asked.

"Miss Eilidh Fyffe." The low husky timbre of her voice skittered down his spine.

"Your age?"

"Nineteen."

"Your father didnae arrange a guardian for ye then?"

She snorted, those silvery-green eyes flashing icy fire. "No, I am sorry tae say. He was a bit too busy being ill and dying and waiting for cherished friends tae respond to requests for assistance. If anyone would have been appointed my guardian, it would likely have been yourself." Her tone clearly indicated what she thought about *that* idea.

Kieran narrowed his gaze, a stinging retort on his tongue.

But before the words escaped, he noted her fingers curled into tightly balled fists on her lap.

Something within him . . . panged.

She was not as flippant as she appeared. Her curt words were surely a defensive maneuver.

"Again, as I have explained many times, I am eternally sorry that I was not a better friend to your father. I wish to make amends." Kieran kept his voice even. "Now . . . please explain how ye came tae be aboard this ship."

She squirmed, not quite meeting his eyes.

Good.

She should be uncomfortable. Her choices had landed him in a damned hard place.

"My father and James both contracted consumption. My father lingered for years, but it sent Jamie tae his grave quite quickly. Jamie died on a Tuesday. My father passed the next day, thinking Jamie was still alive and well." Her accent softened as she spoke, her voice becoming more melodic. The tones of a gently-born, Scottish lady, not a lowly carpenter's mate. "There was nothing for me. I was raised a gentlewoman, but without a father, brother, or some other family to take me in, it was immediately obvious that my options were limited. I could marry or find employment. There were no young men clamoring for my hand in marriage. So employment was my only choice. But as I had no references, finding honest work was nearly impossible." Her eyes lifted to his, flashing with that fire again. "Have ye ever faced such desperation? The terror of not knowing where your next meal might come from? Afraid what morals hunger might lead ye tae compromise?"

Kieran rubbed his breastbone with the heel of his hand.

Yes, he did know that desperation. That had been his lot when Charles first found him all those years ago.

"I had your letter for Jamie," she continued, "promising him a place aboard ship. I know a bit about woodworking and the idea simply . . . came to me. I could *become* Jamie. So I cut my hair, put on Jamie's clothing, and presented myself on ship, just as Jamie should have done."

Kieran listened to her recitation with stoic calm, though his leg bounced in time to his thrumming nerves.

"I see," he said. "A ship is an extremely risky place for a woman. Not because of the work, per se—though that is often dangerous, too. It is rather . . . men can be savage beasts. You seem to understand this, based on your comments tae me not thirty minutes ago. Though despite your low opinion of myself, I have never taken anything from a woman that was not freely offered. I will do everything I can tae protect ye here."

She nodded. Her fists clenched tighter.

"Because of this," he continued, "I will be putting ye on the first ship back to Scotland once we reach Rio de Janeiro—"

"No!" Her head snapped up in alarm.

"No? What do you mean, *no*?" Kieran pitched his voice into the tone he used for insubordinate crew members. The tone that made grown men squirm.

She didn't so much as wriggle.

"No, ye cannot send me back. What will I do? How will I provide for myself?"

"I will arrange a suitable situation for ye. Surely, Andrew or Rafe know of a lady who could use an agreeable companion, such as yourself—"

"But I don't *want* tae be a lady's companion. Do ye ken how monotonous that is? Day after day, reading to an elderly woman, taking tea with her equally elderly friends, and attempting to embroider handkerchiefs? I hate embroidery. I haven't the patience for complicated chain stitches and French knots. No, thank ye. I want to remain aboard ship."

"That is clearly impossible, lass."

"Why? Women have done such things in the past—"

"I assume ye refer to that memoir by Mary Lacy? *The Female Shipwright*?"

"Aye, among others. I am hardly alone in my wish to remain aboard."

"But . . . why? Ye were raised a lady." Bafflement rattled in Kieran's chest. "Why would ye wish tae remain aboard ship, risking physical harm and subsisting on salted beef and hardtack, when ye could be sipping tea and nibbling shortbread with the vicar?"

She snorted. "That's precisely the point! I may have come aboard this ship out of desperation, but now I want tae stay out of love of the job. I had no idea it could be so satisfying working with one's hands. I'm bored to tears when faced with an embroidery hoop but, turns out, I can work miracles in wood. Can ye not understand? Ye have spent your life being permitted to explore the things that most interest ye. But women are not granted that luxury. Yes, my mother raised me tae be a lady. But I've realized that isn't all life can be. On this ship, I feel reborn in more ways than an adopted name."

"That's all well and good," Kieran narrowed his eyes, "but the risk to yourself is too high."

"Yes, but it is *my* risk to assume." She tapped her chest. "Mine tae choose."

"And what happens when others realize you're a woman?" Kieran hissed. "What will Mr. Chen do?"

She stilled, her gaze abruptly absorbed in the contents of his bookshelf.

Kieran's expression sank.

"Mr. Chen knows ye are a woman." It wasn't a question.

She sighed and nodded, turning her eyes back to him. "Please don't be angry at him. But we share a cabin, and he is perceptive. He realized within a day or two. He says I am like a daughter to him."

Kieran stared at her.

If he expected her to feel the weight of his gaze, he was again disappointed. She met it with steady courage.

"If ye send me back tae Scotland, I'll just run away again. I've found a freedom I didn't know existed for a woman." Her chin raised a notch, taking on a decidedly stubborn look. "I won't be thrust back into a cage."

Admiration rose and stretched in his chest.

Charles had probably been prescient to keep this fascinating creature out of Kieran's reach.

He admired her spirit and courage far more than was wise.

"We shall see," he hedged. "I dinnae know how we're going tae keep this from the rest of the Brotherhood, though."

Again, her eyes slid sideways away from his.

Kieran's heart sank. "Bloody hell, woman! Who else knows?"

"Well . . ." Her voice drifted off, lips pursing.

Kieran beckoned with his fingers. *Out with it.*

"Alex, as a doctor, is most perceptive. He confronted me about it just a day or two after we formed the Brotherhood."

"Is that all?"

"Uhmm, Ewan asked tae sketch my face and realized that my bone structure matched that of a woman, not a man. Something about my brow bone not being properly mannish." She pointed at her dark, finely-sculpted eyebrows.

Kieran raised his own brows, waiting.

She licked her lips. "Andrew and I—"

"Andrew, too?!"

"Aye," she sighed. "We were watching a pair of pelicans fish alongside the ship. I leaned too far over the edge and would have tumbled overboard if he hadnae grabbed me. He said it was obvious I wasnae male."

Kieran pinched the bridge of his nose. He was almost afraid to ask. "Rafe?"

"He got too close when showing me how to properly dislodge an opponent's rapier."

"Anyone else?"

She shook her head.

Silence.

"So . . . in summation . . . you've been terrible at keeping your sex a secret." Kieran folded his arms.

As usual, his glacial stare and stern expression had no discernible effect on her.

"Nae, we simply have observant friends," she countered. "*You* didn't realize I was female—"

"Logic dictates that it's only a matter of time before everyone aboard this ship knows."

"I think ye are wrong there. The Brotherhood has already begun tae help me hide my sex. Mr. Chen, too. If my friends stand by me—as *I* will stand by them—then all will be well."

"Perhaps." Kieran frowned, hating the logic in her words. "Regardless, nothing can be done until we reach Rio. Until then, I shall ponder all options."

She studied him.

The ship rocked. Somewhere, a cow lowed. Sailors called to each other on the deck above their heads.

"Ye willnae send me home," she finally said. "I'll make sure of it."

"We shall see, Miss Fyffe—"

"I'm Jamie now." She pushed to her feet and turned for the door. "Ye best remember it."

She left his cabin with a boyish toss of her head, shutting the door with a resounding clack.

"And that is all you remember, Miss Fyffe?" Mr. Patterson—the procurator fiscal—pushed his spectacles up the bridge of his nose. The glasses promptly slid down again. "Nothing at all aboard ship?"

Mr. Patterson shuffled papers atop the hastily-placed gate-leg table before him, marking something with a pencil.

"No, nothing beyond the brief memories I mentioned of Dr. Whit—ehr, Lord Lockheade," Jamie replied, shooting Alex an apologetic look. "I have no memory of anything that led up to the sinking of *The Minerva*."

Kieran's leg bounced as Mr. Patterson questioned Jamie.

Eilidh.

Miss Fyffe.

His *wife*.

Jamie sat isolated in a chair in the center of the room, hands fisted in her lap, all of her looking so small and alone. She had always been short and petite, but without the fire of Jamie animating her, she had somehow shrunk.

Kieran had thought that after that first meeting between them, things would improve. That she would slowly begin to remember. That her icy distrust and seeming revulsion of him would ease.

But if anything, after the passage of nearly thirty-odd hours, she was even more withdrawn. All of her Miss Eilidh Fyffe.

It was as if no trace of his Jamie remained.

Instead, a stranger inhabited her body.

A stranger who wore fine dresses and spoke like an Englishwoman and didn't remember how she had grown and laughed and loved—loved him!—aboard a merchant ship on the opposite side of the world.

Worse . . . she didn't understand the value of what she had lost.

To the question, *Why did you assume your brother's identity and board the ship under false pretenses?*, she had recounted the reasons Kieran already knew—her feelings of terror and desperation, her strong desire to avoid the workhouse.

But beyond that, she could answer little.

Why did you continue the charade?

I don't know.

Who did you tell you were a woman?

I can't remember.

Did Captain Cuthie know?

I don't know.

With each answer, more of Kieran's hope died—her memories were well and truly absent.

She had been his lodestar for so many years. He had prayed for her, that she had lived, that she was well.

And God had granted them both that miracle.

Her body *had* lived.

But the person who had been Jamie . . .

Where had that woman gone?

"Ye must prepare yourself for the reality that she may never regain her memories, Kieran," Alex had warned him more than once over the past few months. *"Jamie may never wish to return to a life as your wife."*

The words felt nearly prophetic now.

She sat unnervingly still before Mr. Patterson, her posture rigid and ladylike and very un-Jamie-esque. His Jamie had been a constant blur of motion, her shorn curls a whirling halo around her face.

Now, her hair had grown long, the wild curls tamed and teased into an intricate knot with ruthless precision. The fine wool of her pelisse accentuated her creamy complexion, the tanned skin of her time aboard *The Minerva* having long ago faded.

In short, Miss Eilidh Fyffe was every whit the genteel captain's daughter she had been raised to be.

The only trace of Jamie that Kieran could see were the rounded fists in her lap. His Jamie had clenched her hands when she was upset or incensed or readying herself to defend those she loved.

He stared at her achingly familiar face, the one that he cherished and loved and longed to cup between his hands and bestow a trembling kiss. His eyes dropped to her mouth, the lips that had spoken marriage vows on a beach at dusk in Sydney Harbor, promising to never let him go.

As if feeling the weight of his regard, she turned her head and met his gaze. Her silvery-green eyes burned with emotion—fear, apprehension, wariness—but no recognition. No love.

Not even a flicker of memory of their handfasting. Of the strength in her fingers afterward, as she snatched his hand and led him by starlight along a glistening path, giggling over her shoulder, "Ye better adore the surprise I have planned for ye!"

He looked away.

The weight of memory was too heavy, and he was too alone in shouldering its burden.

The rest of the Brotherhood sat in various places around the room, watching Mr. Patterson with Jamie. Were their thoughts like Kieran's? A torrential reminder of what had been lost?

Kieran suspected so.

Though each of his friends appeared calm, wee discrepancies leapt out—Rafe's rigid spine, Alex's folded arms. Andrew kept shifting his weight. Ewan paced in a circle.

Mr. Patterson removed his spectacles, cleaning them with a handkerchief, oblivious or perhaps uncaring of the tension in the room.

"Your missing memory poses a significant problem to this inquiry, Miss Fyffe," the man said. "As a procurator fiscal, it is my job to determine the cause of any suspicious deaths. *The Minerva*, though a private merchant vessel, was sailed from Scottish waters and, therefore, is under the jurisdiction of the maritime courts in Aberdeen. One hundred and twenty-seven men lost their lives at her sinking. That is not an insignificant number, as I am sure you can all appreciate." He perched his glasses back on his nose and peered over the lenses at Jamie. "The untimely deaths of so many are of deep concern to the Judge Admiral. I have already questioned all other known survivors of the voyage—most of whom are in this room. I was hoping that you, Miss Fyffe, could provide more clarity on the issue. But as is, I fear I shall have to draw conclusions and make recommendations to the Judge Admiral based on the information I *do* have at my disposal."

Mr. Patterson reached into his brief bag and removed a clutch of papers. He shuffled through them, placing several on the table before him and returning the rest to the bag. He pushed his glasses up his nose yet again.

The man struck Kieran as less of a firebrand and more of an unyielding bureaucrat. The sort who would not mount a campaign of vengeance but who would inexorably work his way toward the conclusion that facts and evidence supported.

A man who would never permit the spirit or intent of an action to supersede the letter of legality.

For men like Mr. Patterson, the law was the law.

"I interviewed Captain Cuthie and Mr. Massey and received their version of events before they departed for the Caribbean. That was nearly three years ago." Mr. Patterson tapped the papers before him, studying them. "Since that time, as no new information had come to light, the Judge Admiral had allowed the matter to lapse. However, that was before any of us knew that you—Miss Fyffe—had survived." Again, he peered at her over his spectacles. "Naturally, your survival changes matters."

"How so?" Andrew leaned forward from his seat on the sofa, eyes narrowed. "She cannot remember—"

"So she says." Mr. Patterson raised an eyebrow and gave Jamie a rather pointed look.

Ire, hot and potent, rose in Kieran's chest.

Was this man calling Jamie a liar?

Kieran opened his mouth, but a sharp glance from Andrew had him shutting it again.

"Please explain yourself, Mr. Patterson," Rafe said, adopting his loftiest I-am-the-son-of-a-duke expression.

"As I was saying, Captain Cuthie and Mr. Massey separately provided me with an account of the sinking of *The Minerva.* Their versions of those events closely align, which is what the Admiralty looks for when prosecuting a case—corroborated evidence. Despite circumstantial reports of the ship having wrecked on a reef, both the captain and his first mate insist that a deliberately-caused explosion sunk the ship." Mr. Patterson clasped his hands atop the papers on the table and fixed his gaze on Jamie. "Miss Fyffe, I will not go into details of their recitation, as I still wish to hear your version of events, free and clear of other influences. However, I will say that both Cuthie and Massey named yourself, Miss Eilidh Fyffe, as the party responsible for the explosion."

A rather dreadful silence followed Mr. Patterson's words.

Jamie's jaw, quite literally, dropped. Her mouth hung open in a blankness that mimicked the shocked horror of Kieran's own brain.

"Myself?" she whispered. She shook her head, brows drawing down in bewildered horror. "I am but a woman, Mr. Patterson. I cannot countenance it. That I, no matter the state of my lacking memory . . . that I would . . . that I would *destroy* a ship . . . to knowingly cause the deaths of so many innocent men . . ." She pressed a trembling hand to her mouth.

Kieran lurched to his feet, as if Cuthie himself were present and he could bury a fist in the liar's face.

Alex shot him an alarmed look. *Get a hold of yourself.*

"That is what Cuthie and Massey have asserted, Miss Fyffe," Mr. Patterson said, uncaring of Kieran's reaction. "They were most clear in laying the blame at your feet."

"But . . . ," Jamie frowned, "can I be held responsible for something I don't remember?"

"Yes. A self-proclaimed inability to recall committing a crime does not exonerate one from consequences. Otherwise, every thief and murderer in the kingdom would claim to have no memory of their offenses. If witnesses present corroborated, sworn evidence against yourself, then yes, you can and will be brought to justice, Miss Fyffe."

The words landed like a fist to Kieran's stomach.

If she were found guilty of killing so many people . . .

Jamie would swing for it.

She obviously understood the same, as her hand wandered up to her neck.

"I would *hang* for such an offense," she whispered.

Mr. Patterson said nothing, the silence speaking for him.

It was too much. Too much to bear. Too much to accept.

"This is such utter rot." Kieran took a step forward. "Cuthie has always been a lying—"

A heavy hand landed on his shoulder, stopping him. Kieran looked up to find Ewan at his side.

His friend shook his head, the pressure of his palm a silent command. *Stand down. You're not helping.*

Andrew and Rafe sent him similar warning looks.

Kieran folded his arms which, as a method of corralling frustration and anger, felt woefully inadequate.

"Ye said, *sworn evidence*," Alex said into the quiet. "So Cuthie and Massey have not officially sworn this testimony then? Not under oath?"

"You are most perceptive, my lord." Mr. Patterson grimaced. "I do not, at the moment, have Cuthie and Massey's corroborated account as *sworn* testimony. I merely questioned them and took notes, but the men were not under oath. They named Miss Fyffe as the guilty party. Obviously, at some point, they learned she was a woman. However, as Miss Fyffe was believed dead at the time, the information was moot. Therefore, I did not press the matter of her guilt.

"However, once Miss Fyffe's survival was brought to my attention last autumn, I sent a request through the Admiralty to have Cuthie and Massey restate their claims as sworn testimony. It is my understanding that they are currently aboard a ship in the West Indies. I am not requiring the men to return to Scotland, as they are merely witnesses to the events, not the ones being investigated. A sworn statement under oath before a judge admiral in Barbados or Jamaica will suffice as corroborated evidence. I want the full weight of Scottish law behind their accusations to ensure their veracity and legality in court, particularly as Miss Fyffe claims to have no memory of the events. I expect an answer within the next month or two. Once we receive their sworn testimony and if a formal inquiry shows sufficient evidence of an intentional crime on the part of Miss Fyffe, the matter will be sent to the maritime court for trial."

Kieran swallowed. So soon?

His Jamie had already been dealt so many blows in life. But this? It was intolerable. Only Alex's stern look and Andrew's faint head shake stopped Kieran's tongue.

"What am I to do in the meantime?" Jamie asked. The quiver in her voice nearly shattered Kieran's composure.

Again, Mr. Patterson said nothing for a moment.

"Ye cannot think to *arrest* Miss Fyffe," Andrew said into the silence, his voice rising syllable by syllable.

"That would be the Admiralty's preference, Lord Hadley." Mr. Patterson pursed his lips. "She has been accused of killing *one hundred and twenty-seven* men."

Kieran hissed in a breath.

Bloody hell.

Prison? *Now?*

His Jamie?!

To the devil with her remembering their marriage. That was a minor issue, now.

The woman he loved would not be subjected to a criminal trial for murder. She would not climb the wooden steps of the gallows and stand with her hands bound as a noose was fitted around her wee neck—

A torrent of words climbed his throat. He looked to his friends. *Now* could he shout his objections?

Alex once more shook his head, even though the rest of the

Brotherhood appeared equally concerned. Ewan had taken to pacing once more, and Rafe stared ahead with down-turned lips.

Andrew spoke first. "Surely, we can come to some other arrangement, Mr. Patterson. At the moment, Miss Fyffe is merely suspected of wrong-doing; the investigation seems to be ongoing. No official warrant has been issued, I take it."

"You are correct, my lord. The maritime court will not come into session until September, so of course, no trial would happen before then. I am merely gathering evidence." Mr. Patterson looked between them all, taking in Andrew's stern frown and Alex's raised eyebrows. His eyes darted to Rafe and Ewan, who still paced beside Kieran.

In short, the man was weighing his sense of legal duty against the might of aristocratic power assembled in the room.

The man's shoulders slumped, as if admitting a small defeat. "Assuming these illustrious lords will vouch for your person, Miss Fyffe," Mr. Patterson waved his hand, "I will allow you to remain free for now on your own recognizance, provided you stay here at Kilmeny."

Jamie nodded, face blanched white.

"Thank ye," Alex nodded.

"Aye," Andrew nodded. "We shall ensure that Miss Fyffe remains here. Ye have our word."

For her part, Jamie merely swallowed.

"You are fortunate in your friends, Miss Fyffe," Mr. Patterson fixed Jamie with a stern stare. "As for how you spend your time . . . well, the best defense, Miss Fyffe, would be to recover your memories and provide the courts with your version of the events that transpired."

"JAMIE IS . . . ALTERED," Andrew said, swirling the finger of whisky in his glass.

Rafe and Ewan nodded their agreement, sipping their own drinks.

"Aye," Kieran whispered, forcibly not reaching for a glass of whisky himself. Though as he stared at the bottle, there was no denying that a finger or three of whisky would ease the jittery ache in his chest.

But that way lay madness.

He feared if he started drinking now, he wouldn't stop until he was drunk. He had already taken to the bottle once to deal with his pain over Jamie.

Never again.

Unfortunately, his friends noticed his too-long contemplation of the whisky bottle. Rafe shot Andrew a weighted look.

"Och, youse dinnae have to dance around me like I'm some fragile bit of porcelain," Kieran snorted. "I willnae crack if things go sideways. I ken that I need tae stay strong for Jamie, so stop your clucking."

"Are ye sure?" Andrew asked. "Ye were raging there for a wee while after Mr. Patterson left."

"Aye," Ewan said. "I believe ye cursed every aspect of Cuthie's life, from his parentage tae his reproductive habits."

"O'course, I did. Cuthie is a right bastard, and it needed tae be said. He never liked my wife."

The four of them—Kieran, Ewan, Rafe, and Andrew—were still seated in the drawing room of Kilmeny Hall, picking at the remains of a late luncheon. Mr. Patterson had departed two hours before.

Alex had taken Jamie aside, requesting a private medical consultation to ascertain her general state of health, both physical and mental. Violet, Lady Kildrum, had accompanied them.

Kieran shifted in his seat. How much would Alex learn? Would he be able to recommend any treatments to help Jamie regain her memories?

"Have ye told her then?" Ewan asked, reaching for the last steak-and-kidney pie from the tray before him. "That you're handfasted?"

"No," Kieran said. "Alex is insistent that we need tae let her remember as much as possible on her own."

"Probably wise of ye, for now." Rafe stood and splashed another finger of whisky in his glass.

Kieran nodded, but the agitation in his chest continued to churn. He pushed to his feet, pacing in front of the fireplace. His mind raced with possibilities.

"If Jamie cannae remember that we are handfasted, are we even married?" Kieran had to ask it.

"'Tis a fair question," Rafe nodded. "When we encountered Reverend Gillespie last autumn, he was of the opinion that your marriage was not binding. Handfasting is considered a legal marriage in Scotland. But if a couple handfasts outside of Scotland—even if they both happen to *be* Scottish—the handfasting is likely not binding by law."

"Aye, and I fear it's further compounded by the fact that your handfasting was done in secret with only Ewan as a witness," Andrew added. "I have to be honest—I don't think the handfasting would stand in a court of law."

"We considered ourselves married, though." Kieran ran a hand through his hair. "It never even occurred tae me to think that we were not."

"Well, it's all easy enough tae remedy," Ewan said, swallowing a mouthful of meat pie. "All ye have tae do is claim one another as husband and wife in front of witnesses here in Scotland. That would be sufficient to cement the legality of it."

"Even better, convince Jamie to marry ye in front of a vicar," Rafe said. "Not even an Englishman would gainsay a kirk marriage."

Kieran snorted, feet still pacing. He could scarcely get his wife to *look* at him. She flinched away anytime he got too close.

He had forgotten how little she had trusted him when they first met. His reputation had preceded him then. Only proximity and time had convinced her that most of his supposed 'wild ways' were exaggerated and long since passed.

How was he to re-earn her trust? Much less convince her to claim him as her husband?

Granted, Jamie not knowing they were married was of lesser concern at the moment.

One battle at a time . . .

"It will come right, Kieran." Andrew sipped his whisky. "Jamie hasn't come this far and suffered this much tae hang for a crime she can't remember committing."

"I cannae believe Cuthie has done this. Tae accuse Jamie of murdering so many men—" Kieran nearly spat. "Cuthie always hated our Jamie. She made him look a fool in the end, so of course he has twisted the events tae suit his own ends. The man would perjure himself before man and God afore allowing Jamie to walk free."

"The captain can be viciously vindictive." Ewan set down his plate. "But are we convinced that Cuthie would perjure himself just to spite Kieran and Jamie? Swearing false testimony under oath is a serious crime, and Cuthie has appeared keen to avoid prosecution these past several years."

"Perhaps." Andrew grimaced and tossed back the rest of his whisky. "Regardless, I'll start tugging on some strings in Lords. If the situation deteriorates with Jamie, Alex and I will petition the King for a pardon."

Silence for a moment.

Kieran wiped a weary hand over his face. "Of course, this all assumes that my Jamie is innocent."

Andrew set down his glass, waiting until Kieran met his gaze. "Ye know she wouldn't have blown up that ship without a justifiable reason."

"Aye," Kieran agreed, "but the fact remains that Jamie would have done it, had it felt warranted."

"Och, I hate him, Kieran!" Jamie stormed into the night, her feet sinking into the wet sand of the beach. "I cannae believe he planned this all along."

"Cuthie is an opportunist—"

She whirled around and tapped his chest. "We need a plan. Something needs tae be done to stop him—"

Kieran bit his lip.

What had happened aboard *The Minerva*?

"That's the rub, is it not?" Andrew said. "Cuthie *may* be telling the truth."

"Or a partial truth," Rafe offered.

"But until Jamie remembers . . ." Ewan's voice drifted off.

"Aye." Kieran swallowed back the acidic taste of despair in his throat, walking to stand in front of the window. A sliver of gleaming ocean glinted on the horizon. "Miss Eilidh Fyffe needs tae remember being Jamie. That's all there is to it."

SEPTEMBER 1815

"Youse all should have told me." Kieran pointed a finger at the other members of the Brotherhood. They lounged around the table in Andrew's quarters, dinner spread before them. "I thought we were friends. We pledged a brotherhood and everything."

If Kieran thought to guilt his friends into showing shame, he was disappointed.

"It wasnae our tale tae tell, Kieran," Andrew said, sopping up the last of his ragout with a bit of bread, blithely ignoring Kieran's death stare.

In fact, all of his supposed friends ate on, unconcerned and irritatingly cheerful.

The bunch of *bawbags*.

"Aye, it was," Kieran said. "I'm master of this ship and responsible for her crew. Therefore, I need to know secrets of this magnitude."

"Jamie asked us to keep the confidence," Rafe chimed in, pouring himself more ale from a pitcher.

"The lass doesnae get tae make such far-reaching decisions." Kieran tapped his chest. "I do."

"Och, and how were we supposed to tell ye?" Alex asked.

"It's simple," Kieran snorted. "Youse just open your mouth and say, *Why Kieran, ye know that wee laddie you've taken under your wing? Well, she's actually a bonnie lassie—*"

"Bonnie, am I?" Jamie laughed.

Kieran turned to glare at her.

"Please continue." She clasped her hands under her chin and batted her eyelashes at him. "I *adore* it when men blether on about me like I'm not in the room."

Ewan chuckled, scraping more ragout out of the earthenware bowl and onto his plate. "You're not going to win this one, Kieran."

Glowering, Kieran slumped back in his seat. He ran a hand over his face. "This is a disaster."

"It'll come right," Rafe said.

"Quit your whinging," Andrew nodded. "We will see Jamie through."

"Aye," Alex agreed.

"I must say, I didnae take ye for the worrying sort, Kieran," Jamie piped in. "I always thought ye were more *carpe diem* than a strict advocate of law and order. Why does this have ye twisted into knots?"

Kieran shot her his sternest I-am-master-of-this-ship look.

She, of course, remained utterly unperturbed. She simply poured herself more ale from the pitcher, leaned back in her chair, and propped a booted foot on the cabin door.

She met his gaze squarely.

A frisson of . . . something . . . passed between them.

The spark was as surprising as it was unwelcome.

She wasn't wrong.

He *was* tied into knots.

Just not in the way she supposed.

"I am thorough in my work," he replied. "Ignorant sailors can easily end up dead sailors. I would prefer it if no one dies on my watch."

"Well, I shall try not to let my gender kill anyone," Jamie deadpanned, drinking her ale with rather irritating calm.

The rest of the Brotherhood laughed.

Kieran knew he should be irritated with her. He should find her attitude cavalier and her manners obnoxious.

It was just . . .

Her silvery eyes sparkled like sunlight shimmering on a summer's day as she spoke. Her voice fair vibrated with *joie de vivre.*

Such charm was nearly impossible to withstand.

Kieran shook his head and, to his endless frustration, . . . *smiled.*

He had no business developing a tendre for this woman. It would be a disaster in more ways than he could quickly count.

But . . . it was hard to cast the image of her bathing from his mind, the expanse of creamy skin, the delicate arch of her spine. He was a man, was he not? Images of half-naked women had a tendency to stick.

Though if his attraction to her had been merely physical, even *that* he could have easily mastered.

No . . . it was the fire of her that drew him in. The sense that she would always meet him as an equal.

Perhaps sensing his thoughts, she paused, her gaze tangling a bit too long with his.

He smiled wider, perhaps a smidge challenging now.

True to her nature, she didn't flinch.

But her fingers tensed around the mug she held.

As if she, too, were fighting the unexpected current that threatened to drag them both out to sea.

10

Eilidh woke the next morning, dread sitting like an albatross on her chest.

How many mornings had she awakened to this heavy sensation? How many years had she lost to melancholy and despair?

Her carefully constructed numbness was crumbling.

She rose and paced over to the window, pulling back the curtains, and opening the shutters. The window was small, as was typical for a medieval Scottish castle, she supposed. But if she pressed her forehead to the glass and looked to her right, she could see the ocean. The wind whipped the water into a turbulent froth, sending plumes of sea spray crashing into the cliffs.

It felt too much like a portent. A shadow of the emotional maelstrom headed her way.

One hundred and twenty-seven men.

The numbers spun incessantly in her head—1-2-7.

Dead.

Fathers. Brothers. Sons. Husbands. Friends.

Men who had been known to her. Some had likely been her friends.

Men whose deaths certainly left gaping holes in the lives of those who loved them. She couldn't fathom the depth of such collective grief and pain.

And now . . . she was accused of being the cause of it all.

It felt impossible.

She would never have done such a thing. Never. No matter what Captain Cuthie claimed had happened.

And yet . . .

Overnight, vague memories had wormed their way through her consciousness. Images that her mind labeled as Captain Cuthie—a grizzled sailor with dark eyes and a hooked nose, skin leathery from his years at sea.

Cuthie yelling at a cabin boy for mopping the deck too slowly, cuffing the lad upside the head and sending him sprawling.

Cuthie's onyx eyes wide and mere inches from her own, shouting unintelligible words before pushing her down a ladder.

Cuthie advancing on her with a knife in hand—

She took in a slow breath.

This was the problem with the dark chasm of that missing year.

Every time she plumbed her missing memories, scenes rose, wraithlike, from the murky depths. Ghoulish images that were ugly and frightening and best left undisturbed.

Why? She shook a fist at the specter of memory howling at her back, clawing at her vision. *Why can you not let me be?*

She had finally—finally!—crafted a space of light and safety with Simon. A numbed white void where such darkness did not intrude. She had a future before her, one of hope and hard-won peace.

Why could she not simply continue forward with her life, leaving the bleak depths of that year far behind?

Lord Lockheade's examination of her yesterday had been . . . painful. Not physically, of course. He had merely checked her pulse and asked about her bodily health.

But the rest of his questions . . . those had scrubbed her raw.

Are ye sleeping well?

No.

Do ye have unexplained moments of fear or anxiety?

Yes. Constantly.

Do ye struggle tae feel positive emotions at times?

I prefer not to feel at all.

Have ye talked with someone else about what ye remember?

No.

Do ye wish tae remember?

No.

Never.

She had no desire to ever remember the entirety of her voyage aboard *The Minerva.* The phantom glimpses she had of it were already terrifying. Why would she ever wish to summon the wraiths in earnest?

A plate clinked somewhere lower in the castle. A maid's voice called.

So there were other people about.

That was a blessing, as least.

She and Master MacTavish had returned to the castle yesterday alone. A fact that made her desperately uncomfortable.

The other members of the Brotherhood treated her with kindness and respect, and yet, not one of them accompanied her from Kilmeny Hall to Kilmeny Castle.

Why was she given a new wardrobe but not a chaperone? Did everyone here view her as utterly fallen then? A disgraced woman who did not warrant the protection of a chaperone?

Though technically correct, the thought . . . stung.

She had finally asked Master MacTavish about it the night before.

"Why is there no chaperone here? This situation is highly improper. I am a lady, despite everything." She had turned to face him on the main staircase of Kilmeny Castle. "Why have the others left me alone with you?"

He had grunted and replied, "It's not their place tae be here."

"And it *is* yours?" She was a step above him, the added height bringing her nearly eye-level with him. So close she could see the flecks of darker blue in his pale eyes.

"Something like that," was his enigmatic reply. "Ye will be safe with me."

He crossed his arms and her eyes dipped—entirely without her permission—to the muscles straining against the upper arms of his coat.

"*Your* actions are the ones that concern me the most." She mimicked his folded arms. "Your reputation precedes you, Master MacTavish."

As usual, her biting words affected him not at all. He merely studied her with those formidably blue eyes. "I will never harm ye, lass."

The open honesty in his gaze unnerved her. Even more unnerving was her inability to stop cataloging the pieces of him—the smile lines permanently etched into his cheeks, the way his hair curled over his ears, tempting her fingers to twine—

Eilidh looked away, immediately bid him goodnight, and all but bolted for her bedroom door, hoping that morning would provide some clarity.

It had not.

In short, this entire situation would be more tolerable if *he* were not involved.

Yes, she could admit the obvious—Kieran MacTavish was an alarmingly attractive man. That had never been in doubt. *Of course* she would find it difficult to stop staring at him.

It was how he behaved with those good looks that was the problem. The way his chin had dipped in the stairwell, eyes gazing up at her, broody and stark and searching. The way his hand sometimes lifted as they walked together, as if, almost, to press into the small of her back.

The very thought of such things trembled and quivered, and the logical part of her had no idea why.

After washing and dressing and waiting for the chipper maid who insisted on styling her hair—"Ye have to have lovely hair tae match all your fine, new clothes, miss. Ye simply must!"—Eilidh arrived in the great hall for breakfast.

Like the morning two days ago, Master MacTavish was already seated at the large table, his back to the fireplace. He didn't notice her at first, his attention on a newspaper and the breakfast placed before him.

He had not donned a kilt today. Instead, he appeared the perfect gentleman. His shoulders filled out the breadth of a green tailcoat, the superfine wool neatly tailored to his lean frame. His dark hair flopped across his forehead and over his ears, giving him a boyish appearance.

Why had God granted such a reprehensible man so large a portion of beauty?

"If sin were ugly, we would not be drawn to it," Reverend Gillespie was fond of saying. *"Usually, the more attractive something appears, the more damaging it is to our souls. Do not allow your foolish eyes to lead you again astray, Miss Fyffe."*

If attractiveness were a measure of wickedness, then Master MacTavish would be the devil incarnate.

At the table, MacTavish froze, as if her presence stirred something in the air. He lifted his head and met her eyes.

He set down the paper and shot to his feet, his expression the very definition of delight.

"Jamie!" His smile spread wide, creasing his cheeks and lighting sparks in his pale eyes. "I trust ye had a good night's rest?"

It was too much. Eilidh's jaw instantly tensed.

"Miss Fyffe, if you please. I have a name of my own, Master MacTavish. I am more than my brother's impostor." She gritted her teeth as she sat at the table, disliking how her tongue instantly leaped to incivility with this man.

The smile on Master MacTavish's face remained, but the warmth in his eyes faded.

Be a lady, Eilidh.

She swallowed, took a deep breath, and tried again.

"Master MacTavish—" She clasped her hands primly in her lap. "—I would appreciate being referred to as Miss Fyffe."

"I beg your pardon, Miss Fyffe." He bowed, polite and formal, before retaking his seat and folding the newspaper. "I will attempt tae remember, but as I knew ye as Jamie, it's a difficult habit to break."

Eilidh nodded, but a trickle of unease chased her spine as she spooned coddled eggs and slices of black pudding onto her plate . . . the thought that perhaps she had spoken too harshly, judged him too quickly.

They ate in silence for a few moments. She tore open a still-warm bap and reached for the butter. He drank his coffee and polished off the last bite of his bacon.

The far-off call of servants and the clatter of a wagon in the fore-court filtered through the room.

Finally, he pushed his plate back and reached for the coffee pot, pouring himself another cup. "I fear you and myself have gotten off on the wrong foot. Let's start again. I am here tae help ye remember what ye can about the sinking of the ship."

"Yes, but I don't *want* to remember." Eilidh swallowed back the churn of emotion that swelled at the very thought.

No. She would make no attempts to remember. None.

Master MacTavish set the coffeepot down with more force than was strictly necessary.

"Ye *have* tae remember, lass," he said, his tone irritatingly agreeable. "I willnae watch ye hang simply because you're being stubborn."

Eilidh wanted to rub her forehead. It seemed like she had been in this place just two days ago.

Oh, that was because she *had* been.

"We already had a version of this conversation when I arrived." She set down the bap and placed her hands on the table, staring at him.

"Yes and no." He mirrored her, his hands also on the table. "We spoke, yes, but that was before we discovered ye might hang for actions ye dinnae remember doing. Now, we need tae help ye recall—"

"Why yourself? Why are you the man who is here?" she interrupted. "Why are you the one who meets me for breakfast and sends me to my chambers at night? Why not Lord Lockheade? He is a physician *and* someone I trust. Why was it decided that *you* have to be the one to assist me in this?"

She didn't add that MacTavish lurked most inconveniently . . . in the dark recesses of her memory, in the unwanted puzzle of her sentiments.

"Why myself?" He stirred two lumps of sugar into his coffee. "I suppose because the rest of the Brotherhood know I had—*have*—a close relationship with yourself—"

"Close? Us?" Eilidh's eyebrows flew upward, her accent disintegrating right along with her sense of equanimity. "Ye may think ye know me, but *I* don't know you. Aside from the unsavory bits and bobs my father mentioned over the years, ye are, more or less, a stranger to me."

"That's why ye need tae get to know me." MacTavish sipped his coffee with an annoying slurp, clearly unruffled.

Eilidh did not want him composed and calm.

She wanted him seething and frustrated like the coiled knot currently tightening under her sternum.

"Get to know ye? Why would I?!" She leaned toward him, ticking off on her fingers. "Ye abandon my father in his hour of greatest need, leaving him to a pauper's grave. Ye bring me here by paying off my friends. Ye bribe me with new clothing, but thumb your nose at all propriety, depositing me in this castle, alone with yourself. And then, as if that all weren't enough, ye ask me to plumb the most painful moments of my life with your untrustworthy self as my guide. No, thank ye."

Again . . . she got little reaction from him.

He merely shook his head. "Now, lass—"

"No! Enough!" Eilidh took in a deep breath. "I understand you and the others think me to be in danger. But I know myself. There is *no* chance that I deliberately had anything to do with that ship exploding. The very thought is appalling. This is simply a mistake, and Captain Cuthie's account of what happened will likely show that I am innocent."

Master MacTavish laughed, a dismissive crack of sound. His composure crumbled—brows frowning, eyes narrowing, shoulders bunching.

"Captain Cuthie *despised* ye, lass," he said, leaning forward on his hands. "Ye pulled the wool over his eyes for nearly eight months. He only realized ye were, indeed, a lass right before ye were parted from us. Ye made him look foolish. And a man like Cuthie is most dangerous when he feels humiliated. He would perjure himself tae spite ye. Dinnae think tae receive any respite from that quarter."

Eilidh sat back in her chair and folded her arms across her chest, as if they could stand as a barrier against . . . *all* of it.

Angerfearshamepainhorror churned just beneath her sternum. It was lava—fiery and scorching. It choked her breathing and stung her eyes.

"I cannot do this. Not with yourself," she said, shaking her head, proud that her voice didn't tremble. "If I must remember, leave me to it. Allow me to remember on my own and in my own way."

Master MacTavish sat back himself, arms crossed, again mirroring her. "Ye dinnae have the time tae wait. Alex has suggested that perhaps engaging in activities that ye did aboard ship might help ye—"

"No!"

The lava burst from her chest, painfully clawing up her throat.

Images flooded her mind. Snippets of memory she never wanted to relive.

Her brother, Jamie, lurching upright in bed as he died, vomiting a river of blood all over his chest, the counterpane, her hands.

Herself, curled up on a mat in a villager's hut, drowning in shame and horror, her head an endless drum of pain, the metallic tang of blood in the air.

So. Much. Blood.

Her past ran red with it.

She feared someday she would wake to find the world itself pulsed red—

Eilidh pushed back from her chair, her only thought to get away, away, away—

"Jamie . . ." Master MacTavish's voice reached her.

"Jamie is *DEAD*!" she all but screamed, pausing to whirl back to face him. "Why cannae ye stop saying his name?!"

She swiped at her eyes, the world foggy, her eyesight narrowing. She turned and ran for the door, anything to escape *him*.

She only made it to the central staircase.

"Lass. Stop." His hand snagged her elbow, turning her around.

She yanked free of his hold, staggering backward.

"I won't speak of it," she gasped. "I refuse to remember!"

"Your life depends on ye remembering!"

"It's *my* life. Mine!" She stabbed a finger at her chest. "It is *my* choice to attempt to remember or take my chances with Cuthie. It doesn't affect ye at all. In fact, I absolve ye of any lingering sense of duty toward me—"

"It doesnae affect me?!" His eyes flared wide, and he pressed a palm to his chest. "Of course, it affects me! I care about ye!"

That was it. The very end of her tether.

Every last ounce of her numbness shattered, disintegrating and taking her ladylike manners with it.

"Care about me?! How *dare* ye mock me!"

"Pardon?" He rocked back.

"I was pregnant!" She hurled her deepest shame at him. "I was aboard that ship, and I was pregnant!"

He blanched, color leaching from his skin.

An expression skittered across his face.

Something like regret . . . or pain.

He did *not*, however, look surprised.

"Ye knew?" she hissed. "Ye knew I was increasing?!"

He floundered, as if searching for some platitude to justify himself.

Eilidh would have none of it.

"Ye knew," she repeated, pointing at him. "I may have forgotten much, but *who* I am as a person has not changed. I know I would not willingly lie with a man who was not my husband. So ye say ye care, but where were ye aboard that ship? Where were ye when I was ill-used?!"

"Jami—Miss Fyffe . . . ye werenae ill-used. We kept ye saf—"

"You lie!" she spat.

He raked a hand down his face, his expression so . . . weary.

"What happened tae the babe, lass?" he asked.

"Gone. The baby is gone." Words sliced her throat as they forced their way out. "I was already bleeding when the islanders fished me out of the water and delivered me to Reverend Gillespie. I bled and bled."

"Ah, lass . . ." His hand reached out, as if to touch her again.

She shrank back, choosing to hurl words at his head instead. "My body rejected the babe, thank goodness—"

"Thank *goodness*?!" Master MacTavish rasped.

Agony and shock flashed across his face. As if her words had been a stiletto strike between the third and fourth ribs.

"Aye!" she huffed. "Ye don't think for one breath that I wanted that babe, do ye? What woman would? A child conceived in sin and pain?

What life would such a child have had? Even Reverend Gillespie said that it was a mercy from God that the babe died. And I'm glad of it!"

KIERAN STARED AT Jamie.

Her words were a blow to the solar plexus, punching the air from his lungs and leaving him gasping.

The reverend had told him the babe was no more.

Logically, Kieran had known this.

But . . .

He had assumed that Jamie would have loved their child, no matter her circumstances. After all, the babe was an innocent life.

But this?

Ye don't think for one breath that I wanted that babe, do ye?

The babe died, and I'm glad of it!

To *know* that their baby had passed on—unwanted, unloved, and unmourned.

He swallowed back what felt like the whimper of a wounded animal.

She doesnae know, a part of him whispered. *She doesnae remember. She will feel differently when she does.*

But would she? Feel differently? Or even . . . remember?

His Jamie swiped the tears from her face with a clenched fist, as if eager to rid herself of any memory of their child.

Their child!

He had to tell her, did he not? No matter Alex's warning?

She had to know that she was his wife. That she had once thought differently about their bairn. That this anguish she carried—assuming their baby resulted from an illicit liaison—was unwarranted.

But . . .

Would she believe him? And would he be telling her for her sake? Or merely to assuage his own pain and guilt?

Focus on her.

Kieran bit his tongue, stopping the words.

"I'm *glad* I lost that baby," Jamie repeated. "The shame of being a fallen woman is bad enough. But having a constant reminder of my sins in the form of a child would be—" She paused, shaking her head. She straightened slightly, as if regathering the scattered shards of herself. "I have fought for *six* years to put that episode behind me. That girl—the one who found herself disgraced, pregnant, and abandoned on the underside of the world—is no more. So perhaps ye can appreciate why I am not eager to go rushing into remembering even more of that chapter of my life! Why would I want to recall the horror that led to me being battered, increasing, and left for dead? Perhaps I forgot for a reason!"

Light raked her from the lone window at the end of the hall, turning her face into a harlequin mask—half light, half dark.

Kieran wanted to drag all of her into the light, to tear open the shadow of her memory.

Cannae ye see how much ye are loved?! he longed to yell. *How much* our babe *was loved?!*

But would that convince her to try to remember?

No. No, it would not.

He ran a hand over his face, forcing himself to take a slow breath, in and out.

Patience.

He could be patient.

The jittery anxiety banding his chest did not need to be expressed.

He could rebuild her trust. He could wait for her to come to him.

To remember their love, their baby . . . their *everything.*

"You were not ill-used," he repeated, keeping his voice measured. "I wouldnae be so sure that all the memories are bad."

"I don't want them regardless . . . those memories. I want them to stay gone."

"Ye cannae mean that, lass."

"Of course, I mean it!" She huffed in surprise. "I have moved on from the horror of *The Minerva.* I am forging a new life for myself, one that my mother and father would have approved. I have the regard of a good man who wishes to marry me—"

"Pardon? A good man?!" Surprise raised Kieran's voice a solid two octaves. "What the hell does that mean?!"

Jamie flinched, as surely as if he had struck her. "It means I have a beau."

"Ye cannae be serious?" Blind fury coated Kieran's mind. "Another *man*—"

"His name is Simon," Jamie spat at him. "Mr. Simon Fitzpatrick. He is a curate, and he loves me—"

"Like hell he does!"

"How dare you? Who do ye think ye are?!" She raked him with scathing precision, her eyes chips of frost. "Simon is the only good thing to happen to me since my father and Jamie died. He does love me! More to the point, Simon accepts me even knowing I was forced to be a *whore* aboard a merchant ship! Had he been there, he would have protected me. Unlike yourself! Ye *were* there and did nothing to stop it!"

Jamie spun around, dashing up the stairs, her feet slapping on the stone.

Kieran raced after her. "As I keep saying, ye weren't forced tae be a whore, Jamie! No one coerced ye—"

"*Oh!* No one forced me? So you're saying I *wanted* tae be a whore!" She pivoted and glared down at him, her tone dripping acid. "Please tell me more about all the lovely experiences just waiting to be remembered!"

"If ye would just listen—"

"Leave me alone!" She whirled and continued to race up the stairs.

"Nae! I care too much tae leave ye be! The Jamie I knew would fight to remember. Not give up her future tae the first man who promised her security—"

"One last time. I. Am. Not. Jamie!" She reached her bedroom door and threw it open, spinning to face him, one hand on the door jamb, one on the latch. "The woman ye thought ye knew is gone. I am here the now. And I want peace. I ache for it. And I praise God every day that he sent a good, kind man like Simon into my life. I've finally found a measure of contentment after years of heartache. I will not allow yourself or anyone to take it from me!"

"Jamie—"

"For the last time, Jamie. Is. Dead! Leave me be!"

She slammed the door in his face, the lock clacking with brutal finality.

It felt a wee bit like the closing of a casket.

He stared at the door, chest heaving, hands in his hair.

He wanted to bang his fists on the thick oak.

To shout her name until he was hoarse.

Until she disavowed this *Simon Fitzpatrick*.

Until she opened the door, threw herself upon his chest, and dragged his lips down to hers with greedy hunger.

Until she promised to remain his *wife*.

But then . . . this had always been Jamie's way, had it not? Slammed doors and biting words?

He had forgotten this.

That his Jamie could be difficult to love.

That she kept emotion in until it came spilling out in a ferocity that could shake him to his core.

His wife had changed . . . but, somehow, she was utterly the same.

He took a step back, his shoulders hitting the wall opposite her door. He slid down the stones until he was sitting, wrists resting on his knees.

Simon Fitzpatrick.

Simon the curate.

Simon the Sassenach, more like it.

Blech.

How could she think to marry another? And an Englishman, no less?

She was Kieran's wife, dammit!!

But . . .

What if she never remembered?

They were handfasted, yes, but if she didn't remember, then . . .

Were they even married?

The law would say *No*, just as his friends had asserted. In Scotland, both parties had to acknowledge the marriage in order for the handfasting to be legal.

Kieran's heart begged to differ.

But a marriage required two people.

And it appeared that right now . . . she was moving on from him.

She had turned away from their past and embraced the vista of a vastly altered future.

One in which he was barely a speck on the fast-fading horizon at her back.

11

Eilidh sat for hours on her bed, staring out the window, sightlessly watching the sun creep across the sky.

She had written a letter to Simon, which now sat atop the small desk in the corner, folded and addressed and ready to be posted. She hadn't gone into any detail about her current predicament. Just a vague discussion of the weather and the kindness of Lady Kildrum and Mr. Campbell.

Nothing more. No mention of the Gillespies leaving her. Nothing about the investigation of *The Minerva.*

She couldn't bring herself to write it out on paper, to vividly relive the horror of the past few days.

Besides, Simon was the worrying sort. The man would work himself into a state of agitation over the accusations against her, and Eilidh did not want to cause him undue alarm, particularly when she anticipated it would all come to naught.

Moreover, who knew how soon the Gillespies would be returning to their village in Yorkshire? The reverend and his wife had a habit of traipsing around Britain, visiting wealthier friends in the hopes of drumming up more donations for their return trip to the South Pacific.

Knowing this, Eilidh could very well return to their small village before the Gillespies did . . . before the awkward questions of their split from one another could be raised.

She could simply collect her belongings, marry Simon, and move forward with her new life with him, leaving the past . . . passed.

She missed Simon.

He was kind, learned, and a true gentleman with soulful blue eyes that earnestly studied her as she spoke and a soft voice that soothed the rough edges of her heart.

He was precisely the sort of man her parents would have wished her to marry.

Eilidh considered Simon to be a gift from God. Here was a man who knew she was a fallen woman, who knew the horror of her behavior aboard *The Minerva.* And yet, he still accepted her. He loved her without judgment, without condescension.

She would never forsake such a precious treasure.

They had met the previous autumn. Simon and his mother had let a house near to the Gillespies, as Simon was to take up the position of curate to the local vicar. Reverend Gillespie, despite his bonafides, did not have a congregation of his own.

Initially, Simon had expressed interest in joining the reverend on his next voyage to the South Pacific. But Simon's mother, Mrs. Fitzpatrick, had quickly quashed her son's hopes, though not before Simon and Eilidh had developed a friendship. The Gillespies, Eilidh was quite sure, had never realized the depth of her relationship with Simon.

Two days before she left for Kilmeny Castle, Simon had proposed to her.

"I am not the wealthiest or most charismatic of men," he said, "but I have a genuine regard for you. No matter your past, I wish to be your future. I will cherish you all your days, Miss Fyffe."

As usual, his forthright honesty had touched her.

But . . . something made Eilidh hesitate to accept his offer of marriage immediately. She thought she loved him, inasmuch as she *could* love.

That was the problem with the frozen white numbness of her mind—it made feeling anything difficult. Or, perhaps, she simply was not given to romantic notions.

But as she had never been in love, it was hard to say.

Did marriage require grandiose feelings?

Eilidh thought not.

Marriage required trust, affection, and respect. And those three things, she and Simon had in abundance.

The farther she journeyed from Simon, the more she ached to return to the peace of him. She liked the person she was around him—calm, collected, reserved. Life with Simon would be one of quiet simplicity: a wee cottage behind the village church, parishioners to visit and the poor to help, a fire in the hearth and Simon writing a sermon on a snowy winter's eve.

She planned to accept Simon's offer of marriage when next she saw him. It felt like something she should tell him in person, not in a letter.

Simon was a safe harbor after a terrible storm.

He would never force her to remember things that she wished to remain buried. He would not challenge or upset her.

He accepted that she wished her emotions to remain encased in frozen white, safely floating above the unpleasant memories that lurked in the deep.

He was delightfully English that way—strong sentiments were to be avoided, at best, and then ignored, at worst.

By comparison, Master MacTavish was a cyclone of unwanted turmoil. He invoked a whirlwind of stinging emotions and confused thoughts that spun too quickly for her to pinpoint only one: frustration, anger, desire—

Ugh.

She threw herself backward onto the counterpane, staring up at the plastered ceiling.

Why was she even thinking upon the man? She still did not like him. Case in point . . . merely conjuring his name had set her pulse thumping.

Had she actually yelled at him? Screaming like some shrill fishwife?

She inwardly cringed, setting the heels of her hands to her closed eyes and pressing until a kaleidoscope spiraled in her vision.

This wasn't who she was.

Or, rather, it wasn't who she wished to be.

Her mother had not raised her to behave in such a manner.

Ye weren't forced tae be a whore.

Master MacTavish's words were a battering ram, pummeling the walls of her sense of self—who she was, what she valued and treasured.

The man was wrong, completely and utterly wrong.

She opened her eyes, throwing her hands down to her sides.

How could she have *chosen* to share a man's bed? Whenever she thought of the man who had impregnated her—because clearly there *had* been one—he was always a faceless, nameless brute. Someone she did not wish to *ever* remember—

Oh! Did the other members of the Brotherhood know?

She cringed at the thought of asking Dr. Whitaker—ehr, Lord Lockheade—or Mr. Campbell about her pregnancy.

But . . . what if they *didn't* know? Then, just the question alone would reveal too much. It was too humiliating to contemplate.

She pressed her fingers to her eyes once more.

No. She was not that sort of woman, no matter her missing memories. Surely there was some other explanation, one in which she hadn't *willingly* allowed herself to become with child, that she had somehow been coerced.

And yet . . .

Unbidden the memory rose of those grief-stricken days after Jamie and her father's back-to-back deaths. The terrible bleakness of the future abruptly facing her. The realization that being raised in gentility did not keep one from penury and homelessness. The terror of being a lone woman thrust into the world with little more than the clothing on her back.

But had those emotions alone changed her? Forced her to become such a different version of herself? The woman who had taken on Jamie's name, donned his clothing, and left for foreign lands aboard a merchant ship? And, if Master MacTavish were to be believed, she had *welcomed* it all.

He likely knew who the father of her child was.

Just thinking upon it tightened her breathing and left her hands shaking. She never wanted to associate a name with those forgotten acts.

Yes, Master MacTavish needed to leave her be. To understand, once and for all, that she absolved him of any lingering debt to her family.

She simply wanted his equilibrium-disturbing presence out of her life.

Or, at the very least, a chaperone for herself here at the castle.

Be a lady, even if the way is not easy.

She might be a fallen woman, but she still saw herself as a lady. Mrs. Gillespie had been insistent in that, bless her. That if Eilidh had not chosen to lie with a man willingly—but had instead been assaulted against her will—the sin was not on her head. But, of course, she knew that not everyone was so generous in their thoughts. Most would condemn her, regardless of her actual wishes.

Her stomach growled, reminding her that she had only had a sparse breakfast earlier in the day.

Eilidh sat up in bed with a grimace. She had to leave this room sometime, she supposed.

She placed Simon's letter in her pocket, donned her pelisse, and picked up her bonnet.

She would walk up to Kilmeny Hall and see if she could speak with Lady Kildrum about arranging a chaperone. Her ladyship had been kind the day before. Perhaps if Eilidh explained the situation, her ladyship would assist her in making other arrangements.

She opened her bedroom door.

Master MacTavish sat on the floor opposite—shoulders slumped, wrists dangling over his knees, hair askew.

His gaze drilled her in place, frozen within the door frame.

She had been in her room for *hours*. And yet, he appeared to have remained precisely where she had last seen him.

Moreover, his pale eyes were bloodshot and red-rimmed.

Had he . . .

Had he been . . . *weeping*?

She shook the thought away.

A man such as Master MacTavish did not weep.

Or if he did, why would he weep over her? Why would he care?

He slowly pushed to his feet, shoulders against the wall, his eyes never leaving hers.

"Master MacTavish, this is absurd." She raked him from head to foot. "Why are you still here?"

His shoulders deflated, and he tilted his head back, meeting the wall behind with a soft thump. His pale gaze glittered in the low light of the narrow hallway.

"I will always be here for ye, lass," he said, voice raspy and gravel-edged.

"No—" She held out a staying hand. "This is more than mere politeness. As I have said repeatedly, I absolve you of any debt to myself. Done. Vanished. You can leave me be now."

He shook his head, those red-rimmed eyes watching her with that same unnerving intensity. "I'm not going to leave ye."

The sheer weariness of his tone tugged and pulled at her, until some part of her heart ached to sit and weep with him.

It was the height of absurdity.

"Actually, I don't wish to know why you are still here," she said. "I simply want our private association to stop. I am going to see Lady Kildrum and request a chaperone. It is beyond appalling that I reside here with yourself and no other company. How could her ladyship, of all people, think it wise to house us both together? I cannot continue to betray Simon's trust in this way."

That shot a bolt of life through MacTavish. He lurched fully upright.

"Simon." He all but spat the name.

"Aye, *Simon*."

"Ye cannae marry Simon."

"Of course, I can marry Simon." She moved to pass by Master MacTavish, intent on the stairs. "If you will excuse me—"

"A moment." He placed a hand on her arm. As usual, the casual touch burned.

She flinched away, her knees bending and her left forearm instinctively coming up to defend herself, her right hand fisting around the ribbons of her bonnet.

A fighter's stance, she realized with horror. Her breathing went tight.

Master MacTavish held up his palms, a universal sign for parley.

"Please," he continued. "Just a moment."

Bewildered and terrified that her body had reacted so precisely to a perceived threat, Eilidh instantly straightened. She pressed her back against the doorjamb to her bedchamber, putting as much space as possible between her and Master MacTavish in the narrow hallway.

He sighed and, once more, leaned back against the wall opposite her, as if he needed the strength of the stone to buoy him up.

She clasped her hands in front of her, bonnet ribbons looped around her trembling fingers.

"Well?" she asked.

He continued to regard her, his expression so open she could clearly see a wounded animal within.

He looked . . . ill. A man on the brink of devastation.

"We—meaning myself and the other survivors—have kept certain facts from ye," he began. "We had all hoped that ye would remember them on your own. But I fear we do not have time for subtlety."

Eilidh licked her lips. "Facts?"

"Aye. Facts. Ye are making plans for your life without knowing an important wee bit of information. And I cannae let ye continue on without . . ." His voice trailed off.

He scrubbed a hand over his face, his eyes glittering with what she suspected were unshed tears.

Abruptly, she was terrified of what he would tell her.

What information about herself could make a man such as Kieran MacTavish weep?

Blood roared in her ears.

"Two things." He held up two fingers. "One—"

"Maybe I don't wish to know it," she interrupted. "Must I know?"

"Aye."

"What could possibly be so important?" She threw up her hands. "You're practically *greiting* over it!"

"O' course I'm greiting!" He dragged a knuckle across his eyes. "Ye would be greiting too if your wife didnae remember that she was your *wife*!"

His words were a vicious slap to her senses. Eilidh recoiled, taking an involuntary step back into her bedchamber.

Silence.

Deafening, thunderous silence.

The word reverberated between them—*wife, wife, wife.*

"Pardon?" she whispered, bracing a trembling hand on the doorjamb.

"You, Miss Eilidh Fyffe, are my *wife*."

Eilidh's knees threatened to buckle. She swayed.

He lurched forward, an arm instantly around her waist, pulling her upright, his body pressed to hers.

Every point of contact burned with a fiery heat—his chest under her palm, his thigh against her hipbone, his fingertips on her spine—

She pushed away from him, forcing them both back against opposite walls once more.

But not before she felt a frisson of . . . something.

A roil of current bucking the white numbness.

A flashing hint that perhaps she had been here before.

That perhaps . . .

"No." She shook her head. "I don't believe ye."

"Ask Ewan. He witnessed the ceremony himself."

"Ye think I would remember if I were your wife!"

"Aye! I couldnae agree more! Ye *should* remember. I keep hoping that ye will look at me and just . . ."—his voice cracked—"just . . . *see.* See the emotion in my eyes as they watch ye, recognize how my hands ache with your lack . . ."

More silence.

Her mind spun and spooled.

No.

This can't be.

"Willingly?" she asked. "I married ye . . . willingly?"

He exhaled a breath that sounded trapped between despair and laughter.

"Aye, lass." He gestured a hand toward her. "Ye married me *most* willingly. *Eagerly*, even."

She stared at him anew, trying to picture it.

That she . . .

And this man . . .

That they had . . .

She blushed, the sensation scalding her cheeks and pinching her chest.

"But if we were married, then that means . . ." She pressed a hand to her stomach, her eyes closing.

Kieran MacTavish was the father of her child.

She feared she was going to be sick. How could she have made such a choice?

She opened her eyes.

"Aye—" His voice broke, his pale blue eyes peering intently. "Aye, lass. Your baby—*our* baby—was loved. *So* loved. And so very, *very* wanted. The morning on Vanuatu when ye told me ye were increasing, ye nearly pitched headlong into the surf, ye were spinning with such happiness—"

"Stop!" Eilidh covered her ears with her hands. "I don't want to hear it."

"Ye *loved* our babe, even though it was barely more than a wee body of hope between us."

"Enough!"

"Lass, please. Listen." Master MacTavish pressed his hands together. "Ye keep running from your memories out of fear, worried that ye will remember horror—"

"Yes! Because what I do remember *is* horrific."

"Perhaps, but if ye truly pull back the veil on your past, ye could also find happiness and tremendous courage. Ye might remember laying under foreign stars, tracing the southern cross with your fingertip. Or clinging to a guyline and laughing into the wind as sea spray flared across the ship's deck. There are beautiful memories just waiting tae be uncovered."

"Like being married to yourself?!" Her scathing tone echoed the repugnance in her chest. "A debauched lothario? Was I merely another conquest for ye? The one who managed to slip a parson's noose around your neck?"

He flinched.

He swallowed and looked away, dragging another knuckle beneath an eye.

A bilious emotion churned and seethed in her stomach.

She hated herself like this—shrewish and cruel and fractious.

She wanted peace. Calm. Nothingness.

But . . .

But . . . his wife?! Kieran MacTavish?!

Was she mad?

You idiotic girl! What could you possibly have been thinking, to have made such a choice?!

She could scarcely fathom it.

Had she loved him?

Had she—

Stop.

Enough.

Shaking her head, she dashed past MacTavish, racing for the stairs.

"Jamie . . ." he called to her.

But she kept running.

Down the stairs.

Out the heavy oaken door.

Across the forecourt and onto the path that ran along the ocean cliffs.

Anything to outrace the pounding of her heart and the chasm of decisions she had no memory of making.

October 1815

Kieran rapped on the wall of the open door to the carpenter's cabin. "How fares the repair?" he asked.

Chen and Jamie looked up from the timber they were currently working. A piece of the decking had begun to rot and needed to be replaced. Chen was steadying the board as Jamie shaved it to size.

"It is coming," Chen nodded. "Jamie here is capable with a wood plane."

Jamie raised her head, a crooked smile on her face.

How could everyone not immediately tell the lad was a lass? It was beyond Kieran's ken. She was a wee fey pixie of a woman—delicate cheekbones, thick lashes framing silvery eyes, an adorably pert chin.

There was absolutely nothing lad-ish about her.

But, he supposed, people saw what they were told to see. After all, he himself had been utterly fooled.

"Thank ye." She shot Chen a smile and then turned her piercing eyes back to Kieran. "Mr. Chen has promised if I complete my work to his exacting standards, he'll show me how tae make a firework."

The husky timbre of her voice sent a frisson of sensation down Kieran's spine and flared gooseflesh along his forearms.

Unfortunately, this unwelcome physical reaction had become normal when he found himself in her company.

"Fireworks, eh?" Kieran asked. He knew that Mr. Chen's father had been a firework master in Shanghai. Chen had even apprenticed as one for a while before deciding carpentry and a life at sea suited him better.

Jamie nodded. "Luckily for us, we have the supplies on board to make them."

Like any other ship of *The Minerva*'s size, they were armed with cannon and gun powder. Only fools circumnavigated the globe without being able to defend themselves against pirates.

Apparently, word had reached the crew that Mr. Chen promised to make a few fireworks for lighting once they arrived in Rio. Setting off fireworks at sea would be a bit too hazardous, as a single spark in the rigging could spell disaster.

"Would you be willing to help stabilize the board?" Chen asked Kieran, pointing to the wood they were working. "I need to go check the measurement of the space to be repaired."

Kieran nodded and took Chen's place.

Chen grabbed a measuring tape from a hook and left, half closing the door behind him.

Kieran thought nothing of it until that moment—until he knelt across from Jamie, hands pressed to one end of the wood to steady it, his head scarcely a foot from hers—

He was essentially within easy kissing distance of a bonnie lass.

A bonnie lass that he would very much like to . . . kiss.

Steady, man. She's made it clear how she feels about ye.

His pulse drummed in his throat.

"How are ye getting on then?" Kieran asked, careful not to say anything that indicated her true gender in case there were ears listening. "Have the other members of our Brotherhood been helping ye?"

"Aye. Mr. Campbell showed me how to mark a block of wood for carving, how tae see the potential shape inside."

Kieran snorted. "Ye know that's not precisely what I meant."

She laughed, a soft breath of sound.

Kieran studiously kept his gaze fixed on her hands, working the plane over the wood, but he could feel her eyes on his face.

He often felt her eyes on him.

"It feels endless, sometimes, this relearning of myself," she said after a moment.

"Pardon?" He lifted his head. "What do you mean?"

She rubbed the plane back and forth, her curls bobbing against her cheeks. "Just that the world is rather different from what I had thought before taking to the sea as Jamie. My own abilities are greater than I had supposed." She paused, those silvery eyes of hers lifting to his. She licked her bottom lip. "You . . . are different."

The punch of her gaze left Kieran light-headed.

"You've been kind tae me," she said. "Ye are not the man I thought ye were, Kieran MacTavish. Ye are . . . gentler. Responsible. More professional."

"So you're saying I'm not quite the reprobate you've been led tae believe?" he chuckled.

"Something like that. I likely owe ye an apology."

"Thank ye."

"Oh, I didnae say I was *actually* going tae apologize—"

"Are ye not?" He couldn't help the lilt in his voice, the upturn of his lips. "It's quite easy tae do. Allow me tae demonstrate." He sat up straight and cleared his throat. "Ye simply say, 'Why Kieran, I was so utterly wrong tae doubt your magnificence. Can ye forgive me?'"

She laughed, just as he hoped.

"Your ego doesnae need my bolstering words." She rolled her eyes and returned to working the plane.

"Your father was not necessarily wrong in his opinion of my behavior," he said, voice softer. "But the sins and follies of my younger self dinnae need to direct my course in the present or mold the future shape of me. I can step in a clearer direction, carve a new shape, just as ye do with the wood here."

"Aye," she nodded. "I ken you've done that. Dinnae let it go to your head."

"Too late."

She smiled.

Kieran felt stupidly proud of that smile.

The air between them hummed with electricity . . . like ship rigging in a thunderstorm, the air laden with humidity and portent.

"Well . . . no matter what the others say, the offer tae return to Scotland once we reach Rio remains," he said. "I'll see ye cared for—"

"Nae. I'll be staying aboard ship." She regarded him with those silvery eyes, a grin still tugging at her lips. "After all, where else would one such as myself learn how to make fireworks?"

Kieran snorted. "I cannae see how a knowledge of fireworks will help ye once ye return to a life of gentility—ye cannae knit with a fuse or embroider wee flowers with black powder."

"Oh, I beg tae disagree." She smiled more broadly. "What man wouldn't want a woman who knows how tae light a spark?"

Kieran's hands nearly slipped off the wood, a startled gasp sticking in his throat.

Was this lass . . .

Was she . . .

Was she *flirting* with him?

Her abruptly averted eyes and the blush climbing her cheeks made him think that . . .

Yes.

Yes, she was.

Perhaps . . . she didn't dislike him as much as he thought.

Perhaps . . .

Kieran knew there were a thousand reasons why he should keep his distance—he was her commanding officer, he had made a promise to her father to protect her, any romantic entanglement threatened her safety.

And yet, this woman was a siren—beckoning him closer. The sort of peril a wise sailor would view through a spying scope from a furlong at sea.

But he feared it was too late for him. Her song had already ensnared him.

He stared helplessly at the fan of her lashes as she bent over the board, working the plane back and forth.

"A spark, eh?" he said. "The right lass shouldnae have tae resort to pyrotechnics for that."

Her head snapped upright, sending dark curls tumbling onto her forehead.

"Is that so?" A delighted smile spread across her face. "If only I had a teacher . . ."

"Careful, lass," he murmured, leaning forward, halving the distance between them. "A good teacher would remind ye that sparks can lead to a conflagration."

They stared at one another. Kieran willed her to close the remaining gap between them, to put her siren lips on his.

Awareness pulled and stretched, a cat uncurling from a nap and reaching out its paws, pricking the rug.

"Well," she smirked and went back to moving the plane, "I *am* more capable than I had supposed. I imagine that along with learning to create fireworks, I could also learn to control the fire itself."

Kieran felt color climb his own cheeks.

Bloody hell.

He was in so much trouble.

13

Eilidh ran along the clifftop path, lungs near to bursting, feet pounding in time with her pulse.

If only she could run faster and farther . . . so far away that *The Minerva* and the events aboard would never find her.

Her thoughts beat a frantic tempo with her heart—*wife, wife, wife.*

It couldn't be true.

She had been *married?*

She wasn't sure if the thought comforted her—she hadn't been a woman of loose morals! her child had been conceived in wedlock!—or terrified her even more.

Of all the men on Earth, how could she have taken *Kieran MacTavish* as her husband? Yes, the man was alluring and handsome—that was a biological fact—but surely she was intelligent enough to marry for more than basic animal attraction.

In all the pain of her memory loss and the shame of finding herself with child, she had never once considered that she might have taken a husband.

Why would she have thought as much? She was not wearing a wedding ring when she was dragged, half-drowned, from the ocean. Had Master MacTavish not provided her with one, then? Did he not esteem her enough as his wife to give her a wedding ring?

Wife, wife, wife.

How could she have forgotten about a husband? That seemed like something a woman would remember.

Could Master MacTavish be misleading her in some way?

She finally slowed when her body screamed in protest, air leaving her lungs in great, gusting gasps. Clouds raced across the sky, the sun winking in and out, turning the ocean into a mottled patchwork of light and dark.

She pressed a shaking hand to her forehead.

Oh, merciful heaven!

If she truly were married . . . what about Simon? What about the simple, peaceful life she planned with him? What would become of them now?

The thought rendered her nauseous.

How could she unravel this tangled knot her impetuous younger self had snarled half a world and a lifetime away?

She wiped the tears gathered in her eyes. The white numb threatened to utterly collapse. Panic thrummed in her blood and a jittery ache hammered in her chest.

What was her future to be now? The unwilling wife of Kieran MacTavish?

She pressed a hand to her stomach, as bile rose in her throat.

Turning in a circle, she spotted the chimneys of Kilmeny Hall peeking above the grassy headland. Beside the elegant, honey-stone of the hall, something winked in the intermittent sunlight.

Eilidh frowned and squinted.

It was . . . a glasshouse. A large glasshouse.

Ah. Was this Mr. Campbell's studio? The one the gentlemen had discussed?

Ask Ewan. He witnessed the ceremony himself.

Mr. Campbell claimed to be a friend, but could she depend on him to tell her the truth?

Her footsteps turned toward the building, and she soon discovered a well-worn path through the grass, as if Mr. Campbell traipsed between his glasshouse studio and the ocean with some regularity.

The glasshouse was a modern wonder of architecture—the entire front wall a bank of glass, interspersed at regular intervals by supporting arches of stone.

As Eilidh approached, she could see Mr. Campbell dressed in a great kilt, standing with his back to the glass, a palette in one hand and a paintbrush in the other. Lord Hadley lounged on a stool to one side, Sir Rafe in a chair to the other. Lord Lockheade leaned against the wall, legs crossed at the ankles.

Eilidh paused, her courage failing her. Emotions churned through her so quickly—fear, anger, panic, worry—it was hard to grasp just one.

She couldn't interrupt the men. Such a gathering could easily turn more confrontational than she wished—

Lord Lockheade spotted her standing before the glasshouse, hesitating like a nitwit. He beckoned to her and pushed open the door.

"Miss Fyffe!" Lord Lockheade smiled, holding the door wide for her to step inside.

All four men turned her way, Sir Rafe and Lord Hadley instantly coming to their feet to greet her. As if she were a lady come calling. As if they respected her.

Something hard and aching lodged in her throat, but she managed a wan smile as she walked past Lord Lockheade into the room.

However, her expression was not convincing. Or, perhaps, these men did indeed know her better than she remembered.

Their welcoming smiles quickly turned to concern.

"Och, what did Kieran do, lass?" Lord Lockheade shook his head.

"Aye." Mr. Campbell nodded. "He promised he would be patient with ye, but I'm wondering now."

"Ye look ready tae pound something into a pulp," Lord Hadley agreed.

Oof! That was unnervingly accurate. She *did* want to hit something. To beat her fists and shriek her fury and vent her churning feelings like steam from a kettle.

Be a lady.

She settled for swallowing and clenching her fingers tightly.

But their kindness and concern gave her the courage to say her piece.

"Am I married?" She was proud of how she asked the question, no quaver to her voice, no anger or shouting. "Did I marry Kieran MacTavish?"

To a man, they sighed. A collective heaving, in and out.

Had Eilidh been in a more cheerful frame of mind, their reaction would have been humorous.

But as it was . . .

"I take that as a *yes*," she said.

"Kieran wanted to tell ye immediately," Lord Lockheade said, "but I told him to wait. That ye weren't yet ready—"

"As much as it pains me to admit, Master MacTavish had the right of it," she snapped, agitation finally slipping out of her mouth. "I should have been told such vital information immediately."

"We were all hoping ye would remember on your own," Lord Hadley said, bracing his hands behind his head. "That if ye just spent time with Kieran, ye would gradually remember."

"So *that's* why I have been relegated to the castle with him without a chaperone? Because he is my husband?"

The men nodded, looking all too much like scolded school boys.

A scene flashed through her mind.

These four men and Kieran lounging around a table in a ship's cabin. They were laughing, passing around a bottle of whisky and saying something that set Mr. Campbell to blushing.

The memory was . . . light-hearted.

An ache rose in her chest, and along with it, an intrinsic understanding that these men *did* care about her. The sense that perhaps, like Simon, they could offer her safe harbor.

And why, why, *why* did this entire situation have to be so unsettling and confusing?!

Eilidh took a step forward and sat on a chair.

"Did I go willingly to the altar?" She asked the question to the floor as much as to the men around her.

"Ewan is the only one who witnessed the ceremony," Sir Rafe said, retaking in his seat. "The rest of us didn't learn of your marriage until long after."

She frowned. "You all weren't there? You were not invited?"

"Kieran wished tae keep it private," Lord Hadley said, also sitting back on his stool. "It was a tremendous risk, marrying yourself. But ye clearly cared deeply for our Kieran. *That* . . . we all noticed."

"Aye. Ye wouldnae have handfasted with him otherwise." Mr. Campbell nodded.

"A handfasting?" She looked up, up, up to Mr. Campbell. "So it wasn't a proper ceremony then? Nothing recorded in a parish record or captain's log?"

Mr. Campbell shook his head. "Nae. It was quite secret. But ye married of your own free will, lass. That I can promise ye. The rest . . ." He looked away, rubbing the back of his neck. "Ye should likely ask Kieran for details."

"I cannot say I wish to." The less contact she had with Master MacTavish, the better.

Besides, her mind had lunged at the word *handfasting*, searching for a loophole. She and MacTavish had an irregular marriage, one that had never been properly recorded. Was it even a marriage then? Perhaps she would not be forced to tie her life to his. Perhaps there was a way out of this predicament.

Perhaps . . .

"I would prefer to remain here, if I could, at Kilmeny Hall, not in the castle." Eilidh looked at each of them. "I do not need Master MacTavish's help. You all could tell me about the trip—"

"That's not possible, lass," Lord Hadley said gently.

Eilidh frowned.

"Aye." Lord Lockheade nodded. "We all leave in the morning, as we were only here to answer to Mr. Patterson's summons. But we will return for the Midsummer Festival on the summer solstice."

"And though Ewan here is far too polite to say so," Sir Rafe said with a rueful twist of his lips, "it would be inconsiderate to continue to impose upon Lady Kildrum's hospitality, given her current condition—"

"Och!" Mr. Campbell waved a hand. "Youse are all welcome tae stay, ye ken that—"

"Aye, we know, but you've this fine painting tae finish—" Lord Hadley waved a hand at the colorful canvas before Mr. Campbell, swirling with reds and blues. It appeared to be an image of a Highland family sending a soldier off to war. "—and your lady has a child tae birth. Not to mention, Lady Aster and Lady Rose arrived back home only an hour ago—"

"Lady Kildrum's younger twin sisters," Lord Lockheade whispered to Eilidh.

"—and the twins will tax whatever energy Lady Kildrum can muster."

"Honestly, it's why we're all out here with Ewan and not in the house," Sir Rafe said. "The twins can be . . ."

"Delightful?" Mr. Campbell supplied, a warning tone in his voice. "My fair sisters-in-law can be delightful? I'm quite sure that's what ye were going tae say, aye?"

Sir Rafe chuckled. "Yes. They are refreshing, I'll give ye that."

"The point, as I'm sure ye have realized, Miss Fyffe," Lord Lockheade said, "is that we feel it best to give Lady Kildrum and her family space during the remainder of her confinement and delivery. You, however, must remain here, per the orders of the Judge Admiral."

"Of course, I had not realized." Eilidh pursed her lips. "But I simply *cannot* remain with Master MacTavish alone, the impropriety of it . . ."

"A chaperone could be arranged," Lord Hadley said.

"Aye." Mr. Campbell gave Eilidh a warm smile. "But for now, come up to the house. Violet likes a late afternoon snack before her dinner. And I'm sure the twins would like tae meet ye."

Eilidh nodded and waited as Mr. Campbell stowed his paints and washed his brushes, setting them out to dry. The other members of the Brotherhood filed out, but Eilidh waited for Mr. Campbell. Though the man was a giant—and Eilidh was so short, the top of her head barely reached his sternum—he radiated calm and comfort.

He motioned for her to go through the door.

"Kieran is worthy of ye, lass," Mr. Campbell said as she passed by, earnestness in his words.

Eilidh turned to him.

Mr. Campbell fixed her with his hazel eyes. "Ye can trust him."

"Can I?"

"Aye. I ken ye have a lot going on in here." He tapped his temple. "But dinnae neglect your own heart. It remembers. At least attempt tae reclaim what ye once had."

She swallowed and looked away. "Sometimes, remembering comes at too high a price. The more I learn, the more I think I forgot for a reason."

A long pause.

"Perhaps," he said. "But I can promise ye this—Kieran MacTavish isnae the reason ye forgot. And if ye can find it in your heart to trust me, even just a wee bit, then know this: I dinnae think ye will ever regret recovering the memories ye have of him. Give him a chance, lass."

Eilidh found she couldn't answer. The words stuck in her throat.

So instead, she nodded and walked through the door.

KIERAN FOUND EILIDH hours later sitting in the grass, staring out over the ocean.

She looked so tiny and alone, framed against the vastness of the sea, it nearly broke something inside him.

He knew she had taken the long route along the cliffs to Kilmeny Hall before returning back the way she had come.

But she had not returned to the castle.

Instead, she had continued to walk the path that snaked along the clifftop. He had watched her from one of the castle's upper towers, wending her way through the yellow gorse in bloom, the wind whipping the blue of her pelisse and tugging at her bonnet.

When she had disappeared from sight, he finally went after her—round and round the corkscrew castle stairs, down the main staircase, out through the forecourt, and onto the path.

He couldn't bear it. To know she suffered with no one beside her.

She merely looked up as he neared, her expression lifeless and controlled, as if all the fire of her had been banked.

He sat beside her, not a word passing between them.

His wife felt like a stranger. As if another had taken on Jamie's form but had neglected to include the spark that made her so uniquely . . . *her.*

The North Sea stretched before them, a rippling mass of shadow and light. The ocean currents and the near-constant wind conspired to create a crosshatch pattern on the water. In Scotland, the water itself bore the stamp of a tartan.

But as a sailor, Kieran understood only too well the danger of a crosshatch sea. It spoke of strong, competing currents that could easily drag a man down to his death.

Was that what he and Jamie faced now? A swirling tartan sea that would spell the doom of their love?

"We used to sit like this, you and myself," he finally said.

"Did we?" Her voice was monotone.

"Aye. On Vanuatu. We were married by then, ye see . . . nearly two months. It was like a honeymoon. We would sit under the stars and listen to the cacophony of a tropical island at night—frogs and bugs and birds and scuttling things in the brush. We would talk about bonnie Scotland. The smell of heather after a rain. The odd quiet of a summer's evening. The sounds of moments just like this—wind and seagulls. We missed it."

He dared a glance at her. She sat so rigidly, her back agonizingly straight. The posture of a lady.

Of the woman she had been before life forced her to forge a future as Jamie Fyffe aboard *The Minerva.* Before she had realized her own capabilities. Her own tenacity and innate courage.

Had her experiences on the ship transformed her into the brave woman he married?

Or had life since then conditioned her to become this cautious, withdrawn person?

Heaven knew, he had changed.

Her loss—and his subsequent descent into grief—had carved deep fissures into the bedrock of his psyche.

"I visited Mr. Campbell's studio and Kilmeny Hall earlier today," she said, her tone once more constrained and English sounding. "I had tea with Lady Kildrum and the Brotherhood. I met Lady Kildrum's sisters, Lady Aster and Lady Rose, as well. They have returned."

Kieran said nothing, waiting to see where this would lead.

"Lady Aster and Lady Rose seem . . . young," she continued.

"The twins *are* young. I think they are scarcely nineteen."

"The age I was when I boarded the ship. Their heads are full of romantic whimsy and an almost foolish sense of optimism."

Kieran allowed himself a small smile. "I understand they are quite a handful for Lady Kildrum."

Silence for a moment.

He kept his eyes on the gray tartan sea.

"Was I ever similar?" she asked.

Kieran pondered the question. "Were ye similarly whimsical and romantic? No. But were ye high-spirited and plucky? Aye."

More silence.

More crosshatch seas.

The wind tugged at his hair. A pair of cormorants quarreled in the distance.

"I spoke with the Brotherhood about . . . us," she said.

"Aye?"

"They confirmed that you and I . . . well . . ." She swallowed. "They confirmed our . . . marriage, but Mr. Campbell said I needed to ask yourself for the full story."

The full story?

How could mere words capture the vibrance of their love? The hope of her?

Kieran took in a slow breath.

"We decided tae marry when we arrived in Sydney," he said softly. "We first thought tae find a vicar, but they all required three weeks of banns to be read, and we didnae have three weeks of time. A special license wasnae possible. Aside from myself and the other members of our Brotherhood, no one aboard the ship knew ye were a woman. So we couldnae ask the captain tae do the honors. In the end, we invited Ewan to witness a good, old-fashioned handfasting. We're Scots, after all. Our lot have been marrying that way for centuries. We figured we'd solemnize our union in a church once we returned to Scotland."

He picked up a pebble and threw it, watching as it arced over the cliff's edge. Rather like the sensation currently sinking through his chest.

"How was the actual ceremony?"

He paused, an ache rising in his throat.

"It was truly lovely." His voice went hoarse. "Ye looked an angel, lass. I couldnae believe I had convinced ye tae marry me."

"And yet, you didn't value me enough as a wife to seal our vows with a wedding ring," she said, tone flat and challenging.

"A ring wasn't possible. The boy, James Fyffe, could not appear on deck with a gold wedding ring on his left hand without raising difficult questions—"

"Perhaps not," she replied, "but I could certainly have worn a ring on a chain around my neck. *Something* physical to denote our supposed connection—"

"And I wanted to, lass. But ye were concerned about someone seeing it. Instead, ye made me promise to buy ye a ring once we returned tae Scotland."

She rolled her eyes, making a scoffing noise before turning her face to the sea once more.

"I kept my promise." Kieran reached a finger past his neckcloth and tugged on the chain around his neck, pulling it over his head.

Jamie sat back in alarm, one hand braced on the ground as if poised to flee.

He held the chain between them. A gold ring dangled from it, winking in the sunlight.

"As soon as I returned to Scotland, I bought ye the ring I promised."

"But you thought me dead."

"Aye," he nodded. "I did. But not even death could quell my devotion tae yourself." He extended the ring on its chain toward her. "It is yours now."

She stared at the ring as it spun in a slow circle.

"I do not wish to be your wife." She shook her head, going back to studying the ocean. "You are a stranger to me."

Her words were a knife to his senses, hurting all the more for their dull delivery.

"Then get tae know me, lass. Give me a chance tae prove myself." He tucked the chain and ring into his fist. "To earn the right tae place this ring on your finger."

Silence.

She continued to sit unnervingly still, her profile to him.

He had once understood her so well. Every move, every glance . . .

But now?

He had not a clue.

"I must be honest, Master MacTavish—"

"Kieran. Please, lass. Call me Kieran."

Her eyes snapped to his.

Ah.

There was turbulence there, as if her fiery self battered the walls of her self-control. Perhaps some bits of *his* Jamie remained.

"I cannot countenance such familiarity." She shook her head. "You will remain Master MacTavish to me. I would prefer to be called Miss Fyffe—"

"Despite your present feelings, ye are my *wife*. I cannae call ye Miss Fyffe, as if we never meant whole worlds to one another."

Her shoulders slumped, the smallest of reactions to his words.

More silence.

"I will accept the familiarity of Eilidh," she finally said, regal, ladylike. "But I simply cannot be Jamie. That is my brother's name. It does not feel like myself, and every time I hear it, I imagine him—"

She broke off, abruptly turning back to the ocean. Her bottom lip trembled.

Ah, my love.

She took in a slow breath before looking at him once again. "His death was not . . . pleasant. It is one of a thousand scenes I would prefer not to remember."

Kieran nodded. "I know."

"You do? You know how Jamie died?"

"Aye. Ye told me." He leaned toward her, willing her to believe. "You're my *wife* . . . Eilidh. I know ye."

"I cannot countenance that we are married. More to the point, if I have no recollection of the handfasting, how could it possibly be legally binding? It is an irregular marriage, not recorded in any place but our memories. And as I have none . . ."

The pit in Kieran's stomach spun and churned.

He said nothing.

"So though *you* may consider us married, I would ask that you cease to refer to me as your wife. I do not recognize our union. And without my consent . . ." She spread her hands wide. "Without my consent, it is as if it never happened."

Kieran let out a long gust of air. He clenched the ring tighter in his fist, the edges biting into his palm.

Her words were not unexpected.

But that didn't remove the agony of them.

What was worse?

That the Jamie he knew and loved had died?

Or that her form lived on with another version of her inside?

"However, along with that," she continued, "I said some unkind things to you earlier today. They were most unladylike, and for that, I apologize. I hope I will have your forgiveness."

Kieran froze.

And just when he thought this woman could no longer surprise him—

Jamie would not have apologized. His wife was many remarkable things—fearless, reckless, fiercely courageous—but humble?

Not so much.

Had she ever apologized so readily?

Kieran rather thought not.

"Apology accepted," he murmured. "And I apologize for any of my own heated remarks that might have inflicted harm."

She nodded her head.

And that was . . . that.

"I requested a chaperone," she said. "Lady Kildrum said that someone suitable would be sent down. As I consider myself an unmarried woman, it is only proper. I will maintain my reputation as much as possible. Simon deserves as much."

Ah.

Kieran pinched his lips shut, stemming the words that bit and stung his mouth.

No good would come from lashing out at her.

The woman he had known and promised to love, cherish, honor, worship . . .

That woman?

She had vanished as surely as if she had never been.

She existed only as a figment of memory. A wisp of thought and a kaleidoscope of color.

The irony.

He had too much of memory.

She . . . too little.

And now they faced a future not unlike the ocean before them—

A gray expanse extending to the horizon, the crisscrossing lines warning the wise to venture no further into the deep.

What if Jamie—*his* Jamie—truly was dead after all?

Eilidh was delighted by two arrivals the following morning.

The first was Mrs. McKay from the nearby village—a rosy-cheeked, white-haired widow who was only too happy to act as a chaperone.

The second was a letter from Simon, who had received her direction from the Gillespies before they left.

I find the days long and tedious without you, Miss Fyffe, he wrote.

She smiled. Here was a true gentleman—one who respected the formalities of gentility and did not give way to overly familiar terms of address without permission.

The rest of his letter was similarly soothing.

> *Mother sends her regards. She hopes that you will return soon, as summer is always the most glorious time of year. Reverend Smith has been taken with gout again, and so I find myself preaching more. With each sermon, I imagine you here, in the pews, looking up at me in your earnest way. It is easy to envision our life together.*

Ah, Simon.

It *was* easy to envision their life together.

He would continue as curate and replace Reverend Smith as vicar when the man retired in a few years. Eilidh would be a diligent wife, visiting the poor and assisting Simon with his sermons, all the while tending to their own children and household.

It was the future her parents had wanted for her—respectable, genteel, secure.

She ached for the peace of such a life.

A life that existed as placidly as an English lake in summer.

The life of a lady.

Master MacTavish—she steadfastly refused to call him Kieran, even in her mind—was more akin to a Scottish loch in the midst of a winter squall: tantalizing in its wild beauty but utterly terrifying.

As for the staggering revelations from the day before . . .

She had lain awake half the night, thoughts spooling obsessively in her head.

Why *had* she married Kieran MacTavish on a summery December day in Sydney? Had she truly loved him, as the Brotherhood and MacTavish himself insisted?

Again, Eilidh supposed she could see the appeal—Master MacTavish was a handsome man. There was no doubt she found him attractive.

But . . .

She felt no peace in his presence.

No serenity. No repose.

Instead, he evoked tumultuous emotions that tossed her to and fro.

At times, she wished to beat her palms against his chest and shriek her anger.

While at others, she fought back tears and longed to seek shelter in his arms.

And then just as quickly—and, quite frankly, against all logical thought—she yearned to fist her hands into his hair and drag his lips down to hers.

But mostly, she longed to ruffle his composure, to cause him to behave as unsettled and angry and confused as she felt.

None of these impulses denoted love, it seemed.

A sort of crazed madness, certainly.

But not love.

And knowing this, why would she wish to remember *more* about the man?

Give him a chance, Mr. Campbell had pleaded.

Oof.

She didn't want to give him a chance.

She might have married Kieran MacTavish, as Mr. Campbell witnessed, but surely she had done so out of some pressing necessity.

She had been alone, orphaned, and on the opposite end of the world. Kieran MacTavish had offered her the protection of his name. And she had accepted it.

She valued safety, after all.

Worse, if she *did* eventually remember their marriage, what then? Would love for him magically accompany her memories?

Or, if she remembered their union had been driven by desperation on her part (as she suspected), was she then obligated to acknowledge their handfasting? Even if she didn't love him? Even if she had plighted her troth under personal duress?

The thought set her stomach to churning.

If she did *not* remember, she was safe in her affections for Simon. Tucked securely into the harbor of his calm love and caring heart. Protected within her numbness.

As for the accusation that she had blown up the ship . . .

She continued to refuse to give it any credence. She might have lost her memories, but she certainly hadn't changed so much that she would have killed 127 innocent men. The thought was as nauseating as it was absurd.

Despite the Brotherhood's insistence that Cuthie would accuse her of the crime no matter the truth, she was not so sure. When Cuthie had thought her dead, he had no problem naming her as the guilty party because who would gainsay him? The man had taken one last vicious jab at the Brotherhood and their affection for her.

But now that she was here, the landscape had changed.

Swearing false testimony under oath was a serious offense. Based on what she had heard so far, Cuthie appeared eager to avoid His Majesty's court system. Was he willing to risk gaol himself in an attempt to spite her?

The more she had touched on her few brief memories of Cuthie, she recalled a man who was vindictive, yes, but also self-serving in the extreme.

In short, Cuthie was a survivor. He would do what he must to live another day. If naming her the guilty party did not serve that purpose, he would not do so.

And knowing all this—her wish to *not* remember her marriage to Master MacTavish, the certainty of her own character and the uncertainty around Cuthie's behavior—was it even necessary to plumb her memories?

Eilidh spent the morning with Mrs. McKay in the great hall. The older woman cheerfully knitted away, telling Eilidh all about her dear departed husband, Robert, who had been a solicitor in Aberdeen.

For her part, Eilidh wrote another letter to Simon—still choosing not to burden him with her current predicament. Then she worked on her embroidery and ignored needling thoughts of Kieran MacTavish.

Of course, the man himself joined them after luncheon.

"I spent the morning mapping out a plan for attempting to recover your memories." He sat down opposite her at the large table and nodded a greeting to Mrs. McKay.

"Good afternoon to yourself, too," Eilidh replied dryly, tugging to free a tangled embroidery thread.

If she thought to irk him by pointing out his bad manners, she was disappointed.

He gave her a smile before rising from his seat again.

"My apologies, Miss Fyffe." He bowed extravagantly, presenting her with one leg and sweeping a hand down it, as if he were a courtier from centuries past. "Allow me tae say, ye look as lovely as a picture today."

Eilidh rolled her eyes, still trying to untangle her threads. No matter how many samplers she stitched, her embroidery simply did not improve.

But for Simon's sake, she continued to try.

Mrs. McKay chuckled. "When I spoke with ye yesterday, Master MacTavish, I didn't realize ye were a charmer."

Master MacTavish, the wretch, fixed Mrs. McKay with a positively melting smile. The sort of smile that dimpled his cheeks and set Eilidh's heart to pounding.

"Mrs. McKay, with such beauty before me—" He spread his arms wide. "—it's nearly impossible for a man tae behave any other way."

Mrs. McKay giggled.

She *giggled.*

Master MacTavish had reduced this grandmotherly, respectable matron to a puddle of giggling goo in less than two minutes.

Eilidh was torn between feeling appalled or impressed.

And to think . . . she had *married* this man?!

Honestly, the more she learned, the more Eilidh doubted the sanity of her past self.

What had that girl been thinking?

Past Eilidh had made some decidedly questionable choices.

Had she been so lonely and afraid that she had latched onto Master MacTavish like a lifeboat? Or had she, too, fallen under the spell of his easy charm, silver tongue, and rakish good looks?

How could she have so thoroughly disregarded her father's warnings?

Eilidh pinched her lips, frowning as her clumsy fingers struggled with her tangled embroidery threads. The wretched man tied her very fingers into knots.

Her mood had been so lovely before Master MacTavish arrived.

No turbulent feelings.

No hum of awareness in her blood.

No tingling of her skin or flare of gooseflesh.

Just . . . the simple calm she craved.

She pulled at a thread, snarling her stitches further.

She huffed and resisted the urge to throw the whole lot—hoop and all—at Master MacTavish's head.

He tsked and held out his hand. "May I?"

With another roll of her eyes, she sent the embroidery skimming across the table to him.

He studied it, turning it this way and that. “Ye arenae much of a dab hand with a needlework, are ye?”

“Master MacTavish—”

“Ye always said how much ye hated embroidery. Ye can sew a straight seam like a professional, but this? It doesnae suit your personality at all, I ken.” He waggled the embroidery hoop in his hand, tangled threads dangling down. “You’re a bit too high-spirited to tame all that energy into fancy stitches on linen.”

Eilidh breathed in and out.

For one, she hated the sense that he might be right.

Two, she deeply disliked that this man knew her so well, and yet, she knew him not at all.

Three, she detested how readily he aimed another winning smile at Mrs. McKay.

He was far too free with those deadly smiles. He was likely to incapacitate an unwary widow or blind a debutante with them.

“Mrs. McKay,” he said, “I have set up a memory test for Miss Fyffe down in the forecourt. Ye can see it through the window.” He waved a hand to the small window to the right of the fireplace. “I was hoping tae encourage Miss Fyffe tae join me.”

Eilidh shot a wide-eyed look at Mrs. McKay, hoping against reason that the lady would object.

“Outside over yon? I cannot imagine that would be a problem,” Mrs. McKay smiled, dashing Eilidh’s hopes. “It’s most gallant of ye to assist Miss Fyffe in recovering her memories. I’ll sit by the window to keep an eye out. The sea air doesn’t quite agree with my old joints.” She flicked her fingers at Eilidh. “But nothing cheers a young heart like a bit of sun.”

THIRTY MINUTES LATER, Eilidh stood before a carpenter’s bench in the sunny forecourt of Kilmeny Castle, wearing one of her old, cast-off dresses.

She had been utterly outmaneuvered.

Master MacTavish, in shirt sleeves, neckcloth, and a blue linen waistcoat, beamed triumphantly at her side.

The sun beat down on the forecourt, the high walls trapping the radiated heat. The bluebell sky had Eilidh squinting and pulling her poke bonnet lower to shield her eyes. Servants called back and forth from over the wall . . . something about fetching cheese and eggs from the cold cellar.

Eilidh all but glared at Master MacTavish, disliking how the wind tousled his dark hair into a boyish mop and pressed the fine cotton of his shirt against his upper arms, molding to the lean muscle there. And why did a *lack* of a coat make his shoulders appear even broader?

Ugh. This was utterly ridiculous—

"You cannot have everything your way simply for asking," she muttered to him, turning to wave at Mrs. McKay looking down on them from the window above.

Mrs. McKay waved back, beaming happily.

"You prey upon the trusting nature of an elderly lady," she continued, turning back to him.

"I cannae help it that the lasses find me so charming." He grinned, wicked and unrepentant, his pale blue eyes flashing. "It's always been my lot."

"Aye. *That* I remember well. The stories my father used tae tell . . ."

His smile didn't so much slip as morph from charming to ardent. His gaze focused entirely on her, as if there were nothing so fascinating in the world as herself.

"Those stories are my past, lass, a past I had repented of long before I met yourself. Only one woman holds my heart now, only one whose trust matters tae me." The heat in his gaze left no doubt as to *whom* that was. "I have been a true and faithful husband to ye."

Eilidh's eyes dipped to the shadow of her wedding ring, dangling on its chain under his shirt.

A symbol of her own past trust.

She looked away.

"Why?" She wrapped her hands around her elbows. "Why did I believe you had changed enough to trust your word?"

He stared at her, silent for a moment.

"Time, I suppose," he finally answered, reaching to place a piece of wood on the table. "Time and familiarity. Ye saw the harmony between my words and actions and that created trust."

"And now?"

"Now . . . I have the tremendous honor of earning your trust all over again."

She longed to snort and roll her eyes, but the profound sincerity of his gaze held her fast. Like looking into the eyes of a wild stallion that had allowed itself to be caught.

She had *owned* all that power and passion for herself—

Her heart clogged her throat.

She looked down at the carpentry tools resting beside the wood—a plane, a drill, a saw, three chisels of varying sizes. "I take it you think to jar my memory with these?"

"Aye. I thought perhaps ye could work on repairing this chair here." He motioned toward a stool that was missing a leg. "See if your muscles and fingers remember the movements, even if your head does not."

She darted a glance at the stool and then returned to the carpentry tools, even touching a finger to the wooden plane before pulling back.

"They willnae bite ye," he said, laughter in his voice.

His easy, almost flippant, manner was like a lit fuse in her chest.

Her emotions were a turbulent froth, and yet, he appeared utterly unaffected.

She wanted him as off-kilter as herself.

She touched a chisel, more deliberately this time. "Why did I marry you?"

It was the one question she had neglected to ask him the day before, the one that looped in her brain.

She looked up from the woodworking tools.

That was likely a mistake.

He still watched her with those sincere pale eyes.

Piercing eyes.

Too-*seeing* eyes.

"Ye married me because ye loved me." His simple words cut her.

"Are ye sure?"

"As sure as any man can be of a woman's affections, I ken." He rubbed the back of his neck. The gesture was abruptly familiar and therefore equally unsettling.

Unbidden, she wondered at the memories he might keep—a stolen kiss behind casks of wool in the ship's hold? his arm wrapped around her waist as they whispered under a star-lit sky?

"What did I claim to like about yourself?" The question tumbled from her.

He grinned at that, hands spreading wide, shirt sleeves tugging in the breeze. "My handsome face? My delightfully quick wit?" He spun in a slow circle, forcing her to appreciate the tight cut of his trousers around his thighs. He paused and looked at her over his shoulder. "My ravishing physique?"

She was torn between smiling and throwing a chisel at his head.

He finished turning around, lifting his eyebrows.

"I'd like to think I'm hardly so shallow as to be turned by a pretty face," she said dryly.

"Hah! I knew ye found me handsome!"

Eilidh lost the battle with propriety and snatched up a chisel, tossing it at him.

He caught it easily—of course, he did—his laughter bouncing off the courtyard walls.

The man was her nemesis.

"Ye aren't answering my question." She folded her arms.

He sobered, his eyes turning soft and thoughtful . . . which was, again, somehow even worse.

She was rapidly realizing that underneath the charm and flirtation rested a sincere and earnest heart.

Her pulse beat a frantic tattoo in her chest.

He stepped toward her.

Eilidh instantly backed up, not because she abhorred the thought of his touch, but because she feared she might invite it.

He paused, hands up as if petitioning for peace.

"Why did ye love me, lass?" he repeated her question. "I think ye loved me because we are kindred souls, yourself and me. I admired your spirit and fire—your courage and kindness even in the direst of circumstances. Ye appreciated my candor and fierce devotion tae those I count as mine. And you, lovely lass, ye are without question . . . *mine.*"

Mine.

The word landed with ruthless brutality.

That she had been so beloved, so prized.

That this man—who commanded men and conquered oceans—had been and would continue to be so devoted to her.

He extended a hand to her, a wordless invitation.

Take it. Remember me.

She swallowed, staring at his outstretched fingers.

It was a well-worn hand, long-fingered with callouses along the pads of his palm, but not . . . *un*attractive.

A hand that had held her, embraced her, pulled her to him with fingers pressing dimpled indents into her hips—

Her own hands clenched into fists.

She tore her eyes away from his hand, unequal to the torrent of *feeling* which scoured her.

It was too much.

She would not rise to his bait.

She would not touch him.

And yet . . . her skin burned, as if singed by the buried weight of it, by caresses she could not remember.

"I do not recognize myself in the woman you describe." She turned her back to him, staring across the forecourt to the blue sky beyond. "I simply cannot fathom that I evolved into such a different person aboard the ship."

"Ye initially adopted your brother's name in order to be safe among men." His words lashed her from behind. "But over time, it became a new identity for ye. Ye became *Jamie*—a brilliant fierce light who cast off past grief to embrace a new and uncertain future. That same lass is still within ye. Ye can find her."

"Yes, but I don't *want* to find her. My current self is appalled by the decisions that girl made." Eilidh pivoted to face him, the carpentry tools between them. "Moreover, you're assuming that there is anything of that girl left within me."

Blindly, she picked up the plane and a bit of wood off the table, as if determined to show him that, like embroidery, she would fumble at this, too.

Instead, almost unbidden, her hand set to smoothing the rough piece of wood with the plane. As if she had done this very thing a thousand times.

The movement felt natural.

Worse, it felt . . . compelling.

Her mind instantly began assessing the wood on the table, seeing the scattered bits as a puzzle, how this piece could be formed to slot into that, which would create a—

No!

She dropped both items, her hands shaking as if scalded.

She scrubbed her palms against the worn fabric of her dress. The threads caught on her palms. She lifted her hands, studying them. She hated the callouses there. Evidence that she had known hard labor.

Hers were not the hands of a lady.

The shape of the plane had fit right against the callouses, reddening the skin.

No.

She didn't want this knowledge, this tangible proof of everything she had forgotten.

Bands of anxiety squeezed her chest.

Where was her numbing calm? Where was the white void?

She reached for it in her mind, but it was no use.

She bit her lip and pressed the heels of her hands to her eyes.

Memories pounded at the door, forcing their way in.

A dark-haired man, his hair in a long queue down his back. *Mr. Chen*, her mind labeled him.

The scenes skipped and stuttered.

Mr. Chen laughing, holding her hand to show her how to smooth a piece of wood.

Mr. Chen placing a kind palm on her shoulder, pointing to something on the ship deck.

Mr. Chen, his head bent, guiding her hand to pack a firework tube—

She recoiled from the last image.

It was simply too much.

She was no longer the woman aboard that ship. That creature overflowing with pluck and verve as Master MacTavish described.

She was afraid and anxious and weary.

So very weary.

Her thoughts winged to Simon.

If he were here, he would gently touch her elbow and whisper that all would be well. That she was safe. That the past was past. No need to dwell on it.

And then he would hold her hand and talk about the dreary weather and Mrs. Bryant's upcoming garden party until the fear eased. Until the blank numbness reasserted itself, and she felt equal to face her future once more.

But Simon wasn't here.

How was she to manage this nameless terror on her own?

She swallowed back a lump in her throat.

"Eilidh," a soft voice murmured near her ear.

She jumped and twirled to find Master MacTavish standing close beside her, eyes concerned. He clasped his hands behind his back, as if forcibly restraining himself from touching her.

"What are ye afraid of?" he whispered, leaning toward her. "Why this anxiety?"

She hated him in that moment. That he knew her so well that he could nearly pluck the thoughts from her head.

"Why do ye cringe from these memories?" he continued. "As I've said, I promise ye—there is *good* in them."

She shook her head. "No. Ye may have known me aboard the ship, but ye didn't see me in that villager's hut, trying tae come to terms with it all. Ye didn't see the aftermath of my injuries—my miscarriage, my headaches, the terrors that would grip me. I don't want it." She hugged her arms to herself. "I don't want those memories!"

"Eilidh—"

"No! What does it even matter?" She threw her arms in the air. "Why does it matter if I remember or not?"

"Because ye will *hang*," he sputtered. "I have not searched and scoured and *suffered* in order for ye to hang for this crime!"

"Why are ye convinced I will hang for a crime I didn't commit? You are not without friends and connections, men who claim to be *my* friends, too." She pointed a finger to her chest. "Why not have more faith in our justice system? You claim to know me so well, so why not trust that the truth will prevail? Let Cuthie say what he will, but we both know that I didn't blow up that ship—"

"Are ye so sure?"

"Of course, I am!" she nearly shouted. "The very idea is preposterous. I would never deliberately harm so many men."

"Even if your memories are as dark as ye suspect?"

She hissed, flinching back, his words striking true.

"No," she said, though her words were more bravado than knowledge. "Not even then. I have recovered a few memories of Mr. Chen. He was a good, kind man—"

"Aye. He was."

"I would never have harmed him. This entire accusation is absurd. I didn't destroy *The Minerva* and her crew."

Master MacTavish placed his hands on his hips, head shaking back and forth.

He lifted his pale eyes to hers.

"That's the problem, I ken," he said. "The woman ye are right now—the person ye see yourself as—she likely would not have blown up a ship. But Jamie? The woman I know? The woman I love?" He tapped his sternum. "*That* Jamie absolutely would have blown up *The Minerva* had she had a good enough reason—"

"Pardon?" The sheer audacity of such a statement stole her breath, sending her accent tumbling. "Ye actually think *I* did it?!"

"I dinnae know." He took a step closer. "That's why I keep pushing ye tae remember. Would you have done it if ye deemed it necessary? Even with Mr. Chen aboard? Aye. Ye would have weighed the facts and made a decision."

Eilidh struggled to rally her thoughts beyond *huhnnnnnn*.

Finally, she straightened her shoulders. "In that case, is it any wonder I don't wish to remember? If that is the woman I was, then good riddance."

October 1815

Again," Kieran called. "Faster this time."

"My arms are jelly." Jamie sagged, chest heaving, the tip of her rapier dipping. "You've managed tae liquefy them."

"Jamie," he growled, aggravation rolling in his chest. "Ye have to be able tae defend yourself from attack. When you're tired, most particularly. Now, *en garde*."

This beautiful, brave lass *needed* to know how to protect herself. Kieran would accept no other outcome.

Jamie rolled her eyes, but she lifted her blade and parried his attack. He beat her back against the deck railing, but instead of standing her ground, she darted to the side and danced away from him, laughing.

"Jamie," he warned, spinning to follow her. "This isnae a game."

"It isnae?" she chuckled, her accent rough, matching that of the other Scottish sailors aboard. "My wee arms are never going tae be strong enough for this."

"They will be. Ye just need tae practice more."

The ship bobbed at anchor in the vast harbor of Rio de Janeiro. The town clustered around the water's edge, but mountains rose behind, impossibly green and exotic. The air hung with the perfume of tropical flowers and the call of wild parrots and toucans.

Kieran had always considered Rio to be one of the most beautiful places on earth.

Most of the crew had already gone ashore, including Captain Cuthie and the rest of the senior mates. Kieran was left in charge with only a few able-bodied men as guards against thievery.

And Jamie, of course.

She had wanted nothing to do with "the tomfoolery that sailors get into while ashore."

Or rather, she recognized that maintaining the fiction of her gender would be fraught were she to find herself in a bathhouse.

The crew would only return to the ship in order to sleep.

The rest of the Brotherhood, as they were passengers and not crewmen, had rented rooms in a hotel along the harbor.

"I intend to be waited upon hand and foot for the next few days," Rafe had chuckled.

"Aye, and eat a meal with fresh fruits and vegetables," Andrew had agreed.

This meant Kieran and Jamie practically had the ship to themselves during the daylight hours.

To while away the time, they fenced and practiced hand-to-hand fighting skills. Jamie had learned much from Rafe, but Rafe's approach to fencing assumed his opponents would be civilized and orderly.

However, a true fight was rarely 'civilized and orderly.' It was, at best, terrifying chaos.

Jamie didn't just need to know how to fight. She needed to learn how to fight dirty.

But the time Kieran spent alone with her was fraught, as it magnified the tug of attraction between them.

Yes, she was friends with all of the Brotherhood.

But Kieran was the only one she singled out.

Three weeks.

They had been at this dance for three weeks.

Flirtatious banter when no one else could overhear. Long talks under the cover of darkness. Hours of laughter with the others in Andrew's cabin.

There had been no further mention of her returning to Scotland.

"Come along, Jamie," he motioned with his own rapier. "Why are ye refusing tae push yourself today?"

"I dinnae have it in me," she said. "I was up too late last night assisting Mr. Chen."

She leaned against the opposite deck railing, breathing heavily.

He sheathed his sword and walked over to her, stopping only a foot away. Her silvery eyes flashed under the mop of her dark curls. Like his own, her skin had bronzed in the constant sun of sea life, scattering new freckles across her cheekbones—wee flecks he traced in his mind, imagining how it would feel to press a shaking finger to her soft skin.

He swallowed.

"So the fireworks will be lit tonight?" he asked.

"Aye." She grinned. "Andrew even sent word to the governor tae let him know. We dinnae want any of these fine folk tae think they're under attack."

"A lot of good you'd be in an actual attack." He tapped the rapier still in her hand. "Ye need to become stronger."

Her eyebrows flew upward, wrinkling her brow. She swept her eyes up and down his body, a blatantly feminine perusal of appreciation.

His breathing hitched in his chest, fire spreading in his veins.

"If only I had the proper motivation," she whispered, her accent reverting to the softer lilt of her birth. She licked her lips. "Pity that."

She handed him her rapier and pushed past him, disappearing down the aft ladder to the deck below.

Kieran stared after her, mind a maelstrom.

Once more, he rehearsed all the reasons why he needed to keep his distance. They rolled through him like beads on a rosary—he was her senior officer; she trusted him to behave honorably; he had promised her father that he would protect her from harm, himself included.

To that end, he did the sensible thing—he returned to his cabin, sheathed her sword, and stowed it alongside his own.

He would stay in his cabin, maybe read for a bit, write a letter to some friends in Edinburgh.

He continued with this list, even as his feet left his quarters and followed the path to the cabin Jamie shared with Mr. Chen. The carpenter was ashore with everyone else.

Jamie, of course, was alone. She was bending over, placing some tools in a trunk.

He slid the door shut.

What he had planned to do . . . he wasn't sure.

Talk? Listen to the husky timbre of her voice?

Instead . . .

She stood and turned around, chin notched high.

Her chest heaved, as if she had been running.

He didn't know who reached for whom first.

But between one breath and the next, Jamie was in his arms, rising on tiptoe to fist her hands into his hair, her mouth hungrily finding his lips.

He hitched her against him, desperate for the feel of her body against his.

Kieran had known want in his life.

He was no stranger to desire.

But *this* . . .

This was the promised conflagration.

A torch tossed onto spilled tar pitch, flames instantly erupting.

Though such a wee thing, she pushed him back against the door, never once taking her lips off his.

Kieran smiled.

She felt his expression.

"Ye better not be laughing at me," she whispered against his mouth.

"Never." He smiled more broadly.

"Then why are ye smiling?"

"Cause when I'm with ye, I cannae help it. Ye make me proper *fou* on happiness."

"Your answer is acceptable," she replied, tone as haughty as a duchess.

He laughed.

She kissed him for that, a hungry nip of lips that pulled a groan from his throat.

"Are ye going to take advantage of me, lass? Compromise my honor with your kisses?"

She snorted. "Ye seem rather willing, MacTavish."

"That I am." He kissed her again, savoring the feel of her smile against his lips.

And somehow, he knew in that very moment—

He wasn't just kissing a beautiful, fiery lass.

He was kissing his future wife.

16

Kieran allowed Jamie a day of reprieve.

One day without him haunting her every step.

Or rather . . . Eilidh.

He had ceased to think of her as Jamie, truth be told.

She stubbornly refused to even *try* to remember.

And now . . . there was the specter of Simon Fitzpatrick.

Simon the Curate.

Simon the *Sassenach*.

The man seemed a veritable milksop just from his name alone.

Kieran hated Simon with vitriolic passion. He wished death and destruction upon the man's house and a pox upon his person.

It didn't help that the *haar* had rolled in off the North Sea, blanketing the landscape in dense fog. Kieran felt as if the world itself were collapsing in on him.

In short . . . he wasn't coping quite as well as he should.

Ewan, ever the sensitive soul, walked down from Kilmeny Hall the afternoon after Kieran's disastrous conversation with Eilidh in the forecourt. He cornered Kieran in the small library on the second floor of the castle. Though to call the wee room a library was perhaps a bit of a stretch. It was more like a study lined with books. But given the dreich weather out the window, the warm wood paneling and crackling fire at least didn't further aggravate Kieran's mood.

"Ye look like someone's been stomping on your grave," Ewan said with no preamble.

"Probably because someone has." Kieran rolled his eyes. "It's likely my wife, happy tae be rid of me."

"Ah." Ewan sat in a chair beside Kieran, stretching his hands toward the hearth. The days were less cold in June, but Scotland was rarely ever genuinely *warm*. Fires were still a necessity, particularly when fog and misting rain rolled in off the ocean.

Ewan looked around the room. "Where is our Miss Fyffe?"

"Hiding from me in her room." Kieran rested his head against the back of his chair. "Dinnae ye have a lovely wife at home, ready tae burst with child? Why are ye here with me?"

He did not manage to strip the bitterness out of his tone.

Ewan couldn't help the blessed fortune of his fate any more than Kieran could help the acidic pain of his own.

But it still hurt. To see his friends happily married to women who remembered that they were, indeed, happily married.

Funny, the silly things one took for granted.

That a person's sense of self would remain constant.

That a wife's affection would not disappear overnight.

If Ewan found Kieran's snippy tongue offensive, he didn't show it.

"I'm here because ye need a listening ear." His friend stretched out his long legs. "And tae be even more honest, I think Violet could use some space. She accused me twice today of hovering."

Kieran doubted the truth of that. That Violet needed space. Or that Ewan had been hovering.

More likely, Ewan was attempting to turn the tables, to make Kieran feel like *he* was doing the favor and not the other way around.

Kieran asked after Ewan's painting and got a grunt and shrug as an answer. They spoke of the midsummer festival that Violet still insisted on hosting. It sounded much like a traditional Scottish clan gathering with a fair and contests of prowess.

But eventually, Ewan circled back to the topic weighing on them. "So . . . how is Miss Fyffe?"

Kieran sighed. "Physically? I ken she's hale and hearty. But emotionally? That I cannae say."

"Och, go easy on the lass," Ewan said. "She's had a series of shocks. She's scarcely been here five days, but she's already learned she was married and may have blown up a merchant frigate and her crew. It's understandable that she needs a wee bit of space tae assimilate it all."

"Aye, and I'm trying tae be patient."

Ewan snorted. "Not your strongest character point . . . patience."

"Dinnae I know it." Kieran sighed. "But with Jamie . . . ye ken how she is . . . stubborn to the point of madness. She has a tendency tae form opinions that nothing can shake her from."

But even as the words left Kieran's mouth, he wondered.

That *was* true.

For Jamie.

But what about Miss Eilidh Fyffe?

Miss Fyffe was Jamie as she had been before the ocean voyage changed her. As such, she was more retiring and cautious than Jamie had ever been.

But on the other hand, Eilidh had apologized, unprompted. She was more attuned to other's feelings. She definitely exhibited a greater sense of fair play.

Perhaps, he was going about this all wrong.

"You're doing quite a bit of thinking over there," Ewan nudged Kieran with his booted foot. "Planning your attack."

"Aye. Perhaps my wife needs less of an attack and more of a concerted wooing." Kieran stared into the flames.

"Ye remember how long it took for her tae develop a tendre for ye the first time around?"

"Forever, it seemed. Months. The distance from Aberdeen to Rio."

"Well, there ye are, then. Woo her in earnest."

"I think I shall." Kieran rubbed his hands together. "Now I simply need tae decide how tae go about it."

"I WOULD LIKE tae try to jog your memory with another activity," Kieran said the following morning over breakfast.

Eilidh lifted her head from where she sat across from him.

He had experienced a rather sleepless night, but just after midnight, he had finally formulated a plan to woo his wife. It had required an early morning to procure what he needed—the result of which sat at his feet—but he hoped his efforts would pay off.

Eilidh merely reached for a dish of poached eggs and black pudding, spooning some of both onto her plate.

Mrs. McKay was on duty in the corner of the great hall, knitting a scarf for her grandson. The clack of her needles set a steady rhythm.

"As I have repeatedly stated," Eilidh said, pouring herself some tea from the pot on the table, "I do not believe I was responsible for *The Minerva*'s demise. Therefore, I am not eager to plumb my memories from the trip."

"Aye. I ken that." Kieran sat back in his chair.

She looked lovely this morning, dressed in a white gown of the finest muslin. The cut was simple but immaculate, as only the best seamstresses could manage. Her dark hair was piled atop her head in yet another complicated fashion, the whole banded with a strip of orange silk. A similarly bright Paisley shawl with whirling blue-and-orange flowers draped her shoulders.

In short, she looked nothing like his Jamie. She was every inch Miss Eilidh Fyffe, the gently-bred daughter of Captain Charles Fyffe.

And even now, her aching loveliness set his heart to thumping and fanned a burning sensation in his chest.

She lifted her head, pinning him with her silvery eyes. "If you understand that I do not wish to remember, then why are you thinking to convince me otherwise?"

"'Tis a fair question, though as I have said more than once, I adore your lovely neck. I would greatly dislike tae see a noose around it." Kieran pushed his empty teacup toward her. "Would ye be so kind as to pour me a cup?"

She froze, clearly attempting to parse the prosaic nature of his request with the harsh reality of his words.

Of course, being the clever lass that she was, she didn't pause for long.

She looked at his teacup and then the teapot by her elbow. Frowning, she reached farther down the table for the silver coffeepot, pouring him a cup. She then added two lumps of sugar to the coffee and pushed it back toward him.

A blissful sort of pain punched Kieran in the sternum. She had bypassed the tea for coffee and then prepared it exactly as he liked.

"Thank ye," he said.

Something in the worshipful nature of his tone reached her. "You are quite serious about your coffee, are you not?"

He was.

But how did Miss Eilidh Fyffe know that, unless she had remembered it?

"Aye. And ye added sugar, just as I like." He sipped gently at his cup, not wanting to scald his tongue.

A wee dent appeared between Eilidh's brows. Her eyes drifted back to the coffeepot, as if it had somehow betrayed her.

Ye be in there somewhere, my lass. Ye will remember me yet.

Kieran set down his cup, moving on, but a gladness hummed along his skin. "As you've said, it's not fair that I know yourself, but you dinnae know me. So, I'd like tae even the playing field, as it were. I am prepared to give something, too."

Eilidh dragged her gaze from the coffeepot and back to her own plate. "I cannot imagine what you might have that would sway me—"

Kieran hefted the burlap sack that had been sitting at his feet and set it on the table.

Eilidh's eyebrows lifted upward. Mrs. McKay stopped her knitting in the corner.

He reached into the sack and pulled out an orange. The orange fruit mimicked the color in Eilidh's shawl and hair ribbon, glowing in the morning light.

Her eyes widened.

Kieran presented the fruit to her, resting it on the tip of his fingers.

"Where did you get that?" she whispered.

"Lady Kildrum has a neighbor with an obliging greenhouse. She called in a favor."

Eilidh swallowed, her eyes never leaving the fruit.

"Ye remember?" Kieran asked, voice soft. "Me peeling ye oranges in Rio de Janeiro? We walked along the beach and skipped rocks in the waves and had a lunch of local smoked fish, *pãozhinos*, fried plantains, and . . . fresh oranges."

She shook her head, but her chest moved in quick breaths.

He continued, "Ye told me then about the time your father brought home oranges from a trip to Jamaica. He had picked them right as he left and kept them cool during the long voyage, just for ye tae have a drop of tropical sunshine, he said."

"They were the sweetest thing I'd ever tasted," she murmured.

"Aye. Just like the oranges in Rio." He set the fruit on the table between them.

"You think to bribe me with tropical fruit now?"

Kieran smiled. *Nae, I plan to woo ye with oranges.*

"Isnae that obvious?" He laced his hands together on the tabletop. "I'm not so unscrupulous as tae wield the might of my irresistible self upon ye. I wish tae win ye, fair and square. Not through chicanery."

She rolled her eyes in earnest at that, but he could sense no real irritation in it.

Eilidh went back to eating her eggs and black pudding, but her eyes kept wandering to the orange.

"Here is what I propose," he continued. "I have five more oranges in the bag. For each day that ye try to remember, ye get an orange—"

She snorted. "You vastly overestimate my love of oranges, Master MacTavish."

"No. I dinnae think I do." Kieran smiled. "You're convinced ye won't hang, but I ken it's more that the thought of hanging is too abstract. Ye need something tangible as a motivation to remember. And so—" He rolled the orange around the tabletop with his fingers before lifting it. "It smells lovely."

He extended the orange toward her.

She regarded it warily.

"Why do I feel like Eve in the Garden of Eden? Eyeing fruit offered by a serpent?"

"How ye wound me!" Kieran mock-gasped, pretending her words were a dagger to his chest. "Do ye hear this, Mrs. McKay? How the fair lass slanders me?"

The older lady chuckled. "Ye know yourself tae be handsome enough tae tempt the Devil hisself, Master MacTavish."

"You're quite the flirt, Mrs. McKay," Kieran laughed.

She winked at him. "I turned the head of many a lad in my day."

"I can leave you both to your flirtation, if you would like?" Eilidh sipped her tea. "You can plot your wicked deeds in peace."

Kieran tossed the orange back and forth between his hands. "I'm hardly tempting ye to sin, lass. Only to try tae remember."

Or, rather, to fall in love with me once again.

She pursed her lips and studied him for a moment.

"I want more than oranges. This isn't just about you giving me something physical in exchange for my efforts. I want more than that." She poured herself a spot more tea. "If I am going to actively try to uncover painful memories, I need to not feel so alone in my vulnerability."

Excellent.

She had moved to bargaining. Always a sign of capitulation with Jamie.

"What do ye propose?" Kieran barely suppressed a triumphant grin.

"For every question you ask me, I get to ask one of yourself in return."

She paused, as if expecting him to back down.

Hardly.

"Deal," he said.

She narrowed her eyes. "*Any* question."

If she thought to scare him, she was utterly mistaken.

"Any question. Anything." He would lay bare any hurt, confess to any emotion, anything to win her heart once more. "But ye have tae try to remember. And ye have to try in the ways I request."

"I am certainly not going to agree to *anything* you request—"

"Within reason." He held out a staying hand. "I willnae ask ye to do anything untoward."

She continued to stare at him.

Or rather, she tried, but her eyes struggled to stop staring at the orange.

Finally, she nodded. "Very well."

"Excellent," he smiled. "Let's start this afternoon."

Kieran extended a hand across the table.

She hesitated and then took it, sliding her palm into his.

The shock of touching her warm skin sent a jolt up his arm.

He noted the pulse fluttering in her throat. Her own emotions were not as calm as she supposed.

He would rekindle their love.

Simon the Sassenach would not win Eilidh's affections without a battle.

And in time-honored Scottish tradition, Kieran intended to fight dirty.

November 1815

"Well, we may be a week late for Bonfire Night," Jamie laughed, folding her arms, "but we will make up for the time in sheer spectacle."

Kieran grinned at her infectious enthusiasm.

"Aye," Andrew smiled.

"Does Mr. Chen need help?" Ewan asked, looking down the hill to the beach where the ship's carpenter was pushing sticks affixed with firework rockets into the sand. A bonfire burned farther on down the shoreline, flames lighting up the dark night. Crew members gathered around the flickering fire, laughing and passing around a bottle of gin someone had unearthed from the ship's hold.

"Nae," Jamie replied. "Mr. Chen said we were tae leave him to it."

She peered over her shoulder, her eyes instantly finding Kieran's. As usual, the smoldering tension of her gaze sent heat spiraling through his veins.

Damn, but he was the most fortunate of men to have this lass's regard.

They had left Rio two weeks ago. Mr. Chen's fireworks had been such a success there, the crew had begged to be able to do another round of fireworks for Guy Fawkes Night. As Captain Cuthie refused to allow fireworks to be lit on ship—for good reason—they had postponed the event until landing in Tristan da Cunha, the last island stop before sailing into the Roaring Forties that would eventually lead them on to Sydney.

The Brotherhood now stood together beneath a stand of palm trees at the edge of the sand. The dramatic slopes of an extinct volcano rose behind them, green and vibrant in the wet tropics.

Kieran stole another glance at Jamie. She grinned at something Rafe said, bouncing on the balls of her feet in excitement.

Unable to bear being so far from her, Kieran slipped around the men and moved to stand behind Jamie. She acknowledged his presence by reaching back and wrapping her fingers around his, the dark night and looming shadows easily hiding the connection from prying eyes on the beach. After all, as far as Kieran knew, no one else aboard *The Minerva* suspected that James Fyffe was a woman. He intended to protect her from discovery.

Mr. Chen lit the first fuse, and a rocket hissed into the inky sky.

A boom of orange sparks soon followed.

The crew cheered.

Jamie added her own voice, once more bouncing eagerly on her tiptoes.

Kieran laughed.

How he adored this lass.

He loved how she giggled while telling a joke, unable to hold the laughter in.

He adored the wee dent in her brow when she concentrated on a task.

He loved how she rolled her eyes and shimmied her hips when she ate something she liked.

He worshiped the saucy upturn of her nose, those fine freckles that dusted her cheekbones, the way sunlight caught reddish highlights in her dark curls.

He loved how she met each day with fire and determination.

He loved . . . her.

The feeling washed over him, humbling in its intensity.

Bright. Pure. Clear.

Kieran MacTavish loved Jamie Fyffe.

How had it taken him this long to realize it? He should have known he would love her from that first conversation after discovering she was a woman. It was so obvious to him now.

How he loved her!

As if to punctuate the moment, another series of fireworks exploded overhead.

Boom. Boom. Boom.

The sound echoed the thundering of Kieran's own heart. Love scoured his soul.

It all expanded upward to his mouth, words swelling and multiplying until he had to loose them.

He leaned forward and pressed his lips to Jamie's ear.

"I love ye, *mo chridhe*," he whispered. "Now and forever."

She gave a hiccupping gasp and pivoted, staring up at him.

Kieran could see the fireworks reflected in her eyes.

And then . . . she smiled as bright and incandescent as the fireworks at her back.

"I love you, too," she mouthed to him. "Always."

18

Eilidh feared she had been hoodwinked.

Honestly.

She stared at the trousers, shirt, and waistcoat laid out on her bed.

I willnae ask ye to do anything untoward, he had said.

Why had she believed Kieran MacTavish?

The man truly was the Devil incarnate. A snake in the grass.

She picked up the note lying atop the shirt.

Put these on and meet me in the great hall.

Trust me.

K

She snorted.

The man was dogged beyond tolerance and reason.

Clearly, he thought that donning trousers—which she had surely worn aboard ship while, no doubt, losing her foolish heart to him—would help jar her memory.

Eilidh eyed the innocent-looking shirt and waistcoat apprehensively.

She didn't have to do it. She could simply refuse.

But the oranges . . .

They conjured a brightness, a lift in her soul. A luminous sweetness that hung just beyond the reach of memory.

In short . . . she adored oranges.

Curse the wretched man for knowing her so well.

The fruit was a blinding weakness for her, but one that she very rarely indulged. Oranges, after all, were ghastly expensive and far outside her meager finances.

Still, as deeply as she craved those oranges, she hated how Master MacTavish's constant pestering rattled her peace of mind. The man was as relentless as the ocean waves below Kilmeny Castle, slowly eroding her ability to remain numb.

Her mind still reeled from the revelation that he considered her capable of blowing up *The Minerva*. She refused to accept it.

She would never have knowingly sent 127 men to their deaths.

Impossible.

Kieran MacTavish was mistaken.

She crumpled the note and stared down at the shirt and trousers.

Finally, she straightened her shoulders.

Very well.

She would meet his demands, but she would not make the path easy for him.

TEN MINUTES LATER, Eilidh walked into the great hall.

The trousers, shirt, and waistcoat did not feel as odd as she might have thought.

But they did not feel as comfortable, either.

It's been six years since you wore such a thing, part of her pointed out.

Or . . . perhaps she hadn't been as 'boyish' as others claimed.

The thought died on her lips as she caught sight of Master MacTavish.

Kieran.

He was similarly dressed to herself—trousers, waistcoat, and a shirt open at the throat and cuffed up his forearms.

But it was the fencing foil in his hand that stopped her short.

Surely, he didn't think . . .

That she would be interested in . . .

But a glance around the great hall confirmed they were the only two present. The dining table had been pushed to one side and the carpet rolled up, leaving an enormous expanse of wood floor in the center of the hall.

"Ah! There ye are, lass." He saluted her with his blade, surveying her up and down.

Frowning, Eilidh crossed to him.

She meant to administer a blistering set-down.

Truly, she did.

But his state of partial undress disrupted her breathing. Yesterday in the forecourt, he had at least retained his cravat and kept his shirtsleeves buttoned.

But today, her eyes were distracted by the ropes of muscle rippling in his forearms. Worse, a V of his bare chest peeked out from the top of his shirt. She could see hints of the planes of muscle, and even a glint of the chain around his neck, the wedding ring swinging to press against the linen as he moved.

Had she *touched* that chest? Run her hands over those broad shoulders? Pressed kisses against—

Stop!

She gritted her teeth and pulled her eyes up to his.

He looked amused.

Because . . . of course he did.

She clasped her hands behind her back, itching her palms with her nails. Anything to banish the phantom sense of him.

She shot a pointed look at the blunt-tipped fencing *épée* in his hand.

"I'm not going to fence with you." She got right to the point. "The very thought is absurd."

"Ye promised ye would try to remember, lass. Ye gave your word—"

"And where is Mrs. McKay?" Eilidh scowled, looking around the room once more. "You are breaking faith with me at every turn."

"Mrs. McKay is taking a nap," he all but sighed. "The door is open. There are servants about. I assure ye, we are meeting propriety."

Her eyes narrowed on him. "I like Mrs. McKay, but I am starting to suspect that she was chosen as my chaperone because she is elderly, permissive, and easily swayed by flirtatious compliments."

The twitch of Kieran's lips was all the confirmation Eilidh needed.

"I'm not fencing with you," she repeated.

"Ye promised. And I have . . . *oranges*." He pointed his *épée* at the burlap sack still sitting on the table.

Eilidh glanced at it and then looked back to him.

"I may have promised, but all I've seen is you testing that promise—pushing my cooperation to its limits. If you want me to fence, you will have to give me an orange first, as a show of good faith." She snapped her fingers and held out her hand. "An agreement is an agreement."

He shook his head, closing the distance between them. "Ye have done nothing to try to remember yet."

She folded her arms. "Then we are at an impasse, Master MacTavish."

If she thought to unsettle him, she found she was mistaken.

Shooting her a rather smug smile, he set down his rapier and fetched an orange from the sack. Leaning back against the edge of the ancient oaken table, he crossed his feet at the ankles and began peeling the orange, the muscles of his forearms flexing and retreating.

"That's *my* orange." She crossed to him. "You cannot simply eat it yourself."

That roguish smile stretched wider. "Consider this a bonus orange. A show of good faith, as ye requested."

The heady smell of citrus filled the air. He peeled the fruit in a bright narrow strip, round and round, his long fingers expertly skimming off the rind in one continuous corkscrew of summery color.

Eilidh watched, her gaze helplessly tangled in the orange spiral.

His actions felt simultaneously novel and, yet, achingly familiar.

She took another hesitant step forward, halving the distance between them. With a grin, he finished peeling the orange and then deftly reassembled the long corkscrew back into a sphere. He held both oranges out to her—one on each palm—the bright orange hollow peel and the pith-speckled ball of its interior.

Eilidh reached for the fruit.

Grinning even wider, Kieran snatched it out of her reach, holding it over his head.

She narrowed her eyes at him.

His smirk said he would welcome her climbing his body to grasp the prize.

That was *not* going to happen.

She held out her palm, a silent demand.

He looked at her hand, shook his head, and then split the peeled orange in half, sending a small spray of juice into the air. The scent of citrus assaulted her.

Her mouth watered. The smell was so intoxicating, Eilidh contemplated snatching the fruit from his grasp and racing off with it.

Kieran peeled off a slice and held it out.

She reached for it with her fingers.

He pulled it back.

She frowned.

"Stop playing games," she hissed.

"Let me feed you."

"Like a baby bird? I think not." She folded her arms once more. "This bonus orange appears to have stipulations. That renders it less of a bonus and more of an . . . an *onerous* orange."

He chuckled, still holding the orange wedge out to her. Enticing. Luring.

She glared at it.

"I don't like *onerous* oranges," she deadpanned. "You tell me to trust you, but then you behave in this flirtatious manner. As if you're attempting to *woo* me."

His expression didn't change. "I *am* attempting to woo ye."

"Wooing wasn't part of the deal."

"Consider it a bonus wooing, as well." He dangled the orange slice. "You get oranges, flirtation, *and* help recovering your memories."

He waggled the orange, tempting. Probably knowing, too, that the smirk on his lips and the rakish angle of his shoulders would be equally enticing to her.

She pursed her mouth. Drat him for knowing she would commit mutiny in earnest for an orange.

Fine.

Two could play at this game.

If she was going to eat this orange from his fingers and tolerate his open flirtation, she would not make it pleasant for him.

"What is your greatest weakness?" she asked, arms still folded.

She leaned forward and swiftly snatched the offered orange section with her teeth, careful not to touch him in any way.

The tart juicy sweetness detonated in her mouth. She barely stifled a moan.

"My greatest weakness?" he repeated, watching her chew, pupils dilating. He slowly peeled off another slice. "The sound of your laughter."

Eilidh swallowed. "Please be serious."

"I *am* being serious. Wooing, remember?" He looked at her before glancing down at the orange wedge in his fingers. He popped it into his own mouth, groaning in appreciation.

She growled and took a step closer. "That one was mine. You're stealing now."

"Ye always were bad at sharing," he tsked around his mouthful of *her* orange.

"This wooing is going rather poorly."

"I'll be the judge of that." He peeled off another slice and held it out to her.

"What is your greatest regret?" She ate it from his hand again, eyes rolling back in their sockets.

Heavens, but she loved oranges.

"My greatest regret?" He paused, a shadow passing over his expression. "I regret that I wasnae there in that villager's hut with ye when ye miscarried our bairn. That ye had to experience such suffering without me."

His eyes dropped to Eilidh's flat stomach.

She felt the weight of his gaze, a sinking through her midriff. She pressed a hand there, as if that could stop the potency of . . . whatever was happening between them.

She needed to ask questions that were not parried as easily as the swords lying at their feet.

"What is the thing you dislike the most about me?" She ate another segment of orange.

"That ye dinnae remember me," he replied, again popping another section in his mouth. "That ye dinnae remember I *love* you."

Love.

Present tense.

The verb—active, immediate, longing—joined the sinking tug just below her sternum.

This would not do.

"Allow me to rephrase the question. What is the thing you disliked the most about me when I was Jamie?" She ate another slice from his fingers.

His answer was immediate. "I loved everything about ye."

"Try again. Be honest."

"I am!" he snorted. "Ye were the light of my life, lass."

"*Ooof!* Cease this flirting!"

"I cannae help it when I'm around your fair self." He spread his arms wide, showing her far more of his attractive forearms than was wise for her sanity. "Bonus wooing, remember?"

"Kieran!" She stamped her foot. "Be serious—"

"Och, ye can be a wee bit stubborn, ye know!"

His aggravated growl sent a thrill chasing her spine.

He dropped another slice in his mouth.

They were down to two orange slices.

She ate one of them. "Do you want me to be Jamie again?"

Instead of popping the last piece into his own mouth, he offered it to her.

She readily accepted it. It tasted of sweetness and hope, despite the chasm of loss and forgetting between them.

He watched her chew.

"I want ye to remember how much ye love me," he whispered. "I want ye to let *me* love you."

She swallowed, that leaden weight in her stomach sinking further.

How did he do this?

How did he turn every conversation back at her, leaving her unsettled and unsure?

His eyes dropped to her lips.

She tensed.

The silence stretched and strained.

But he did . . . nothing.

He merely looked away, wiped his hands on a handkerchief, and walked past her, picking up his *épée* again. He tested the square blunt on the tip, ensuring it was solidly in place.

She pivoted with him.

"Here." He snatched a second *épée* and tossed it to her, hilt first.

Without conscious thought, she snagged it out of the air.

He nodded his approval.

"Come," he beckoned with his blade. "Let us see what ye remember."

"Remember? I fought?" Eilidh paused. "Or are you thinking to begin teaching me as more of your *bonus* wooing?"

"Nae, no bonus wooing in this, unfortunately," he grinned. "Ye learned tae fence, lass. Ye were quite the swordsman by the time we reached the New Hebrides."

She learned to fence?!

Eilidh hefted the blade in her hand—half-wondering, half-terrified of its vaguely familiar weight.

"*En garde.*" He raised his sword.

She ignored him and instead tested the sword. It felt . . . balanced.

How did she know that? How a balanced sword felt?

Did she truly know how to use it?

He misread her hesitation.

"Ye promised me, lass," he warned, pointing his blade at her. "I've never known ye to go back on a promise."

She bit back the sarcastic words crowding her tongue, *"Well, that was before ye dressed me in trews and handed me a sword."*

"If it helps, think about how satisfying it will be tae jab the fencing foil into my chest," he continued.

"A bonus stabbing?"

His pale eyes flared. "Aye, if that comforts ye."

He mimed taking a rapier hit to the stomach. Of course, the motion tipped his body forward, giving Eilidh a clear glimpse of corded pectorals, a smattering of chest hair, and her wedding ring spinning round.

She looked away, forcing her breathing to remain slow.

"Very well." She lifted the blade, mirroring his stance. "I cannot say that I remember how to fence. But . . . *en garde*."

He darted forward, feinting to the right.

She flinched and skittered back.

He jabbed left.

She shrieked and dropped her *épée*.

His expression studiously neutral, he flicked his sword toward hers. "Pick it up. Keep your eye on my *épée*."

Her pulse thrummed in her ears and her hands shook slightly. But some part of her refused to back down from this.

Biting her inner cheek, she did as he asked.

Again, he charged.

Again, she lost her nerve and dropped her sword before making contact.

"You're braver than this. There is a fighter in ye, lass." He motioned for her to pick up the sword again. "Try again. I'll go more slowly."

Taking in a deep breath, she picked up the sword.

"You're over-thinking," he offered. "Shut your mind off. Allow your body to take over. Your muscles will remember, even if ye do not."

The fencing foil *did* feel familiar in her hand, balanced and smooth. She could envision it as an extension of her arm.

He attacked once more.

She managed to hit his blade one time, but the metallic clang and vibration along her arm startled her into dropping her *épée* again.

He waited patiently for her to pick it up.

Abruptly, she saw him on the deck of a ship, sword in hand, the same quiet intensity in his eyes.

"Come along, Jamie." Fire flashed in his pale eyes as he swished his rapier. Dressed in only shirt sleeves and trousers, she decided it was a sin for any man to be so lethally handsome. One glimpse of the bunched muscle of his shoulders and her mind instantly rolled into the gutter. "Why are ye refusing tae push yourself today?"

She took in a slow, stuttering breath, forcing the memory back. The rogue sense that she had found him just as powerfully attractive then as she did now.

She could not allow this.

"*En garde*," he said.

She nodded and raised her own weapon.

She would fight the siren call of him, metaphorically and literally.

This time when he attacked, she allowed her body to take over, to react instinctively.

Their swords clashed. She blocked his slash to the right, retaliated to the left, and then darted out of reach.

"Good," he barked. "Again."

She dashed in and the battle was on. Their blades crossed, in and out, as they circled one another. Her mind noted that he was moving more slowly than he could, that he could disarm her, but he was choosing not to.

Some unknown part of her responded.

How dare he assume her so weak! She could best him.

She *would* best him!

She began to move faster and faster—slicing left, feinting right—her movements more sure.

She was pure instinct.

No thought.

No words.

Just air moving in and out of her lungs, the *shush-shush* of her feet on the wooden floor, and the twang of their blades crossing.

Blood pulsed in her ears, clogging her throat and banding her chest.

The faster she went, the more precisely he matched her.

She had thought to banish the allure of him.

But . . . the opposite happened.

The hotter her blood flowed, the more flashes of her former self floated to the surface.

The thrill of adventure. The allure of a different life.

He was stunning in motion—liquid and lithe.

Her eyes kept darting back to the V of his chest at his throat. To the muscles rippling underneath his shirt. To the wedding ring swinging on its chain underneath, pressing against the fine cloth.

Did she, disgraced sailor and future vicar's wife, truly own this ship master's heart as he claimed? Had she willingly accepted him as her husband? And had he counted himself lucky for it?

It felt . . . impossible.

And yet . . .

Watching him move . . .

She wanted.

She yearned.

He took advantage of her momentary distraction, tangling her blade in his. The action should have stripped the *épée* from her hand, but instead, he held the blades together, essentially trapping her in place.

He stepped forward, so close scarcely a half a foot separated them.

His pale eyes snared her.

"Anytime," he whispered.

"Pardon?" she gasped, lungs burning for air.

"I know that look on your face."

"What look is that?" She licked her lips. His eyes followed the motion.

"The look that says ye wish tae touch me." He lifted his eyes back to hers, his gaze so very . . . hungry.

Lungs, words, breath, thought—*every* part of her froze.

"And my reply—" He halved the space between them, his body so close the heat of him singed her, so close that his breath brushed her mouth. "—is that ye can touch me whenever ye would like. Anytime. Anyplace. Anywhere. I will *always* welcome your hands on my person."

He flicked his wrist at that, the final gesture to pull the *épée* from her hand, sending both their blades clattering to the floor.

The abrupt motion caused her to tumble forward, her palm pressed to his chest, pressing tight against the wedding ring there.

He caught her against him, one hand banded around her waist, the other pressed between her shoulder blades.

The sensation was too much.

He was too much.

His head dipped down, lips seeking hers.

Eilidh . . . panicked.

She had let too much in and wandered too far outside her habitual numbness.

That's when it struck.

Terror engulfed her, a tidal wave of fear, obliterating the last vestiges of her numbness and drowning her in emotion—*frightpainhorrorhelphelphelp.*

A vise gripped her lungs, squeezing out the air, leaving her gasping.

The world went black.

She was trapped. She couldn't free herself from the steely arms encasing her.

She devolved into a wild creature, shrieking and hitting.

"Let me go! *Letmegoletmego!*"

Kieran hissed and released her immediately, leaping back, palms out.

She wrapped one arm around her stomach and pressed a shaking hand to her mouth.

He stared, eyes wide and horrified.

"Eilidh . . ." he whispered.

She pivoted and fled from the room, the very hounds of hell at her heels.

December 1815

"Ye have tae leave, lass," Kieran whispered to Jamie, pulling her off her feet as he hugged her tight. "Things cannae continue like this."

The hour was late. She had waited until everyone was asleep and then sneaked into his cabin, as was her wont. The room was dim, lit only by a slit from a dark lantern in one corner.

"But I just got here," she murmured, arms a vise around his neck. "Besides, ye tell me to go, but your actions say *stay, stay, stay.*"

He breathed out a soft laugh, setting her gently back on her feet. "Ye know what I ken."

"Do I?" She rose to her tiptoes and pressed her nose into the crook of his neck.

She was so fierce and determined, he often forgot how truly wee she was. The top of her head barely skimmed his shoulder.

He bent his head and caught her lips with his, nipping at them.

As usual, his heart drummed in his chest. After a day of arguing with Cuthie over supply issues and disciplining a wayward boatswain, he was unbearably relieved to have her in his arms once more.

Why had this brave, beautiful, spunky lass chosen him?

The thought regularly filled him with wonder.

But loving Jamie Fyffe came with obstacles.

Foremost . . . he was terrified.

Afraid that she would decide she was too young to become involved with him, that her father had been right to reject Kieran as a suitor for her.

Afraid that she would realize that she did not, in fact, love him as thoroughly as he loved her.

So very afraid that her gender would be exposed, no matter how carefully they all guarded her.

Terrified that he would be unable to protect her.

Though it was not illegal for a woman to work aboard a ship, impersonating her brother could have consequences. Cuthie would likely extract a pound of flesh from them all for such a deception.

"I'm not leaving ye," she whispered, answering his thoughts.

Her fingers slid through his hair, sending a cascade of gooseflesh down his spine.

"I cannae protect ye here, not aboard ship." He clasped her tighter against him. "We dock in Sydney tomorrow. We will hire a companion for ye and arrange passage back tae Scotland. Andrew has already said he will front the money."

"Only if ye come with me." She pulled back to press a row of kisses along his jaw, utterly scattering his wits.

"You're trying to distract me with your wiles, lass." He placed his hands on her shoulders and gently coaxed her to take a step back and put six inches of space between them.

She grinned and ran her palms over his chest, clearly pleased that her fingers had more freedom of movement. Her touch burned his skin.

He snagged her hands with his, intending to simply shackle them. But instead, found himself lifting them to his lips and pressing kisses to the callouses on her palms.

"Ye'll be the death of me yet, Jamie," he muttered.

She smiled, a beam from the flickering dark lantern catching the curves of her face. "Mmmm, the romantic things ye say. Woo me more, my noble knight."

He grinned at her dry tone, pulling her back into his arms, trapping her hands against his chest. "I'm happy tae tell ye how fetching ye look in trousers, lass. Women would never wear dresses again, if I could help it."

"Trousers *are* infinitely more practical," she agreed. "Have ye considered starting a petition? I am sure Lords—"

"No more distracting me." He kissed her. "I am trying tae have a serious conversation."

"No, ye are having a silly conversation. There is a decided difference."

"Jamie—"

"I will hear no talk of us being parted. I love ye too well to bear it."

"But the risk tae your person aboard ship . . . sailors can be savage brutes. I couldnae live with the guilt if something were tae happen—"

"What will happen?" She sighed and snuggled against him. "You are here. Our friends are here and not without significant power. Even if my gender is uncovered, I will be safe."

Kieran held her for a long moment, trying to silence the worried voices in his mind that offered up an endless string of nightmarish scenarios.

Finally, he could take no more of the uncertainty.

"Marry me?" He whispered the question against her hair.

He felt more than heard her gasp.

"Pardon?" She pulled back, peering up at him, her silvery eyes wide in the soft light.

He pressed a kiss to her plump lips.

"Will ye marry me?" he repeated. "Become my wife. Allow me to give ye the protection of my name."

He didn't add that as his wife, she would have reason to be aboard even if Cuthie found out the truth.

"Is that all ye want?" she asked. "To protect me?"

Kieran nearly laughed at the absurdity of the thought.

Protection? Hardly.

"Nae, lass. I only said protection because it's a logical reason for us tae marry. But there are a thousand illogical reasons for us tae marry." He pressed his forehead to hers. "I love the way your eyes crinkle when you laugh. How ye tease me out of my bad humor. But the simplest reason is this—ye are my best friend. And I cannae bear the thought of facing even one more day of my life without yourself firmly at my side."

Jamie said nothing for a long moment.

So long that Kieran feared he had overstepped. That he had perhaps misread their situation.

But staring down at her, Kieran realized that her lips were trembling. A tear splashed onto her cheek.

Oh!

She said nothing because her heart was too full to speak.

"Ah, lass." He swallowed against the telltale sting in the back of his own throat. "Nod your head if ye mean tae say, 'Yes.'"

She vigorously nodded and then launched herself into his arms, burying her nose once more into his neck.

He held her for a long while.

Allowing the soft sound of her happy sobs to melt into the rocky swish of waves lapping the ship.

Eilidh lay still on her bed, her body curled into a ball, terror raking her insides with vicious claws.

Her numbness had shattered into jagged shards, and she had no idea how to remake it.

After racing to her room, she had immediately stripped, hands shaking so badly she tore a button off the waistcoat and tripped on the trousers.

She now wore one of her old dresses—a blue muslin gown that never failed to kindle a smiling light in Simon's eyes.

Anything to quell the sense of otherness within her.

To purge that wild, foolish girl who had made such recklessly *stupid* choices and allowed herself to be trapped aboard that ship.

To ground herself in the reality of her life *now,* to the future she wanted *now.*

She shook and trembled on the bed for a long while, trying desperately to rebuild emotional walls around her heart. Anything to stop the agony lashing her chest, the ghastly tension that banded her lungs and made breathing nearly impossible.

This was why she avoided the past.

This was why she could not risk remembering.

Such black terror had not visited her in nearly four years, not since returning to Britain.

The first year after the wreck of *The Minerva*, Eilidh could scarcely sleep. She moved through days on New Caledonia with the Gillespies, dragging the leaden weight of her missing memories behind her. Her unknown past felt dark and oppressive, rendering her weepy one moment and utterly despondent the next. Melancholy was a constant companion. Something had irreparably broken within her, and she had no idea how to fix it. How to silence the never-ending cacophony of pain.

On the ship back to England, she had stood more than once on the deck, staring down at the deep ocean, pondering the lull and dark of it. How easy it would be to just fall, allow the water to cocoon her—to render her mind and body as weightless as starlight as she sank down, down, down—stopping the pain forever.

She had not succumbed to the urge. And miraculously, the black terror had gradually receded once she landed in Britain.

Eilidh thought that perhaps the reprieve had something to do with returning to an environment that was familiar and so unlike the wet, tropical heat that had stolen her memories.

Reverend Gillespie was less sanguine. He called it a gift from God. A blessing for her righteousness, for repenting of the wickedness she had no doubt fallen prey to while aboard *The Minerva*.

Regardless, after a year or two, Eilidh had finally been able to subdue the horror of the events after *The Minerva* sank. She had accepted the unknown weight of her missing year and moved on, skimming along the surface of life, never delving too deep into memory or emotion.

Anything to avoid stirring up the pain of the black terror.

And she had been doing well, particularly since meeting Simon.

Kind, gentle Simon.

Soothing, *safe* Simon.

Her hand reached for his letter on her bedside table.

> *Mother and I visited Sir Michael Allan and Lady Allan Monday last. They send their regards. Lady Allan inquired twice as to when you might return. I told her that no specific date had been set, but I do hope it will be soon. I miss the soothing sound of you reading to Mother and me of an evening. You always render the voices in such a way that brings the tale to life.*

Eilidh wiped a tear from her cheek.

She wanted *this.*

The simplicity and quiet of an uncomplicated relationship. One where she slipped in and out with ease, safe and secure.

No current of electric feeling. No bruised longing. No magnetic Scot teasing or prodding in order to know her better.

A future without terror lurking, waiting to pounce.

Simon accepted what Eilidh was willing to give and demanded nothing more.

Anything else—persistent questions, flirtatious innuendo, a scalding fingertip brushed along her cheek—

Eilidh stopped her thoughts right there, forcing a steadying breath in and out.

Yes, anything beyond genteel companionship was too difficult. It invited in a deluge of emotions that she could not control or understand.

Avoiding them was the only way forward. The only way to even *have* a future.

She had been a fool to even *attempt* to remember—

A quiet knock sounded on her door.

She stared at the door handle from where she lay on the bed. Her entire body felt sore, her limbs too heavy to lift themselves.

"Eilidh," Kieran's voice was muffled but distinct.

Her heart sped up.

"Please, Eilidh. Open up. Let me see ye, *mo chridhe.*"

Mo chridhe.

My heart.

She swallowed.

His words challenged her, both physically and metaphorically.

She didn't wish to see him.

She didn't want to let him in. Not into her room. Not into her thoughts. Definitely not into her heart.

She wanted to be alone.

She wanted the blessed numbness to return.

She wanted the black terror to retreat and never bother her again.

"I ken that ye dinnae want to see me, lass. But I cannae leave ye be. Not when I know ye are hurting so. I promise I will do nothing. I willnae touch ye." A soft *thunk*, as if he had rested his forehead against the door. "Just . . . dinnae shut me out."

She could see it so clearly in her mind's eye. Kieran leaning against her door, his palm on the wood, as if he could reach her by the strength of his affection alone.

It tugged at her. A need to go to him, to soothe his fears.

Why?!

She pressed the heels of her hands to her eyes.

Why, why, *why* did he pull at her, call to her? Why could he not be vile and ridiculous so she could hate him and move on?

Instead, he plied her with oranges and sweet words and made her wish that maybe, for once, she could find the courage to fight her desolate brokenness.

That she did not have to choose between two undesirable options—living trapped in the pain of black memories or compressing her emotions into a frozen white glacier.

That somehow, she could be whole.

He made her *want* to be whole. To live again—

Give him a chance.

No. It felt . . . impossible.

The more she came to know Kieran, the more she poked a cautious finger into the blankness of her missing memories, the more fear and darkness swarmed out to torment her.

She simply couldn't do it. She didn't have the courage—

"You're stronger than ye ken," Kieran said from the other side of her bedchamber door.

Eilidh let her hands fall from her eyes.

At the very least, Kieran MacTavish could stop reading her mind.

But he continued on, voice muted but still clear through the heavy oak between them.

"Cuthie and that voyage took too much from ye. Why continue to let him hold your future hostage? Why allow the fear of hidden memories to dictate your path? Take charge, lass. Remember in truth and prove Cuthie's accusations wrong."

Eilidh bit her lip.

Remembering was the problem, was it not?

At least at the moment, her memories were unknown.

But what happened when she knew?

When the unspecified terror she felt had defined edges—a voice, a face, a body?

How was *knowing* going to do anything other than varnish her pain in colors as vivid as one of Ewan's paintings?

"There is beauty in your memories, lass," he continued. "I know I keep saying it, but it's true. It might not be all good, but I believe that if ye were tae remember . . . if ye could just see in your head the way I cared for ye . . . ye would say . . ." A deep breath sounded, followed by another soft thunk of his head against the door. ". . . ye would see that the good outweighs the bad. Ye would not be so . . . *afeart*."

Quiet.

So quiet, she thought he might have left.

A buried part of her panicked at the thought, that he might have left her alone once more.

It was what she wished, after all, was it not?

So why, then, did it worry her?

But then . . . another thunk of his head—

"Please, Eilidh. Please let me in."

KIERAN NEARLY STUMBLED forward when the door unexpectedly opened.

He truly thought Eilidh would refuse him entry.

Jamie certainly would have; she would have ignored him and licked her wounds in silence.

The terror on Eilidh's face right before she had run from the great hall . . .

She had been a feral animal, trapped and caught, lashing out.

This had been his own fear, had it not? That some sort of physical assault lurked in the chasm of her missing memories. She had been alone aboard *The Minerva*, after all. Unprotected. At Cuthie's mercy.

And Cuthie had no reason to treat her kindly.

But the man had to have known that if even one member of the Brotherhood survived being marooned, he would hunt Cuthie to the ends of the earth to avenge Jamie's wounds.

It was the reason Cuthie and Massey had not returned to Britain in nearly three years. The Brotherhood were men of power, and Cuthie had hurt, if not broken, one of their own.

Part of Kieran had hoped that Cuthie, being self-preserving and shrewd above all else, would have at least not brutally assaulted Jamie directly.

Even so, Eilidh had been without Kieran for nearly six years. Anything could have befallen a woman during that time. He hated that he knew so little of her recent past, that he did not understand all the forces that had shaped her into the reticent, fearful woman she had become.

But . . . she *had* opened the door just now.

He righted himself and met her gaze.

She had been *greiting*, his lass, her face splotchy and pale, eyes stormy and red-rimmed. Her dark hair had tumbled from its pins and now hung in a riot of curls around her face.

But she faced him with her jaw stubbornly clenched, her gaze holding traces of the brave woman he had married.

"Thank ye for opening the door." He nodded. "May I come in or would ye prefer to speak elsewhere?"

She paused, as if the courtesy of his words caught her off-guard.

"Here will be fine." She stepped backward, allowing him to enter. "I cannot imagine our conversation will last long."

She left the door fully open and motioned for him to take a seat in a chair before the fireplace. She grabbed a shawl from off the trunk at the foot of her bed, wrapping it tightly around her shoulders.

"What must ye say to me?" Picking up her hair pins from the counterpane, she sat opposite him. She gathered the heavy weight of her hair over one shoulder and then proceeded to twist and twirl the mass into a knot, pinning the lot to her head.

It was hard not to see symbolism in her actions. That she was containing her internal, feeling self as ruthlessly as she flattened and smoothed her rebellious curls.

She had utterly withdrawn, retreating into the blank-faced woman who had arrived just a week ago.

Kieran feared even the minimal progress he had made with her was now lost.

And so, he gave her the only words he had left.

"I love ye, Eilidh." He waited until she met his gaze. "And because I love ye, I want ye tae be your fullest self. So I have tae ask it—are ye happy with who ye feel yourself to be at the moment?"

She took in a slow breath, her head turning back toward the fire. She pulled the shawl tighter about her.

"Am I happy?" she asked, voice low. "Ye keep talking about Jamie, about this mythical woman I once was. Was I happier then? Neither of us can say with any certainty." She shrugged. "But are ye so sure that the 'Jamie' version of myself is the true me? Why are ye so confident that who I am right now is not my truer self?"

That took Kieran up short.

How to respond?

"That is a possibility," he agreed. "But I sense a lot of fear in ye."

"How could I not be afraid, given my current predicament?" she snapped.

"But that fear *controls* ye," he countered. "Being afraid isnae the problem. It's what that fear propels ye to do. In your case, I watch ye hide and cower and shiver in pain. Do ye want to live your life like this?"

"It's this constant pressure to remember that is causing my terror to resurface." She all but glared at him. "How can you not see this? I long for safety. I ache for *peace.* Simon—"

"Simon!" Kieran spat.

"Aye, *Simon.* He offers me this peace. He understands that I want a quiet life. He respects that. He does not pester and poke and dredge up the monsters lurking in—"

"Och, Simon offers ye a life of avoidance and complacency, lass, not peace."

"Sometimes the only solution to a problem is to simply . . . leave it behind." She made a fluttering motion with her fingers. "Sometimes, avoidance is the only way to achieve serenity."

"And just how do you picture serenity, lass? Sitting in a cushioned chair gazing out a window over a pasture of sheep and trying for the thousandth time to wrangle your embroidery threads into submission? *Blech.* 'Tis hardly a life, if ye ask me." Kieran leaned forward in his chair, elbows on his knees. "You're a lass who has known fierce wind in your face—wind so relentless, ye might have lifted your arms and flown clean away. And ye wouldnae have feared it, either—ye would have soared."

Eilidh licked her lips, as if his words meant little, but the white knuckles clenching her shawl told a different story. "There is nothing wrong with numbness, with windows, or . . . or *sheep.*"

"Except that you're only watching, lass! To fully live, ye must be open to a full range of feeling. Something keeps threatening to surface. Alex has said that often the best way to tame overwhelming feelings is to talk about them, to relive the memory that caused them, and by so doing, gain a measure of control over—"

"Enough! In order to 'tame' feelings, I need memories. I don't *have* memories," she said, voice sharp. "I *did* suffer a head injury. Headaches plagued me for nearly two years afterward. It's just as likely that my memories have been erased, never to be retrieved."

He swallowed, sitting back in his chair, foot tapping out the jittery tension constricting his chest.

"We go in circles, you and I, and I weary of it," she continued, the weight of her silvery eyes boring through him. "This is my life. These are my choices. If I continue to attempt to remember, I wish to do it on my own terms. Not yours or Lord Lockheade's or anyone else's."

Kieran tossed his head back, rocking it from side to side along the top of the chair. He wanted to argue with her. He wanted to rant and shout and help her understand that her choices affected him.

But . . .

She was not wrong.

To remember or not was, in the end, *her* choice alone.

So even though a voice in his head howled in protest—she was his wife! she needed to remember him!—he would respect her wishes.

"Very well," he nodded.

"I also ask you to refrain from touching me," she continued.

That was easier for him to understand, given her earlier reaction.

"Absolutely." He let sincerity shine in his gaze. "I willnae touch ye unless ye invite me to. As I keep saying, I will do whatever I must to re-earn your trust."

Silence hung for the space of a heartbeat.

She nodded, as if the deal were done.

He would not touch her unless invited.

She would—possibly? maybe?—continue to try to remember on her own.

She had left him with nothing to cling to. No plan. No action. And in a sense, no real hope.

She turned her head, going back to watching the flames dance.

He continued to study her, his heart thudding in his chest.

Who was this woman, in the end?

Were they even suited anymore?

Or would it be better for them both if he waved goodbye and wished her well with Simon the Sassenach?

Burying his Jamie once and for all?

DECEMBER 1815

Jamie was impossibly lovely.

How had he convinced this bonnie, brave lass to marry him?

Kieran stared at her, wonder and awe fizzing in his veins.

She smiled back, eyes shy for once, a blush climbing her cheeks.

They stood on a secluded stretch of beach along the endless shoreline of Sydney Harbor, the warm sun sinking toward the rolling hills of the hinterland, rays of light fanning upward, painting the clouds in pink and orange.

They had rowed across the inlet from Mrs. Macquarie's Chair—a bench carved into the sandstone where the current governor's wife could sit to watch arriving ships—and then picked their way through the rocks until they reached a sandy stretch hidden by a stand of eucalyptus.

"Are ye ready then?" Ewan asked. Their friend held a silk ribbon in his hand, prepared to witness their handfasting and solemnize it by tying Kieran's hand to Jamie's.

"Aye," Kieran said.

Jamie nodded.

His Jamie was a proper lass today, dressed as fine as any lady.

"I want to feel pretty, Kieran," she had whispered to him that morning. "Just for today. Just for a wee while. I want to remember what it feels like to be Miss Eilidh Fyffe. I want to be a lady marrying her gentleman."

He had purchased her a gown at a second-hand shop in Sydney—a pretty blue frock that clung to her figure and sent his thoughts tumbling.

Here on the beach, Kieran took Jamie's hands in his, staring into her quicksilver eyes and the vibrant sunset colors reflected there.

Before they could begin the handfasting ceremony, she popped up on her tiptoes and whispered into his ear. "I have a surprise for ye later."

He pulled back and wiggled his eyebrows at her.

She blushed more deeply and squeezed his hands. "A different sort of surprise. You'll like it."

He smiled, but then it felt as if he hadn't stopped smiling in weeks. Even Cuthie had commented on it.

"Are ye sure there isnae something I should know about?" the captain asked. "Ye seem a bit too happy."

Kieran had brushed it off. "I find Sydney agrees with me."

That was true.

There was an energy in Sydney—from the nearly-constant building activity around the Customs house to the flood of new immigrants following the end of the war with Napoleon. The city pulsed with life, with an optimistic rush to embrace its future.

In short, it was not a bad place to anchor.

Every day, it seemed, he and Jamie had the same conversation—he refused to call it an argument, though it perhaps drifted into that territory more often than not—about her possibly remaining in Sydney.

Kieran wished it.

Jamie refused.

"I will not remain behind without ye," she said each time he suggested it.

Kieran didn't want to leave *The Minerva*, but he also couldn't stomach the risk they took by keeping Jamie aboard ship.

Finally, he had broached the topic of his leaving with Cuthie, hinting that he had been offered another position with a ship in Sydney. After all, Kieran could hardly tell Cuthie the truth—

Surprise! The carpenter's mate is a woman and my wife!

Cuthie had been intransigent. "I need ye here, MacTavish. I cannae navigate the Great Barrier Reef without your assistance. You've made a study of Mr. Flinders' map. You've sailed these waters before. I need your expertise if we're to survive the voyage. Ye would not want your wealthy friends tae perish, would ye now?"

Kieran had gritted his teeth in frustration.

Cuthie was correct. Kieran had been hired specifically for his navigational knowledge of the waters surrounding Australia. He could hardly leave the Brotherhood to the mercy of Fate. And Andrew and the rest of the Brotherhood would not leave Andrew's own ship, should Kieran announce he was staying in Sydney. That would be ridiculous.

But even then, Jamie had refused to listen.

"I will not be separated from ye," she had snapped just the day before. "Ye must cease speaking of this. I willnae discuss it further."

Sometimes terror clamped down on Kieran's heart. What if something happened to her? How would he survive her loss?

Marriage, even this irregular one, would bring a measure of protection if her true gender were discovered. As a Scot, Cuthie would recognize their handfasting as a legal marriage.

Kieran just had to hope it would be enough to safeguard her.

"Shall I begin then?" Ewan asked. Waves sloshed at his back, the water shimmering blue and orange with the reflected light of the sunset.

"Please," Kieran breathed, never taking his eyes off Jamie. "I cannae go another minute without knowing this beautiful lass is my wife."

22

Eilidh had lied a smidge in her words to Kieran.

She had said she would attempt to remember in her own way, on her own terms.

But that was untrue.

She had no intention of trying at all.

The fear of summoning the black terror was too great.

If a memory rose of its own accord . . . fine. She would accept it.

But she would do nothing to push herself.

Kieran perhaps sensed this, as the following morning, the remaining oranges were left in a basket outside her door with a simple note:

Oranges are only one of many happy memories that await you.
Please try, lass.
K

Eilidh ate the oranges, each one more delicious than the last. Despite

Kieran's words, no memories came of it. Just the smell of citrus and bright orange juice licked from her fingers.

And for a moment—a *very* brief moment—Eilidh regretted that she hadn't shared the moment with Kieran.

AS THE DAYS dissolved into a week and then two, Eilidh's sparse efforts at remembering yielded equally sparse results.

Just a handful of memories worked their way free.

Mr. Chen carefully watching her pack a firework tube, talking about the fireworks they would let off in Vanuatu.

Captain Cuthie scowling and threatening to have her flogged if she didn't have his favorite footstool repaired by nightfall.

Kieran laughing, his head thrown back, eyes crinkled shut, teeth flashing.

Ewan sitting on a beach, his head bent over a sketch of a bird mid-flight.

Yet for every scene, there was no emotional memory. No sense of affection for Mr. Chen. No loathing for Cuthie. No love for Kieran.

They were simply scenes from a play acted before her eyes.

Eilidh passed the days with Mrs. McKay, chatting and reading. Occasionally, they would walk up to Kilmeny Hall and visit Ewan as he painted in his studio.

She saw Kieran every day, too. They talked and interacted but little more. She deliberately didn't ask him any further personal questions.

It felt like the more she knew, the more the black terror loomed.

Kieran was wrong.

Sometimes, numbness was better than feeling.

Sometimes, the pain was simply too much to bear.

And no matter how much Kieran insisted the opposite, she still doubted the veracity of Cuthie's accusations. She simply had not been responsible for *The Minerva*'s demise. She had not deliberately killed all those men, no matter what anyone said. Moreover, the captain would not commit perjury—and risk gaol himself—to falsely name her the guilty party.

The one thing she did embrace, however, was the revelation that she was handy with a knife and wood.

As Mrs. McKay embroidered away the hours, Eilidh whittled.

She took a block of rosewood Kieran gave her and carved a wee kelpie—a creature of Scottish folklore. The mythological water spirit had the head of a horse, a mane of serpents, and the body of a fish. It was whimsical and when rubbed smooth, gleamed in the sunlight.

Kieran had studied it with reverent awe.

"It's bonnie work, lass." He turned it over, running a hand over the burnished sides. "Ye havenae lost your touch."

"Do you think it would be appropriate to give it to Ewan? He is the one who taught me how to see a shape within wood. I remember that much, at least. Perhaps it could be a gift for the new babe?" she asked. "Or would that be too odd?"

"I ken that Ewan and Violet would treasure it."

Additionally, another letter from Simon arrived—usually a joyous thing—but this time, its contents sent Eilidh's thoughts into disarray.

> *I heard word earlier today that Reverend Gillespie and his wife had returned. Overjoyed, I immediately trekked over to their cottage to call upon them (and therefore, yourself). But imagine my dismay to learn that you had not returned with them. They did not tell me why. In fact, the Gillespies were uncertain as to when, or even if, you would return. The reverend went entirely tight-lipped when I broached the subject of our potential nuptials. He even went so far as to encourage me to abandon my suit of you. I left their house in a bit of a state, as you can well imagine.*
>
> *My dearest Miss Fyffe, clearly something is amiss. My heart is all anxious palpitations for your safety. I pray that you are happy and well. I*

also pray that you have been honest with me, as I have been with you. A marriage can only go forward if both parties trust and hold faith in the other.

You know of the depth of my regard for yourself. I long to spend the rest of my life with you. You have always been, first and foremost, a good friend. If my affections are only a diversion or amusement for you, please set me free. Or at the very least, let me know the state of your heart as it pertains to myself.

Eilidh pressed her hand to her forehead, letting the foolscap fall.

Guilt pounded through her.

She should have said something to Simon, even just a brief mention of having to answer questions for the procurator fiscal.

But because she hadn't, now poor Simon was left to his anxiety and worst-case catastrophizing.

She was a terrible person.

But how was she to answer this?

Well, you see, Simon, it is all rather complicated. I am (possibly) being accused of murdering one hundred and twenty-seven men, and without my memories to defend myself, it has left me in a bit of a muddle. My (sort of) husband has been attempting to help me remember information that might exonerate me, but that also is fraught . . .

She could already see the horror on his face.

But good, sweet, earnest Simon was right—

He did not deserve to have his affections abused or trifled with.

If she intended to marry him, she needed to tell him everything. She could not keep such information from her betrothed. It would not be right.

She had to tell him.

And she would tell him.

She *would*.

She simply had to find the right words.

She looked at the whittled kelpie sitting on her bedside table, waiting to be delivered to Ewan and Lady Kildrum.

Perhaps . . . perhaps she could seek some guidance.

EILIDH CLUTCHED THE cotton bag with the kelpie, nodding at the butler who showed her into the drawing room of Kilmeny Hall.

Three heads turned her way—Lady Kildrum and her two sisters, Lady Aster and Lady Rose.

Lady Kildrum greeted Eilidh with a weary smile from her seat on a sofa opposite her sisters.

"Forgive me for not rising to greet you, Miss Fyffe." Her ladyship waved a hand to indicate her distended belly. "I am told that I will be delivering a child any day now."

Eilidh managed a smile in reply, even though her heart lurched and panged to see Lady Kildrum rounded with child and glowing. Eilidh was infinitely happy for her ladyship and Ewan. But the premature end of Eilidh's own pregnancy still pulsed hot and feverish when touched upon.

One of the myriads of memories she wished to never relive.

"I apologize Ewan isn't here to greet you," Lady Kildrum continued, motioning for Eilidh to be seated. "But as you know, he is frantically working on his submission to the Academy for this year, trying to get it done before the baby is born."

"No bother, your ladyship." Eilidh sat in a chair placed between the women—Lady Kildrum to one side of her, the twins on a chaise to the other. "I've come to see yourself anyway."

"Please, call me Violet," her ladyship said. "I feel as if we have been friends for years, after all the tales I've heard."

"You are too kind, your lad—uhm, Violet." Eilidh resisted the urge to squirm. She might have new gowns and a maid to style her hair in the latest fashion, but she had never mixed with such august company as the Countess of Kildrum. "You must call me Eilidh then."

"Not Jamie?"

A bit of a pause. Eilidh resisted twisting her hands in her lap.

"I don't . . . I don't *know* Jamie, if that makes sense. I don't really remember being her and so, it is difficult for me to associate the name with myself. Jamie was my brother, not myself."

Violet studied her for a moment, gaze pensive.

"I like Eilidh," Lady Rose said into the silence. "It's pretty and traditional."

"Truly?" Lady Aster looked at her sister. "I was just thinking how romantic Jamie is for a woman. Jamie is the name of an . . . an *adventuress*."

Lady Rose cocked her head. "That is true."

"Girls. Please." Violet shook her head and then pressed a hand to her belly. "You will make our guest uncomfortable."

Eilidh considered that unlikely but said nothing.

Though twins, Lady Aster and Lady Rose were nearly opposites physically. Lady Aster was dark, dainty, and petite. Lady Rose, by contrast, was fair-haired, tall, and lushly curvaceous. That said, what the twins lacked in physical similarities, they more than compensated for in sameness of thought and behavior. They were both equally outspoken and freely mannered.

"We are merely commenting on Miss Fyffe's various names, Violet." Lady Rose looked at her older sister with wide, innocent eyes. "I mean, we haven't said a word about how exciting it must have been to don trousers."

"And sail the Seven Seas aboard a merchant frigate." Lady Aster wiggled excitedly in her seat, turning to her sister. "Ewan told me that Jamie was a master swordsman by the time they reached Vanuatu. Can you believe it? Jamie, fighting men, aboard a ship!"

"Is that true, Miss Fyffe?" Lady Rose clutched her sister's arm. "I cannot imagine stabbing another person. I fear I would swoon."

"That is only because you dislike the sight of blood," Lady Aster pointed out.

"True," Lady Rose nodded earnestly. "Do you swoon at the sight of blood, Miss Fyffe?"

Eilidh froze at the sheer casualness of the question.

"Girls!" Violet said, her tone that of a woman nearing the end of her tether.

"That's a foolish suggestion, Rose," Lady Aster scolded. "Of course, Miss Fyffe doesn't faint at the sight of blood. She is far too courageous to allow a wee spot of blood to stop her."

"She would just slash right through a murderous mob." Lady Rose mimicked the action with her arm.

"Yes, Miss Fyffe." Lady Aster turned to Eilidh. "Do you think it likely you may have killed a man?"

"Rose! Aster! Enough!" Violet's voice cracked through the room, the tether-end clearly having been reached. Her ladyship looked at Eilidh. "You do not need to answer that, Miss Fyffe."

Eilidh managed a weak smile. "I certainly hope I have not taken anyone's life, Lady Aster. I have no memories of violence. Nothing specific, that is. It is all well and good as a joke, but deliberately causing someone else such harm . . . well, I cannot imagine myself being that sort of person."

In fact, Eilidh trembled at the thought. At 127 men who would never live to see another day.

"Well said," Violet nodded her head, shooting her sisters another repressive look.

"I have recovered a handful of memories about my time as a carpenter's mate, however." Eilidh stood and handed the cotton bag to Violet. "They have resulted in a wee gift for the bairn."

"Oh!" Violet's eyes lit with delight. "You are too kind." She tugged open the draw string on the bag and pulled out the kelpie. "It's beautiful!"

Violet turned it over in her hands, inspecting every detail, before handing it across to Lady Aster and Lady Rose who cooed in delight.

While they were still passing the wooden sculpture from hand to hand, a footman brought in a tea tray laden with biscuits and finger sandwiches.

Lady Rose poured the tea.

Thankfully, the twins' conversation moved on from fighting and blood.

Eilidh nibbled on a shortbread biscuit while they spoke of the upcoming midsummer festival. Lady Rose and Lady Aster were insistent that buntings must be hung across the lower gardens.

"The buntings will be festive," Lady Rose said, passing a cup of tea to Eilidh.

"They will take far too long to make," Violet countered.

"But *you* will not have to make them." Lady Aster pointed at her sister's belly.

"Yes." Rose nodded. "You will be too busy with my new favorite niece or nephew."

Violet shook her head and grimaced, pressing a hand to her side once more.

"So what else brings you here today, Miss Fyffe?" Lady Aster gave a decidedly wicked smile, reaching for a pickle sandwich. Clearly, the twin's spirits could not be repressed for long. "Please tell me it involves the handsome Master MacTavish—"

"Aster! It is hardly polite to bring up the subject in such a manner—" her ladyship broke off mid-sentence, wincing and rubbing a palm along the outside of her belly. She panted for another moment.

Eilidh set down her teacup and half stood, extending a hand out. "Are you poorly, Violet? Shall I summon—"

"I am fine." Violet took in two deep, deliberate breaths and waved Eilidh to sit back down. "Just the skin of my belly tightening over and over. It isn't painful, just uncomfortable. Alex said it's the body's way of preparing me for birth. Anyway, where were we?"

Lady Rose poured Lady Aster more tea. "Eilidh was going to tell us about how delicious Master MacTavish is—"

"Rose! Honestly. Not you, too." Violet rubbed the space between her brows, as if she were too weary to say more.

Eilidh wasn't sure if the twins' enthusiasm for the opposite sex was humorous or alarming. But they were not necessarily wrong about the purpose of Eilidh's visit.

"Uhm, actually—" Eilidh nibbled on a biscuit. "—I was hoping for a bit of . . . advice."

The twins both perked up.

"Romantic advice?" Lady Aster leaned forward.

"*Please* tell us it's romantic advice," Lady Rose agreed.

"Yes, it is." Eilidh closed her eyes for a second, gathering her thoughts.

She then spent a solid ten minutes outlining the gist of her problem—Simon, marriage, Kieran—ending with a distressed, "So I do not know what to do. How much do I tell Simon right now? He is justifiably concerned about me, but I feel I should tell him the specifics of my current situation in person, not via letter. But I need to tell him *something* and do not wish to abuse his trust—"

"Is Simon handsome?" Lady Aster asked.

"Handsomeness is not the only noteworthy criteria when it comes to a gentleman, Aster." Violet all but sighed. "How many times must I tell you this?"

"That is true," Lady Rose agreed, tapping her lips. "Do you swoon when you kiss him, Miss Fyffe?"

Eilidh blinked. "I haven't kissed Simon."

"Pardon?" Lady Rose was aghast.

"But . . ." Lady Aster floundered. "But how can you possibly consider marrying a gentleman whom you have never kissed?"

"Simon is far too much of a gentleman to kiss a woman who is not his betrothed. Though he has kissed my hand a number of times." Eilidh thought for a moment. "And he did kiss my cheek once, after politely asking permission. Does that count?"

"That does *not* count," Lady Aster said.

Eilidh shook her head. "We are veering off track, I fear. I merely wished advice as to how much I should tell Simon about Kieran."

The twins stared at Eilidh for a moment.

Violet set down her teacup and rubbed her belly again.

"I beg to differ," Lady Aster said. "How much you tell Simon depends entirely upon how serious you are in marrying him. So first, we must determine that."

"I agree." Lady Rose returned to nibbling on a biscuit, but a dent had appeared between her eyebrows. "So aside from his calm demeanor and staid nature, what else do you like about Simon, Miss Fyffe? Does he make you laugh?"

Eilidh paused, frowning. "I cannot say that Simon is much given to laughter. He is a curate and takes his duties to the parish quite seriously. He is very attentive to his mother, however. My own mother always said that a man will treat his wife much as he treats his mother. And based on that, any wife of Simon's could expect to be lavished with kindness and forbearance."

The twins went back to sipping their tea.

Silence hung again.

"You have come for advice, so I must be honest with you . . ." Lady Aster paused.

"Simon sounds boring." Lady Rose filled the silence.

Lady Aster deflated, nodding emphatically. "He definitely sounds boring."

"Girls!" Violet managed to scrape together some outrage, though Eilidh suspected that after accusing their guest of killing a man, talk of kissing and marriage was small potatoes. "Really, that is hardly helpful."

"We're just being honest, Violet." Lady Aster turned to her older sister. "Master MacTavish is a remarkable man—handsome, adventurous, charming. Oh! Have you noticed how nicely his shoulders fill out his coats—"

"In short . . . the *opposite* of boring," Lady Rose added. She looked at Eilidh. "You chose Master MacTavish once, Miss Fyffe. Why aren't you giving him more of a chance now?"

Eilidh bit her lip, hesitating, and then decided that if the twins were going to be forthright, then she could be, too.

"I fear you are perhaps missing the point," she said. "I *like* Simon's boringness, as you put it. When one has already experienced far too much of life, boring and staid and predictable are balms to the soul. I have already had a lifetime of adventure. To you both, it might sound exciting, but it was actually just exhausting, to both my mind and my body. Now, I simply crave . . . home."

Violet studied her for a long moment. "I hear your words, Eilidh. And I can even relate to your wishes. But I do wonder if you are perhaps being somewhat short-sighted." She paused, pressing on her belly once more. "I have been married long enough to understand how glorious marriage to the right man can be. Such a union can feel like the safest, most wonderful of homes. But because of this, I also clearly see how truly terrible it would be to marry the wrong man."

"I agree. This is why I have focused my affections on Simon. He may be somewhat boring, but he is also kind and patient—"

"Marriage is a life-long commitment. Such a decision should not be made lightly." Violet shifted on the sofa, still trying to get comfortable. "I, myself, struggle with decision making. Odd, I know, for a countess to admit as much, but it is simply my nature. However, when it came to marrying my Ewan, I had no doubts. It was a breathlessly easy decision to make."

"Truly?" Eilidh asked.

"Yes. And from everything I understand, you once made a similar commitment to Kieran, without hesitation. You leapt into it joyously . . . doubting nothing."

"Perhaps, but that was Jamie. That was a woman I have no real memory of being. Even if I regain my memories, I will never be that woman again. Jamie may have loved Kieran, but I do not know if the woman I am now can ever feel that for him. I have changed too much."

Violet looked pensive. "That may very well be true. But before walking away from Kieran forever, I think you owe it to the memory of Jamie to be sure that he is not who you want. How is it phrased? 'Marry in haste; repent at leisure.' Just . . . do not let that be you. Make sure Kieran is not the home you wish."

"But if you do end up kissing Master MacTavish," Lady Aster added, "you must tell us every delicious detail."

"Aster!" Violet gasped and then winced, emitting a low moan.

"Violet?" Eilidh shot to her feet, noting the water darkening Violet's skirts and the sofa.

"It's time," Violet said through clenched teeth. "I believe my waters just broke."

February 1816

"Jamie! Dinnae walk away from me!" Kieran picked up his pace, trying to catch up with his wife as she nimbly darted through the thick underbrush. "I'm trying tae have a conversation with ye."

"No," she shot over her shoulder. "You're trying tae scare me. There's a difference."

"Aye! Ye should be scared. I'm frightened out of my wits."

She ignored his words and continued to race through the forest jungle.

Kieran swallowed his frustration and ran after her.

The New Hebrides were a lush paradise. *The Minerva* had sunk anchor in a picturesque natural harbor just a few days before. Cuthie intended to bargain for access to the island's rich supply of sandalwood, something to fill the hold for the eventual return trip to Britain.

Today, Kieran and Jamie had escaped into the forest surrounding the village, ostensibly to find wood to repair a damaged deck railing.

But it was mostly a chance for them to have a modicum of privacy to discuss their looming issue . . . both literally and figuratively.

If only his recalcitrant wife would stop.

"Ye cannae run from this, Jamie," he continued. "Please, stop."

She paused and turned around, hands on her hips. "Why must we discuss this now? We are *months* away from my condition even being noticeable." She poked her still-flat stomach.

Kieran covered the ground to her. "Aye, but at some point, we will have to tell the Brotherhood, as well as Cuthie and, well . . . everyone! A pregnancy can only be hidden for so long. We need a plan, a way to proceed."

"And like I've been saying, we will cross that bridge when we arrive at it. You're being a wee too much Master-of-the-Ship at the moment. *Order supplies! Make a schedule! Plan for contingencies!*" Jamie threw her hands in the air. "Worrying about the end now won't solve anything."

"*Jamie*," his voice fell to a low growl, "you're saying that simply to avoid talking about it. Cuthie is up to something. He and Massey have been spending hours closeted together, talking. He's supposed to be negotiating with the village chiefs to purchase sandalwood, but he hasnae begun tae do so. I'm concerned."

Jamie frowned, *finally* pausing. "That is . . . odd. All Cuthie has done the past month is talk about the sandalwood to be had in the New Hebrides."

"Precisely. What if his plans involve ye? What if he knows?" Kieran motioned toward her body, indicating both her gender and their growing child.

"I cannot think how he would know." Jamie folded her arms. "Cuthie and I rarely talk. He has never so much as touched me."

"Perhaps, but something isnae quite right. I'm not irrational tae be concerned about ye! We need a plan."

"Och, we're talking in circles, Kieran. Look at me." She swept a hand down her body, indicating her trousers, shirt, and waistcoat. "I am a woman who will don breeches, hop a ship, and then master carpentry and fencing while sailing the world. Do ye honestly think I willnae be a *tigress* when it comes tae protecting our bairn? Me, the babe, and yourself . . . we will find a way. No matter what Cuthie knows. No matter what he has planned."

She popped up on her tiptoes and pressed a lingering kiss to his lips before snaring his hand. She pressed his palm to her stomach.

"Have faith in me," she continued. "Trust my courage. All will be well. I will make sure of it."

The chaos in the drawing room was instantaneous.

Violet staggered to her feet with a moan, hands clutching her belly.

Lady Aster ran to fetch Ewan.

"Let us get you to your bedchamber," Eilidh said.

Violet nodded, panting.

Lady Rose wrapped an arm around her sister. Eilidh took the other side, but as both Violet and Lady Rose were significantly taller, Eilidh felt herself to be merely an elbow rest for Violet more than any actual help. Lady Rose bore the brunt of her sister's weight.

They slowly helped Violet walk toward her bedchamber, pausing on the grand central staircase as a labor pain hit.

Ewan burst through the front door, taking the stairs two at a time, eyes wild but lit with a fervent excitement.

"A groom has gone for the midwife," he informed his wife, scooping her into his arms as if she were a wee babe and not an exceptionally tall woman in her own right. "What can I do?"

Violet moaned and cuddled into him, secure in the safety of his arms. Ewan carried his wife up the stairs and into their bedchamber, cradling her against his chest.

Eilidh followed, hovering nearby, unsure what to do.

The housekeeper and a pair of maids rushed in.

Eilidh found herself pushed more and more into the corner of the room, observing.

Ewan fussed over his wife, kissing her head, making sure she was comfortable.

Finally, Eilidh bit her lip and looked away, unequal to witnessing the tenderness between them. The entire scene calcified the anguished catch in her chest.

Would this have been her lot? Had she had her baby with Kieran at her side? Would he have been so attentive? Would she have behaved like Violet—clinging to her husband one minute, then pushing him away the next?

Her frail numbness crumbled once more.

But this time, the culprit was not the terror of her unknown memories.

Instead of fear . . . loss swamped her.

Eilidh pressed a hand to her chest, anything to stem the flood of grief.

She wanted to run away, fast and far. But there was no outrunning this pain.

It was nearly a relief when Violet banished Ewan from the room.

Eilidh followed him out the door.

They returned to the drawing room.

Kieran arrived only moments later, a burst of sea air billowing into the room behind him. His chest heaved as if he had run the whole way from the castle. His hair was certainly windblown, askew and adorably rumpled.

But it was his instant concern for Ewan that tugged at Eilidh the most.

"How fares your lass?" he asked.

"Fine, I suppose." Ewan paced before the fire. "I've been banished."

"Ah, it's likely for the best—"

"No!" Ewan shook his head, looking longingly at the door. "It's not for the best. I cannae believe Violet has tae go through this without myself beside her. It's unbearable." He raked a hand through his hair. "We began this together. I want to finish it together."

"Yes," Kieran sat down, looking up at Ewan. "It is unbearable tae watch the one ye love most suffer."

Eilidh made the enormous mistake of looking at Kieran just then.

His gaze shifted to hers.

She could see it there . . .

The double meaning in his words.

The grief mirroring her own.

She looked away, but the pulse in her throat continued to pound and the raw ache in her chest did not abate.

VIOLET'S LABOR SEEMED never-ending.

Kieran had no idea how Ewan was dealing with the strain of it.

He and Eilidh kept Ewan company in the drawing room—playing cards and listening to Eilidh read *Ivanhoe.* Ewan and Kieran spent nearly two hours swapping stories about their time aboard *The Minerva.*

Ewan paced occasionally, clearly agitated.

His words kept to one theme and one theme only.

"It is absurd that the father isnae allowed to attend the birth," he said. "It feels wrong. This is my child, too. This is something the person I love more than anything must suffer through. Why should Violet do this alone? Why not allow me to take part in the birth of our child?"

Every hour or so, one of Violet's sisters would arrive with an update.

"Violet is in good spirits," or "The pain grows worse, but she is managing."

Afternoon melted into evening. Kieran and Eilidh had dinner and then supper, but Ewan ate little.

"I cannae remember a time when ye didnae have the appetite of an ox," Kieran noted.

Ewan shrugged and sent another longing look at the door. "I still cannae believe she banished me."

They had just summoned a servant to retrieve the supper tray from the drawing room when a scream rang from the upper floor.

Violet.

Ewan was out the door like a shot, taking the stairs two at a time.

Kieran and Eilidh exchanged tense looks.

A few minutes later, Lady Aster and Lady Rose entered.

"Well, I would never have thought of Ewan as implacable," Lady Aster said, "but he stormed into the bedchamber, crawled right onto the bed, and inserted himself between the headboard and Violet's back. Our sister is currently using her husband as an armchair."

"The midwife only laughed, thank goodness," Lady Rose added. "I doubt even explosives could dislodge Ewan now. The man is a mountain of determination."

"I think it for the best," Lady Aster nodded. "Violet may never admit it, but I know she is glad to have him at her side."

Lady Rose looked at Eilidh and Kieran. "You both might want to return to Kilmeny Castle, as the midwife feels our sister's labor might last throughout the night."

One glance at Eilidh was all Kieran needed to understand that she wished to stay.

And he certainly would not be leaving without her.

The twins excused themselves, leaving Eilidh and Kieran alone.

Kieran paced over to the window, looking out over the garden. Twilight still lingered in the blue sky, even though the hour was well past ten o'clock.

The weight of Eilidh's gaze pressed against his shoulder blades.

He could feel the heaviness of her thoughts.

The air between them hung with the memory of their lost babe.

Kieran swallowed back the ache in his throat.

Who knew how it might have played out . . . had Eilidh not been separated from the Brotherhood, if she had not been injured, if their child had not been born far too soon?

Or, at the very least, if she had not miscarried the baby alone in that villager's hut, believing the child to be the result of an unwanted liaison. If he could have been there—tucked behind and arms around her—to share the grief.

"Would ye like tae talk about it?" he asked, not turning around.

"No," came her reply. Decisive. Unwavering.

He clasped his hands behind his back, contemplating the irony of the moment—how this Eilidh was so vastly different from the woman he married . . . and yet, so utterly the same.

His Jamie would have refused to talk about it, too. She had avoided unpleasant topics while aboard *The Minerva*, whether it was her pregnancy or the constant threat of discovery.

He said nothing more on the topic.

They stared in silence, each turned away from one another.

The gulf between them had never felt wider.

A SHARP CRY rent the air.

Eilidh woke with a start, jerking upright.

Weak morning light filtered through the drawing room windows.

Oh, dear.

She had fallen asleep on the sofa.

Well, she had fallen asleep on *Kieran*, to be more precise.

He had taken over reading *Ivanhoe* aloud and then . . .

. . . nothing.

She had slumped against his shoulder.

And he had simply sat, letting her sleep on him.

And she had felt . . . safe. Comforted.

Mmmm.

Safe. Comfort.

Those were two words she did not associate with Kieran MacTavish.

And yet . . . the emotions lingered.

He slept still, his head lolled on the back of the sofa.

No surprise there. He's a sound sleeper, after all.

The thought flitted in and out.

Eilidh swallowed, unnerved that any part of her understood Kieran MacTavish's sleep habits.

Yet she remained beside him, unable to look away from his face.

He was always in motion. Quick with a smile or a quip. His expression never slack.

But now . . . she could catalog the unique pieces of him.

The ray of lines fanning out from the corners of his eyes, the result of too many years squinting into the sun.

Two vertical grooves dented the space between his brows, as if even in sleep he pondered heavy things.

Whiskers stubbled his chin. Her palm itched with the sensation of them, as if the memory of caressing his stubble-laced cheeks was burned into her flesh.

His cocky attitude and over-the-top flirtatiousness aside, he was undeniably attractive.

And you supposedly married him.

Had she truly loved him as the Brotherhood all claimed?

The sensation of safety, of comfort, lingered. And it lent her courage.

For the first time, she mentally reached for memories of him.

Anything.

Any hint that affection for him had once ruled her heart.

Perhaps he was right.

Perhaps there might be comfort in talking through some of the things she *did* remember.

Perhaps she could find some harmony between the black terror and the white numbness . . . a narrow space she could inhabit that allowed for some feeling, just not the emotions that so terrified her.

Abruptly he opened his eyes. Those impossibly-pale blue eyes, like looking into a sun-bathed winter sky.

Some part of Eilidh's brain pointed out that she was close to him.

So close.

Close enough to—

The shrill cry of a newborn babe rent the air again.

Eilidh blinked and all but lurched away.

Reality crashed in behind.

The baby.

Violet had finally had her baby.

TWO HOURS LATER, Ewan walked into the drawing room, the tiniest of bundles cradled in his massive arms. He looked as exhausted as Eilidh felt, but the smile on his face was euphoric.

"I want ye both to meet my new daughter, Lady Dahlia Campbell," Ewan said the words without taking his eyes from the babe's face.

Eilidh couldn't see much of the baby from where she stood near the fireplace, just the tip of a pert nose.

Kieran smiled and immediately crossed the room to join his friend, bending over to inspect the wee girl.

Eilidh felt cemented in place, her heart a frantic beast in her chest.

The baby was so small. How was Ewan to protect her? To keep her safe?

Blood roared in her ears.

Why had she not anticipated this particular pain? This swooping dip in her stomach and vise around her lungs?

This was not the black terror per se, but something akin, equally aching and raw.

Yes, it was the grief of losing her own babe.

But it was also a thousand *what ifs*.

What if her body had been strong enough to heal her own injuries and carry the child to term?

What if Kieran had been at her side?

What if her memories had not fled?

Would she—as Jamie and with Jamie's memories—have been strong enough?

But . . . no. She had failed—

"Congratulations. She is right bonnie," Kieran was saying, clapping his friend on the shoulder. If he shared Eilidh's pain, he hid it. "And how is Violet?"

"Tired but otherwise in good spirits. The labor and delivery went as well as could be expected, the midwife says. It's only us that felt the birth lasted far too long. It was miraculous to witness. Every man should be in the room when his child is born, I believe. My wife is a goddess!" Ewan laughed at that, a baffled sort of wonder in his tone. "Do ye want tae hold her?"

Kieran nodded and carefully took the babe. Little Dahlia squawked and a tiny hand appeared, waving above the blanket.

The sight nearly did in what remained of Eilidh's heart.

Would Kieran have held their own child with such reverent awe? Would the same wide smile have creased his face?

A scene flared through her mind's eye.

Not a memory but a flash of a future that would never be. Of Kieran laughing, chasing a wee girl with black curls across the lawn of Kilmeny Hall, catching her around the waist and spinning her in a circle. Eilidh could almost hear the lass's shrieks of delight.

Kieran raised his head, fixing her with pale eyes. "Come see, Eilidh. She is beautiful."

She wanted to refuse.

She wanted to shake her head and run from the room.

Instead, her feet moved, leading her to Kieran's side.

The baby was gently slipped into her arms.

Oh!

Lady Dahlia was so unutterably tiny. And yet, perfect, as well. A button nose. A swoop of forehead.

"She's already got red hair," Ewan pointed out in awe.

So she did. Eilidh ran a finger over the sparse red-gold fuzz.

Ye are so loved, little one, she thought. *Never forget how loved ye are.*

That same feeling of loss and *what if* squeezed tighter.

Vividly, the interior of that villager's hut surfaced. The sun winking through the palm fronds of the roof, as she stared upward, day after day. The smell of blood mixed with that of the sea. The quiet voice of Mrs. Gillespie reading aloud from Psalms and the *shh-shh* of the elderly island woman who would pat Eilidh's hand in comfort.

The aching feeling of emptiness. The sense that more than just memories had been stripped from her.

"Do not grieve the child. It is for the best," Mrs. Gillespie had murmured. *"A child conceived in such sin would not have had a fortunate life. God has blessed you both in this."*

Eilidh had chosen to believe Mrs. Gillespie's words. She had only allowed herself to feel relief.

Relief that she would not have to care for a child who would have been an outward symbol of immoral choices or trauma or *something* she had no memory of.

Relief that the baby would not be subjected to the hardship of life as the illegitimate child of a missionary in the South Pacific.

But when Eilidh stared into the wide, gray eyes of Baby Dahlia . . .

It was hard to remember that relief.

Dahlia would have every advantage that life could give a child—love, stability, wealth.

Eilidh had only had love to give to her babe.

But . . . the Gillespies had been wrong to think that would not have been enough.

Love would have driven her to protect her child.

She would have suffered all the horrors she suspected lurked in her missing memories, if only she could have kept her baby, if only her battered body had not rejected it.

It was what a mother did, was it not?

Sacrificed anything for the life of her child.

And now, knowing that her baby had been wanted, had been celebrated . . .

Grief replaced her relief.

Swallowing against the surge, she turned and carefully handed wee Dahlia back to Ewan before the sentiments could overwhelm her.

She pressed a shaking hand to her forehead.

"Eilidh?" Kieran's voice reached her, as if through a fog.

Eilidh swallowed, biting back the tears that threatened to fall.

This was a happy occasion. Ewan's joy and good fortune should be celebrated.

Her past was done and gone.

She hadn't been able to save her baby, in the end.

She tried to imagine if Kieran had been there. Would she feel differently now? Would the pain and grief be lighter for being shared?

And if she supposedly loved Kieran MacTavish so fiercely, why could she not remember?

Why can I not remember?!

Again, she reached for memories of him. How many times had he promised her that there was good in her missing memories, things she would be happy to recall?

She mentally pushed and prodded at the black miasma that shrouded an entire year of her life.

Nothing surfaced.

It was as if the blast that destroyed *The Minerva* had blown away all the moments she had lived upon it.

The thought caused something to shift abruptly within her, a lurching roil of the blank recesses of her memory.

Eilidh blinked.

And there it was, a glowing snippet of memory, as mesmerizing as moonlight on the ocean . . .

A chaotic mix of emotions churned in her chest.

Please, please let everything go as planned, she silently pleaded. There is no room for error. This has *to go off perfectly.*

She picked up a lit taper, grimacing at the tremor in her hand.

Steady now.

She lit the end of a fuse.

An explosion sounded.

The scene played through Eilidh's mind, an endless loop of memory.

The dark of night.

Emotion pounding through her.

A plea that everything would go as planned.

Her hand picking up a lit taper.

The sizzling hiss of the taper igniting the end of a fuse.

And then . . . the cacophony of a horrific explosion.

Again and again.

Once remembered, it wouldn't stop.

The memory felt . . . important. Like it had presaged something significant.

But what?

A knot coiled in her stomach.

She was being willfully obtuse.

She *knew* what she had to be seeing.

She simply could not countenance it.

Yet . . . what was it that Kieran had said?

My Jamie absolutely would have blown up The Minerva *had she had a good enough reason.*

The very thought nearly sent Eilidh racing for the nearest chamber-pot, bile rising in her throat.

As she and Kieran walked back to Kilmeny Castle in the midmorning sun, Kieran kept glancing at her, the dent between his eyebrows deep and concerned.

Eilidh hastened her footsteps, unequal to his probing questions.

Upon reaching the castle, she immediately retired to her bedchamber and stayed there, refusing entry to everyone, taking luncheon and then dinner and then supper from a tray sent up from the kitchens.

Her mind churned, her chest devolved into a maelstrom of agitation.

After a maid took away the supper tray, Eilidh found herself pacing the floor between the fireplace and the tiny window—*flames, pivot, step, step, step, sea, pivot, step, step* . . .

Had she done it? Had she murdered 127 men? Blown up the ship, risking her unborn baby's life, and killing Mr. Chen along with everyone else she had known?

She could scarcely fathom it.

If she had blown up the ship . . . why? *Why* would she have done it? Yes, Captain Cuthie was a despicable human being by all accounts, but why would she have felt the need to do something about it?

Could it have been an accident on her part?

But even the memory negated that thought, did it not? She had been intent on lighting the fuse.

She dared to test the memory, pushing at it, trying to recall a wee bit more.

Surely, it wasn't as deliberate as it seemed—

Agitation and nervousness pummeled her chest. This was it. This was the culmination of all her plans. It had to work. Please, dear Lord, let it work.

She picked up the taper. Her hand was shaking so badly, she could scarcely light the fuse. It hissed when it caught. She lurched back, scrambling for safety before—

BOOM!

The memory, more vivid and intense this time, had her racing for the chamberpot in earnest, emptying the contents of her stomach.

She sat on the floor for a long while after, one hand loosely pressed to the porcelain pot, the other mopping tears from her cheeks.

All those men. Gone. Killed. How many widows still wept their grief over husbands who had gone down with *The Minerva*? How many fatherless bairns *greited* for fathers they would never know?

How could she have intentionally caused such tragedy? Created such far-reaching pain?

It took nearly an hour for Eilidh to gather her wits enough to change into a night rail, bank the fire for the night, and close the shutters.

But as she crawled under the counterpane, the trembling started. A dreadful quaking that chattered her teeth and chilled her fingers. Emotional pain made manifest.

Her numbness had shattered into crystalline splinters, each more cutting than the last.

This was what she had feared, was it not? That once the numbness utterly vanished, she would be a quivering mass of *terrorpainfearhorrorhurthurthurt—*

She burrowed further under the counterpane, but it did little to stem her shivering. In fact, the more tightly she curled into a ball, the harder she shook.

Would she ever be warm again?

Terror banded her chest. Each breath hurt, as if pulled through glass shards.

She wrapped her hands around her head, her forehead nearly touching her knees as she lay, but it didn't help.

She couldn't manage another moment with this pain, this fear, this anxiety.

Help!

This *was* the black terror in its truest form.

The pain that had driven her to the ship's railing on the return home to Britain. The feeling that had her staring at the ocean, thinking how easy it would be to fall, fall, fall and leave all the pain behind forever.

How could she continue breathing until morning, suffering through this blackness, this anguish raking her with fiery talons?

She couldn't.

Curled inward on her bed, fighting the blinding panic, she remembered the comfort of waking up with her head on Kieran's shoulder.

She had felt safe with him. So safe.

Ye will always find a safe haven in me, lass.

She staggered from the bed, dragged on her dressing gown, and lit a candle from the coals in the fireplace. Her feet padded up the central staircase, winding higher in the castle until she stood before Kieran's bedroom door.

Her hand clenched into a fist, wrapping around the wool of the dressing gown. The candle wobbled in her still shaking hand.

She shouldn't be here.

But . . .

She would merely slip in and rest in a chair in the corner. Just sitting in the same room would be enough. It had to be. He was a sound sleeper, after all. She would leave before sunrise.

He would never know that she had sought solace here.

That when the pain in her heart had felt too heavy to bear, her only thought had been to come to him.

She tried the door handle.

Not locked.

She tentatively pushed it open and stepped inside, closing the door silently behind her.

The room was much larger than hers, likely the principal chamber of past lairds of the castle. An enormous tester bed took up most of the space to the left. The shutters had not been closed; weak moonlight spilled from a window beyond the bed. A pair of wingback chairs sat before a fire smoldering in the hearth.

The candlelight flickered from the tremble in her hand. She looked at the bed and the Kieran-shaped lump slumbering there. He hadn't moved. It took more than the weight of her gaze to disturb him.

She blew out the candle, set it on a small table, and quietly moved toward the closest chair, sitting soundlessly. She pulled her knees up to her chest and curled into a ball, trying to feel the comfort of him from across the room.

But she continued to shake, violent palpitations that hitched her breathing and left her hands clammy and cold.

"Jamie?" Kieran's voice rumbled through the quiet.

Oh.

Perhaps she had not been as silent as she had thought.

She looked toward the bed. He was sitting up—a man-shaped shadow of broad shoulders, a nightshirt, and sleep-mussed hair.

"Eilidh," she whispered, as if needing to remind them both that Jamie no longer existed.

"What's happened, lass? Are ye poorly?"

His instant concern caused her eyes to sting.

She bit her quivering lip.

"I can't be alone tonight and ye s-said—" she hiccupped. "Ye s-said I would be safe with ye. That ye would be my h-haven."

"Och, ye be *greiting*, sweetling. Why ye be over there?" He threw back the bedcovers beside him. "I cannae bear tae see ye suffer so. Allow me tae comfort ye."

Eilidh hesitated.

But she was so cold. The kind of chill that came from deep within. She feared she would do anything at the moment to stem the panic threatening to overwhelm her.

Perhaps that was what emboldened her.

Or perhaps part of her knew that she had once slept at his side.

She stood and crossed to the bed.

"This is j-just for a m-moment. I haven't remembered ye." Words spilled from her. "But ye p-promised and—"

"Hush, lass. I willnae do anything untoward. I promise."

She slid under the counterpane.

He reached for her, touching her finger. "Your hands are proper ice. Come here." He tugged on her wrist.

She closed the distance between them, desperate for the warmth of him. Anything to banish the chill freezing her heart.

He pulled her into his chest. The smell of comfort and sleepy masculinity assuaged her, warming her senses like a finger of bolted whisky.

She burrowed into him.

He said nothing more.

His strong arms banded around her, holding her tight.

Her own shaking continued, however, dreadful tremors that spasmed through her muscles and made her want to crawl out of her skin.

Eilidh clung to him, a life-raft in a storm. As if somehow, she could transfer the cyclone battering her onto him.

Through it all, he said nothing.

Not a word of recrimination.

Not a single empty promise.

Not '*It will all come right*' or '*Hush now, it's not as bad as all that.*'

He was her rock, her safe harbor, his heart a slow and rhythmic *thump-thump* under her ear.

Eventually, the heaving gasps of her lungs softened, the warmth of him finally seeping through her.

How wonderful to just be . . . held. She couldn't remember the last time she had been hugged or embraced in any meaningful way.

That unnamed black terror had always lingered.

But now, knowing and trusting that Kieran would do nothing physically without her permission, the fear had retreated.

And within the vacuum it left, she could finally understand.

Her body was starved, as if her very skin required the sustenance of another's touch. And maybe not just anyone else's. Maybe just . . . his.

She closed her eyes, allowing herself to melt into Kieran, to give him the weight of her body, her heart, her thoughts. She pressed a hand to his chest, her fingers feeling the round metal of her wedding ring beneath his shirt. The promise of it.

He answered with the steady thump-thump of each heartbeat—one hand on her waist, the other pressed between her shoulder blades, his chin resting on the crown of her head.

Her body greedily drank the comfort he offered.

Finally, she found the courage to return to the snippet of memory that had surfaced.

She had lit a fuse. Had it truly been the fuse that caused the explosion which destroyed the ship?

And if not, why else would she remember it with such excruciating detail? As if it were some vital memory?

She simply could not fathom that she would . . .

That she had . . .

Surely, she had loved her unborn baby enough not to do something so risky? Hadn't she?

She swallowed, taking in a long, slow breath.

Kieran mimicked the motion. She could hear the air rushing in and out of his lungs.

"Tell me . . ." She trailed off.

He stilled, his chest seizing under her cheek.

"Tell ye?" he whispered.

"Aye." She licked her lips. "Tell me how much I loved our babe."

EILIDH'S WORDS WERE a punch to the stomach.

Tell me how much I loved our babe.

How could Kieran give words to that? To relive those days when he had thought he would be a father?

But she was *here*. In his bed. In his arms.

She had willingly come to him, seeking solace.

Come back to me, he longed to beg her. *Let us be one again. Come be my wife.*

But that was the selfish part of him speaking.

Eilidh did not need more guilt heaped upon her.

No, she needed understanding.

He wondered if she had been as gutted as himself, watching Ewan with wee Dahlia. Kieran had never understood how he could simultaneously feel so much happiness for a friend and yet so much sorrow for himself.

"Our babe?" he repeated. "Our bairn?"

"Aye."

He filled his lungs and released the breath slowly, forcibly telling his hand not to rub circles on her back or caress her upper arm or press a trembling kiss to her head.

Her trust was fragile. He would do nothing to jeopardize it. So even though part of his mind begged him to pull her close and kiss her lips, to feel the press of her soft curves melting into his body, he did nothing.

He forced himself to lie still, to accept what she was willing to give.

"Ye were ecstatic," he began. "We were on Vanuatu by then, if just barely, and had been married about two months. Ye had missed your menses the month before, but ye waited until the following month tae tell me, just tae be sure. The weeks that followed on Vanuatu were some of the happiest of my life. Ye were a wee bit nauseous from time to time, but not so much that anyone commented. After all, every sailor is sick on occasion. Ye were giddy at the thought of being a mother. Ye kept talking about what we would name the bairn—James or Charles, if it were a boy—"

"I should like to name a boy James." She snuggled into him.

Bloody hell, he had forgotten how marvelous it felt to simply *hold* her.

"Aye, James would be an excellent name for a lad," he agreed. "Of course, we were both concerned about the baby, too. There was no way we could keep your pregnancy a secret, long-term. But no one besides Ewan knew that we were married, much less that ye were increasing."

"What did we decide to do?"

Kieran nearly snorted at her question.

"Ye refused to talk about it. Ye just insisted that everything would somehow magically come right." He jostled her on his chest. "Sound familiar?"

He felt her answering wan smile against his chest.

She said nothing for a few moments, his words lingering between them. Then, she sucked in a stuttering breath and pressed her face to his chest, as if bracing herself.

"We wouldn't have named our baby James," she whispered, words muffled. "Because . . . the babe was a girl."

Oh!

Kieran closed his eyes, allowing the anguish of that simple sentence to wash over him.

A girl.

A wee lassie.

"She was so tiny," Eilidh continued. "So impossibly small—barely the length of my hand—but still clearly female. After she was . . . born . . ." She paused. Kieran felt her swallow. ". . . Mrs. Gillespie wouldn't let me see her, didn't tell me the baby's gender. Nothing. She said . . . she said it was better to not think of it as a child, but instead as a . . . a trial that had been miraculously taken from me. But . . . my heart couldn't bear it—" she gasped. "I couldn't *bear* the thought of my cold, lifeless babe not knowing me, not feeling her mother's hand just one time. Mrs. Gillespie had wrapped the body in a rag to dispose of it the next day, but I sneaked out that night. I took the tiny wee bundle deep into the jungle. How I managed that in the state I was in, I don't know. I was bleeding and weeping, my head a pounding mass of pain. I remembered nothing before arriving on the island the week before. But something in me knew I *had* to give my babe a proper burial."

"Ah, lass," he managed to whisper around the grief lodged in his throat. "I should have been there. I would have done anything tae be there."

Eilidh squeezed him tightly, but continued on with her story. "I dug her a grave as deeply as I could, kissed her wee head, and said a prayer over her remains. And then I buried her. Mrs. Gillespie noticed that the babe was gone the next morning and that my feet were dirty and scraped. She just l-looked at me with sad, knowing eyes. She n-never said a word."

Eilidh hiccupped and pressed closer, her body shaking again.

More than anything, Kieran wanted to shine light and love into the battered corners of her heart. To assure her that happiness would come again, that there would be more children, more joy, more hope—not just for her, but for them both.

Yet in this moment . . .

All they had was their shared grief.

For their wee baby girl who had been born far too early and laid to rest in an unmarked grave on a distant tropical island.

A telltale sting began in his own eyes.

He felt more than heard the sob leave her, the silent shaking of her shoulders.

No—

He was the one trembling, as if he were truly absorbing her anguish into himself.

A great gusting breath left him.

And then another.

He pressed his face into her hair.

Oh, my love.

That was all it took for her own tears to flow in earnest.

Great wrenching sobs that tore from her lungs and drenched his chest.

They clung to one another, each weeping their pain.

For a past that could never be recovered.

For a shared loss they had each faced alone.

For an uncertain future that loomed, large and terrifying.

He had no idea how long they clung to each other.

But eventually, the sobs turned to hiccups and then to sniffles.

Kieran dragged his knuckles over his eyes.

Eilidh wiped her tears on his shirt.

They lay together for several long minutes, so still he would have thought her sleeping if not for the ragged gusts of her breathing, the repeated swallowing he could feel against his chest.

Only then, did certain things click together for him.

Something was not quite right. There was a disconnect between what he supposed her emotions to be and her words.

Why would Eilidh abruptly want to be reassured that she had *loved* their child? Up until tonight, she had given every indication that she resented their bairn. Why would she abruptly need *Kieran* to tell her how much she had loved their child, how much she had anticipated the baby's birth?

His brows drew down further and further until he had to say something.

"What else are ye not telling me, lass?" he asked into the gloom of the dark room. "There is some piece of this missing."

Would she answer?

Jamie would have avoided the question. She would have kissed him and made him forget what he had asked in the first place.

But then, Jamie would have hesitated to pour her grief onto his chest, as well.

However, Eilidh relaxed further into him.

"A bit of memory returned," she said. "I saw my hand lighting a fuse."

Kieran froze, breath seizing in his chest. "What do you mean?"

"Just that. I saw my hand grasp a taper and then light a fuse. The sort of fuse one uses for explosives."

He blinked, mind scrambling, unsure how to interpret this.

"Ye liked building fireworks with Mr. Chen, lass," he finally said. "I would imagine ye are just remembering one of those incidents."

She paused, as if this possibility had not occurred to her.

"Perhaps," she began slowly. "It *feels* more important than that. As if . . . it is tied to emotion somehow. In my memory, my heart is beating rapidly, and I feel jittery—worried but determined. So . . ."

She stopped, swallowing again. When she continued, her voice was once more thick with tears.

"So . . . I have to know if I loved my baby. You said that Jamie was the sort of person who would have blown up the ship if she deemed it necessary. I need to know. I need to believe that I loved my baby and other people, like Mr. Chen, enough to not do something like that.

"Part of me admires this Jamie ye speak of. She sounds courageous and self-sacrificing. But I worry that she was also hot-headed and impulsive. That she m-might have h-harmed those she l-loved."

Eilidh burrowed into him again, quiet sobs rocking her shoulders.

Kieran held her.

He said nothing.

Jamie would have blown up the ship, if she felt it necessary. Of that, he was certain.

But—

"Ye survived, lass," he murmured. "That is proof enough that ye loved your babe. Ye did what ye must to protect yourself and her."

"B-but what about Mr. Chen? W-what about the others?"

Kieran held silent.

He didn't have a satisfactory answer there.

"I still strongly doubt that the memory you have recalled involves setting powder alight to destroy the ship."

She sniffed. "B-but you cannot say it is *not,* either."

In her wisdom, Eilidh was not wrong.

Jamie had been many brilliant, fierce things, but she could also be rash and reckless in her decisions.

Like the one that had left her alone on that damned ship in the first place.

But Eilidh . . .

The seeds of Jamie were still there.

She was, despite everything, the same person.

But her courage was a quieter thing now.

The strength of someone who had known agonizing loss.

A woman who faced fear and uncertainty every day with a stoic verve.

A lass who had the mettle to not only be brave, but to be vulnerable. Jamie—for all that he loved her—had never allowed herself to be vulnerable.

As Eilidh spilled her grief onto his chest, a new truth flooded Kieran's heart—

He had loved Jamie with every sliver of his soul.

But he saw with abrupt clarity that Miss Eilidh Fyffe threatened to own depths of him that even Jamie had not reached.

Heaven help him.

What if he came to love this new version of Jamie even more than the old?

March 1816

Terror pounded through Kieran's blood.

He parried a midshipman's knife with his rapier, kicking the man in the stomach and sending him sprawling. At Kieran's side, Jamie sliced through another man's arm.

Around them both, island villagers pummeled the crew with staffs, spears, and wickedly-curved knives.

Kieran grunted, looking for Cuthie but not seeing him in the mayhem.

Bloody hell, how had they come to this?

Cuthie had a plan, all right, the bastard.

The Brotherhood had spent the last month blissfully thinking that Cuthie would be bringing sandalwood aboard ship for their return voyage.

That had been a lie.

Instead, before leaving Britain, Cuthie had struck a deal with Andrew's financial backers to capture some of the villagers and sell them into slavery in South America.

The sheer barbarity of the plan still rendered Kieran nauseous. The Slave Trade Act had banned the practice in the Atlantic Ocean, but unfortunately, not in the Pacific. A loophole Cuthie had been eager to exploit.

Cuthie had waited until Kieran was off the ship, visiting the villagers with Ewan and Alex, before informing Andrew of his plans. Kieran supposed the captain had thought to bully Andrew into submission without the support of his friends nearby. Andrew, not the sort to be intimidated, adamantly refused. Rafe was aboard and added his voice to the mix, supporting Andrew in denouncing Cuthie's plans.

Cuthie, incensed by the insubordination, had Andrew and Rafe taken up in chains. Jamie, bless her, had slipped off the ship to warn Kieran and the others.

Kieran and Jamie had organized a rescue party that included all the capable warriors from the village.

So while Cuthie had assembled the crew on the deck of *The Minerva* and had them watch as both Andrew and Rafe were beaten nigh to death, a group of warriors, led by Kieran and Jamie, had stolen aboard the ship.

Now they fought the crew, hand-to-hand, desperate to rescue Andrew and Rafe still lashed to the main mast. Kieran parried another attacker and saw, out of the corner of his eye, that Ewan, Alex, and two burly villagers had reached Andrew and Rafe, cutting them free.

Hallelujah!

Kieran jerked his chin at Jamie, indicating that they should fight their way toward the ship's railing. She nodded and disarmed her attacker.

As they pressed forward, Kieran finally caught sight of Cuthie fighting near the forecastle. The captain looked at him, eyes wide and desperate.

Kieran read the man's expression clearly. Cuthie had miscalculated and made an enemy of Kieran. The problem, of course, was that Kieran was the entire crew's passage home. The captain didn't care what happened to the rest of the Brotherhood, but his sailing master *had* to remain. Kieran was the only one who knew how to navigate *The Minerva* through the enormous reefs that abound in this part of the world. After all, Kieran had prepared and studied maps for a solid year. Cuthie was rightly concerned that the ship might flounder.

At the moment, Kieran didn't care. He simply wanted his friends to be safe.

He parried another sailor's attack. Out of the corner of his eye, he noted Ewan hefting Andrew's body over his shoulder. Rafe staggered with help from Alex. The village men cleared a path to the ship's railing.

Kieran pressed closer to Jamie and they renewed their efforts, keeping crew members busy until Ewan and Alex had disappeared over the railing with the badly injured Rafe and Andrew. Noting that the injured men were rescued, the village warriors also began to abandon ship, diving overboard in droves.

Kieran turned his back on Jamie for only a briefest of seconds, looking toward the railing, plotting their path to freedom. That was all it took.

When Kieran glanced back, Cuthie had wrapped an arm around Jamie, lifting her squirming body clean off the ground.

"Stop, MacTavish!" Cuthie shouted.

Kieran froze, his eyes winging to the ship's captain.

Cuthie shifted his hold on Jamie, the man's eyes flaring.

Realization sank in. Kieran could see it in the man's gaze.

Cuthie knew.

He *knew* that the person he held was not a boy, but a lass. That Kieran had been aware there was a lass aboard and had said nothing.

Kieran's hesitation gave Massey time to disarm him. Rough hands grabbed Kieran from behind. Cuthie said nothing—just held the squirming Jamie—and stared at Kieran with that deadly look of his.

"Take him tae the brig, lads. Be sure to chain him," Cuthie ordered.

The crew were not gentle.

They wrapped Kieran's wrists in manacles and dragged him deep into the ship, shoving him in the dank, dark brig.

Kieran staggered against the wall, sinking to the floor and resting his bound wrists on his knees. He stared at the door opposite, hands sweating and heart pounding.

Where was Jamie?

What was Cuthie going to do to her? To them?

This was all his darkest fears made manifest.

After what felt like an hour, steps sounded outside. Cuthie's face appeared at the barred window.

He threw open the door and shoved Jamie inside.

Kieran nearly wept in relief. She was wide-eyed, bedraggled, and shackled but otherwise whole.

"Does this one belong tae yourself?" Cuthie nodded toward Jamie.

"We belong tae each other," Jamie spat, using her manacled hands to push her hair out of her face.

"I wasnae asking you, brat," Cuthie said. "Well, MacTavish?"

"Aye. Jamie is mine." Kieran nodded, playing the only card he had left. "We married in Sydney."

Cuthie's eyes narrowed.

Kieran held his gaze.

That's right, he wanted to say. *She has the legal protection of my name, and a ship's master would be permitted to bring his wife aboard ship, if he wished.*

Cuthie stared in silence, clearly weighing his options given the chess board situation before him.

Kieran knew Cuthie was in a bit of a bind. The man may not care what happened to the rest of the Brotherhood, but Kieran had to remain. And Cuthie had to ensure that Kieran felt like cooperating.

"Here is how this is going tae play out, MacTavish," Cuthie said, his voice holding an eerie calm. "We are going to weigh anchor as soon as the tide turns. But first, the men will pay a wee visit to the village. The islanders cannae go unpunished. As for your obstinate friends, they can remain here, for all I care. *Jamie*—" He leaned on her name, mockery in his tone. "—will remain chained in the brig until ye see us safely through the surrounding reefs and islands to the open ocean. If ye do that, I will have the courtesy to deposit ye both at the first convenient port. But the slightest waver in your determination, MacTavish . . . I would just as easily toss ye both into the sea. Dinnae test me."

Cuthie slammed the door shut and turned the lock with a loud *clack*.

"Lass," Kieran whispered.

"I'm not hurt," she said, intuitively knowing that was his first thought.

She curled into his side, her shackled hands twisted to the side between them, her body squirming to get as close to him as possible.

Kieran wished desperately there were some way to hold her, to comfort her. "We'll find a way out of this, *mo chridhe.* We can return tae England once Cuthie deposits us in a port. It will all come right—"

Jamie grunted.

Kieran frowned.

She continued to writhe.

"Lass?"

"Cuthie is a lout," she hissed, wriggling beside him. She sounded more frustrated than upset. "He won't set us free. Instead, he'll use me as leverage to get ye to do all sorts of dastardly things and then 'deposit' us in a watery grave when he is done. The man only behaves morally when there is a distinct threat of retaliation."

"Cuthie is an opportunist, a survivor of the worst sort."

"Aye." She squirmed, her manacles clanking. "He will always find a way to cheat or brutalize or manipulate his way out of trouble. We have to get off this ship afore it sets sail."

Kieran nodded in agreement. "That's all well and good, wife, but the tide will turn before morning. By the time the sun rises, *The Minerva* will be out to sea. Unless the rest of the Brotherhood mount an assault, I fear we are stuck—"

"Got it!" Jamie abruptly sat back.

Kieran looked down at her.

She held aloft a thin, metal pick with a hooked end.

"How?" He shook his head.

"Mr. Chen slipped it into my pocket as I was being shackled. Let me see your hands."

Kieran proffered his chained wrists and watched in amazement as his clever wife set to picking the lock.

"How did I ever convince ye tae marry me?" He shook his head in wonder. "You're a marvel."

"Thank ye." She kissed his lips. "But fair warning, I'm going tae remind ye of this moment for the rest of our lives." Her voice went sing-song. "*Oh, ye thought ye were going tae pop down to the local for a pint with Tam, did ye? I think not. Remember that time I saved ye from sure death aboard a merchant ship in the South Pacific? Well, you've now got a babe with a nappy that needs changing. You'll be staying in tonight.*"

Kieran chuckled, soft and low.

Heaven above, only Jamie could make him laugh at a time like this.

"Ye get us out of this mess, lass, and I'll gladly forgo all pints with this mythical Tam."

His brilliant wife grinned and continued to pick the lock.

She had him free in ten minutes. It took another twenty for her to talk him through picking the locks on her own wrists.

Kieran's heart hammered in his chest so loudly, he worried others could hear it.

But the ship was quiet.

He heard Cuthie call to Massey in the distance, something about most of the men having gone ashore to "teach those savages a lesson."

Jamie looked at Kieran. He nodded.

She bent down and made quick work of the door lock.

Carefully opening the door, they noted the empty space beyond. Kieran led the way as they crept up the stairs from the steerage to the berth deck. There they had the misfortune to encounter a pair of midshipmen, set to guard that portion of the ship. Kieran overpowered the men but not before they raised the alarm.

From there, it was a fight. Jamie snatched up one of the men's daggers. Kieran grabbed a heavy staff. He and his brave lass hit and hacked their way up to the top deck. It helped that the men didn't really want to harm Kieran. After all, he was the source of their safe navigation home.

Once they reached the top deck, Cuthie and Massey were all that stood between them and the safety of the ship's rail and the ocean beyond.

Flames lit up the night sky.

Cuthie had ordered the crew to set the village afire, it appeared. A knot of horror rolled through Kieran's chest, fueling his anger and launching him into the men.

Kieran engaged Cuthie, countering the man's blows with his wooden staff, while Jamie led Massey on a chase around the deck. She was quick on her feet, weaving in and out of coiled rope and barrels, evading Massey's reach.

"Jump," Kieran yelled to her, parrying Cuthie's advance. "Save yourself! They willnae harm me."

"I'm not leaving without ye," she called back.

Stubborn lass!

Kieran inched his way toward the railing, both he and Cuthie panting. Jamie was only a few feet away now, darting in and out of Massey's reach.

Pushing Cuthie back, Kieran sent the older man sprawling. He turned for the railing, looking for Jamie, when Massey grabbed him from behind, pinning Kieran's arms.

"Ye'll no' be leaving," the man hissed.

"No!" Jamie screeched.

"Jump, Jamie!" Kieran roared, struggling against Massey's hold.

But Jamie wasn't listening. Instead, she lunged forward, stabbing Massey in the shoulder.

The man howled and released Kieran.

Jamie continued forward, pushing Kieran hard in the chest, sending him tumbling over the ship's railing.

He reached for her hand as he fell, only to have it slip through his grasp.

"*No!*" he screamed as he plunged downward, hitting the water hard, sinking deep.

He swam for the surface.

Had Jamie managed to jump, too? Had she escaped?

His lungs burned.

His head broke above the water, and he heaved in a breath of air.

He treaded water in a circle, looking frantically.

A cackling laugh had him looking up.

Cuthie peered down at him, Jamie struggling against his iron grip.

"Come back aboard, MacTavish," Cuthie shouted down to him. "Ye wouldnae want me tae hurt your wee pet carpenter, would ye?"

"Dinnae do it, Kieran," Jamie called. "He's bluffing. Bargain for my release."

"Oy!" A voice called across the water. "Ye want us tae grab MacTavish, Captain? Bring him to ye?"

Kieran spun to see crew members approaching in two row boats.

A thousand thoughts winged through his head—plans to rescue Jamie, ways to punish Cuthie—but he recognized that the odds of either were against him at the moment.

Surely, Cuthie wouldn't leave without him. Kieran and his navigational knowledge were the ship's safe ticket home. Jamie was right. The information in his brain was the best bargaining tool the Brotherhood had to get back aboard the ship.

Without Kieran, Cuthie would be sailing blind. The captain was too self-serving to risk his own life like that.

He wouldn't leave Vanuatu without Kieran aboard.

And so, Kieran made a decision.

He kicked off, swimming away from the rowboats and *The Minerva.* He would reach the safety of shore and wait for Cuthie to begin negotiations.

He swam, the light from the burning village guiding his way. The waves washed him ashore. Exhausted, Kieran lay on the sand for a long moment before pushing himself upright.

He turned to look back at the harbor and then howled in horror.

The Minerva billowed before him, her sails unfurling in the reflected firelight. He could hear the 'heave-ho' call of the anchor being raised.

Cuthie was leaving.

Taking Jamie with him.

Eilidh woke to sunlight thrumming against her closed eyelids.

She was cocooned in warmth. Flooded with a profound sense of security.

How long had it been since she had felt so safe? So comforted?

She closed her eyes, sinking deeper into that sense of safety, the heat that seeped through her skin and warmed the chill deep in her soul.

A heat that was so palpable, it nearly had a heartbeat of its own.

Eilidh stilled.

Wait.

Heartbeat?

The warmth *literally* had a heartbeat.

Not her own.

Her eyes flared open.

She stared at the foot of a large tester bed.

A heart continued to thump a steady rhythm under her ear.

She blinked.

Memories of the night before rushed in.

Baby. Hand. Fuse. Terror. Kieran. Comfort.

In precisely that order.

Right.

She was still sprawled across Kieran's chest, all but wrapped around him.

Hardly the behavior of a lady.

Good grief.

How had she abandoned thoughts of Simon so quickly? Was it only two days ago that she received his letter, asking her why she had not returned with the Gillespies?

She carefully pushed upright, staring down at Kieran, studying his face. His whiskers were even longer now. But the dark stubble only highlighted the sharp angles of his jaw and the slash of his cheekbones.

Yes, he was handsome.

Yes, she felt a strong pull of physical attraction to him.

Those things may have drawn her to him in the past—may have even been the primary reasons why she married him—but lust and physical longing were insufficient for her now.

Moreover, the comfort she felt with Kieran was not the same as what she experienced with Simon.

Simon offered her solace and safety without complications, without restraint. *Avoidance*, Kieran had called it. But was it truly avoidance? Or merely a lack of weighty obligation?

By contrast, Kieran's comfort was laced with portent. It *required* things of her—effort and dialogue and midnight confidences.

Though he had been right. There was relief in talking about their shared past.

She felt . . . lighter after their conversation the night before. Like the pressure within her chest had eased slightly.

Perhaps talking through her pain had some merit.

Not, however, in Kieran's bed at one in the morning. Or even whatever time it was now.

She winced at the impropriety of her behavior.

A glance at the clock atop the mantle told her the hour was still quite early, despite the cheery sunlight streaming across the rug—the reality of being so far north and approaching the summer solstice.

She needed to leave. If a servant caught her in here, her hard-won reputation would be in tatters. She might be forced to accept Kieran as a husband, regardless. How comical that she insisted on having a chaperone only to steal into a gentleman's bedchamber in the dead of night.

She looked down again at Kieran as she eased away.

That might have been a mistake.

He appeared younger in sleep, hair tousled and askew. She could clearly see the boy he had been—wide-eyed and bold. She even had vague memories of him as a youth. Though her father had never brought Kieran into their home, Eilidh had seen him occasionally when she and Mamma would visit Papa's ship. At six years her senior, he had seemed sophisticated and worldly, walking across the deck with swagger in his step.

Kieran had been a child when her father had taken him on.

What happened? she wondered. *What forces led you to be in my father's care at such a young age?*

Why did she not know?

Kieran opened his eyes then, as if the weight of her gaze had pulled him from slumber.

A slow smile wreathed his face, his pale blue eyes electric in the morning light.

"Now this is a bonnie sight." He reached up to touch her hair, his gaze going soft with wonder. "How I've missed waking up beside ye."

He said the words quietly, as if almost to himself.

Eilidh flinched.

She pulled further away.

"I still don't remember ye," she whispered. "I didn't come here to resume . . ." She trailed off, ending on a hard swallow.

"I understand that, lass," he said, eyes still unnervingly steady. "But I find it encouraging that in your hour of distress, your feet brought ye tae me. I think part of ye remembers."

She stared at him, heart galloping once more in her chest.

She hated him right then.

Hated that he was likely correct.

Hated that she still had no real memories of him, not as Jamie.

Hated that her missing memories lurked beneath the surface, threatening to upend everything she planned for her future.

She felt like a new lamb, tottering around on shaky legs, trying to decide if Kieran was a helpful shepherd or a fearsome wolf in disguise.

"Ye dinnae have to find your way in the dark, lass," he continued, once again easily reading her thoughts. "Part of ye knows that I will always be your safe harbor."

Safe.

That word again.

Was he safe? Particularly when his version of safety came with so many requirements attached?

No matter how safe and comforted she felt in his presence, he would never stop pushing her. He would never cease encouraging her to be more, do more, remember more.

Unlike Simon Fitzpatrick, Kieran MacTavish would never let her simply . . . *be.*

She felt infinitely tired even contemplating it.

"I must go." She turned away from him, pushing off the bed. "I cannot be found here."

She pulled her dressing gown tight around her chest as she crossed the room. But she paused with her hand on the door handle.

"Thank you." She half-turned back to him. "Thank you for lending me comfort when I needed it."

He nodded, sitting up in bed. "Always, *mo chridhe.* Always."

She turned away, but the image of him in that mussed bed—leaning on one hand, rumple-haired, shirt open and revealing half his chest—burned behind her eyelids.

IT WAS AFTERNOON before Eilidh trusted herself to see Kieran again.

They lived in the same castle. It was not as if she could avoid him permanently.

But she did try.

She needed a little distance. To ponder the events of the past twenty-four hours. To decide how she wished to proceed.

She took breakfast and then luncheon in her rooms, trying to come to terms with her instinctive actions the night before.

Part of ye knows that I will always be your safe harbor.

And yet . . . Kieran MacTavish was decidedly *not* a protected cove.

He was a storm-tossed sea—wild and terrifying and breathtakingly beautiful.

Wee memories pummeled her.

The hitch in Kieran's breathing when she first sank the full weight of her body onto his.

The way his hand trembled as he cradled her head to his chest.

The catch in his throat as he wept for their baby girl.

It was too much.

Too much feeling, too much unknown.

To calm her thoughts, she reached for Simon, reading and re-reading his most recent letter until her eyes began to cross. She wanted to feel the soothing peace of Simon, the unconditional solace that a life with him promised—comfort without the weight of obligation.

But all she felt was guilt. Guilt that she considered Simon to be a dear friend, and yet, still hadn't told him the barest outline of her present situation.

What was she to do?

She hated the thought of putting the mess of her current predicament on paper. But Simon knew the basics of her history since landing in the Gillespie's care, and he had accepted her. He would understand this situation, too.

And yet, sweet Simon would worry himself into a dither if he thought she might hang for a crime she could not remember committing.

She couldn't do that to him.

Nor could she tell him about Kieran, for the same reason.

It was one thing to believe herself assaulted against her will. It was something else entirely to find she had a (sort of) husband.

What if after telling him all, Simon considered her married? What if she were doomed to live her life in this in-between place—not quite 'married' to Kieran, but unable to marry anyone else?

The thought was nauseatingly upsetting. She sighed and mentally added it to the long list of nauseatingly upsetting things she currently faced.

But . . . she could not, in good conscience, leave Simon to stew in his justifiable concern. To do so would be *avoidance* in truth.

In the end, she wrote Simon a kindly letter, telling him all was well, that she still cared for him, and she would return soon. She simply was waiting to answer some questions for the Judge Admiral.

She sanded the ink and then studied her words once more, making sure there was nothing alarming in them. Satisfied, she folded and sealed the letter, leaving it to be posted.

Now, what to do about Kieran?

Violet's words came back to her:

Make sure Kieran is not the home you wish.

As advice, it was not . . . ill-informed.

As she had noted earlier, talking about her lost babe *had* brought relief. A small piece of her that had been so broken had . . . if not healed, per se, at least scabbed over.

She felt less fractured. Lighter.

The first step in true healing she had experienced since the wreck.

For once, it felt possible to drift away from her numbness, if just for a wee while.

Perhaps, she should have listened to Alex's medical advice sooner.

Could other ghosts be similarly exorcised?

But what if the process of exorcism brought absolute confirmation of her guilt? She didn't think she could ever recover from the horror of having deliberately killed 127 men. The very thought set her hands to trembling once more—the black terror loomed, ever eager . . . waiting to pounce.

She pressed her fingers to her forehead.

When could she stop going round and round like this?

What was she to do?

At the very least, perhaps a day spent with Mrs. McKay would help clear her head.

But she found only Kieran in the great hall.

"I gave Mrs. McKay the day off," he said by way of greeting. "Her daughter is visiting from Aberdeen."

Her eyebrows flew up at his high-handed comment.

If he was nonplussed, it did not show.

"So given that there is no true chaperone inside the castle," he continued, "I wonder if you would care to join me for a walk?"

"A walk?"

"Aye. 'Tis far too glorious a day to be spent indoors." His grin was endearingly lopsided. "The cliffs are lovely. The sun is shining. And I promise to flatter ye with the purplest of prose."

The idea of spending such an afternoon sounded . . . thrilling and upsetting and cheering and *worryhappysadsad*—

In short, a jumble of contradicting emotions, each of which tugged at her. Eilidh was still unsure if she wished to court them.

Numbness was simpler. It required nothing from her. It simply . . . existed.

But this . . .

All the *feeling* that Kieran pulled from her, the way he coaxed her to actively pursue comfort . . .

It hurt, but within the pain, she could also sense hope.

And hope had been too long gone from her life.

"Very well," she swallowed, "as long as the prose is the purplest, I cannot refuse. Let me fetch my bonnet and pelisse."

THE WIND TUGGED at Eilidh's bonnet, coaxing her to lift her face to the sun.

Kieran had not lied. The day was glorious.

A blue-sky, puffy-cloud, you-cannot-help-but-smile kind of day.

Sea birds whirled and spun along the sandstone cliffs, chattering in their nests, the cacophony melding with the crash of the ocean on the rocks below.

She and Kieran walked along the clifftop path. The North Sea furrowed in blue waves to her left, while grasses mimicked the undulating expanse to her right.

It rendered the world an endless rippling flow and made everything feel so very alive.

She felt alive.

Newly born and scrubbed raw.

Last night's emotional storm had whipped away her cloak of numbness as surely as the sea wind currently threatened to tear off her bonnet.

"Will ye attempt to remember anything more with the fuse?" he asked.

"No."

He said nothing more, but she nearly heard his unsaid words regardless—

Could I convince ye tae change your mind? I like your wee neck too well to see it marred by a hangman's noose.

"I grow weary of this conversation. We need to cease having it." She sighed into the silence. "The problem with remembering is, of course, the possibility that I am guilty. It's one thing to not know and simply say as much to Mr. Patterson and the Judge Admiral—*I do not know. I do not remember*. It's something else entirely to know and either lie about it or try to explain away my actions."

They walked in silence for a moment.

"Ye wouldnae have blown up the ship without good reason, lass," he said.

Oof!

She stopped abruptly. "Ye keep saying that, but what reason could possibly be good enough to justify killing innocent men? Can ye think of one?"

He paused, too, turning to face her. "Nae, I cannae, but that doesnae mean it doesnae exist."

"Mr. Patterson does not strike me as the sort to accept *extenuating circumstances* as an excuse. The man is a bureaucrat through and through."

"The Judge Admiral will have a say, as well. Moreover, Andrew and Alex are powerful men—"

"I thought I was promised flirtation. Purple prose, ye said. The purplest." She fluttered her eyelashes at him, anything to change the topic.

"You're trying tae bewitch me with your wit and beauty." He folded his arms across his chest. "Trying tae get me to drop this."

"Is it working?"

He ran an appreciative look up and down her body, her skin goosebumping to attention wherever his eyes landed.

"Aye," he nodded. "It is."

Eilidh's breathing hiccupped. The memory of the night before reared up—the steady *thump-thump* of his heart, the scalding heat of his skin—

She shook the memory away.

"Excellent." She moved past him, continuing on the trail.

He gave a huff of frustration.

"Ye are maddening, lass," his voice reached her from behind.

"You've mentioned it as one of my many enchanting traits," she replied, tone so very dry.

"Eilidh." He tugged on her arm. "Please stop running."

She allowed him to pull her to a stop.

She snorted. "Pot, meet Kettle."

"Pardon?" He reared back, eyes flaring.

"You're just as bad as myself. You run from your emotions and memories, too."

"No, I don't."

"Aye! Ye do!" Her accent slipped right along with her temper. "Oh, you're quick with a quip and appear open and affable, but ye rarely disclose anything too deeply intimate. Don't act like this is solely my problem—"

"All I've been is open and personal with yourself." He took a step toward her, his voice a growl. "What do ye think I am afraid of?"

"Of letting people too close. Of disclosing your secrets." She rolled her eyes. "Did Jamie know all the dark corners of your heart?"

More silence.

The rather damning sort.

"I thought not," she nodded. "Well, let's start easy. Why did ye end up in my father's care at such a young age? How old were ye?"

"Nine." He shifted on his feet. "I was *nine* years of age when Charles Fyffe took me under his wing."

"And where was your family?"

He swallowed, eyes darting over the sea and then coming back to her.

"Ye think tae call my bluff, lass, but I will not keep secrets from ye. When ye were Jamie, ye didnae know much about my past because ye didnae ask, and, to be fair, I was a bit of an arse and didnae bother to tell ye. You're a finely-bred lady from a genteel family. No need tae remind ye that ye married beneath your station."

"I was a woman pretending to be a boy aboard a merchant ship. Hardly a paragon of ladylike femininity."

He smiled at that. "That was your circumstance, lass. Not your identity."

"You're stalling. Answer my questions, if ye please."

He shook his head—more rueful than frustrated, she thought—and motioned for them to continue walking. "Very well. My father was a sailor. He died when I was eight. My mother took in sewing and washing, but it was never enough tae see us through. I spent time in the harbor, begging for what work I could get. Your father took pity on me. I'm sure I chattered his ears off and looked pathetic for long enough that he eventually took me aboard. My mother died soon after, and I was essentially in your father's care after that."

Eilidh looked at the rippling ocean.

A memory surfaced. Not one lost to her injury, but a scene simply . . . buried by time.

Eilidh stood on the deck of her father's ship while it was into shore, her hand tucked into her mother's. She pulled her new cloak around her, feeling pretty in the red wool. She turned her head and met the gaze of a dark-haired boy, glaring at her. He seemed to be all lanky limbs and was dressed in only a thin jacket, despite the cold. He turned his head and spat into the ocean before stalking off.

He didn't look back.

Kieran. Or, rather, the angry boy he had been.

"He was a good man, your father," Kieran said. "I would have done anything for him."

"The best of men," she agreed. "It's why it stings that ye didn't visit during those final years of his life. It was unkindly done."

He said nothing for a moment. Had she offended him then?

"It was fear, I ken, that held me back," he finally said. "I wanted to remember your father as the strong, capable captain he had been."

"Not the weak, crippled man he became? That *was* cowardly of you."

"Aye. It was. I valued my own emotional comfort higher than supporting your father through the last months of his life."

"Is that your deepest shame then?" she asked. "Give me an honest answer."

He said nothing for a minute. Then two.

Her heart sank.

He would not answer, would he? He was willing to let her into his heart, but only so far—

"My deepest shame . . ." he repeated slowly. He stopped and turned to look at her. "My deepest shame is my behavior after thinking ye might have lived."

"What do ye mean?" Eilidh frowned. "Your behavior when I might have . . . *lived*?"

EILIDH STARED UP at him, her silvery eyes holding hints of the blue sky in them.

In her fashionable bonnet and expensive pelisse, she looked as far from his Jamie as possible.

And yet . . .

His chest panged to look at her.

She was *his*.

It was as simple as that.

And when he had thought her gone, and yet, not . . .

"What happened?" she asked, her voice quiet.

He looked away. He hadn't lied when he said it was his deepest shame. The depths to which he had sunk—

"Ye have tae understand. I had grieved ye. I had accepted for three long years that ye were gone, that there had been no survivors. I had grieved and mourned and thought I had begun to heal from your loss. But then . . . Cuthie surfaced. And it was as if . . ." Kieran took in a deep breath, allowing the memory of the anguish to wash through him.

That was the only way through such pain, he had realized. To allow it to come and then help it flow out again.

". . . it was as if I had not healed at all. The wound of your loss was slashed open, and I couldnae stitch it back together again."

"But why would finding out that I might have *survived* been so painful?"

He swallowed past the ache in his throat. "Because . . . because I figured ye would have found a way back tae me. Ye were resourceful and spunky and so very clever. But ye hadnae returned. Which meant that either ye were dead in truth, or something potentially even worse had befallen ye."

She stood in silence for a moment, allowing the implications of his words to sink in.

"Like . . . captivity? Slavery?" She voiced his deepest fear for her. "There are caliphates in the Indian Archipelago who traffic in such things. Reverend Gillespie heard tales of European women being sold into harems."

"Aye. A woman like yourself would fetch a hefty price. Just the thought that ye might have survived and been forced into such a life. I couldnae sleep. I couldnae eat . . ." He dragged a palm over his face. "It nearly drove me mad."

She lifted her hand, as if to touch him, to offer reassurance. But then dropped it just as readily. As if unable to bring herself to touch him.

"Why are such emotions your deepest shame?" she asked instead.

"Because in my despair, instead of channeling my terror into action to find ye, I turned more and more to whisky tae ease my pain."

Her eyes widened into two Os of understanding.

"I became the worst of drunkards," he continued. "Angry. Bellicose. It became so bad that I was let go of my position aboard ship. If it hadn't been for Alex forcibly dragging me back to his house in Edinburgh . . . I dinnae know if I would have survived. I think part of me was determined tae kill myself."

"Oh, Kieran." She did touch him at that.

The warm weight of her gloved hand on his arm burned.

He managed a wan smile. "So there ye have it. My deepest shame. That instead of setting sail immediately for Sydney to assist ye, I wallowed in self-pity and recriminations. Hardly stellar husband material, now, am I?"

He tried to keep his words light and humorous, but they came out razor-edged and ringing of truth.

"Will ye return to the bottle if things do not go well with the Judge Admiral?" she asked.

The question gave him pause.

"Things will go well for ye, lass. I am sure of it."

"Kieran, please stop saying that—"

"But it's true. Ye havenae suffered and conquered so much tae end up swinging for a crime that either ye were justified in or didnae do. I willnae countenance it."

"Indulge me. Will you return to the bottle?"

Kieran closed his eyes and looked back over the ocean.

Could he resist the call of whisky if he had to witness her hang?

Or if she were exonerated but chose a life with Simon the Sassenach?

He couldn't answer that.

He turned and continued walking.

"You're running away," her voice called to him. "You need to face this, Kieran."

"Face what?!" He whirled back to her.

She had been walking briskly, but she skidded to a stop in front of him. The wind whipped her pelisse and tugged at her bonnet and sent a rosy blush glowing in her cheeks.

She was so impossibly beautiful.

"The brutal reality," she panted, eyes pleading. "I cannot see a way back to . . . *us*. At least, not as we were."

Her bold words seized his chest. "Why? Why cannae ye imagine a life with me?"

"Because I long for peace and quiet. And though you offer me comfort and safety of a sort, those things come with the cost of remembered pain. They come with obligation. You and I may have suited once, but I don't think we are so similar anymore. I lost my memories, and you lost your . . . your wife—" She stumbled over the word, as if unequal to saying *me*. "These losses have changed us. You want to return to the past. I simply want an uncomplicated future."

Kieran winced.

Despite the successes of his career, she wasn't wrong to crave the unencumbered security that Simon the Sassenach offered.

Kieran had never been a brilliant choice for her. His struggles with whisky aside, he was a lower-class urchin at best. She was a genteel captain's daughter, raised as a lady. As much as it burned him to admit, Simon the Sassenach was an infinitely better option.

But Kieran couldn't let her go. Despite her hesitance over the word, she was his *wife*.

And he had always reached for things above and beyond what he deserved.

"Ye took a chance on me once, lass." He closed the space between them. "Why not trust your past self and try again?"

He took the final step to her. She had to tilt her head back to look him in the eye.

But she, true to *her* nature, did not back down. Her chin jutted out in such a familiar, Jamie-esque expression it made him want to smile and weep simultaneously.

Her accent slipped once more. "Ye mean the past self who also thought it was a good idea to hop a merchant ship, learn to fence, and set off fireworks? *That* past self?"

"Aye." Kieran did smile at that.

"That woman had *terrible* judgment."

He chuckled. "O'course, she did. She married me, did she not?"

"I thought ye wanted to aid your argument, not give me more reasons to leave ye?"

That sobered him quickly.

"Eilidh." He lifted a hand, thinking to wrap it around her waist, to draw her into him. The instinct felt as natural as breathing.

The freezing scowl on her face stopped his hand midway between them.

Right.

No touching.

He had promised.

He rubbed his hand through his hair instead.

"Will ye claim me as your wife?" she asked.

He frowned. "What kind of question is that?"

"An intelligent one," she shot back. "If ye are determined to claim me as your wife, then it won't matter what future I wish to have. No one will marry me—not Simon, not anyone—if there is a risk that I might legally be married elsewhere."

"Eilidh, I willnae force ye tae be my wife. I will not claim ye unless you wish it."

Silence.

"Give me a chance," he repeated. "Open your heart to the possibility. Ye say I do give ye some comfort. Lean into that. See if that comfort and safety can be turned into true healing."

Another long pause.

Emotions flitted across her face too fast for him to identify them.

"Very well," she finally said. "After last night, I see the curative benefits of allowing myself to be more accepting of yourself, despite my reservations. But I require a reciprocal promise from yourself."

"Anything."

"In the end . . . if I decide to go with Simon—" She paused, eyes drilling into him. "—I need ye to love me enough to let me go."

The next two weeks passed in a blink of rushing lethargy.

Kieran recognized the paradoxical ridiculousness of the thought, and yet, it was true.

Time with Eilidh whirred passed, days blending quickly one into the other. And yet, he felt as if their relationship was mired in toffee, unable to make any forward progress.

True to her promise, she was more open, taking tentative steps to truly get to know him. He regaled her with stories about his life aboard ship, and she told him about her years with the Gillespies.

However, the threat of Cuthie's impending testimony loomed large.

I need ye to love me enough to let me go.

Her words gutted him.

Because he knew the answer.

Yes.

Yes, he did love her enough to let her go.

Even though the thought made his soul howl and his heart pace restlessly, a caged beast pressing against bars.

He loved her and he wanted her happiness more than his own.

But with every passing day—their shared laughter over the antics of a stable cat, the way her head tilted as he told a story of fighting a gale off the coast of Nova Scotia—he hoped.

He hoped that she might return to him in earnest.

Yet . . . she had gone no further in her affections than a general sort of friendship.

Similarly, she had given up any attempts at remembering. A few more snippets of their trip had surfaced, but nothing more.

Though her recalcitrance frustrated him, Kieran understood her apprehension. If she had been responsible for blowing up the ship, perhaps not remembering *was* the better choice.

Of course, that meant not remembering him either.

Thoughts of Simon the Sassenach haunted Kieran. He hoped the man was paunchy, elderly, and hideous. Or perhaps young and fit enough for Kieran to not feel an utter lout for besting the man in a round of fisticuffs.

How could she consider marrying another?

And so, he had gone on the offensive. She had said she was open to his courtship, had she not?

He had made this woman fall in love with him once. He would do it again.

He included wee gifts on her breakfast tray—a bouquet of posies, an engraved knife for whittling—and took to complimenting her outrageously.

She accepted it all but did not reciprocate.

Stubborn lass.

And still . . . they simply waited.

Until Cuthie's sworn testimony arrived, they were able to float in limbo. To exist in a liminal space where he could pretend that a future with her was possible, even if she never remembered him.

"What will ye do when this mess with Cuthie is cleared up?" he asked one bright sunny afternoon, extending a hand to help Eilidh over an uneven bit of ground.

They had descended the cliffs today, taking a narrow path down a steep slope to a small cove. The beach here was part pebble, part sand.

"*If* it is cleared up," she sighed, dropping his hand and stopping beside him.

He stared out at the ocean. Waves rolled over and around the pebbles, sending the stones tumbling and rumbling. The sound of the rocks clacking mixed with the call of seabirds and the low hum of the never-ending wind.

Beside him, she spun slowly in a circle, surveying the ocean and cliffs. The weather was so warm, she had dispensed with a pelisse and left her bonnet behind, saying she wished to feel the sun on her face. The wind tugged at the loose curls framing her face and threatened to upend her hair from its pins.

Kieran adored her like this, unbound and unfettered. A charming blend of all the women she had been.

"Let's pretend Cuthie exonerates ye," he said. "Then what do ye do?"

She motioned for them to continue to walk.

"What do I do?" she repeated. "I return to Yorkshire, most likely. It has been my life for the past few years." She didn't mention Simon by name, but Kieran heard echoes of the man just the same. "And what about you? What do you imagine when you find yourself awake in the wee hours of the morning?"

"Us," he said without hesitation. "I think about us. I used to ponder how we were, but lately, I have been thinking about you as ye are now. How we could build a future together."

They walked in silence for a bit. The cliffs loomed overhead to their left, the pitted stone covered in yellow lichen and flocks of birds. He even saw puffins, their distinctive colorfully-striped bills visible even at a distance. A thin waterfall tumbled through the mix, leaving a trail of mossy green down the red-black rock. The cliffs along the coast here appeared a blank canvas, one that birds and plants and wind sculpted into art.

He helped Eilidh over another outcropping of tide-worn boulders.

"And how could we be?" she asked at his side. "What would you envision for our life, if I were to agree to claim you as husband?"

Husband.

Kieran savored the word on her lips.

Granted, he wanted to savor anything that had to do with her lips, preferably their presence pressed against his own—

He took in a deep breath of lung-cleansing sea air.

Small victories. He needed to focus on small victories. The fact that she was here, listening to him, entertaining the idea at all.

Patience.

"That's a fair question," he said. "It partially depends on what ye want our life tae be. Would ye like tae sail with me? Andrew has been begging me tae captain one of his large merchant frigates, to be both master and commander of the vessel. And as ye know, a ship's captain can bring his family aboard with him. We could sail the world together, you and myself."

She said nothing for a stretch.

Kieran envisioned it with bright clarity—Eilidh writing at a desk in his captain's quarters, light from an open porthole kissing the side of her head. He would steal up behind her and place a kiss in that soft hollow where her jaw meets her ear . . .

He clasped his hands behind his back, anything to stop himself from reaching for her.

"And if I don't want a life at sea?" she finally said. "What then?"

He darted a sideways glance at her. Nothing in her expression tipped her thoughts.

"I willnae sail without ye," he said. "I couldnae be parted from yourself for months at a time. I love ye too well. My preference is to work as a ship's captain—with the aim of being able to own my own ship one day. But your happiness is my greatest concern. So if ye dinnae want a life at sea, Andrew has said I could supervise his fleet for him. He has purchased five merchant vessels over the past three years, and he needs a man of affairs to manage them. His business interests are widespread, and he doesnae have time to oversee the lot. Such work would likely be based out of Aberdeen or Edinburgh. We could let an elegant townhouse in whichever place pleases ye best."

More silence.

Up the beach, a dark patch in the cliff face hinted at the presence of a sea cave.

"It would be a good life," he continued.

"Aye," she nodded. "It would be."

He could practically see the gears working in her brain. He had to point out the obvious.

"Moreover," he said, "is it *so* very different from the life ye envision with Simon?"

"Husbands are hardly like bonnets, Kieran. I am not the sort to decide upon one on a whim."

"Then why do ye speak about returning to Yorkshire when this business with Cuthie is done? Why are ye discarding me without a test?"

"Excuse me?"

"Have ye kissed Simon?"

"I beg your pardon!" She stopped and pressed a hand to her chest. "That is a most personal question—"

He all but rolled his eyes. "I think we are past the point of niceties, Eilidh. It's a relevant question—have ye kissed him? Have ye felt that spark of attraction? How can ye contemplate marrying a man if ye havenae kissed him?"

EILIDH FROZE AT Kieran's words.

Part of her wanted to turn right around, march back up the trail, and tuck into the safety of her castle bedchamber.

Anything that permitted her to dissipate the ache that thrummed through her blood.

She had been allowing Kieran into her heart, bit-by-bit, over the past two weeks.

And she had discovered that . . . she liked him.

He awakened a restless hunger within her, an emotion unlike anything she felt around Simon. Whereas Simon was calm and solace and creature comfort, Kieran was . . .

Oof.

Kieran MacTavish was an endless tug and pull on her senses—wild wanting mixed with aggravation and frustration.

But she had to admit, he was more than that, too. He made her long to curl into his side at night, to feel his strong arms banding around her, to hear the soothing rhythm of his breathing.

How can ye contemplate marrying a man if ye havenae kissed him?

Kieran's words were an echo of Violet's.

Her pulse was a drum in her ears.

She had never really contemplated kissing Simon. It seemed like far too much intensity for their relationship, too much desire, too much . . . *everything.*

But with Kieran? She sometimes felt hard-pressed to think of anything *but* kissing him.

"Did *we* kiss before we . . . ?" She threw the question back at him, hating the breathlessness of her voice.

"O'course, we did," he laughed. "There were a great many kisses afore we tied the knot of our handfasting."

Eilidh was unsure how to respond to that.

The thought of a *great many kisses* was like the waves beside her—a large upwelling that, if it came too close, threatened to drag her out to sea.

Her pulse quickened.

She sped up, making for the sea cave in the cliffs, ordering herself to disregard the electric sizzle of *him* at her side. The endless temptation he presented.

The knowledge that, as he had said, she could place her lips on his at any time . . . and he would welcome them.

The cave was a jagged crack in the cliff face, cool and damp. She took a few steps inside, running a hand over the wind-smoothed rocks. The cave ended just beyond the reach of daylight, retreating into a crevice of rocks and battered seashells.

Finally, she turned around.

Kieran stood at the mouth of the cave, rimmed in golden sunlight, glowing like an archangel. As if Mother Nature herself bestowed a blessing on Eilidh claiming this man.

He waited, one patient shoulder leaning against the cave wall. As if he would outlast the weight of everything crowding her skull.

The brief memories she did have of him washed over her—striding across the ship's deck, beckoning her to fight faster with his sword, looking down at her with those impossibly blue eyes.

The terror that recovering more memories of *him* meant perhaps remembering her own perfidy. That she had indeed destroyed *The Minerva* and killed 127 men.

But along with that came another worry—what if she left Kieran and went with Simon, only to remember that Kieran was her love?

Or, what about the opposite? She left Simon, stayed with Kieran, and regained more of her memories, only to realize that she had changed too much, that a life with Kieran was no longer what she wanted?

And how could she know until she made a decision?

He had asked her to be open to the possibility of him. But what that really meant was . . . love.

Was she open to the possibility of loving Kieran MacTavish?

Fear held her feet in place.

And still . . . he waited.

"I'll be here when you're ready." His voice echoed in the tight space. "Take all the time ye need."

How easily he read her.

It was horrific and wondrous all at once.

To be so known.

To feel so cherished and . . . and *loved*.

She did love how Kieran loved her.

It was not, of course, the same thing as her loving him. But it was a start, was it not? And no matter what came, she would like to keep this man as a friend—

Oof! She was a fool to think that. She could not choose Simon and keep Kieran as a friend. It would be impossible.

And yet, her heart hammered at the thought of banishing Kieran from her life entirely. Surely that meant something.

Where did friendship end and attraction and romantic love begin? Were the two even capable of being separated, in the end?

After all, she considered Simon to be a friend, as well.

The sea frothed on the beach outside the cave, churning in time with her pulse.

Could she remain a coward? Could she continue to run from the unsettled feelings Kieran evoked?

Or could she . . . act? Could she test the budding friendship between herself and Kieran and see if love could blossom there?

As Jamie, she had acted. Sometimes when Kieran described her former life, it felt as if Jamie were *all* action. As if Eilidh had so thoroughly thrown off the strictures of her past, she had devolved into another creature entirely.

But that wild lass still existed, did she not? She was still part of Eilidh.

Perhaps . . .

Perhaps . . . she could try being Jamie in truth.

Perhaps, she could take a taste of the love they supposedly shared.

Her feet moved before she consciously commanded them to.

Kieran watched her approach, eyes hooded, his face reduced to shadows by the sun haloing him.

The way he leaned against the cave wall reduced his height by several inches. Eilidh was short, but she would not have to stretch too far to kiss him.

His expression said that he knew this, that he planned to make his lips as accessible as possible to her.

He shifted, placing both shoulders on the wall, opening his face to the light. His eyes gleamed, a pale reflection of the water and sand beyond.

She stepped between his legs, so close that she saw the hitch in his breathing. The frantic flutter of the pulse beside his Adam's apple.

He swallowed.

She placed a hand on his chest, as if every part of her wished to confirm how thoroughly she affected him.

It felt vital, somehow, to know that he was as unmoored and out to sea as herself.

His heart pounded under her palm, his breathing shaky.

Her eyes fixed on his mouth.

"Lass . . ." he said.

She shook her head.

"This is just me . . . testing," she whispered.

"An experiment?"

"Aye," she nodded.

She closed the remaining inches between them, pressing her body to his. His hands wrapped around her waist, holding her close.

Reaching on her tiptoes, she brushed the barest feather of kisses across his mouth.

Oh.

A tremor shuddered through him, every muscle taut underneath her palms. As if he shook from the effort of doing nothing.

She pressed her free hand to his jaw, closed her eyes, and rose upward once more—a wave of sensation propelling her.

She kissed him again, pressing her mouth more firmly this time.

Oh!

Tears pricked.

Heaven help her.

He felt familiar. Agonizingly so. The pressure of his mouth, the warmth of his touch.

He *tasted* familiar.

Every sense roared, battering and pulsing, as if desperate to remind her that this was something she treasured.

Something she craved and needed and wanted more than—

Eilidh moaned.

His control broke. He pulled her hard against him and set to plundering her mouth.

All thought fled.

She was out to sea in truth, drowning in sensation, in the raw pleasure of him.

His hands roamed her body, as if desperate to reacquaint themselves.

Familiar. So gloriously familiar.

As if they had done this a thousand times and each moment had been more perfect than the last.

Her hands knew what to do in return, how to shape themselves to him. One threaded into his hair, hitching herself that much closer, holding his mouth against hers. The other hand pressed to his chest, fingers slipping under his neckcloth, feeling the circle of her wedding ring beneath his shirt.

No wonder she had married him.

She was a fuse, and he had just supplied the flame.

How brightly would they blaze in the ensuing conflagration?

More. She wanted more.

The hot, feverish energy of him scorched her mind, pushing past barriers.

Flame.

Burning.

Images billowed to the surface, like memories seen through smoke, her eyes blinking at the sting.

Kieran, staff in hand, turning to yell at her. "Jump, lass. Save yourself!"

Blink.

Cuthie leering down at her, his leathery smile as cruel as the glint in his eyes. "There's no one who can save ye now, girl. You're alone and at my mercy."

Blink.

Mr. Chen grabbing his chest and falling, vomiting a river of blood, a gaping wound in his chest.

"Noooooo!!" she screamed, thrashing against hands that held her. "Let me go! Letmego!"

Blink.

Her hands packing gunpowder into a tube. Faster. Must go faster. *But her clumsy fingers were shaking too badly. She had to do this. She had to be strong. Mr. Chen could not have died in vain. How much gunpowder would be enough?*

Blink.

Her hand picking up a lit taper and lighting the end of a fuse.

At last!

At last, his wife was in his arms.

At last, he was kissing her.

Kieran nearly wept from the sheer joy of it.

Bloody hell, he had missed her. He had missed this.

Them. Together.

The way she fit against him, her soft curves filling his emptiness.

The lift of her body, rising to meet his lips.

The wondrous gift of her trust.

He loved her so much it hurt.

He trembled with it, hands shaking, tenderness slicing him like a blade.

Love me, mo chridhe, he silently pleaded.

He pressed soft kisses across her jaw, down her throat . . .

And then . . .

. . . everything warped.

Something fractured within her.

One minute, she was pliant and eager in his arms.

The next . . . he was fending off a wild cat, just as had happened those weeks before while fencing.

"Let me go!" She pushed against his chest, beating her fists. "*Letmegoletmego!*"

He instantly released her.

She staggered back.

"Eilidh? Lass?" He reached out a hand to steady her.

She scrambled out of reach, face white and horror-stricken, one hand pressed to her stomach, the other covering her mouth as if attempting to block a scream.

"What is it?" he asked. "Are ye remembering?"

She shook her head, not looking at him.

She pivoted round . . . hitched up her skirts . . .

And ran.

Kieran was so startled by the turn of events, he required a full second to react.

And then he raced after her.

"Eilidh! Wait! Talk tae me!" he yelled.

She was quick and nimble on her feet. But even so, she slipped and staggered over the rocky outcroppings striating the beach.

He could hear the sounds of her sobs above the waves.

Her distress was no match for his determination.

He caught up with her and snagged her elbow.

"Talk tae me, lass," he begged.

He expected her to pull away and keep running. Or to lash out, to hit and scream.

But that had been Jamie.

Eilidh . . . looked up at him with anguished eyes and then collapsed against his chest, seeking comfort.

The force of her unexpected capitulation caused Kieran to stumble back, nearly tumbling them both into the churning surf. He barely managed to keep upright.

She wept, *greiting* her anguish onto his chest. Heaving gusts wracked her, body shaking, as if willpower alone were holding her together.

Kieran said nothing.

He simply held her and let the wave of her pain crash over him.

"They k-killed him," she hiccupped, her face pressed to his sternum. "Someone k-killed Mr. Chen."

"What?" he gasped. "Who killed him? What do you remember?"

"I d-don't know. But I saw him d-die. Vomiting blood. Like my brother did. B-blood. S-so much blood."

"Oh, lass!" He pressed a kiss to her head.

She wept and cried and mourned. But it was more than grief, he realized.

Her body vibrated, a vicious trembling that shook them both. As if anxiety was pounding her to shards.

He could nearly taste her fear.

"What is it, *mo chridhe*?" he whispered. "What else did ye see?"

She shook her head against his chest.

"I'll just hold ye then," he continued. "Tell me when you're ready."

They stood there on the beach, locked in a tight embrace, for a long while. The sun and waves and wind soothed even as fear and panic churned in his chest.

Eventually, Kieran had to scoot them farther up the shore, as the tide began to roll in.

Finally after what felt like an hour or more, Eilidh pulled out of his arms and, wiping her cheeks, turned away, sitting on a wind-smoothed rock well back from the water's edge. Her face was splotchy and mottled from her weeping. An elegant crier his lass was not. She wrapped her hands around her elbows and looked toward the sea.

"Will ye tell me?" he asked, sitting down on the sun-warmed sand beside her. He pulled his knees up toward his chest.

She sighed, wiping another stray tear from her cheek.

And still, she said nothing.

EILIDH'S HEART HAMMERED in her chest.

She didn't look down at Kieran.

He remained seated at her feet, his eyes turned toward the ocean.

She longed to crawl into his lap, rest her head against his shoulder. To seek the comfort she knew he could give her.

But fear kept her frozen in place.

She could feel her memories lurking, waiting to pounce.

"I th-think I did it, Kieran," she hiccupped.

He turned to look at her, eyebrows raised.

"I think I *did* b-blow up the ship," she continued.

"What suddenly convinced ye?"

"Mr. Chen's death." She took in a slow, stuttering breath, desperate to stem the chattering of her teeth, the hitch in her lungs. "And the few thoughts that have filtered up around that. I remembered packing explosives, being terrified but so determined. That I didn't want Mr. Chen's death to be in vain."

Kieran closed his eyes at that. He swallowed.

"So, if I blew up that ship—"

"Ye *cannae* say that for certain," he interrupted, pushing himself upright, brushing sand off his hands. "Not until all your memories return—"

"No!" The crushing fear forced Eilidh to her feet. "I keep speaking, but ye aren't listening. I don't think I had a reason. I think I willfully murdered one hundred and twenty-seven men! I was scared and angry and, perhaps, vengeful. Ye were gone. Mr. Chen was gone. Who was I protecting at that point?"

"Our bairn?!"

She flinched, wrapping her hands around her elbows once more. "I don't know, Kieran. I don't know that I thought about the baby as a living entity. It was all so abstract. Ye need to leave me be."

She spun and stalked away from him, from the memories, from the crack in her heart that only seemed to be getting larger and larger.

She did care for Kieran. She did. She wanted more kisses and more long talks and more confidences whispered into the night.

But it all came with a high cost. Her greatest fear.

That the closer she got to Kieran, the more likely the dam was to burst. And given the snippets of memory that had surfaced, she absolutely did not want to remember more.

"Eilidh! Stop this!" His voice called from behind her. "Ye are braver than this!"

"No, I'm really not," she called over her shoulder. "I'm not brave. I'm terrified."

She reached the narrow path which led to the top of the cliffs. Lifting her skirts, she took it at a near run. By the time she reached the top, she was panting and out of breath and had to stop to rest.

So much for outrunning Kieran MacTavish.

He was right behind her, rounding to stop in front of her.

"Without a true version of the events to tell, ye will surely be convicted," he hissed.

"Have ye ever considered that perhaps I *should* hang?" The words tumbled from her. Horrific and raw and so agonizing they cut her throat. "That if I am responsible for the deaths of all those men, that perhaps I *should* be brought to justice."

"No!" Kieran all but shouted. "I willnae allow ye tae nurture such dark thoughts."

"Precisely!" She glared at him. "That is the problem here. The more I remember, the closer I come to the cliff's edge." She waved a hand, indicating the drop beside them. "Bad things happened, Kieran. I feel it, but I don't *remember* it, and that's the important difference. Right now, I have the luxury of believing that *maybe* I didn't do it. That maybe I am innocent. But once I know, I know. And there is no going back." She shook her head.

"You could *hang*—"

"Yes! But it is my choice to make. *Mine.*" She tapped her chest. "And I expect ye to respect my freedom to make that choice."

She pivoted and walked along the path, heading toward the castle.

He paced beside her.

"Jamie would fight." His words lashed out at her. "Like ye did on the ship. Like ye did saving my life. Jamie wouldnae run away and bury her head in fear—"

"But I'm Eilidh." She clenched her teeth. "I've always, *only* been Eilidh."

She continued walking.

Kieran kept pace with her.

Unsaid words piled between them.

She could feel the *angerdespairfrustration* rolling off him.

The forecourt to the castle appeared. A farmer's gig was pulled up before it. A gentleman in a top hat and tight coat helped an older woman down from the wagon bench, saluting the farmer as he drove on.

A familiar gentleman.

A familiar woman.

"Who on earth?" Kieran muttered.

Eilidh wasn't sure whether to laugh or cry.

Of course.

Of course, this would happen at this precise moment—

When the memory of Kieran's lips still singed hers, when the heat of his hands yet burned her skin.

When panic loomed and she could scarcely think a coherent sentence.

"Simon." Eilidh pressed her fingers to her forehead. "Simon has come."

Kieran hated him.

He detested Simon Fitzpatrick with the violent heat of a thousand suns.

"We simply could not go on without ensuring that our Miss Fyffe was well," the man was saying, shooting a devoted look at Eilidh.

They were seated in the arrangement of chairs and two sofas on the north side of the great hall. Eilidh and Mrs. McKay sat on one sofa. Simon and his mother on the other.

Kieran occupied a chair between them—the odd, unpaired outlier.

It felt rather like a portent.

"Yes, yes," his mother agreed, placing a hand on her son's arm. "Oh! The anxiety we both felt for our dear Miss Fyffe. I feared my heart would succumb to palpitations."

"Myself, as well." Simon beamed at his mother, expression affectionate and kindly. He looked back at Eilidh. "It is such a relief to see you in good health and among friends."

Kieran nearly snarled at the man's genteel goodwill.

Simon the Sassenach was supposed to be a loathsome fellow—balding, paunchy, pompous.

Instead, a paragon sat opposite.

Simon was every inch a curate with a wee bit of an inheritance to supplement his living. He exuded gentlemanly kindness. His clothing, though not the first stare of fashion, was elegantly tailored and of clear quality. Furthermore, he possessed all his teeth and hair and, with golden locks and soulful eyes, was decidedly *not* unhandsome.

In short, given the impoverished, dubious circumstances in which Simon the Sassenach had found Eilidh, the advantage in the match was entirely on her side. She had reached above her station in engaging Simon Fitzpatrick's affections. He was precisely the sort of gentleman Captain Charles Fyffe would have liked his daughter to marry.

She had repeatedly told Kieran this. Yet, somehow it took finally seeing Simon to viscerally understand it.

Kieran and Eilidh had just spent the past twenty minutes allaying the Fitzpatrick's fears and concerns. Apparently, Eilidh had written a letter explaining the basics of her situation, but it must have passed the Fitzpatricks heading south while they were traveling north.

"Thank you for your concern." Eilidh smiled at her friends, pouring them all tea. Kieran hated the slight tremor in her hands, the only wee sign of her internal agitation. "As you can see, I am in the company of friends. Master MacTavish was a close compatriot of my father's, and Mr. Ewan Campbell—who resides in Kilmeny Hall with his wife, Lady Kildrum—was a shipmate aboard *The Minerva*."

Eilidh had already informed them that she had been asked to remain in the area, pending an inquest by the Judge Admiral. The way she cleverly spun the tale—never telling a lie, but also not disclosing the whole truth—was so very Jamie-esque, Kieran nearly smiled.

But he only *nearly* smiled, because nothing about watching his wife make doe-eyes at another man was remotely humorous.

"Again, I apologize that I did not write in a more timely fashion," she said, handing a teacup to Mrs. McKay. "It has all been a rush, you see, with the Judge Admiral requesting I remain here for a wee while in order to determine what I can remember."

Eilidh poured another cup of tea and passed it to Kieran. The brief weight of her gaze pleaded with him to go along with her subterfuge, and please, please, please not disclose the information she had not articulated to Simon—namely that she was under inquest for destroying the ship.

Kieran gritted his teeth.

"My dear Miss Fyffe, what an ordeal this has been for you." Mrs. Fitzpatrick reached for a shortbread biscuit on a tray which rested in the middle of them all. Simon's mother was rosy-cheeked and quick to smile and Kieran disliked how much he instantly liked her.

"Yes." Simon balanced his teacup. "I am only upset that we were not here from the beginning to offer you our support."

His mother nodded. "But I am so very glad that you have had the support and care of friends."

The lady spoke with kind openness. In short, Kieran could sense no undercurrent, no insincerity in the Fitzpatricks.

They both clearly adored Eilidh. How could they not? Kieran's lass was easy to love.

Simon, in particular, gazed at her with warmth and affection—the proprietary gaze of a man who considered a woman to be his.

"Thank ye, Mrs. Fitzpatrick. It is lovely to have ye both here." Eilidh shot a smile at Simon. "There is to be a midsummer festival on the night of the solstice."

"In two days' time?"

"Yes. I hope ye will remain here and attend with us."

"I wouldn't miss it, Miss Fyffe." Simon reached for a biscuit, but his eyes never left Eilidh's face.

It was too much.

Too much for Kieran to contemplate, to absorb, to tolerate.

To have come this far.

She was alive.

She was here.

They had wept and laughed and fought and kissed.

Kissed!

Kieran had thought that perhaps . . .

That with a wee bit of time . . .

But . . .

Sitting here, watching Simon watch her—

Kieran now understood with vivid clarity the future that Simon offered her . . . one of calm and peace, of gentility and ease, with her feet deeply rooted in community and family.

Eilidh would be a fool to turn the man away.

Damn but that hurt to admit. It burned and stung and lashed his senses with a cat o' nine tails.

And yet . . . Simon was *good.* A kind man who offered Eilidh safety and refuge from harrowing memories.

Had Kieran ever stood a chance? Or had their love been doomed from the start? Eilidh's decision already made?

Again, she had told Kieran this repeatedly, had she not?

And he, in his arrogance, had assumed she was somehow . . . wrong. That their midnight confidences and hungry kisses were building their relationship anew.

He loved her more than ever.

But was he the *best* man for her?

Or was a quiet life as Mrs. Simon Fitzpatrick perhaps the future Eilidh needed most?

"I WAS SO concerned for you, Eilidh. You do not mind that I came?" Simon asked the words with his usual quiet intensity, but Eilidh could hear the note of anxiety beneath it.

So courteous, her Simon. So gentle, never wanting to misstep.

"Of course not, Simon," she replied. "It is proof of your generous heart."

She said the words unconsciously, a reflexive response.

Oof! She was such a coward. She needed to tell Simon about the implications of Cuthie's looming testimony, that she might stand trial as a murderess.

But she hated to exacerbate his worry.

And it was a moot point until charges were legally made, was it not?

"You are charitable, as always, my dear," Simon replied.

They had finished their tea and now strolled toward Kilmeny Hall, intending to call upon Ewan.

Eilidh had taken Simon's arm, as was appropriate for their standing as a courting couple and his status as a guest.

Mrs. Fitzpatrick and Kieran walked ahead, Kieran politely steadying the older woman along the path. Kieran bent his head and smiled at something Mrs. Fitzpatrick said.

Her mind still stuttered and floundered, attempting to accommodate the revelations of the day.

Her decision to open herself up to the possibility of Kieran's love.

The wondrous euphoria that had been their kiss.

But then, the quick repercussion for her carelessness. The horrific crash of her damning memories—the horror of Mr. Chen's death, her fear and scrambling to pack the explosives.

And then, the final *coup de grâce*—Simon's arrival.

She had thought that perhaps she would feel differently when she saw Simon again. That the revelations of the last few weeks and her growing relationship with Kieran would alter her perception of him.

But . . . that had not been the case.

Just the sight of Simon had caused a lift in her chest, a soothing balm on the painful realizations of the day. A sense that comfort had come. A safe place where she could rest from the frightening memories and worrisome truths that Kieran MacTavish unearthed.

Emotions Simon's presence had always evoked.

This is a sign from God, Miss Fyffe, she could practically hear Reverend Gillespie say. *Peace is often an excellent indicator of God's will. A clear symbol of the path you should choose.*

And she *did* feel peace with Simon.

Even now, her hand was threaded through Simon's elbow, a casual intimacy that proclaimed the closeness of their relationship.

She had yet to take Kieran's arm, for example.

But why was that, she now wondered? Why had she eschewed touching Kieran? There was nothing untoward in taking a gentleman's arm when on a walk.

Was it loyalty to Simon?

Perhaps.

Though if you are loyal to Simon, you have a poor way of showing it.

She hadn't taken Kieran's arm, but she had slept at his side and exchanged decidedly passionate kisses.

And what had been the result of that?

Feelings.

Feelings that required action from her.

Feelings that called up memories she had no wish to ever relive.

However, touching Simon evoked . . . nothing. No rush of confusing emotion. No hum of electricity along her skin. No conflict between love and terror.

No obligations or debts.

Just a quiet sense of safety, of refuge. A hush in her mind like a gentle breeze over meadow grass. A life where words were pleasant and events calm and controlled.

How can ye contemplate marrying a man if ye havenae kissed him?

Kieran's words from earlier rose up.

As did the memory of his kiss.

That dratted kiss . . .

It had been . . . awakening. Rousing.

Shaking her soul from slumber.

Part of her wanted more, more, more.

But the other part retreated in fear, terrified of the hidden depths of her memories.

Was this why she hadn't kissed Simon?

Because part of her intuitively knew that introducing physical passion into their relationship would disturb the safety she felt with him?

But a marriage *required* physical intimacy. So how was she to avoid stirring up the same ache and desire she had felt with Kieran?

Or rather . . . *would* she feel those same things with Simon?

She darted a glance at him.

Simon was frowning at Kieran ahead.

Kieran looked over his shoulder, meeting Simon's gaze. Eilidh knew Kieran's expressions well enough to know he was wishing a pox upon Simon's person.

She sent Kieran a silent rebuke—a flaring of her nostrils, the slightest shake of her head. He narrowed his eyes at her and turned back to Mrs. Fitzpatrick.

"I must say, Eilidh," Simon said, the frown moving into his voice. "I cannot reconcile the rather intense way Master MacTavish regards you. Is there some past understanding between yourselves?"

Again, she heard the uncertainty in Simon's voice, the worry.

But what could she say?

Well, you see, Simon. Kieran and I are married in a way, but then not precisely, either. It's all a muddle. He makes me feel so very many things, most of which are painful, but he does make a comfortable pillow for sleeping. Oh, and I did kiss him, and it felt rather like fireworks shooting off in my veins, explosive and spark-laden . . .

Mmmm.

Well, not that, obviously.

Simon deserved someone so much more devoted than herself.

She settled on, "As I said earlier, Master MacTavish was my father's protégé, but my father was never keen on myself and Master MacTavish establishing an acquaintance. Any undercurrent you sense is likely related to that."

There. A truthful answer. Or, at least, a reply that wasn't a falsehood.

Simon continued to frown. "Has Master MacTavish treated you well while you have been here?"

Ah, sweet Simon. "He has. But . . . if it is all right with you, I would greatly prefer to *not* speak further about Kieran MacTavish at the moment."

"Very well," Simon nodded, saying next exactly what Eilidh knew he would. "Then we will not speak of it."

This is Simon, she thought.

Blessed, tranquil Simon.

Boring Simon, Lady Aster and Lady Rose had called him.

But . . . what was amiss with boring?!

She saw Simon's face and took his arm and all thoughts of *The Minerva* fled.

He never ruffled her.

He never overset her life with kisses and flirtation and insistent encouragement.

Simon just let her . . . be. He allowed her to float in an ocean of numbness, safe from the harrowing depths of her own mind.

So knowing all this, why did she still hesitate to agree to a life with him?

Wait—

Did he still wish to marry her?

"You have not entreated me to give you an answer to the question you asked before I left," she said.

He pondered her words for a long minute, as was his way. Simon was nothing if not methodical in his thinking.

"I know you, Eilidh," he finally said. "I know you will tell me once you have decided what you wish. Until then, I will be patient. I care enough to wait. I want your decision to be firm."

Eilidh nodded, trying to ignore the prick of unease.

Just tell him yes, part of her urged. *Agree to marry him.*

And yet . . .

What if she *had* blown up the ship? Simon did not deserve to be known as the betrothed of the woman who destroyed *The Minerva.* It would utterly ruin him.

Was this why she hesitated?

Or was it more that she had opened up her heart to the possibility of another? And now she struggled to agree to a life without Kieran MacTavish in it?

She looked at Kieran's shoulders ahead—shoulders she had wrapped in a passionate embrace not three hours past, shoulders that had borne more of her grief and anger than Simon even knew afflicted her.

Simon noticed her noticing of Kieran. That wee dent remained in his brow.

She shot him a soothing smile.

Simon trusted her.

He likely shouldn't, but she could hardly say that.

The irony, of course, was that Simon in his retiring way hardly knew her at all. To him, she was a placid sea, no wind or curling tide. And she craved to see herself thus, to embrace the simplicity of it.

That was the problem, though.

Simon didn't know her well enough.

Kieran knew her better than she knew herself.

Both men were unnerving and exhausting in their own way.

But with Simon, she didn't *have* to remember. She could float atop the current-less sea, safe and becalmed.

Sometimes *boring* was a relief.

"DO YOU HAVE a moment, Master MacTavish?"

Kieran turned as Simon Fitzpatrick hailed him from across the parterre garden of Kilmeny Hall. Beyond Simon, voices drifted out from the open doors of the drawing room. Lady Aster laughing over something. The low rumble of Ewan's voice.

Simon strode toward him with an easy grace, immaculately attired, not a single hair out of place—blond, blue-eyed, meticulously English.

Simon the Sassenach.

Simon was every inch as handsome this afternoon as he had been yesterday evening when he arrived. Lady Aster and Lady Rose had certainly noticed. The ladies flirted outrageously with him. But Simon—gentlemanly, good-egg Simon—had batted away their advances with practiced ease, focusing his attention unwaveringly on Eilidh.

Kieran hated that he grudgingly admired Simon for it.

The curate was everything a woman could want in a suitor—a good, upstanding man who would give Eilidh a comfortable life.

The wee *sleekit* bastard.

Kieran scowled as Simon stopped in front of him.

If Simon found Kieran's attitude disconcerting, he gave no indication. Of course, he didn't. Simon was too much the gentleman.

"May I speak with you for a moment?" Simon repeated his question.

"Aye." Kieran motioned for them to walk on.

Simon fell into step beside him, feet crunching on the gravel path.

The petty part of Kieran wanted to walk quickly, to force Simon to scramble beside him, voice puffing as he tried to talk.

But the charitable bit—the one that Kieran focused on for Eilidh's sake—recognized that Simon was as much a victim of this situation as anyone.

The man wasn't deliberately seeking to steal Eilidh away. He simply didn't know the lay of the land, as it were. Moreover, Kieran knew it would shatter whatever trust existed between himself and Eilidh were Kieran to disclose anything of their shared history to Simon.

And so, Kieran walked in silence. It was one thing to avoid spilling painful truths to Simon. It was something else entirely to smooth the man's path into conversation. Kieran bit his lips between his teeth.

Simon cleared his throat. "So . . . you were a compatriot of Miss Fyffe's father?"

"Aye. I was."

More silence.

Again, if Simon found Kieran's silence heavy, it did not show. The man was rather unflappable. In any other circumstance, Kieran would have admired such *sang froid.*

However, at the moment, he rather wished Simon would give him an excuse to deliver a fist to his perfectly-formed jaw.

"As an old friend of the Fyffe family, you appear to have a somewhat . . ." Simon paused, as if searching for the right word. ". . . *avuncular* interest in Miss Fyffe's future happiness."

"*Avuncular?*" Kieran couldn't stop the word from spilling out, laced with disdain.

The men passed from the parterre garden, through a stone wall, and into the rose garden. A small fountain gurgled in the middle, a winged cupid spitting water.

"Well, yes," Simon replied. "You obviously care about Miss Fyffe's future happiness, much as an uncle or some other blood relation would. As she is quite alone in the world, it makes sense that you, as an old friend of the family, would wish to see her well-settled."

Kieran grunted, as Simon was not technically wrong.

Simon took that as encouragement. "Based on your somewhat censorious reactions to myself, I merely wished to assure you of my honorable intentions towards Miss Fyffe. I desire to make her my wife. She is the loveliest of women, so kind, so sacrificing—"

"What is it you want of me, Mr. Fitzpatrick?" Kieran cut him off. His stomach could not tolerate listening to another man extol the virtues of his *wife*. "Miss Fyffe is old enough to make her own decisions for her future. I will not plead your case to her."

"Of course not," Simon quickly agreed. "I, too, wish Miss Fyffe to make decisions based upon her own heart. But I would ask for your blessing."

Kieran stopped, pivoting to face the man. "My blessing? I am not Miss Fyffe's guardian—"

"Yes, I understand that. But I believe she respects your opinion. And I would not wish to encourage Miss Fyffe to go against the advice of her friends. I want her to retain the relationships that are important to her, if she does decide to accept my suit."

Kieran stared at Simon Fitzpatrick. The man's blue eyes dripped with sincerity.

Bloody hell.

Did he have to be so perfect for Eilidh? So conscientious? So well-mannered and gracious? The precise sort of man that Charles Fyffe would have wanted for his daughter.

But *Kieran's* blessing?!

No. He would not take an active part in breaking his own heart.

"I will not stand in your way," Kieran finally said. "As I said, I will allow Eilidh the freedom to make her own choices—"

"Kieran!" A voice called from behind them.

Both men pivoted to see Ewan racing toward them, brows drawn down.

"Please consider my request," Simon said quietly, almost conspiratorially.

"I cannot assist ye in this," Kieran replied, not quite succeeding in keeping the steel out of his voice.

Simon blinked and took a step back.

"Ye are on your own with Miss Fyffe," Kieran continued. "But so help me, if ye break her heart—"

"Mr. Fitzpatrick," Ewan nodded, stopping before them.

"Mr. Campbell." Simon gave a small bow. He turned an intent look to Kieran. "Thank you, Master MacTavish. I will heed your words. If you will please excuse me?"

Simon bowed—shooting Kieran one last pleading look—and took his leave of the two men.

Ewan turned to ensure the man left before pivoting back to Kieran.

"Do I want tae know?" Ewan tossed his head toward Simon's retreating back.

Kieran replied a terse, "No."

Ewan pulled a piece of foolscap from his pocket. "Andrew just sent word from the Judge Admiral."

Kieran let out a slow breath. "Cuthie's testimony?"

"Of a sort." Ewan sighed. "Turns out the Admiralty decided they would like Cuthie and Massey to testify in person."

"Pardon?!"

"Andrew says that, months ago, the Admiralty sent a summons requiring Cuthie and Massey to appear in Aberdeen. They expect the men to arrive within the week."

"What?" Kieran ran a shaking hand over his face. "Why were we not informed of this at the beginning?"

"Andrew doesnae say exactly." Ewan shook his head, scanning the page again. "Just that when the men arrive, the Judge Admiral wishes Miss Eilidh Fyffe to appear before him in Aberdeen to hear Cuthie's and Massey's testimony and present her own version of events."

"They mean to confront her." Icy dread settled in Kieran's stomach. "It feels as if the Admiralty has already made up their mind as to her guilt. That all of this has just been for show."

"Andrew says roughly the same thing." Ewan swallowed, a grim set to his features. "He has been throwing his weight around as Lord Hadley, trying to get the Admiralty to soften their stance, but . . ." His voice drifted off.

"But without Eilidh's memories, there isnae much hope." Kieran finished the thought. "She still hasnae remembered anything that will exonerate her. Worse, the few memories she has recalled are not encouraging her to remember more."

"Aye. That's the rub, isn't it?"

It was too much.

Something angry and raw lodged in the back of Kieran's throat.

He braced his hands behind his neck and turned in a circle, staring up at the sky, blinking repeatedly.

Time.

He had thought to have more time.

His eyes darted back to the still retreating figure of Simon Fitzpatrick in the distance.

Had either of them ever stood a chance?

Because at the moment, it seemed as if every possible path to Eilidh's future led her away from him.

The morning of the mid-summer festival dawned bright.

Eilidh had moved through the past twenty-four hours in a blur of physical activity and mental anxiety.

Ewan had let her read the letter that had arrived from Andrew and the Judge Admiral. Cuthie and Massey would testify in person. She wasn't sure if that knowledge terrified or relieved her.

Surely, it would be harder for Cuthie to look her in the eye and tell a falsehood. But, of course, it was also just as likely that she *had* blown up the ship.

Ewan and Kieran insisted that Cuthie would condemn her regardless of the truth. She needed to remember.

And perhaps that was true, but as of right now, she had run out of time.

It had all sneaked up on her—the Judge Admiral's summons, the mid-summer festival preparations, Simon's return. Over the past forty-eight hours, she had scarcely had a moment to think about her missing memories or truly delve into her future wishes. There was simply too much to be done, and so she had automatically retreated back into her white numbness. The void was effortless to achieve with Simon at her side.

For their part, Simon and his mother had jumped in to help the overworked house staff with the mountain of tasks. The twins' dreams of yards and yards of bunting had been realized. The triangles of colorful muslin now hung in crisscrossed loops across the south lawn, decorating the booths there.

Throughout it all, Kieran had hovered at her periphery, keeping his distance whenever Simon was near and flirting outrageously when he was not.

The Brotherhood had returned yesterday afternoon to join in the festivities. The six members of their band had met in the drawing room of Kilmeny Hall, gathering around Ewan to greet his new daughter.

"Och, she is a bonnie lass," Alex had beamed, smiling at the cooing Dahlia swaddled in Ewan's arms.

"Aye," Rafe nodded, patting Ewan's back.

"Both lasses in this room are remarkably beautiful," Kieran agreed, eyes darting to Eilidh.

She took in a deep breath and looked away.

"Thankfully, Dahlia got her mother's looks," Ewan blushed.

"Well, aye, that goes without saying," Andrew chuckled. "We didn't say that because we didn't want tae hurt your feelings."

The entire household of guests had dined together, everyone achingly polite to Simon and his mother. Eilidh had ensconced herself at Simon's side throughout the evening, her hand threaded through his elbow as they mingled with guests in the drawing room before and after dining.

She had spoken only briefly with Kieran in the dining room over after-dinner tea, the wretch gallantly kissing her hand in greeting.

Hours of small, casual contact with Simon, and yet, it was the pressure of Kieran's lips on her ungloved fingers that lingered into the wee hours of the morning.

Could she trust the intense physical bond she felt with Kieran? Or was the calmer connection with Simon the correct path for her future?

In short, Eilidh was a muddle of confused wishes and contradicting thoughts. And she could essentially do nothing about it, as her entire fate now hinged on Cuthie's and Massey's testimony.

But the mid-summer festival had finally arrived, and Eilidh intended to lose herself in the day.

She dressed and was descending the castle stairs to the great hall for breakfast when a hand snagged her elbow.

Kieran pulled her into the small library on the second floor with its dark paneling and floor-to-ceiling bookshelves. He shut the door behind them.

"Kieran," she said, exasperation in her voice, "I cannot be caught alone with you in here—"

"I just need a moment, lass." He pinned her with his pale eyes, his brows drawn down.

He was wearing the great kilt made of her black-and-red tartan, a contrasting burgundy short-coat underneath, the length of plaid criss-crossing his chest.

She folded her arms. "Very well."

He hesitated, jaw clenching and unclenching. A line creased his brow.

Something was wrong.

Part of her marveled that she knew this man well enough to divine his mood from such small signs.

The rest of her was terrified as to what he had to say.

He did not keep her in suspense. "Cuthie and Massey landed at Peterhead yesterday. The Admiralty has demanded we present ourselves before the Judge Admiral in Aberdeen tomorrow. Andrew managed to convince the government not to send naval officers to escort ye to the inquiry."

"Escort me?"

"Aye. Apparently, Mr. Patterson hinted that Cuthie's testimony will be somewhat damning. There were concerns that ye might try to abscond."

Eilidh's stomach plummeted.

"Mr. Patterson revealed nothing as to the precise contents of the testimony," Kieran continued. "Just that we must present ourselves tomorrow afternoon in Aberdeen. We will depart after breakfast."

She swallowed convulsively.

"Here now." He stepped close and took her hands in his.

Only then did she realize she was trembling.

He pulled her into his arms, as if offering her comfort were as natural as breathing.

It *felt* as natural as breathing, which could be the only reason why she stepped closer and pressed her cheek to the slash of tartan, her hands tucked between them, palms against his chest.

"All will come right, lass. I have faith." His words rumbled under her ear. "Andrew and Alex have both pledged to put the full weight of their combined political power behind ye. If Cuthie condemns ye, Andrew thinks he can convince the King to grant ye a pardon. We will fight with everything we have."

Eilidh swallowed back a whimper.

But even in her distress, she felt the electric pull of him.

The way her body craved to be closer, closer, closer—

As Jamie, she had eagerly embraced the physical chemistry between them. But did she want that now?

The problem with numbness, she realized, was that it was just that . . . numb.

She moved her palms, intent on hugging him, but then . . . stopped. Her fingers splayed against his chest, noting something—

Kieran no longer wore her wedding ring. She couldn't feel its clear shape under his shirt.

The fact should not have surprised her. Did she think that he would remain loyal to her forever?

And yet . . . part of her plummeted at the thought.

Is he giving up on me?

She rested her head against his chest for a moment, so impossibly tired of combating this barrage of feeling.

"Have ye told him?" Kieran asked.

No need to ask whom and what he referred to.

"No." Eilidh pushed out of his arms.

Bad enough that she was alone with Kieran. Even worse that she was hugging him and mourning the loss of a wedding ring she declined to wear.

But to leave kind Simon in the dark over her past with this man?

She was a terrible person.

Perhaps even blow-up-a-ship terrible.

Tomorrow would tell.

She turned away, wrapping her arms around herself. The room was so small, just two steps took her to the single window. The wavy panes of glass rendered the sunny landscape beyond in rippling shapes.

The clock on the mantle chimed the hour.

She felt Kieran shift behind her. The small desk creaked, as if he had leaned against it.

"If Cuthie exonerates ye, what will ye do?"

"It does not sound like Cuthie will exonerate me."

"Humor me," Kieran said. "What will ye do? Will ye leave with Simon?"

She could hear the gravelly edge in his voice and could feel the weight of what the question cost him.

She took in a depth breath. "Simon is easy."

"O'course, he is. He doesnae challenge ye in any way. He's an utter milksop."

She gritted her teeth, hating the truth in his words. "Please, do not speak of Simon like that. We have been over this time and again. Simon has been a pillar of support for me. Moreover, he is a good choice—"

"Is he though? Does Simon flirt with ye? Does he tell ye your eyes are the silver of a new moon on a calm sea? Does he call ye *mo chridhe* and curl your toes with his kisses? Does your knowing of him stretch across years and oceans?"

"Stop." She whirled around, glaring at him where he leaned against the small desk, hands braced behind him. "Please, stop. Simon lets me be. Why can't ye do the same?"

"Because I love ye too well, lass! Security isnae the same thing as love. It's close enough for some people, but I dinnae think it will be good enough for you. Not long term."

"And what if it is?!"

"You're lying to yourself. I know ye, Eilidh Fyffe." He crossed his arms, the motion pulling the superfine of his coat against the muscles of his arms and bunching the sash of tartan on his chest. His long legs stretched toward her, the kilt riding up to reveal his knees, feet crossed at the ankles. The hilt of his *sgian dubh* peeked out from the top of his gartered stockings. "You will continue to grow and evolve as a person. So the affection that offers security right now will eventually feel oppressive—"

"I like feeling secure!" She clenched her teeth, hating the truth in his words.

"Then let *me* be the one to shelter ye!" He pushed to standing. "Let me be the one to hold ye. Living life—*truly* living—involves feeling. Ye *will* feel again. Ye cannae keep yourself numb forever. Eventually, the pain will spill out, as it did with our babe. And what then? Do ye want Simon tae be the one to dry your tears and absorb the weight of your grief? Is he even capable of understanding the depths of ye?"

KIERAN STUDIED EILIDH, his heart thudding so hard in his chest, he feared for his veins.

She met his gaze for one second, then two, before turning away to look out the window once more.

"So knowing all this, would ye truly leave with him?" He had to ask it.

The thought that she would voluntarily commit herself to another was an open wound. The sort that one poked and prodded and could not leave alone, thus ensuring that it never fully healed.

She spun back around to face him. "Ye love Jamie. Not me."

He sighed. "You *are* Jamie."

"I'm *Eilidh*. We've had this conversation, too."

"No! Ye are both—Jamie and Eilidh. A whole person—the woman I love!"

"Am I?" Her eyebrows flew upward. "Is the woman you love still your true love if the life that made her that person no longer exists?"

"Pardon?" He flinched, her question akin to cold water being flicked in his face. "What do ye mean?"

"Just that. Ye loved me as Jamie, as a woman who had cast off society's strictures and brashly laid out a new future for herself. Forces shaped her, cajoled and molded her into that person. But I don't remember any of those forces—the sea, the people, the man Jamie loved. Instead, I am the same woman shaped by *different* forces." She tapped a finger to her breastbone. "I am a woman who has experienced terrible fear and loss without yourself and the rest of the Brotherhood as protectors. I am the woman you loved, broken and battered and utterly altered."

Something harsh lodged in his throat. It tasted of futility and loss.

"I disagree," he said. "Ye keep acting like Eilidh and Jamie are two different people. You've been at this for weeks now. But why? Why do ye persist with this dichotomy?"

"Because Jamie did things I would never have done! And tomorrow I may learn, definitively, that Jamie was a killer! She did all these things, leaving me—the memory-less woman I am now—to face the consequences for her behavior!"

He said nothing more.

She was not wrong.

But then, neither was he.

She pressed her fingertips to her forehead. "Perhaps you and I were once right together." She shook her head. "But I cannot say that anymore."

"And Simon the Sassenach is right for ye?! You dinnae even trust him enough to tell him the entire truth of us. The man isnae capable of understanding your complexity or your past—all the days and hours of living that have brought you to *now*."

But even as he said the words, Kieran doubted them.

The look in Simon's face in the parterre garden rose in his mind. The expression of a man who adored a woman and would do right by her.

"Even *I* don't understand who I am now," she shot back, answering his thoughts. "How can ye fault Simon in this?"

"Ye know who ye are, Eilidh. Ye always have."

She paused, wrapping her arms around her waist. "What do ye mean?"

"Just this—the wishes of our hearts make us who we are. In short, we are what we want. So I ask ye—what do ye want? Ye asked me what I envisioned for our future, and I told ye. But if ye remove the specter of memory from the equation, what do you envision for yourself?"

"Why do ye ask me this?" She threw her hands up. "I cannot see past the 'specter of memory,' as you put it. It's a fog, clouding everything. I feel like this choice ye are presenting me—yourself or Simon—is utterly hypothetical. The most likely scenario, with or without my memories returning, is that I hang for blowing up *The Minerva*. *That* is the future facing me."

She stared at a point beyond his shoulder, looking so lost, so alone.

His arms ached with the lack of her.

Silence.

"And so . . . I don't know what I want," she whispered, voice almost . . . disbelieving. "I cannot choose between a future with yourself or one with Simon. It's all too clouded."

Kieran drank her in.

She was so agonizingly beautiful.

His wife.

The choice of his heart.

And even now, even as Eilidh, she was still the one he wanted at his side.

But . . .

He knew what he needed to do.

"I loved ye as Jamie." His voice rumbled through the quiet room, bouncing off the dark paneling and the books crammed into every nook and cranny. "But I'm here tae tell ye right now—I love ye as Eilidh, too. The lass I've come to know over the past few weeks is every bit as fiery and brave and courageous as Jamie, just in different ways. Ye are not two people, *mo chridhe*. Ye have always, ever, only been yourself—the woman I love."

"Kieran . . ."

"Marriage was never a whim for me, Eilidh." He shook his head—a sharp slice of motion. "I could have married any number of women. But I waited for you. Because in yourself, I found the missing half of my own soul. Ye accepted me with open arms. We raced into our marriage, hand in hand, eager to begin the rest of our lives together."

A tear spilled down her cheek.

He leaned forward and caught it with his finger, holding it between them. The teardrop sparkled in the light, reflecting both their faces back to him.

"But here is my final, barest truth." He shook the teardrop free. "If you're trying to choose between myself and Simon, I *want* ye to choose him. Because if ye truly loved me, there would be no other choice. I dinnae want a crumb of our love. I dinnae want a ghost of it. I want the whole brightness. And if I cannae have that—"

His voice broke at the end.

He swallowed and then continued, tone coarse with emotion.

"If I cannae have that, then I want to be free."

He reached into the pocket of his coat and pulled out her gold wedding ring on its chain.

The one he had purchased for her, believing her dead.

The one he had kept warm with his body for nearly five years.

The one she had never worn.

He held the chain aloft, the ring slowly spinning between them, gold glinting in the low light.

Her eyes fixed on it.

"Ye asked me if I could let ye go?" His voice was the barest whisper. "And the answer is . . . *yes*. Yes, lass."

He reached for her hand and lifted it, cupping it in his, coaxing her fingers open. Her hand felt so slight, so fragile, her pulse fluttering.

Very slowly, very gently, he deposited the ring on her palm.

He coiled the chain, round and round, atop it.

Then, one by one, he closed her fingers around the ring.

He looked at her fisted hand. And then raised his gaze to hers.

"Yes, *mo chridhe*, I love you enough to set ye free."

32

Eilidh was in a shambles.

She drifted through the midsummer festival in a daze, Simon and his mother at her side.

The entire county was in attendance, it seemed.

There were booths of local merchants set up on the south lawn. The haberdasher had yards of silk ribbon and lace collars from Ayrshire. The two local inns were competing to see who could sell the most whisky and steak-and-ale pies. An enterprising pair of widows were raking in the coppers with delicious wedges of clootie dumpling wrapped in paper.

Beyond the booths, children screeched in delight at the scarecrow contest, each effigy more scandalous and terrifying than the last.

The men were gathered around a large, roped-off stretch of lawn, participating in a time-honored Scottish tradition—trying to impress one another by lifting and/or throwing absurdly heavy things. To that end, someone had attached a chain to an enormous stone, and the men were now seeing who could spin fast enough to send the chained boulder sailing. Their calls and shouts of encouragement rang out in sharp bursts of sound.

And through the lot, the never-ending thrum of bagpipes reverberated. A group of elders took it in turns to play, calling out tunes in an attempt to stump one another.

The external cacophony of sight and sound reflected the riot in Eilidh's chest.

Kieran's comments would not let her be.

I dinnae want a crumb of our love. I dinnae want a ghost of our love. I want the whole brightness of it. And if I cannae have that, then I want to be free.

The words had landed with the force of Ewan spinning the chained stone round and round before sending it soaring.

She hadn't needed to ask Kieran, *free to do what?*

She knew the answer—he wished to be free to find that bright love with someone else.

Someone other than her.

The thought . . . burned.

It was acid, churning her stomach and flaring an emotion that felt suspiciously close to jealousy for a woman who did not yet exist.

Eilidh had spent the past several weeks believing that the person she once was—the woman Kieran loved—no longer existed.

But with jealousy burning acidic green in her chest, she wasn't so certain. Her past self felt suddenly more real and bound to Kieran than any future woman could ever be.

And so, she had taken the wedding ring on its chain and hung it around her own neck, tucking the gold into her decolletage.

It was the height of absurdity.

To be with Kieran meant risking remembering everything. It meant a terrifying free-fall into memory and sensation and a morass of confusion.

Things she did not want, right?

What had Kieran said?

We are what we want. So I ask ye—what do ye want?

What *did* she want?

The question rattled through her brain as she sampled the clootie dumpling with Simon and helped Lady Aster and Lady Rose judge the scarecrow contest.

What do ye want?

The question pulsed like a chant as she sightlessly watched Ewan easily win the caber toss—throwing a fully-grown tree end over end—and listened to Simon swap parish horror stories with the local vicar.

The festival spun past in a dizzying burst.

"Are you feeling poorly?" Simon touched her elbow. "You seem rather distracted, my dear."

She pasted on a smile. "I am well. Shall we check on your mother?"

Sweet, dear Simon.

He didn't know her well enough to understand why she had withdrawn.

Kieran, of course, would have understood immediately that her emotions were in turmoil.

Not that she saw much of Kieran.

His only other words to her that morning had been: "I'm not sure I'm strong enough tae be near ye anymore, lass. So pardon me if I'm aloof. Besides, I know what Ewan has arranged for this evening, and I intend tae keep my distance."

Eilidh wasn't sure what to make of that last bit. She knew Ewan had planned something to honor the birth of Lady Dahlia. It was to be a grand surprise for the villagers.

But why would Kieran wish to stay away? Would it be upsetting to him? Should she be worried, as well?

True to his word, Kieran had kept his distance throughout the day.

Yet her eyes didn't stop searching for him.

She watched him help with the cattle judging.

And she clapped when he gracefully lost the hammer toss to Ewan (though *everyone* lost to Ewan, so losing gracefully was generally the only option).

She noted when he lingered and talked with an elegant lady who was a friend to Lady Aster.

Would she, at least, see Kieran tomorrow?

In the morning, she and the Brotherhood would pile into carriages, traverse the two-hour journey to Aberdeen, pause for luncheon, and then meet with the Judge Admiral and procurator fiscal. She would see Cuthie and Massey for the first time in six years and hear their testimony. The Judge would likely ask her questions about *The Minerva*'s sinking, events she still could not remember.

And then, the Judge would decree whether she would be formally charged with murder.

Just that word . . . *murder.*

It shot terror up her spine and chilled her blood.

Murderess.

And not just one man, but an entire *ship* of them—sailors she had worked alongside and laughed with over cups of grog and—

She swallowed.

What do ye want?

She wanted Cuthie and Massey to not condemn her with their testimony.

She wanted to know she hadn't been responsible for sinking a merchant ship and killing 127 men.

She wanted to feel whole again.

She wanted to remember *why* she had wished to marry Kieran MacTavish.

She wanted a future free from the looming black terror and abruptly unsettling memories that lashed her senses.

This was the problem with wanting . . . once you opened yourself up to possibilities, it never ended.

Sometimes, it was safer to want nothing. To aim for the security and safety that a life with Simon promised and let the rest be.

And yet, did she even want that anymore?

Until she knew for certain . . . she waited.

At her side, Simon remained blissfully unaware.

She *still* hadn't told him of the potential charges against her. If she was exonerated, then she would be free. If she wasn't . . . well . . . she would be taken to gaol to await trial, conviction, and hanging.

Simon would surely return to Yorkshire, eternally grateful he had not allied himself with a murderess.

But . . . what if?

What if she were found to be not guilty? Or what if the reasons for her actions were justified by law?

Such an outcome seemed nearly impossible, but . . . what if?

What would you want then?

She could accept Simon's offer of marriage and leave for Yorkshire immediately after.

But did she *want* that?

She walked among the booths at the festival, Simon at her side, a smile plastered onto her face. All the while, the weight of Kieran's ring pressed against her breast.

Oh, it was more of a metaphorical weight than a literal one, to be sure, but it hung there nonetheless. A nearly constant reminder of the differing futures facing her.

Did she look as maniacal as she felt? Did she sport the deranged expression of a woman who found herself one bad decision away from utter despair?

But her smile didn't falter.

Not as Simon and Mrs. Fitzpatrick talked with Andrew and Alex.

Not as Simon bought Eilidh and his mother crispy sausage rolls from the baker and cups of mulled wine from the innkeep for dinner.

Not as everyone gathered on the enormous south lawn after dining for a traditional Scottish ceilidh, dancing and laughing as the sun sank toward the horizon.

Eilidh expected Kieran to be there, swinging the pretty village lasses through a reel.

But as she scanned the crowd—still outwardly smiling while unraveling inside—he was nowhere to be seen.

KIERAN STARED OUT the window of the dining room of The Hart Inn near Kilmeny Hall, watching the sun contemplate descending toward the horizon. Even though the time was well past dinner, sunset was still hours away.

A barely-touched bowl of cullen skink, a thick wedge of bannock, and an unopened bottle of whisky sat before him on the table. The smoked haddock in the skink had been palatable, but the oaty bannock had stuck on the way down, even after he dipped it in the creamy broth first.

As for the whisky . . .

Kieran had thought to down the whole bottle. To drink himself into a stupor before the festivities Ewan had planned for the evening.

But looking at the whisky now . . .

A jittery pain clutched his chest.

The same feeling he experienced after finding Jamie had lived.

The same torment that had driven him to the bottle.

If he downed even one drop of whisky tonight, would he be able to stop tomorrow? Or would he return again to the bottle, seeking anything to banish the suffocating agony in his chest?

He wasn't sure.

And so he stared at the uncorked bottle.

The dining room was empty, but even so, Kieran sat tucked away in a dark corner wedged between the bar and the cold fireplace. The dim, chilly location suited his mood.

A solitary potman had been left behind to man the inn and see to the occasional guest. A group of travelers had just arrived in a pair of carriages, drawing the potman away to help. Kieran could hear them all speaking with the ostler in the stableyard, horse tackle jangling.

Of course, nothing drowned out the sounds of merriment from Kilmeny Hall drifting through the open windows—shrieks of laughter, traditional music, and the occasional whistle or call. His wife—his Jamie—would have loved the events Ewan planned for tonight. Would Eilidh, Kieran wondered?

None of it eased his suffering.

His heart was an angry crosshatch sea, a tumult and crash of disordered waves that he feared would never calm.

He had told Eilidh he would let her go, but saying the words and then actually *enacting* them were proving two very different tasks.

Kieran had loved her as Jamie.

And now he loved her as Eilidh.

He would likely still love her once she was Mrs. Fitzpatrick.

He would leave tomorrow, directly after the meeting with the Judge Admiral, regardless of the outcome.

He respected Eilidh's right to walk away from him.

But he didn't have the strength to stand by and watch it occur.

A rattle near the front door of the inn caught his attention.

"Ho, there!" An English voice called. "Innkeep!"

"Is no one about?" Another voice joined him.

"I cannot say," the first replied. "Innkeep!"

"Ye'll have tae ring the bell, Lieutenant," a familiar voice joined in. "They cannae hear ye."

A sickly sensation crawled up Kieran's spine.

No.

It couldn't be.

And yet . . .

Kieran leaned forward so he could see past the bar and into the entryway.

Two red-coated officers stood in the doorway.

And behind them, a third man—grizzled and older than when Kieran had seen him last, but still unmistakable—

Captain Martin Cuthie.

In the flesh.

Kieran drew in a slow, measured breath.

Of course.

He was an eejit to not have put it all together. If Cuthie and Massey had landed in Peterhead, they would need to travel south to Aberdeen. And that path could send them past Kilmeny Hall.

The officers accompanying the captain were not gaolers, per se. The Admiralty had likely sent them along to pay for travel and ensure that Cuthie arrived on time.

Robert Massey stepped in behind the men.

"The ostler says they're running a skeletal crew tonight, Captain." Massey's voice carried across the empty dining room. "There is a festival at the grand house across the fields."

"Is that what that racket is?" one of the officers snorted.

"Aye, Lieutenant." Massey nodded. "The potman says ye'll need tae speak with him about a room."

The Lieutenant sighed and motioned for his fellow officer to follow him back into the stableyard. The two men disappeared out the door, leaving Cuthie and Massey in the entryway.

"I didn't say the interesting part in front of the lieutenant," Massey continued. "The grand house with the festival? It's owned by Lady Kildrum."

Cuthie's head whipped upright. "Lady Kildrum? Ye mean that countess Ewan Campbell married?"

"I ken it might be."

A long stretch of silence. A roar rose from the gathered crowds at Kilmeny Hall.

"Well." Cuthie rubbed at his graying beard. "Ye dinnae say."

Kieran *knew* that sound in Cuthie's voice.

It was speculative. The tone he used when he realized a wealthy gentleman was too deep in his cups to notice someone dealing cards from the bottom of the deck. Or when a rum merchant might be too daft to haggle a price properly.

In short, the sound of a man who saw an opportunity and exploited it.

Kieran had to do something. To stymie whatever plan Cuthie concocted.

He stood, pushed his way out of his dark corner, and walked toward the men.

Massey saw him first, flinching in surprise and taking a half-step back.

Cuthie followed Massey's gaze but, as he was made of sterner stuff, he didn't react. The older man did nothing more than smile as Kieran approached them. A sinister sort of grin that set gooseflesh skittering down Kieran's skin.

"Kieran MacTavish." Cuthie's grin spread like an oil stain across his cheeks. "I guess that answers our question about Ewan."

Kieran longed to bury his fist in Cuthie's jaw. To wipe that smug expression from the captain's face and unleash his pain on the older man's body.

"How does it feel to be the husband of a murderess?" Cuthie continued and then snapped his fingers. "That is . . . if Miss Eilidh Fyffe *remembers* being your wife."

"I suppose it doesnae matter if she remembers or not," Massey chuckled, but then Robert Massey had always been a toad-eater.

"Aye." Cuthie grinned. "Once Jamie swings for her crimes, ye'll be a free man, MacTavish."

One of the officers shouted something to the other in the stableyard. Cuthie turned his head toward the sound.

Kieran swallowed back the words scalding his throat, shaking the tension out of his fists. But his body still hummed with suppressed violence. He wanted Cuthie battered and bleeding. He wanted the man on his knees, begging for mercy.

Kieran took a deep breath. In. Out.

Attacking Cuthie would only create trouble for himself. It would do nothing to help Eilidh.

"As long as ye tell the truth before the Judge Admiral and God tomorrow," Kieran said, "I think all will be well for Miss Fyffe."

Cuthie snorted. "The lass will hang, MacTavish. Of *that*, I have no doubt."

"Ye dislike us so much that ye will perjure yourself to point a finger at Jamie?" Kieran asked.

"Cuthie! Massey!" the officer called from outside. "We go this way to our rooms."

Massey poked his head out the inn door. "We're coming."

"Perjure myself?!" Cuthie laughed, his gaze darting to the side.

"There will be no *perjury* in my testimony, boy. Massey and I know what we saw."

"I would think long and hard about what did or did not happen to cause *The Minerva* to sink, Cuthie," Kieran said. "Remember, ye directly assaulted both Andrew and Rafe. We would hate for those crimes tae be brought into the light."

Cuthie's smug expression didn't waver. "We both know that we stand at a truce with that. I don't mention *your* mutiny, MacTavish. And Lord Hadley holds his silence about my supposed slight."

"But that silence could end at any time."

"And ye would possibly hang alongside your wife." Cuthie pointed out.

"Aye, but *you* would be in Newgate. Or worse—"

"Pardon me for breaking up this *tête-à-tête*," a dry voice said behind them. "But perhaps you ladies could gossip about the weather at another time."

Kieran turned to see the lieutenant entering the inn.

"We have rooms for the night." The lieutenant nodded at Cuthie and Massey. "Please follow me. The next time I ask, I will not be so polite."

The lieutenant spun on his heel, confident that Cuthie and Massey would follow.

"Better not keep your nursemaid waiting." Kieran jerked a chin toward where the officer had just been.

If Cuthie found Kieran's mocking words cutting, it didn't show.

With a snort, Massey followed the lieutenant out the door.

Cuthie pivoted to follow, paused, and then turned back. He walked across the entryway until he was only a foot from Kieran. The smell of foul breath and stale tobacco smoke clung to him.

"No matter your choice—" Cuthie's smile stretched wider. "—your precious Jamie will dangle from the end of a hangman's noose. There is no escaping that."

"I wouldn't be so sure," Kieran shot back. "Think long and hard about repercussions should you decide to forswear yourself tomorrow. The truth of *The Minerva*'s sinking will come out eventually, and ye would hate to swing for it. That is, if Andrew and Rafe don't prosecute ye first."

Kieran kept his expression blank, but his heart hammered in his chest. His words were a bluff, and he knew it. If Eilidh never recovered her memories, the truth might stay hidden forever.

The gleam in Cuthie's eyes said he understood this. The man took a step back, still grinning widely.

"Youse all can come after me, if ye wish," Cuthie shrugged, "but it will make no difference for yourself. And that, MacTavish, is just one more thing that makes this situation so bloody brilliant. Because nothing ye do will spare her. Rant. Rage. Try tae hurt me all ye wish. But at the end of the day, Jamie will still be dead, twitching at the end of a hangman's noose. And that is a reality ye cannae escape. She is lost to ye." He chuckled and slapped the lintel of the inn's doorway as he turned to leave. "'Til tomorrow, MacTavish."

33

"Would you care to dance?" Simon asked at her elbow.

Eilidh watched the crowd whirl and spin through the steps of 'Strip the Willow,' sunlight blazing nearly sideways along the horizon. She loved dancing but . . .

"Do *you* wish to dance?" She flipped the question back at him.

"Not particularly," Simon sighed.

That sent her gaze snapping to his face.

"I cannot say I enjoy dancing," he continued, darting a glance toward the dancers. "It is inelegant, is it not?"

Eilidh frowned. Simon wasn't *wrong*, per se. 'Strip the Willow' was a whirlwind of swirling skirts and sweaty laughter. But not all dances were so vigorous.

Eilidh thought through the entirety of her relationship with Simon. Had she ever seen him dance? She thought not. He always sat beside his mother at local balls. Eilidh had considered it solicitous and kind of him.

But now . . . it begged the next question—what else did she not know about Mr. Simon Fitzpatrick?

She grimaced inwardly.

Were Lady Rose and Lady Aster correct? Was Simon simply . . . boringly boring? And had she taken this innate boringness and labeled it as 'safe'?

Across the crowd, she noticed Ewan smiling and turning toward Kieran who had just approached him.

Ewan bent his head, nodding as Kieran whispered something in his ear. The men spoke for a few minutes. Kieran turned to leave and then paused, his gaze unerringly winging to hers.

For one solitary heartbeat, they locked eyes, setting Eilidh's pulse to thumping.

Kieran flashed the barest slip of a strained smile and turned away. Eilidh felt the loss of him, an abrupt draining away of the energy he sparked inside her.

Security isnae the same thing as love.

Did she care for Simon *beyond* the sense of safety she felt when around him? Could she feel a similar spark of something with him?

"Shall we sit?" Simon motioned to a pair of nearby chairs, oblivious to Eilidh's moment with Kieran. "I understand Mr. Campbell has prepared a surprise for this evening—"

"Actually, Simon, I *would* like to dance." The words tumbled from her mouth before she could stem them. "It looks . . . invigorating."

Simon paused and pasted a kindly smile on his face. "You know I will deny you nothing, Eilidh. Perhaps dancing with you will be all I need to enjoy the activity."

'Strip the Willow' had ended and the small traditional orchestra struck up the first bars of the Circassian Circle. This particular dance was a good choice for Simon, Eilidh supposed, as each couple stayed together for the entirety of the dance and the steps were more staid.

Eilidh and Simon took their places, bowing and curtsying to one another before joining hands. As the name implied, the Circassian Circle was danced in one enormous circle, couples moving in and out, clapping and spinning in time with the music.

Simon said nothing more. For all his disdain of dancing, he did know the basic steps, easily following as Eilidh directed him where to go.

Throughout it all, he was quiet and calm, as usual.

But . . . the whole affair inspired no sparks for her. And judging by his staid expression, likely none for Simon either.

What was going on in his head? What was he thinking?

Was he upset that Eilidh had dragged him into the dance?

Was he enjoying himself regardless?

What do ye want?

She wanted to *know* the man she married.

She wanted him to know *her.*

She wanted to feel that *zing* of attraction. The thrill of nipping an orange from a lover's hand or holding his gaze as his lips dipped down to hers . . .

She turned in a circle and clapped hands with the woman beside her. Simon did the same with the man beside him.

Then she turned and spun around Simon, his hand sliding into hers. His palm was warm and solid and altered her breathing not at all.

His smile appeared strained.

"Are you enjoying yourself then?" she asked.

Simon's expression remained fixed in place. "For yourself, my dear, I would dance all night."

They separated to clap hands with their neighbors again.

But his words left Eilidh frowning.

Simon hadn't answered her question. He had masked how he felt and, instead, gave her the answer she wished to hear.

How was that a genuine rapport? The sort of relationship to compel people to laugh and argue and love and hold each other through a dark night of grieving a shared loss?

Truly living involves feeling. Ye cannae keep yourself numb forever. Do ye want Simon tae be the one to dry your tears and absorb the weight of your grief?

She blinked, Kieran's words washing over her.

Briefly, she imagined it. Her memories returning, the weight of them towing her under, causing enormous upheaval . . .

Simon would . . .

Well, he would . . .

He would do . . . nothing.

He would wait until the storm of her tears had passed and then pat her on the head and tell her to cease thinking upon such distressing things.

In short, Simon would encourage her to bury her feelings, just as he had about dancing.

She did not want that.

She clasped Simon's hands and let him spin her around.

As the world whirled by in a kaleidoscope of swirling silks and sunset sky, Eilidh realized a simple bald truth—

She did not want a life with Simon.

The knowledge sank deep, the revelation immediate.

Most surprisingly, a warm wave of *relief* followed. As if admitting she did not wish to marry Simon had released a dam of tension within her.

He was a good man. A remarkably good man. As a lady, she knew the importance of marrying a kind gentleman. He fit the mold of the man her mother had wished for Eilidh's husband.

But that very goodness did not necessarily make him the ideal man for her. She could appreciate his wholesome nature and still not wish to marry him.

Security isnae the same thing as love.

Kieran had been right.

Damn him.

What else had she misunderstood? Was Kieran correct in everything?

"Eilidh?" Simon asked, his brows drawn down.

Eilidh looked up at him, finally realizing that she had stopped dancing mid-reel. The townsfolk continued to spin and laugh, eddying around herself and Simon.

"Are you well?" he continued.

She stared up into his earnest eyes, the sunset raking his face from left to right in a glow of orange light.

She had to tell him. It had to be now.

She could not, in good conscience, deceive him any longer in this.

"I cannot marry you, Simon."

He flinched back. "Pardon?"

"I cannot marry you," she repeated. "I am so sorry, but that is the truth of the matter."

"This . . . this is all so sudden, Eilidh." He stared at the dancers still swirling around them.

Shaking his head, he gently took her arm and steered the two of them to the side of the makeshift grassy dance floor. Once there, Eilidh continued walking, leading them past the row of dowagers watching the dancing, finally stopping beside a large flowering rhododendron bush that gave them a modicum of privacy.

"What has happened?" Simon asked, clasping his hands behind his back and looking at her in consternation.

Eilidh bit her lip. "Nothing has happened, Simon. I merely have been thinking about my own future, and—" She sucked in a deep breath. "—I fear you and I will not suit."

"But . . . I thought we were happy together. Are you . . ." Simon frowned deeper and deeper. "Are you sure there is no emotional connection between yourself and Master MacTavish? There seems to be an undercurrent of . . ."

She nearly snorted.

There was nothing *undercurrent-ish* about herself and Kieran. They were more a tidal wave of incoming mayhem and turmoil and endless yearning.

But Kieran *was* a factor in her refusal of Simon. What had Kieran said earlier?

You dinnae even trust Simon enough to tell him the entire truth of us.

She flattened her palm against her chest, feeling the wedding ring there, tucked into her bodice.

The memory of their kiss flooded her senses—the jolt of his lips touching hers, the hitch in his breathing when her body had pressed into his, the possessive pull of his fingers on her hips—

Eilidh took in another slow, bracing breath. She touched a pink flower of the rhododendron beside them.

"My relationship with Kieran MacTavish is complicated, Simon," she said, looking back to him. "I'm sorry I have kept some truths from you. But Kieran . . . he and I . . . we were handfasted while in Sydney, Australia."

"Pardon?!" Simon reared back.

"Kieran MacTavish and I are handfasted," she repeated.

The meaning of the words hit her with brutal force.

Handfasted. Committed. Married.

The idea felt . . . good.

As if, by finally openly accepting the facts of their handfasting, she gave her heart permission to genuinely open to Kieran.

"I have no memory of the event," she continued telling Simon, "and without that, any sort of union between him and myself is not binding. However—"

"You are married?" His expression crumpled. "How could you not tell me?" He looked her up and down, as if truly seeing her for the first time.

Eilidh stiffened her spine. "Well, I only learned of it a few weeks ago myself, and you can imagine, it has been a lot to take in. Yet you are right; I should have told you straightaway. But . . . but I didn't know if I wished a relationship with Kieran MacTavish, and as such, I felt like the point was somewhat moot."

"Moot?!" Simon laughed, an outraged *whoosh* of sound. "Being married is never a moot point, Eilidh. Our marrying would have been a disaster. Do you wish a relationship with Master MacTavish now?"

"I think . . ." Eilidh paused, her fingers once more finding Kieran's ring and pressing it against her sternum. "I think that perhaps I do—"

Fwheeeet!!

A loud whistle snared their attention.

Eilidh and Simon both turned toward the sound.

Ewan stepped up on a small platform, his great kilt ruffling in the slight breeze. He was wearing her tartan, Eilidh noted.

He held out his hands until the crowd quieted.

Simon reached out a hand to her, as if to continue their conversation, but Eilidh shook her head and stepped out of the shadow of the rhododendron bush, focusing on Ewan.

She needed a moment.

Time to accommodate the growing knowledge in her chest.

She *wanted* Kieran MacTavish.

But . . . what did that mean? How was she to navigate caring for him and, yet somehow, manage the horror of the memories that would likely return as she spent time with him?

Granted, if Kieran were there to help her through it . . .

"Thank youse all for coming this evening." Ewan spread his palms wide. "My wife and I are honored. It is always a pleasure to see so many treasured friends in one place. I know word has spread that I have a wee surprise this evening. That is true."

A rustle ran through the crowd. A group of children squealed and began chasing each other, darting in and out of adult hands attempting to rein them in.

Ewan smiled. "My daughter, Lady Dahlia Campbell, has burst into our lives, bringing with her a spark of complete joy. Lady Kildrum and I wish tae share some of that joy with ye tonight. So please join us in welcoming Lady Dahlia."

Ewan waved his hand toward the back of the lawn, signaling to someone.

The crowd rotated *en masse*, people bopping onto tiptoe to see what Ewan was pointing to.

"What is this surprise?" Simon murmured at her side.

Eilidh shook her head, but a terrible sense of foreboding bloomed in her stomach.

The low pop of the rocket igniting was all the warning she received.

BOOM!

A firework exploded overhead, a brilliant ball of orange.

"Oooooh!" a collective gasp went up from the crowd.

Sparks cascaded in an arc.

Children screamed in delight. A smattering of applause rippled outward.

"Gracious!" Simon said, his voice full of wonder, head tilted skyward.

Eilidh, however, was frozen.

Her heart took off like a mad beast, rampaging in her chest.

Another pop.

BOOM!

A starburst cascaded around them.

She whimpered, hands wrapping around her stomach.

She hadn't known this would happen. She hadn't had time to prepare.

And on the back of refusing Simon and opening herself up to the possibility of Kieran . . .

Her barriers were too fragile, too raw.

BOOM!

The sound was cannon fire attacking the blank numbness of her memories.

No. Not this. Not now.

She pressed shaking palms over her ears, anything to stem the sound.

But it was no use.

The noise was too loud, too familiar.

The ache in her chest too strong.

BOOM!

Something collapsed within her, like rocks sloughing off a cliff and tumbling into the ocean.

Scenes flooded her mind.

Mr. Chen warning her of the dangers of packing fireworks. "You must be most careful, Jamie. The slightest spark and boosh.*" He mimicked an explosion.*

BOOM!

Kieran laughing, racing along the beach in Rio, turning to her. "Will ye tell me about the fireworks tonight, lass? Or must I kiss it out of ye?" His face was so boyishly endearing . . . lovewantdesire *raced through her. How could her heart ever withstand him?*

BOOM!

Kieran standing before her, their hands bound together as they plighted their vows. "I will always love ye, lass," he whispered. "There will never be anyone for me but you. I will never let ye go."

Love flooded her, scouring her heart of any other emotion. She threw her arms around his neck and kissed him through her tears.

BOOM!

Her hand picking up a lit taper and lighting the end of a fuse.

"This is your wedding surprise, wife?" Kieran laughed, lounging on the beach

sand, hands behind his head. "I should have guessed ye would have contrived fireworks, in truth, on our wedding night."

Grinning, she sat back, resting her head on his shoulder as the charge exploded overhead, an expanding flower of light. "Only for yourself, Kieran, my love."

BOOM!

Eilidh pressed a shaking hand over her mouth.

The fireworks, the crowd, Simon . . .

The lawn, the estate . . . the whole world receded.

She closed her eyes as a tidal wave of emotion swept through her—colors swirling, her mind expanding and growing and snapping to accept the onslaught.

Image and scene and emotion blasted through every last vestige of numbness, a blurring whir of . . . *everything.*

Kieran racing across the deck, grinning from ear to ear.

Kieran laughing as she pulled him down for a kiss.

Kieran smiling as she slipped into his cabin, hands reaching for her.

Kieran pressing a kiss to her belly, whispering, "You are loved, little one."

Kieran . . .

Kieran . . .

Kieran . . .

Oh!

And there it was.

BOOM!

Love exploded in her heart.

Shining. Bright. Incandescent.

Love.

How could she have forgotten?

How could she have forgotten?!

Something wet hit her hand.

Her eyes flared open, only to realize she was curled in a ball on the ground, weeping.

"Miss Fyffe?" A concerned voice at her ear. "Eilidh?"

She lifted her gaze to see Simon crouched beside her, staring in alarm. She blinked at him, wiping her cheeks.

"Are you hurt?" He pulled her to her feet. "Whatever is the matter?"

She looked up at him.

Simon . . . he was a friend. A *good* friend.

But that was all.

How had she almost agreed to marry him?

Particularly when she and Kieran were *already married!*

But Kieran, the wretch, had let her go.

OH!

He. Had. Let. Her. Go!

How could he?!

To watch her marry someone else knowing that they were . . .

That they had . . .

She pressed a hand to her stomach.

"I have to . . ." She shook her head, emotion clogging her throat. "Forgive me, Simon." She continued to shake her head. "I have . . ."

She felt his hand try to hold her back as she tugged away and rushed into the crowd.

"Eilidh!" Simon called behind her.

But she scarcely heard him.

She had to find Kieran.

Now.

She stood on tiptoe, trying to peer through the crush of people.

But it was futile. She was too short.

The only person she could see clearly was Ewan—the man was part giant after all.

She smiled at that thought. More memories filled her mind—laughing with Ewan, teasing him about a pretty island lass because Eilidh liked making him blush.

And now he was married. To a countess, no less! With a daughter!

Oh!

She had missed so much!

She pushed through the crowd to him.

"Ewan." She grabbed the upper fabric of his kilt. "Where is Kieran?"

Ewan looked down from his great height.

"Where is Kieran?" she repeated, shaking his mammoth arm and moving it not an inch.

"Ah, lass. I thought he told ye." He grimaced. "He's a bit wrecked over everything—"

"I understand that, but I *must* speak with him." She all but ground her teeth. "*Now*, Ewan."

Something in her tone stopped him. He peered at her more closely. His eyes flared and then a wide grin split his face.

"Jamie?" he rumbled.

"Aye?"

Ewan grinned even wider. "Try the library."

"Thank ye—"

"Eilidh! Miss Fyffe!"

Eilidh turned to see Simon bearing down on them, brows drawn down.

"Go, lass," Ewan murmured to her. "I'll explain things tae Mr. Fitzpatrick and send him on his way."

"Tell him I'll write a letter. Bless ye, Ewan Campbell."

Eilidh raced across the lawn, her thoughts as tangled as her poor embroidery threads.

How dare he?!

Lady Aster had asked if she had ever killed a man.

Eilidh wasn't entirely sure.

But if she hadn't, she might start with Kieran MacTavish.

34

Kieran stared out at the dusky sky through the wide library windows. The clock on the mantel chimed midnight. But because it was the solstice, twilight still lingered outside, just light enough to render the sky a deep blue and prevent the stars from appearing.

He lounged in a leather chair facing the fireplace.

Cuthie's words from earlier still rang in his ears—

Jamie is lost to ye.

She was. She was lost to him. In every sense.

The library was deathly quiet. No fire in the hearth. No lit candle.

Just the shadowy gloaming painting the room in featureless shapes.

The dark made the first pop of a firework particularly brutal.

It lit up the entire room, a flash of noonday sun.

Jamie had lit fireworks for him on their wedding night.

"I spent all week making them with Mr. Chen," she giggled. "I couldn't marry ye without a proper celebration. The very sky has to burst with my happiness."

And it had.

He had sat beside her in the sand in Sydney, the lingering heat of the day shimmering in the ground around them, and let the gleaming sparks of the fireworks fill his soul with her happiness . . . with *their* happiness.

One thought alone looping in his brain—

How did I convince this bright flame of a woman to marry me? I am the luckiest of men.

And now . . .

He lived in the opposite of that moment—silence and shadow, despair and desolation.

He dragged a hand across his eyes.

The fireworks continued, illuminating the room, one flash after another. It was hard not to see the bursts of firelight as a melancholy homage to their love.

The past glory of it.

Cuthie's words weighed heavy.

Nothing ye do can spare her now.

Was that true? Surely, Andrew and Alex could use the combined might of their titles to persuade the King to pardon Eilidh, if nothing else?

Surely, not all hope was lost.

Footsteps sounded along the corridor outside.

Wearily, he turned as the door clacked open.

Eilidh stormed in and slammed the door behind her with a loud *smack.*

"*You!*" Her voice vibrated with rage.

In the dim light, she looked like an avenging angel—eyes feverish, chest heaving, hair tumbling from its pins.

Just the sight of her was a dagger between his third and fourth ribs—brutally lethal.

"Eilidh?" He rose from his chair, pushing to his feet.

She stomped toward him.

"How c-could ye?!" she choked.

He shook his head. "What happened, lass?"

He expected her to stop. To stand her ground and spit out whatever she had to say.

Was she angry about the fireworks? He had thought she would love them. A memory of work she adored. Of the happiest moment of his life—the night he married her.

Instead, she kept marching, right into his arms, and beat her wee fist against his chest.

"How. Could. You?!" she gasped, punctuating each word with her hand.

The force of her blows caught him off-guard.

Kieran stumbled back a step, reaching for her elbow. But his heel hit on a footstool, and he ended up tripping, tumbling to the ground, pulling her with him.

She landed on his chest with an *oof*, hair pins scattering.

More to the point, she stayed there.

She did not scramble off.

She did not back away.

No.

She crawled more firmly on top of him and grasped his head between her small hands.

"You idiotic, imbecilic, ridiculous, impossible—" Her voice broke.

She collapsed onto his chest, gusting sobs tearing through her, hands gripping his coat in two fists.

Blinking, Kieran wrapped his arms around her and held her close.

He stared at the ceiling.

Uhmmm.

So . . .

"Eilidh? Lass?" He jostled her with his shoulder. "What has happened?"

She pushed up, a hand on the carpet beside his head, looking down at him through a cascade of dark, tousled hair.

"You w-would have l-let me go!" she hiccupped. "You p-promised me. Never l-let ye go. You vowed!"

Kieran froze.

Never let ye go.

Those words . . .

He *had* promised her that . . .

He pushed upright, heart galloping.

Eilidh slid backward, moving off his chest, easing down to sit beside him.

"What did ye say?" he whispered.

She glared at him.

And that's when he saw it.

She was . . .

It was as if . . .

"Jamie?" It was the barest thread of sound. "*Mo chridhe*?"

She cupped his jaw with one of her wee hands.

"You *promised* tae never leave me. You *promised* that it would only ever be me for ye. You *married* me, Kieran MacTavish! How could ye renege on that? How could ye?!"

Joy blazed through him.

A scouring wildfire, cleansing his soul in its wake.

He raked a hand into her hair. Pulled her to him. And kissed her.

No thought. No finesse.

Just a bone-deep need for connection, for this moment . . . with his *wife*.

She responded with near savage hunger, crawling onto his lap and pressing her body into his.

At last!

She was in his arms, kissing him just as he remembered.

Kissing him as if *she* remembered.

"My love," she whispered, pressing her lips to his cheek, his jaw, his throat. "Husband."

It was too much.

He thought he had lost her yet again . . .

And now . . . this . . .

The pressure in his chest built and built.

A terrible sob tore through him.

Then . . . another.

He clutched her to him.

"My Kieran. Darling." She gathered him close, holding his head to hers.

Her own greiting soon mingled with his.

The relief!

The agonizing joy of it.

She was here.

She had remembered.

They held one another for a long while, until their harsh sobs quieted and Kieran felt equal to speaking once more.

"T-tell me," he whispered, wiping his wet cheeks. "Tell me what h-happened. What changed?"

"It was the fireworks. Or rather . . ." She paused, thinking, resting her head on his chest. "I finally allowed myself to be receptive to the thought of ye. I was so scared of my memories, so paralyzed. But once I opened myself up to the possibility, the fireworks battered through the rest of my barriers, and my memories came flooding back."

As he wiped his eyes, she recounted how the unexpected familiarity of the fireworks triggered a landslide of memories, nearly all of them about him.

He kissed her once she was done, helpless to stop himself.

"Thank you," she choked. "Thank ye for finding me last autumn. For forcing the Gillespies to release me into your care. For doing so much to help me remember. But . . . why didn't ye tell me that I loved you?" She pressed her lush lips to his.

"I did!" he said around their kiss. "Ye wouldnae listen."

She kissed him fiercely and then pulled back to glare at him. "Ye should have tried harder!"

"I did!" he laughed. "You're verra stubborn."

Her eyes narrowed. "Ye should have been stubborner."

"*Stubborner*? I dinnae think that's a word—"

"Kieran." A low warning.

He grinned. "I dinnae ken anyone can out-stubborn yourself, *mo chridhe*. But I will happily listen to ye scold me over it for the rest of our lives."

"I don't think ye are taking this as seriously as ye should."

"I'm trying, but I'm just so happy tae have ye back in my arms, I cannae breathe for the joy of it."

She rolled her eyes. "You're impossible."

"Impossibly charming and handsome?" He kissed her neck. "Impossible tae believe ye married such a paragon?"

She laughed.

Oh, how he had missed making her laugh.

How he had missed . . . this.

The simple pleasure of knowing that she was his . . . that he was hers.

She tucked her nose into the space between his neck and shoulder.

"Why?" she asked. "How could ye let me go? Especially after going through so much to keep me with ye?"

"I meant what I said, sweetling." He kissed her forehead. "I love ye enough tae want ye to be happy. And if I was no longer the man for you, then I wanted ye to be free to find a match that could bring ye happiness."

"But you knew! Ye knew how much I love ye. Why did ye doubt?"

He pressed a kiss to her neck.

"Because ye had changed, lass. Ye were right about that." He cradled her cheek in his palm. "Loss and grief have altered ye. They have formed ye into a woman of such courage and grace—"

"Ah, my love." She kissed him again.

"I scarcely feel worthy of ye."

"That is good tae know," she laughed. "I plan on reminding ye of that fact every day for the rest of your life."

He grinned, joy still wildfire in his veins.

She twined her arms around his neck and curled into a ball against him.

He stroked her back, fingers running up and down her spine.

"So am I tae call ye Eilidh or Jamie now?" he asked.

He felt her smile. "How about simply *wife*?"

"Aye. I can do that."

"Ye were right—"

"Of course, I was."

"Don't be insufferable." She smacked his chest. "Ye were right that I was splitting myself between two people—Eilidh and Jamie. But at the end of the day, I am both at once. Though . . . I am changed. I am more cautious now. Less . . . impulsive."

"I am changed, too. Losing ye . . ." His voice trailed off.

"Did ye truly nearly succumb to the lure of whisky?"

"Aye. If it hadnae been for Alex, I cannae say I would have survived it. I numbed the ache of losing ye. But Alex convinced me tae reach for hope."

She wrapped her arms around him and held tightly.

"I have recovered many memories, it seems . . . large chunks of our trip to the New Hebrides. But I still don't remember what happened to cause *The Minerva* to sink," she said. "I have recovered only a handful of memories past the first week or so on Vanuatu."

"Just Mr. Chen dying?" he asked.

"Yes. And a couple glimpses of us fighting Cuthie aboard *The Minerva*."

They sat in silence for a moment. The fear of Cuthie's testimony and the uncertainty of her future weighed on Kieran's mind.

"Whatever happens tomorrow, I will be at your side," he murmured. "We will see this through together."

She sighed, relaxing into him. "I may be taken into custody tomorrow. We may only have one night together."

He kissed her slowly, lingeringly. "Then we should make it count, wife."

She paused. "Some have argued that you and I are not *precisely* married."

He chuckled and nuzzled her neck. "If only there were a way to rectify that—"

She placed a hand on his chest, pushing him upright. "Kieran MacTavish, if ye are asking me to marry you again, ye need to do a more proper job than that."

"Do I now?"

"Aye." She looked most severe.

Grinning, Kieran set her off his lap and pushed himself to one knee. Clasping her hand in his, he looked into her eyes where she sat on the carpet.

"Miss Eilidh Fyffe, we have experienced a grand journey together, you and I. I would love nothing more than tae spend the rest of my life chasing adventure with ye. Beloved of my heart, would ye do me the great honor of marrying me again?"

She bit her lip, tears pooling in her eyes once more. "Are ye sure, Kieran? Ye might be marrying a murderess. There may not be much more adventure to chase."

"I will always want ye as my wife. Now and forever."

She popped up from where she sat on the floor and kissed him. "I want nothing more than to call ye husband."

Kieran pulled her to her feet, threading their fingers together. Leaning down, he kissed her softly.

And then, hand-in-hand, he led her through the house and out onto the back lawn.

The fireworks had finished, and the villagers were straggling off for home.

But they found Ewan easily enough. He stood with the rest of the Brotherhood—Andrew, Rafe, and Alex.

Their friends smiled as they approached.

"Lass!" Ewan boomed. "Are we tae call ye Jamie or Eilidh now?"

"Och, Ewan Campbell, I will always be Jamie tae yourself."

Eilidh laughed and threw her arms around Ewan's waist, hugging him. She quickly recounted how the fireworks had ignited the return of many of her memories.

"Jamie!" Andrew grinned, opening his arms and all but lifting her off the ground. "It's good tae have ye back."

Alex smiled and kissed her cheek. "Welcome back, lass."

"Glad you're here to set Kieran straight," Rafe laughed, squeezing her shoulders.

Of course, once Kieran and his wife—or soon-to-be-wife-in-truth-this-time—explained what they wished, their friends whooped and clapped their hands.

Ewan instantly pulled his *sgian dubh* from his stocking and sliced a strip from the wrapped edge of his kilt.

When Kieran raised his eyebrows, Ewan snorted. "Ye dinnae think we'd use anything other than Jamie's tartan tae bind your handfasting, did ye?"

Waving goodbye to the last of the guests, Ewan pulled them all into the private, parterre garden.

Like on that beach in Sydney over six years ago, Kieran and Eilidh once more plighted their troth and fasted their hands together.

Only this time, the entire Brotherhood was present.

This time, Jamie pulled her wedding ring from its chain around her neck, wiping tears as Kieran slid it onto her finger.

This time, Alex wrote down their vows on a sheet of foolscap that they signed and the rest of the Brotherhood witnessed.

This time, Andrew would see their vows delivered to the local sheriff and entered into the county marriage registry.

This time, Miss Eilidh Fyffe was Kieran's for keeps.

The Brotherhood cheered and clapped when Kieran capped their vows by kissing his lovely wife.

They whistled and cheered again as Eilidh took Kieran by the hand and led him toward Kilmeny Castle.

As they crested the hill leading down to the castle, the pinks and oranges of sunrise bled over the horizon. The sun never left for long this time of year.

The path was a silvery ribbon of light as Eilidh pulled Kieran along faster and faster until they were both nearly running.

"Mrs. MacTavish, some might call ye overly-eager," he laughed.

She gave him a mischievous look.

"But that person will never be myself," he continued.

She paused and tugged him to her. "I love you, Kieran MacTavish."

"I love ye, *mo chridhe*."

He kissed her once, twice.

And then they ran down the path, her wee hand in his.

The sun peeked over the horizon, sending a burst of rays across the ocean.

Never had a new day felt more full of promise.

Eilidh awakened, the world coming to her slowly.

She lay on her side.

Light leaked through the closed shutters.

A warm arm wrapped around her waist, snugging her spine against an even warmer chest.

Memory quickly followed.

Kieran.

Husband.

Lovelovelove.

She closed her eyes and took in a deep breath, relishing the heady pleasure of waking up in his arms.

How could she have forgotten this?

How could she have come so close to walking away from their marriage?

His breathing quickened behind her.

"Still angry with me?" His voice was a rumble at her back.

"No." She stretched and turned to him, pushing him onto his back so she could put her head on his chest. "More angry with myself. That I didn't trust ye more. That I didn't believe ye sooner."

"Aye. Ye should always trust my word. I'm going tae remind ye of this moment for years tae come—" He left off in a yelp as she deliberately placed her cold feet on his calves.

"Don't be too smug." She cuddled closer, needing to say more. "I am most sorry for the pain I put ye through, Kieran. Though it was born of ignorance, it was still unkind of me."

Kieran heaved a rather put-upon sigh. "If only there were some way for ye to make it up tae me . . ."

She laughed and closed her eyes, relaxing into him.

He stroked his fingers up her arm.

"Nervous about today?"

Kieran had told her about his confrontation with Cuthie the evening before.

"Terrified. And yet . . ." She paused. "Well, I *am* afraid and yet also less so, in many ways. I feel like I have accepted who I was and who I am, and there is a strong measure of peace in that."

"Have any more memories returned?"

"No. Nothing more. The entire voyage is still patchy. And everything before and after Mr. Chen's death is missing. From the week we arrived on Vanuatu until I came to in the villager's hut in New Caledonia is mostly blank. I'm not sure I will ever recover those memories. Or perhaps, my mind will forever protect me from them."

"Whatever the outcome, I promise to always provide a safe haven." He pulled her close. "We'll get through this together."

THE JOURNEY TO Aberdeen was tense.

Eilidh stared out the carriage window, nearly crawling out of her skin with nerves.

Kieran held her hand firmly.

She leaned on him, needing his physical as well as emotional strength.

Alex rode in the carriage, too. The rest of the Brotherhood traveled in Andrew's carriage in front of them.

"The fact that ye recovered so many memories is very encouraging," Alex said. "It indicates that there was a mental reason why ye forgot, not solely a physical head injury."

"Do ye think I'll recover any more memories?" Eilidh asked.

"Only time will tell, unfortunately." Alex shook his head. "It's most likely that your memory loss is a combination of both physical and mental injury."

She turned to stare out the window. "Of course, I may easily hang before anything else surfaces."

"Not if I can help it." Alex's expression was resolute. "There have been precious few times I have been glad to inherit the title of an English marquess, but right now? I am decidedly relieved that I have the power tae do something to protect ye."

"Aye. We'll fight this with everything we have," Kieran nodded.

Eilidh wanted to believe them.

She wanted to believe that Cuthie wouldn't accuse her unjustly.

She wanted to believe that perhaps she hadn't blown up the ship deliberately.

But each mile they drew closer to Aberdeen, her heart rate increased.

Far too soon, the carriage wheels were clattering over cobblestone streets, past shops and fine townhouses and wagons laden with wool bound for the ports.

They rolled by the celebrated Mercat Cross in Castlegate, the ancient monument where the Old Pretender had been declared king in 1715.

The gibbet of Gallowsgate quickly followed, the hangman's noose swaying ominously in the breeze.

The carriages rolled to a stop before the High Court, the gallows still in sight. It was a fitting bit of theater, Eilidh supposed, to make would-be criminals stare at the possible end of their journey—for both the day and possibly mortality—as they entered the courthouse.

An officious-looking man led them all into the Judge Admiral's wood-paneled chambers. Eilidh fisted her hands to stop their shaking.

The Judge Admiral sat behind an enormous desk, his gray hair trimmed with military precision and his neckcloth immaculately tied. Mr. Patterson sat beside him shuffling papers, looking the same as he had previously—bureaucratic and perfunctory. Neither man wore traditional court robes, as this was an unofficial, fact-gathering inquiry.

But it was the two other men seated against the wall to the right of Mr. Patterson who immediately drew Eilidh's attention—Captain Cuthie and Mr. Massey.

Her skin prickled at the sight of them. The men were older and battered—their skin more lined, their bodies hunched—but the predatory gleam in Cuthie's gaze was as chilling as ever. It sent gooseflesh pebbling up her arms.

A burley constable shut the door, standing at attention just inside the room. The Judge Admiral rose and walked around his desk.

"Lord Hadley. Lord Lockheade." He nodded in deference to the two high-ranking peers among them, shaking their hands. If the Judge Admiral was cowed by their presence, it didn't show. "It is a pleasure to have you here."

Everyone murmured greetings in return. Rafe adopted his most upper-crust, English accent. Andrew and Alex exuded aristocratic hauteur. Ewan nodded his head and loomed a full head taller than anyone else in the room. Kieran added a polite greeting. Eilidh bobbed a curtsy.

Cuthie snorted, clearly taking umbrage at the genteel manners on display.

"Let's get on with this," he said.

"Patience, Captain." The Judge Admiral returned to his desk. "Please be seated, gentlemen."

A solitary stool had been placed in the middle of the room.

The Judge Admiral motioned for Eilidh to take a seat on it. She did so gingerly, perching on the edge.

Her heart rattled and lurched in her chest.

She was a prisoner facing the guillotine, praying reprieve would be granted.

She darted a glance at Kieran, sitting behind and to her right.

All will be well, his eyes said. *I am here.*

She bit her lip and looked back to the Judge Admiral and Mr. Patterson.

Mr. Patterson produced a Bible and had Eilidh, Cuthie, and Massey each swear upon it, pledging their eternal souls to tell the truth, as far as they knew it.

Cuthie smirked at Eilidh as he recited his oath, voice gravel-edged and vaguely mocking.

The Judge Admiral clasped his hands on the tabletop. "My goal with this inquiry today is to ascertain what truly happened during those final moments before *The Minerva* sank, taking her crew to an early grave. Before we begin, I'd like to ask Miss Fyffe—"

"Mrs. MacTavish," she interrupted.

The Judge Admiral's eyebrows ticked upward. He glanced toward Kieran, but he otherwise did not falter.

"Mrs. MacTavish, forgive me. I should like to begin with yourself, as you are the accused in this matter. Mr. Patterson informs me that you remember nothing of the events leading up to the sinking of *The Minerva.* Is that still the case?"

Eilidh took in a long breath and looked at Kieran. He nodded in encouragement.

"I haven't remembered anything specific to the sinking of the ship." That was truth. "I have remembered the stabbing murder of the carpenter, Mr. Chen."

"Ah," the Judge Admiral sifted through some papers.

Mr. Patterson handed him a sheet of foolscap, tapping a paragraph inked there.

The Judge Admiral examined it with the help of a quizzing glass.

"Captain Cuthie mentioned this in our previous conversation." He lifted his head. "Would you care to shed some light on this, Captain Cuthie?"

Cuthie snorted. "I had a woman aboard my ship, Your Worship—"

"Please address me as 'my lord,' Cuthie. I am not a mere magistrate," the Judge Admiral interrupted. "Continue." He flicked his wrist.

A splotchy blush crawled up Cuthie's cheeks. "As I was saying, *my lord*, once the crew knew a woman was aboard, the situation devolved into mayhem. As a naval man yourself, surely ye understand that sailors can be savage beasts after months at sea—"

"And had you been months at sea at this point?" the Judge Admiral asked, glancing again at the papers before him.

Cuthie paused. "We were nearly three months out from Sydney, my lord."

"That isn't the question I asked. How long since you had been on land, Captain?"

Cuthie gritted his teeth. "About a week, my lord."

The Judge Admiral noted something in a large book. "Please continue, Captain."

Cuthie cleared his throat. "Jamie—that's what Mrs. MacTavish called herself—was difficult to control aboard ship. She worked the sailors into a bit of a lather with her womanly ways—"

"You were allowing her to interact with the crew at that point then?"

"Ehr, well—"

"I remember being bound," Eilidh offered. "I think I was held captive in the brig."

"Ye were," Cuthie sneered, "but the sailors broke ye out of the brig, intent on having their way with yourself."

"Aye," Massey chimed in. "Figured if ye wanted to act the whore, they were happy tae oblige—"

"What did ye just call my wife?" Kieran said, voice menacing and low behind her.

The Judge Admiral held out a staying hand.

He looked to Cuthie and Massey. "I am merely looking for facts here, gentlemen, not personal commentary. If and when I require that, I will ask for it. So please continue, Captain. Members of your crew broke Mrs. MacTavish out of the brig and then what?"

"They attempted to assault her person. Mr. Chen intervened. There was a scuffle, and Mr. Chen was stabbed in the chest."

Eilidh swallowed.

The burst of her memories settled into a more orderly sequence of events.

Hands binding her, holding tight.

The coxswain leering at her.

Her struggling, wrenching her arms, fighting to get free. Screaming. Kicking.

Mr. Chen yelling, fighting to reach her.

And then blood. So much blood.

She closed her eyes, absorbing the wave of grief.

So senseless for Mr. Chen to die by such violence. Senseless for him to die at all.

And yet, so true to his kind nature—he was killed while attempting to assist a friend.

The Judge Admiral scribbled more in his book. "And then what happened, Captain? I'm assuming the men who murdered Mr. Chen and attempted to rape Mrs. MacTavish were summarily disciplined? Perhaps even executed for their crimes?"

Eilidh heard a scornful exhale from behind her. Rafe, perhaps?

Cuthie had likely encouraged the men in their attack on her. He would have done nothing to avenge Mr. Chen's death.

"Well, my lord," Cuthie hedged, "I figured the men had been driven tae a sort of temporary madness by Jamie's feminine wiles. It hardly seemed fair to punish them for it."

Silence.

The Judge Admiral stared at Cuthie through his quizzing glass. "Your men rose up in insurrection and murdered a member of your crew, and you did . . . nothing?"

Cuthie flushed a deeper red.

Yes, Eilidh thought. *Let the man squirm.*

Mr. Patterson cleared his throat. "Captain Cuthie *was* most censorious of Mrs. MacTavish's deleterious effect on the crew in his previous statement, my lord."

"Of course, he was, Mr. Patterson." The Judge Admiral snorted. "However, it seems to me that if one small woman could cause such chaos, perhaps Captain Cuthie's ability to properly govern his men is suspect."

"Pardon?" Cuthie's voice rose. "Are ye implying I dinnae know my own job?"

"That is *precisely* what I am stating, Captain," the Judge Admiral's voice cracked through the room. "There is nothing *implied* about it. In a well-run ship, a lone woman in the brig would cause no harm, much less a riot. However, under slipshod leadership, sailors can and will find any excuse to behave badly."

"Hear, hear," a voice muttered behind Eilidh. It sounded like Andrew.

"Now see here, your *lofty* lordship," Cuthie snarled, standing up and taking a menacing step forward. "I didnae travel halfway around the world tae have my good name maligned—"

"As ye were, Captain," the constable at the door barked. "Sit down."

Cuthie whirled, glaring at the man. With a harrumph, he returned to his seat, but not before shooting a lethal look at Eilidh.

Her heart pulse drummed in her ears.

"Do you have anything more you wish to add to the official record concerning Mr. Chen's death, Mrs. MacTavish?" the Judge Admiral asked Eilidh.

"No." She shook her head.

"And anything further you wish to say about the sinking of the ship?"

"No. I have no memories beyond Mr. Chen's death."

"Very well, then." The Judge skimmed a page and then moved it off his pile, flipping it over. He did the same with two further pages before lifting up another sheet of foolscap. "Let us get on with the Captain and Mr. Massey's testimony. In the interest of harmony and truthfulness, I will read the statement Captain Cuthie made previously." He looked to

Cuthie and Massey. "If either of you have anything you wish to add, please do so."

The Judge Admiral snapped the paper, lifted his quizzing glass, and began to read.

Two weeks after Mr. Chen's death, the seas rose in a terrible gale as we attempted to navigate a series of reefs. The waves were too high to set anchor, but any movement on our part risked the ship being dashed on a submerged reef. The weather made it difficult to see what lay ahead with any clarity. We were in desperate straits.

Jamie was still in the brig, for her own safety and that of the crew. She suggested a solution—she would take fireworks, climb up the foremast, and send the rockets over the ocean before us, illuminating our path and any dangers ahead. As I considered her to be a dispensable member of my crew (on account of her feminine deceit and weakness), I agreed to Jamie's proposal.

I sent the rest of the crew below deck in case there was an accident with the fireworks. Only myself and Mr. Massey remained on the top deck. Mr. Massey was at the helm, steering the ship. I kept a lookout for hazards. Jamie took a hurricane lantern in her teeth, stashed rockets in an oiled satchel across her chest, and climbed the foremast, lashing herself to it. The ship rolled and pitched, but Jamie managed to light a rocket and send it skimming over the water. It exploded and did as she intended, illuminating the sea before us.

We did this for a while. Between the fireworks and my shouted commands to Mr. Massey, we were able to guide the vessel. Then Jamie released a firework which illuminated a large reef in our path. Mr. Massey pulled the ship hard to starboard. I clung to the deck railing, being tossed with the wind as the ship tilted into the turn. I looked up toward Jamie in the rigging. For some reason, she was lighting another firework. The firework flew from her hand toward the ship deck. Abruptly, the ship shuddered, coming to a halt. And then, it exploded.

The Judge Admiral stopped reading at this point.

Eilidh's hands were fisted in her lap, her heart a battering ram beneath her sternum.

She had risked her life, trying to help save the ship.

And climbing the mast?

That sounded like something she would do, even though she still had no memory of the event.

The Judge Admiral lowered his quizzing glass and looked at Cuthie. "Would you care to elaborate on this chain of events, Captain?"

"It's obvious, isnae it?" Cuthie snorted. "Jamie deliberately aimed the firework at the ship's deck, intent on destroying us all. The firework plunged through the ship's decks and ignited the black powder in the hold. The blast tossed myself and Mr. Massey clear of the ship. I can only assume that Jamie was similarly thrown free. The rest of the crew, being below deck, were not so fortunate."

Eilidh swallowed, certain the hammering of her heart must be audible to all.

The Judge Admiral said nothing for a moment, tapping his quizzing glass against his lips.

He set down the paper. "I must be honest, Captain, I do not see how this all adds up to Mrs. MacTavish deliberately sinking the ship. She was up the mast, trying to save it—"

"Aye! And it was her own idea. She earned a wee bit of our trust and then *boom!*" Cuthie smacked his hands together, causing Mr. Patterson to jump. "The first chance she got, she blew up the ship."

"And what motivation would Mrs. MacTavish have had for endangering her own life like this?"

"Revenge!" Massey spat. "Pure and simple."

"Aye," Cuthie nodded, "she wanted revenge on those who had killed Mr. Chen."

The Judge Admiral pondered this for another moment, brow furrowing.

Eilidh sat stock-still.

Silence hung.

Cuthie glared at Eilidh, eyes mocking and triumphant.

"Do you have anything you might wish to add, Mrs. MacTavish?" the Judge Admiral asked. "You have no memories of the actual wreck, as you said, but do you recall your state of mind after Mr. Chen's death?"

Eilidh swallowed, thinking back. "I cannot say that I wished harm upon the crew members who killed Mr. Chen. I have no memories of wanting revenge. Just sorrow at his death and fear for my own safety. Along with that, I must say that I do not believe I would have intentionally blown up the ship. Not everyone aboard caused me harm. I would never condemn innocent men to a watery death. If I did send a rocket toward the deck, it was likely an accident. Given the lurching of the vessel as Captain Cuthie described, I could have easily dropped it unintentionally. Or even accidentally sent it off-course due to the pitch of the ship."

"Bah! It was deliberate!" Cuthie huffed. "Ye came aboard my ship under dubious circumstances. O'course, ye were capable of killing innocent men—"

"What rubbish! Lying about one's gender is not the same as murder," Kieran growled from behind Eilidh.

Massey lurched to his feet. "She's a deceitful witch—"

"Enough!" the Judge Admiral thundered, his voice thunderous. "Sit down, Massey. This is precisely why I read Captain Cuthie's account rather than have you all tell it. No more outbursts or I shall order you to gaol for insubordination."

Massey glowered at Kieran but retook his seat.

Mr. Patterson nudged the paper before the Judge Admiral. "So, what are we to make about this accusation then, my lord? Do we have enough information to make a decision about bringing formal charges against Mrs. MacTavish? Simply having no memory of wishing someone harm does not exonerate her from having aimed a rocket at the ship's deck."

The Judge Admiral stared down at the foolscap.

Eilidh feared for her veins, her pulse pounded so hard.

Massey continued to send Kieran looks that promised reprisal.

Cuthie simply appeared smug, as if he were certain his testimony would condemn her.

The Judge looked over Cuthie's testimony one more time. And then he raised his head, meeting the gaze of Andrew and Alex beyond Eilidh's shoulder.

Eilidh kept her eyes resolutely forward. She would meet her fate head-on.

The Judge Admiral sat back in his chair, tapping his fingers on the desktop.

"Have you ever spent much time aboard a ship, Mr. Patterson?" The Judge Admiral asked, rather conversationally.

"No." Mr. Patterson shook his head.

"For myself, I fought many a battle aboard ship before Trafalgar. I was merely a ship's captain then—not an admiral—but some memories never leave a man." The Judge Admiral shook his head. "I've watched cannon fire rake the side of a ship at close range, and even then, a cannonball will not always penetrate the thick oak boards of a ship's hull. A cannonball will certainly not crash through three levels of decking to reach the ship's steerage where the black powder is kept. That is precisely why it is kept in the bowels of a ship. It's the safest place to be when bullets and cannons fly."

No one said a word.

The faintest glimmer of hope flared to light in Eilidh's chest.

"My point," the Judge Admiral continued, "is that I cannot understand how a firework rocket, shot from thirty feet above deck, would have sufficient power to penetrate that deeply into the ship. Yes, it's a rocket, but it lacks substance. It propels only air. There is no bullet or cannon within it to punch a hole through something. However, a reef strike at precisely the correct angle could easily slice through a ship's hull, ignite black powder, and cause a ship to explode. Based on this, I see no logical reason why the assertion that a firework blew up the ship would be accurate."

Hope exploded through Eilidh's blood, fizzing through her heart and setting her eyes to stinging.

Would she truly be exonerated? Even with Cuthie pointing a gnarled finger at her?

"Now, see here!" Cuthie erupted, jumping from his seat. "Are ye calling me a liar?!" He took a step toward the Judge Admiral.

Instantly, the burly constable was at Cuthie's side, glaring down at the captain.

"I suggest ye sit back down," the man said.

Cuthie, of course, did not sit.

Nor did he back down.

"I know what I saw," he spat, face bright red. "I willnae be gainsaid by some lordling sitting behind a desk—"

"I am an admiral of His Majesty's Navy, Captain," the Judge Admiral's voice cracked through the room. "I have seen more of war and combat on the open seas than one such as yourself could ever imagine—"

"Ye impugn my honor as a seaman!"

"—and I know what brings down a ship. That's why I'm here, listening to these arguments. Regardless of what you *thought* you saw, a firework shot down from the top of the foremast would not have the power to penetrate through three levels of thick, oak decking to ignite gunpowder in the hold. The very idea is absurd."

"Liar!" Cuthie lunged for the Judge Admiral, reaching across the man's desk.

But the constable reached Cuthie first, tackling the captain to the ground.

Eilidh shrieked and jumped out of the way. Kieran's arms were instantly around her, pushing her behind him.

The constable had a knee between Cuthie's shoulder blades, pinning the older man to the floor with one arm wrenched behind his back. Cuthie swore and fought the constable's hold.

"Right, then." The Judge Admiral glared down at Cuthie and then lifted his gaze to Massey. "Do you have anything you wish to say?"

Massey shook his head, palms out.

The Judge Admiral snapped his fingers at Cuthie. "Take him away, Constable. He'll answer before a magistrate for this attempted assault upon my person."

Eilidh pressed closer to Kieran, threading her fingers through his.

Cuthie struggled and fought, but the constable handily dragged him from the room. Massey watched the whole scene, face pale.

The door shut with a hard *clack*.

Eilidh pulled back and looked at Kieran, the hope blazing in his eyes. A glance around the room showed a similar expression on each member of the Brotherhood.

Was this truly how the saga would end? Cuthie hauled off to gaol and her, free to go?

She could scarcely countenance it.

The Judge Admiral tugged on his waistcoat and motioned for everyone to be seated once more.

"As I was saying," he said, "it is my expert opinion that a reef strike caused the explosion of *The Minerva. Not* Mrs. MacTavish's actions. First, the very laws of physics contradict it. Second, Mrs. MacTavish was up the mast, risking life and limb to save the ship. Why would she then turn around and attempt to destroy the ship? She would not. No. None of this adds up." The man shifted his gaze to Eilidh. "Based on all of that, I hereby decree that Mrs. MacTavish was in no way responsible for the destruction of *The Minerva.* The sinking was a tragic accident, nothing more."

An exhilarated sigh swept through the room. Ewan muttered "Hallelujah!" behind her.

"Thank ye," Eilidh whispered, tears choking her.

"You must be relieved, madam." He smiled.

She nodded.

"I say, this comes as a relief to myself, as well," the Judge Admiral continued, sparing another glance for Andrew and Alex. "I was not eager to prosecute you."

"So . . ." Kieran said from behind her. "Is my wife free to go?"

Mr. Patterson scowled. "There is still the matter of Mrs. MacTavish's impersonation of her brother."

The Judge Admiral smiled. "Given the heroics that Mrs. MacTavish went to in an attempt to save *The Minerva,* I feel inclined to be lenient."

"Perhaps, but sir—"

"Enough, Mr. Patterson. If Mrs. MacTavish will swear to cease using her brother's name—Jamie Fyffe—then I will consider the matter closed." The Judge Admiral turned to her, darting a rather mischievous look at Kieran. "Though I think the point is moot, as Miss Fyffe would be known as Jamie MacTavish now."

Eilidh met the Judge Admiral's gaze, wiping a tear from her cheek. "Absolutely. I swear to never again claim the name Jamie Fyffe as my own."

The Judge Admiral nodded and rose from his seat. "Then I declare the investigation into the sinking of *The Minerva* closed, once and forever."

A sigh of relief swept through the room.

Alex clapped.

Ewan chuckled and patted Rafe's back.

Andrew whooped.

But Eilidh had already buried her face in Kieran's shoulder, sobbing her happy relief.

EPILOGUE

ONE YEAR LATER

Eilidh smiled as she stepped on deck, the sun and sea air delivering a delicious double-punch to her senses.

The sails snapped in the warm breeze. A sailor called from high in the rigging. Someone else answered from below.

She crossed to the railing and looked out.

In the distance, Sydney Harbor was just coming into view, the windows of the Custom's House gleaming in the sunlight.

It felt a bit like a homecoming.

"There is my wife," a voice reached her from behind.

Eilidh turned as Kieran stopped at the rail beside her.

"Husband." She gave him a doting look, noting for easily the millionth time that her husband was a devilishly handsome man. "Or rather, Captain MacTavish."

Kieran slipped his hand into hers, smiling down at her. The look in his eyes said he wished they were below deck in their cabin or some other private place where he could lift her against his body and press a scandalous kiss to her mouth.

But as it was, he was the ship's captain and needed to maintain propriety.

So for now, he settled for holding her hand.

"Are ye excited tae see Sydney again?" he asked.

"Of course. It will always be special to me. It holds beautiful memories. Did ye settle the matter with the cargo?"

"Aye."

This was their first long trip with Kieran as captain.

In the end, they had decided to accept command of one of Andrew's ships instead of managing the entire fleet.

Or . . . more like 'avoided managing the whole fleet for a wee while,' as Andrew had put it.

Kieran had wanted to return to sea, and Eilidh liked the idea of another voyage. As they had no children as of yet, such a journey made sense.

But this voyage was nothing like their first one together.

For one thing, Captain Cuthie was no longer a threat of any sort. He had been sentenced to five years hard labor for openly attacking the Judge Admiral.

For another, Eilidh was aboard ship openly as Kieran's wife.

And yet another, she wore dresses and acted (more or less) like a lady this time around. She was still Eilidh, preferring to go by the name her mother had given her at birth.

Some aspects of being Jamie were forever a part of her, like her courage and risk-taking. But others she had shed, like her younger impulsiveness and resistance to discussing problems. She was not entirely Jamie or Eilidh, but somewhere in between. A woman who was more whole, more complete.

Alex had encouraged her to continue to talk through her memories with Kieran as a way of easing their hold on her. The advice had been helpful and as the months passed, the darkness and grief of her past had lifted. She was healing, slowly but surely.

Moments like this—holding Kieran's hand, a fresh sea breeze tugging at her bonnet, a new land before her to explore—helped.

"Remember our promise to one another?" Eilidh asked him.

"Which one, lass?" Kieran grinned. "I've promised ye a great many things. I've made ye my wife *three* times now."

Eilidh smiled in return.

He wasn't wrong.

After handfasting twice—once in Sydney and once in the gardens of Kilmeny Hall—Kieran had wanted to say their vows before God, as well.

"Never again will anyone doubt that I'm your husband," he had sworn.

She agreed wholeheartedly.

Therefore two months after their handfasting at Kilmeny, they stood before a vicar—the marriage banns having been read three weeks in a row beforehand—and pledged their vows before God.

"I am decidedly your wife, thrice over," Eilidh laughed. "I was referring to the promise of what usually comes *after* marriage."

Kieran wiggled his eyebrows at her, gaze going hungry and eager. "What are ye proposing, wife?"

She laughed harder. "You're impossible."

"Handsome," he corrected. "Ye meant tae say I'm handsome and irresistible, and ye cannae keep your hands off my person."

"Yes, well, that may be true." She took his hand and placed it over her flat stomach. "What do you think? Should we attempt this again?"

Nearly a year had passed without any hint of pregnancy. They had both begun to worry that perhaps Eilidh's prior miscarriage had damaged her in some way. Alex said that infertility was possible after losing a child as she had.

Eilidh and Kieran had weathered the lack of a child together, moving on with their plans regardless.

But now . . .

Kieran froze, his hand atop her still flat stomach, expression almost comically shocked.

"Are ye . . ." He stopped. Swallowed. "Are ye saying what I think ye are, lass?"

Eilidh nodded, partially mortified to realize her eyes had filled with tears. "But we promised we would stop sailing once a bairn came along, and I know how much ye love being at sea . . ."

"Ah, lass." Kieran grinned, his own eyes suspiciously bright. "I have only ever wanted tae be where yourself and our children are. I'm truly going tae be a father? In earnest?"

She nodded again, her smile so wide it hurt her cheeks.

He whooped, a roaring burst of sound.

Kieran swept Eilidh into his arms, spinning her around, before returning her feet to the decking and bestowing a long, lusty kiss to her lips.

The sort of kiss that curled her toes and set their fellow sailors to calling lewd jests and assured Eilidh that she was, indeed, the luckiest woman alive.

Six years later

"HE ALWAYS WINS," Alex was saying. "Every time. Every year."

"Och, your competitive side is showing again, Alex," Andrew snorted.

"Besides, Ewan cannae help winning," Kieran said. "He's the winningest person I've ever known."

"I don't think *winningest* is a word, Kieran," Rafe pointed out, most unhelpfully, per Kieran's point of view.

They were seated on the back lawn of Andrew's estate, Muirford House, for their annual gathering of the Brotherhood of the Black Tartan.

Initially, they had met in March on the anniversary of Jamie's abduction. But as their families had grown, it made more sense to gather in late summer, when the sun was high in the sky and the warm days allowed the children to expend excess energy chasing one another around the gardens.

Today, the men were outside, keeping a general eye on the mayhem (though nursemaids and the odd governess hovered nearby). Their lady wives had retired to the drawing room to swap stories, eat some of Cook's excellent scones, and escape the whoops and shrieks of their combined children for a blissful hour.

Kieran shielded the sun with his hand and looked at Alex, Andrew, and Rafe.

"Of course, Ewan is the *winningest.* How else do ye describe a man who has never lost?" Kieran asked. "His paintings win award after award every year. He never lost a boxing match. And let's not start on the Highland games."

"Maybe . . . Ewan is the most *victorious*?" Rafe offered.

"Och, I don't care what he is," Alex scoffed. "The man just has tae give the rest of us a chance to win sometimes."

Kieran shook his head. "You're just sore because he bested us all in that tug-of-war yesterday."

"We almost had him," Alex grumbled.

"Aye, we did," Andrew agreed, mournfully.

"We'll never win against him. I've accepted my lot," Kieran grinned.

"Besides," Rafe added, "Ewan always wins with grace."

"Aye, though I don't think Ewan is winning at the moment." Andrew pointed across the lawn.

They all turned their heads to watch Ewan drinking tea with his second-to-oldest daughter, Lady Lily. The poor man had scrunched his massive body down, down, down onto an impossibly tiny chair that looked one hasty movement away from collapsing altogether.

Though drinking the tea proved challenging for other reasons, Kieran supposed.

In addition to the teacup, Ewan balanced his twin toddler girls on each knee, while fending off his middle daughter, Lady Fleur, who was presently clinging to his back like a monkey.

Lily was overseeing the wee tea table which had actual china teacups, a teapot, and most importantly, plates with real biscuits upon them. Lady Gabriella, Alex's oldest daughter, assisted, her blond curls gleaming in the sunlight.

Ewan's twins kept reaching for the biscuits, forcing Ewan to grab for their hands. But as was the way with toddlers, the twins were tenacious, squirming and evading their papa's efforts.

Lily's scolding voice reached the men.

"No, Papa, the twins can't have the shortbread. Cook promised them all to me and Gabby!"

Lady Dahlia sat across from her father, watching over the whole with a serious expression, the soft breeze tugging at her red hair.

"Mamma will make you share your biscuits, Lily," she said. "Aren't I right, Papa?"

Ewan didn't answer. He merely scrambled to hold back the twins from toppling the table and then reached a hand out to stop Fleur from falling atop it.

In short, the tea party was a mass of six red heads and one blond one, all jostling for position.

Kieran gave it three minutes before someone devolved into tears.

"Wait until my three hellions realize there are biscuits to be had," Rafe said, shaking his head.

The universe had balanced Ewan's abundance of daughters by gracing Rafe with three sons.

"Where *are* the rest of them?" Alex asked.

A burst of clamor sounded from the sunny, south side of the house. The Brotherhood rotated their heads toward the noise with almost synchronized precision.

Seven little boys and one red-haired tomboy tore across the lawn, racing toward them.

James, Kieran's son.

Andrew's oldest daughter, Isolde, with her two younger brothers.

Rafe's three sons.

And Alex's wee heir, Ian, calling to the older children, "Wait up! Wait up! My legs is too little."

Kieran caught James as he launched himself into his arms.

"Isolde found a snake, Papa!" James said, his voice high and excited. His dark mop of curls and green-gray eyes—so like his mother's—always sent a burst of love through Kieran's chest.

"An adder?" Kieran's brows drew down. Adders were the only snakes in Scotland. They were also, unfortunately, the only venomous animal in all of Britain.

"We were careful," Isolde laughed, wrapping her arms around Andrew's neck and kissing his cheek.

"Yes," Rafe's oldest, John, joined in. "Don't worry. Mamma taught us all about them and how to keep a safe distance. It was just sunning on a log."

"Aye," said his brother, "we left it there."

"I's no touch it," Ian lisped, crawling into Alex's lap.

James twisted in Kieran's arms, looking across the lawn to the tea party.

"Are those biscuits?" he asked.

All seven little heads whipped in choreographed synchronization, mimicking their fathers' only moments before. They were off like launched rockets with cries of "Uncle Ewan!" and "Biscuits!" ringing across the garden.

Poor Ewan disappeared under a pile of children tackling him to the ground and nearly upending the tea table entirely.

Lily and Gabriella initially shrieked in anger. But then decided that jumping atop Ewan as he writhed and tickled the children looked like more fun than a stuffy old tea party anyway.

And for a moment, it seemed as if the combined might of fifteen children might keep Ewan down.

But Kieran merely counted to ten and sure enough, Ewan rose—gently, carefully—from their mass of bodies, a twin clutched under each arm, the rest of the children clinging to him like barnacles.

With a roar of laughter, Ewan looked at his friends where they lounged comfortably in their chairs and slowly started to walk toward them, carrying all the children with him.

"See." Alex pointed toward Ewan. "He always wins."

"The winningest," Kieran agreed with a chuckle.

LATER THAT EVENING, after all the children had been put to bed and the staff had retired for the day, the five couples gathered in the drawing room.

"I think I'm fair knackered," Kieran sighed.

"How so?" Ewan asked, a sandwich in his hand.

"Aye," Alex chuckled, nodding toward Ewan. "Ye didnae fend off the exhausting weight of all our progeny today."

"I'm tired just *thinking* upon it," Kieran amended, cuddling Eilidh against his side on the sofa.

Andrew snorted and passed around a decanter of his finest whisky, his Jane joining the men in pouring some into her tumbler.

Alex, of course, sipped tea. His wife, Lottie, joined him in a show of solidarity.

Rafe sat in a wingback chair, pulling his wife, Sophie, onto his lap.

Ewan was still eating a roast beef sandwich, Violet tucked against his side.

"What shall we drink to tonight?" Andrew asked, lifting his glass.

"To the simple pleasure of us all being here together?" Ewan said.

"To the continued health of your financial ventures?" Kieran suggested.

"I say we drink to our Jamie's safe delivery," Alex said, looking pointedly at Eilidh.

Though Kieran called her Eilidh, to the rest of the Brotherhood, she would always be Jamie.

Kieran smiled and pulled Eilidh tighter against him. It was a bit of a struggle with her rounded belly between them.

He placed a hand on her stomach, waiting to feel their bairn kick.

Kieran feared his heart would burst.

Five years ago, he and Eilidh had returned to Scotland just in time for James's birth. Kieran had taken on managing Andrew's fleet of ships and even investing in Andrew's ventures.

Their finances had blossomed, as a result.

But their family had not.

No more children had been forthcoming.

Until now.

Seeing his lovely wife rounded once more with his child filled Kieran with almost unfathomable joy.

"Aye," Eilidh replied. "Let's drink to not only the safe delivery of this babe." She rested a hand atop her belly and reached for her own cup of tea. "But also to us all. To the sheer wonder that is these gatherings. We are here. We are together. We are blessed beyond measure. Let us never forget it."

Kieran raised his glass. "*Slàinte mhath.*"

To your health.

To a person, each raised the glass in their hand, giving the traditional response.

"*Slàinte*!"

AUTHOR'S NOTE

I always love including some author notes at the end of my books, and this book is no exception. As usual, writing a Regency-era romance is an endless mix of historical fact and imaginative adaptation. I will attempt to separate the two for you here (and, yes, there are a few spoilers in here if you haven't finished the novel yet).

First off, let's start with the obvious: Eilidh/Jamie's memory loss. I knew very early on in the series that Jamie would lose her memories and that the final book would be her remembering Kieran and their love story. Initially, I wanted her memory loss to be very believable from a medical standpoint. That moment when memories come tumbling back for a character (something regularly fictionalized in books and movies), I knew to be a myth. Memories don't ever return like that in real life. Therefore, I spent a lot of time researching different kinds of brain injuries and how they would impact memory. I learned that memory loss is very individual to each patient and, quite frequently, permanent.

Therefore, my preliminary outlines of *Remembering Jamie* had Eilidh/ Jamie slowly regaining a few memories, but never really remembering Kieran and their past together. However in early plot discussions, a friend pointed out that a reader would prefer to have the *ka-pow!* moment of Jamie remembering her love for Kieran over some stodgy nod to medical accuracy, particularly as the trope of instant memory recall is well-worn.

Sigh.

So, I abandoned my plan of medical accuracy and, instead, focused more on PTSD memory loss (also a thing) as the reason for Jamie's missing memories. My research did turn up the fact that memory loss can often be bracketed by traumatic events. So for Jamie, I postulated that the similar, harrowing deaths of her brother and Mr. Chen—experienced a year apart—were triggering events and, along with her head injury and the grief of her miscarriage, caused her to experience PTSD that effectively wiped out her memories between the two events. Therefore, she could regain the emotionally blocked memories in a lump, but the memory loss due to her head injury (the month before the ship sank) would never return. It's weak medically, I acknowledge, but it was a good compromise between believability and dramatic plotting.

Along with that, I endeavored to handle the subject of miscarriage and the loss of a child with sensitivity and care. If you were keeping track of the dates, Jamie would have been around 16-20 weeks pregnant when she miscarried/lost her baby. As a woman who has struggled with infertility and suffered at least six miscarriages myself, I understand the grief of it all too well. The pain of miscarriage is often worse because it's hidden and carried in silence. To all the women out there who have similarly suffered, know that you are seen.

Fireworks, of course, have a long history in China, as well as Europe. In fact, Vauxhall Gardens in London would do a fireworks display nearly every evening during the Regency era, kind of like Disneyland does today. However, fireworks were only orange and yellow until the mid-1800s when chemists figured out how to add other elements to create different colors.

Handfasting is an ancient practice, likely Celtic pagan in origin. In England, handfasting historically referred to a period of engagement before the actual church ceremony. In Scotland, however, handfasting when properly witnessed was viewed as a legal marriage (recognized civilly, though not religiously). It was a prevalent form of marriage in the Highlands and Western Isles for hundreds (if not thousands) of years. The ceremony was simple. The couple would plight their troth and a witness would tie their hands together with a knot (hence *handfasting*), symbolizing the couple's commitment to bind their lives together. From there, a signed statement of the couple's vows was then submitted to the sheriff (not *sheriff* in the American, law-enforcement sense of the word, but more like the governor of an area, like the Sheriff of Nottingham in *Robin Hood*) and the marriage was recorded as legally occurring.

Women were regularly seen aboard ships, historically, both as wives and even as crew members. I based the idea for Jamie off of that of Mary Lacy and her autobiography, *The Female Shipwright*, which was widely circulated at the end of the 18th century. There are numerous tales of women taking to the sea disguised as boys.

Also, I chose to use the more modern meaning of a *ceilidh* (yes, pronounced similarly to *Eilidh*—KAY-lee), as well as modern dance names like Strip the Willow. Historically, the steps would have been called beforehand and not codified and named as they are today. But having to explain all that for the occasional modern reader who understands what a modern ceilidh is . . . well, it felt a bit pedantic.

I owe an enormous debt of gratitude to Amy McGregor for helping me suss out all the Scottish legal issues/terminology. It's helpful that the Scottish courts haven't changed all that much in 200 years, but as Scotland's maritime courts were subsumed into the Court of Session in 1832, I was also extrapolating based on the information I could find. So if there are errors, I apologize.

I know I've mentioned this before, but for those reading one of my Scottish books for the first time, allow me to also comment on Scottish language and pronunciation. It's always a struggle to know how to write an accent, particularly in a historical novel. Scotland today recognizes three distinct languages: Scottish Gaelic, Scots, and English. Historically, Scottish Gaelic has been spoken in the Highlands. Most Lowland Scots in the early 1800s (i.e. those from Glasgow and Edinburgh) would have spoken a mix of Scots and English. (Sidenote: If you want to read some Scots, Wikipedia actually has an entire dictionary written in Scots—sco.wikipedia.org.)

Of course, I realized fairly quickly that a modern, primarily American, audience would struggle to understand Scots.

So, what to do?

After much consideration, I decided to go with a slightly more modern Scottish accent and syntax, simply to aid readability. I write novels, after all, not history texts. I've used modern spellings of Scottish pronunciations and, even then, restricted myself to a few key words to give a Scottish flavor to the text. So at times, the accent as written is not perfectly consistent; this was done to help readability. That said, I have continued to use more common Scots words wherever possible—e.g. *ken/kens/kent* (think, know), *eejit* (idiot), *glaikit* (foolish), *muckle* (enormous), *youse* (you all), *greit/gree*t (to weep), etc.

I have created an extensive pinboard on Pinterest with images of things I talk about in the book. So if you want a visual of anything—including gorse, puffins, the coast north of Aberdeen, etc.—pop over there and explore. Just search for NicholeVan.

As with all books, this one couldn't have been written without the help and support from those around me. I know I am going to leave someone out with all these thanks. So to that person, know that I totally love you and am so deeply grateful for your help!

To my beta readers—you know who you are—thank you for your editing suggestions, helpful ideas, and support. And, again, an extra-large thank you to Rebecca Spencer, Annette Evans, and Norma Melzer for their fantastic editing skills.

I have to give an enormous shout out to Shannon Castleton. As I've said over and over, your comments and suggestions are like Shannon Unicorn Sprinkles™ throughout my manuscript. Bless you, my friend!

Erin Rodabough also deserves another round of applause for her endless help. Thank you for being my writing *and* travel buddy.

Finally, thank you to Andrew, Austenne, Kian, and Dave for your endless patience and support.

And to all my readers, thank you for continuing to read and recommend my work!

Reading Group Questions

Yes, there are reading group questions. I suggest discussing them over lots of excellent chocolate (solid, liquid, frozen, cake . . . I'm not picky about the precise state of matter of said chocolate; chocolate in any form is good chocolate).

1. Why do you think this book was titled Remembering Jamie? How did you see the author playing on the idea of remembering and memory throughout the book?

2. How did you feel about the name Eilidh (AY-lee, rhymes with daily, bailey, etc)? It's weird to look at and is pronounced nothing like it's spelled. Was that off-putting to you as a reader? Did you want her to lose the weird name and become Jamie again?

3. The book deals with themes of self-identity. How much of our innate self do you feel is biologically fixed? How much comes from our lived experiences and memories?

4. Would you love someone enough to let them go if you had to? Is that truly a deep love?

5. Did you want Captain Cuthie to get more of a comeuppance at the end? Did you feel that the ending was satisfying?

6. Clearly, this book contains a lot of information about Scotland and Scottish culture. Did you learn something new or unexpected? If so, what was it?

Other Books by Nichole Van

THE PENN-LEITHS OF THISTLE MUIR

Love Practically (January 2022)
Adjacent But Only Just (May 2022)
Just One Kiss (Autumn 2022)

BROTHERHOOD OF THE BLACK TARTAN

Suffering the Scot
Romancing the Rake
Loving a Lady
Making the Marquess
Remembering Jamie

OTHER REGENCY ROMANCES

Seeing Miss Heartstone
Vingt-et-Un | Twenty-one (a novella included in *Falling for a Duke.*)
A Ring of Gold (a novella included in *A Note of Change.*)

BROTHERS *MALEDETTI* SERIES

Lovers and Madmen
Gladly Beyond
Love's Shadow
Lightning Struck
A Madness Most Discreet

THE HOUSE OF OAK SERIES

Intertwine
Divine
Clandestine
Refine
Outshine

If you haven't yet read *Seeing Miss Heartstone*,
please turn the page for a preview of this
Whitney Award Winner for Best Historical Romance 2018.

Seeing Miss Heartstone

. . . My lord, news of your current financial pressures has reached many ears. I know of an interested party who would be honored to discuss a proposed joint venture. They have asked to meet you along the Long Water in Hyde Park tomorrow morning, where they shall endeavor to lay out the particulars of their proposal . . .

—excerpt from an unsigned letter posted to Lord Blake

In retrospect, Miss Arabella Heartstone had three regrets about 'The Incident.'

She should not have worn her green, wool cloak with the fox fur collar, as Hyde Park was warmer than expected that morning.

She should not have instructed her chaperone, Miss Anne Rutger, to remain politely out of earshot.

And she probably should *not* have proposed marriage to the Marquess of Blake.

"P-pardon?" Lord Blake lifted a quizzical eyebrow, standing straight and tall, rimmed in the morning sunlight bouncing off the Long Water behind him. A gentle breeze wound through the surrounding trees, rustling newly-grown, green leaves. "Would . . . would you mind repeating that last phrase? I fear I did not hear you correctly."

Belle straightened her shoulders, clasped her trembling hands together, and sternly ordered her thumping heart to *Cease this racket.*

Swallowing, she restated her request. "After much consideration, my lord, I feel a marriage between you and myself would be prudent."

Lord Blake stared at her, blinking over and over. Belle was unsure if his reaction denoted surprise or was simply the result of the dazzling sunlight off the water behind her.

Silence.

Birds twittered. Branches creaked. Leaves rustled.

Eternities passed. Millennia ended and were reborn.

Belle gritted her teeth, desperate to bolster her flagging confidence. *You are strong and courageous. You can do this.*

In the past, her passivity over the Marriage Matter had nearly ended in disaster. So, Belle had set her sights on a more forthright course—propose marriage herself. Yes, she struggled to talk with people and preferred anonymity to attention, but her current situation was critical.

She needed a husband. Decidedly. Desperately. Immediately. As in . . . yesterday would not have been soon enough.

At the moment, however, her mental encouragement barely managed to convince the swarming butterflies in her stomach to not free her breakfast along with themselves. Casting up her accounts all over his lordship's dusty Hessian boots would hardly nurture his romantic interest.

At last, Lord Blake stirred, pulling a folded letter from his overcoat. He stared at it, eyebrows drawing down, a sharp "V" appearing above his nose.

"You sent me this message, asking to meet me here?" He flapped the letter in her direction.

"Yes." Belle bit down on her lip and darted a glance behind at her companion. Miss Rutger stood a solid thirty yards off, studiously facing the Long Water. "Well . . . uhm . . . in all truthfulness, Miss Rutger wrote the letter."

Lord Blake raised his eyebrows, clearly uncaring of the minutiae involved. "So you are *not* a gentleman interested in my business venture in the East Indies?" He unfolded the letter, reading from it. "'*I know of an interested party who would be honored to discuss a proposed joint venture. They have asked to meet you along the Long Water,*' et cetera. This 'interested party' is yourself?" He returned the letter to his pocket.

"Yes, my lord." Belle commanded her feet to hold still and not bounce up and down—the bouncing being yet another effect of those dratted nervous butterflies.

Lord Blake's brows rose further. "And you are offering . . . marriage?"

"Yes, my lord," Belle repeated, but she had to clarify the point. Apparently, she had no issue with being thought forward and brazen, but heaven forbid Lord Blake imagine her a liar, too. "Though . . . I *am* proposing a joint endeavor."

"Indeed," he paused. "Marriage usually implies as much."

Lord Blake shuffled a Hessian-booted foot and clasped his hands behind his back. A corner of his mouth twitched.

Was the man . . . amused? If so, was that good? Or bad?

And at this point, did it matter?

Belle soldiered on. "There would be significant advantages to both of us with such a match."

More silence. An errant draft of wind tugged at his coat.

"You have me at a disadvantage, Miss . . ." His voice trailed off.

"Heartstone. Miss Arabella Heartstone."

"I see." He removed his hat and slapped it against his thigh. "And why have we not met in more . . . uh . . . typical circumstances? A ball, perhaps? A dinner party where we could be properly introduced and engage in conversation about the weather and the latest bonnet fashions before leaping straight to marriage?"

"Oh." It was Belle's turn to blink, absorbing his words. *Oh dear.* "We *have* met, my lord. We were introduced at Lord Pemberley's musicale last month. We did discuss the weather, but not bonnets or . . . uhm . . . marriage."

She hadn't expected him to recall everything, but to not even *recognize* her? To not remember their brief conversation—

"How do you do, Miss Heartstone? It's a pleasure to make your acquaintance." Lord Blake bowed.

"The pleasure is all mine, my lord." Belle curtsied. "Lovely weather we're having."

"Indeed, we are."

It did not bode well.

The butterflies rushed upward, eager for escape.

"Right." Blake let out a gusting breath and shook his head, sending his hair tumbling across his forehead. The morning sun turned it into molten shades of deep amber, curling softly over his ears.

Lean and several inches taller than her own average height, Lord Blake was not classically handsome, she supposed. His straight nose, square jaw, and high forehead were all too exaggerated for classical handsomeness.

And yet, something about him tugged at her. Perhaps it was the breadth of his shoulders filling out his coat. Or maybe it was the ease of his stance, as if he would face the jaws of Hell itself with a sardonic smile and casual *sang-froid*. Or maybe it was the way he ran a gloved hand through his hair, taking it from fashionably tousled to deliciously rumpled.

Mmmmm.

Belle was going to side with the hair. Though sardonic smiles were a close second.

Regardless, her decision to offer marriage to him had not been based on his physical appearance. She was many things, but *flighty* and *shallow* were two words that had never been attached to her.

Replacing his hat, Lord Blake studied her, blue eyes twinkling.

Yes. Definitely amused.

That was . . . encouraging? Having never proposed marriage to a man before, Belle was unsure.

"Enlighten me, if you would be so kind, as to the particular reasons why you think this . . . joint endeavor . . . would be profitable." He gestured toward her.

Oh! Excellent.

That she had come prepared to do.

With a curt nod, she pulled a paper from her reticule.

"A list?" His lips twitched again.

"I am nothing if not thorough in my planning, my lord." She opened the paper with shaking fingers, her hands clammy inside her gloves.

"Of course. I should have expected as much. You arranged this meeting, after all." He tapped the letter in his pocket.

Belle chose to ignore the wry humor in his tone and merely nodded her head in agreement. "Allow me to proceed with my list. Though please forgive me if my reasons appear forward."

"You have just proposed marriage to a peer of the realm, madam. I cannot imagine anything you say from this point onward will trump that."

"True."

A beat.

Lord Blake pinned her with his gaze—calm and guileless. The forthright look of a man who knew himself and would never be less-than-true to his own values.

His gaze upset her breathing, causing something to catch in her throat.

Belle broke eye-contact, swallowing too loudly.

"Allow me to begin." She snapped the paper in her hand. The words swam in her vision, but she knew them by heart. The paper was more for show than anything else. She had done her calculations most carefully.

Taking a fortifying breath, Belle began, "Firstly, you have newly inherited the Marquisate of Blake from a cousin. Your cousin was somewhat imprudent in his spending habits—"

"I would declare the man to be an utter scapegrace and wastrel, but continue."

"Regardless of the cause, your lands and estates are in dire need of resuscitation." Belle glanced at him over the top of her paper. "You are basically without funds, my lord."

"As my solicitor repeatedly reminds me." He shot her an arch look. "It is why I am trying to fund a business venture in connection with the East India Company, as you are also undoubtedly aware."

"Yes, my lord. That is why I am proposing an enterprise of a slightly different sort. Allow me to continue." Belle cleared her throat, looking down to her paper. "My own family is genteel with connections to the upper aristocracy—my great-great grandfather was the Earl of Stratton—though we have no proper title of our own, leaving my father to make his own way in the world. I, as you might already know, am a considerable heiress. My father was a prominent banker and left the entirety of his estate to me upon his death three years past."

Belle clenched her jaw against the familiar sting in her throat.

Blink, blink, blink.

Now was *not* the time to dwell upon her father.

"Are you indeed?" he asked. "Though I do not wish to sound crass, I feel we left polite discussion in the dust several minutes ago, so I must enquire: How much of an heiress are you, precisely?"

Did she hear keen interest in his tone? Or was Lord Blake simply exceedingly polite?

"I believe the current amount stands somewhere in the region of eighty thousand pounds, my lord," she replied.

Lord Blake froze at that staggering number, just as Belle had predicted he would.

"Eighty thousand pounds, you say? That is a dowry of marquess-saving proportions."

"My thoughts precisely, my lord."

Her father had originally left her a healthy sixty thousand pounds, but she was nothing if not her father's daughter. Numbers and statistics flowed through her brain, a constant rushing river. She had used these skills to grow her fortune.

It was what her father would have wanted. Refusing to see her gender as a barrier, her father had taught his only child everything he knew—financial systems, probabilities, market shares—even soliciting her opinions during that last year before his death.

By the age of sixteen, Belle understood more about supply-and-demand and the mathematics of economics than most noblemen. Knowing this, the conditions in her father's will allowed her to continue to oversee her own interests with the help of his solicitor, Mr. Sloan. At only nineteen years of age, she currently managed a thriving financial empire.

She could hear her father's gruff voice, his hand gently lifting her chin. *I would give you choices, my Little Heart Full. A lady should always have options. I would see you happy.*

Belle swallowed back the painful tightness in her throat.

Now, if she could only land a husband and free herself from the guardianship of her uncle and mother.

Family, it turned out, were not quite as simple to manage as corn shares.

Her mother, hungry for a title for her daughter, was becoming increasingly bold in her attempts to get Belle married. She had all but forced Belle to betroth herself to a cold, aloof viscount the previous Season. Fortunately, the viscount—Lord Linwood—had asked to be released from their betrothal.

But the entire situation had left Belle feeling helpless.

She *detested* feeling helpless, she realized. And so she used that unwelcome sensation to suppress her inherent shyness and overcome her retiring personality.

Belle would solve the husband problem herself. She simply needed to reduce the entire situation to a statistical probability and face it as she would any other business transaction.

"Eighty-thousand pounds," Lord Blake repeated. "Are husbands—particularly the marquess variety—generally so costly?" He clasped his hands behind his back, studying her. "I had not thought to price them before this."

"I cannot say. This is my first venture into, uhmm . . ."

"Purchasing a husband?" he supplied, eyes wide.

Heavens. Was that a hint of displeasure creeping into his voice?

"I am not entirely sure I agree with the word *purchase*, my lord—"

"True. It does smack of trade and all polite society knows we cannot have *that*."

A pause.

"Shall we use the word *negotiate* instead?" she asked.

He cocked his head, considering. "I daresay that would be better. So I receive a sultan's ransom and your lovely self, and you receive . . ." His words drifted off.

"A husband. And in the process, I become Lady Blake, a peeress of the realm."

"Are you truly so hungry to be a marchioness? Surely eighty thousand pounds could purchase—forgive me, *negotiate*—the title of duchess." His words so very, very dry.

"I am sure my mother would agree with you, my lord, but I am more interested in finding a balance between title and the proper gentleman." She cleared her throat. "You come highly recommended."

"Do I?" Again, his tone darkly sardonic.

Oh, dear.

But as she was already in for more than a penny, why not aim for the whole pound?

"I did not arrive at the decision to propose marriage lightly. I had my solicitor hire a Runner to investigate you. I have armed myself with information, my lord."

Belle wisely did not add that, after crunching all the statistical probabilities, Lord Blake had been by far and away her preferred candidate. She was quite sure that, like most people, he would not appreciate being reduced to a number.

"Information? About me?" he asked.

"Yes. For example, I know you recently cashed out of the army, selling the officer's commission you inherited from your father. All those who served with you report you to be an honest and worthy commander—"

"As well they should."

"Additionally, you are a kind son to your mother. You send her and your stepfather funds when you are able. You visit regularly. Your four older sisters dote upon you, and you are godfather to at least one of each of their children. You are a tremendous favorite with all of your nieces and nephews. All of this speaks highly to the kind of husband and father you would be."

After her disastrous betrothal to Lord Linwood last year, Belle was determined to not make the same error twice. She learned from her mistakes. Her mother and uncle would not browbeat her into accepting one of their suitors again.

If nothing else, eighty thousand pounds should purchase—*negotiate*—her a *kindhearted* husband of her own choice.

Lord Blake shuffled his feet. "I-I really am at a loss for words, Miss Heartstone. I am trying to decide if I should be flattered or utterly appalled."

Belle sucked in a deep breath, her mouth as dry as the Sahara.

Stay strong. Argue your case.

She pasted a strained smile on her face. "Might I suggest siding with flattery, my lord?"

Visit www.NicholeVan.com to buy your copy of *Seeing Miss Heartstone* today and continue the story.

ABOUT THE AUTHOR

THE SHORT VERSION:

NICHOLE VAN IS a writer, photographer, designer and generally disorganized crazy person. Though originally from Utah, she currently lives on the coast of Scotland with three similarly crazy children and one sane, very patient husband who puts up with all of them. In her free time, she enjoys long walks along the Scottish lochs and braes. She does not, however, enjoy haggis.

THE LONG OVERACHIEVER VERSION:

AN INTERNATIONAL BESTSELLING author, Nichole Van is an artist who feels life is too short to only have one obsession. In former lives, she has been a contemporary dancer, pianist, art historian, choreographer, culinary artist and English professor.

Most notably, however, Nichole is an acclaimed photographer, winning over thirty international accolades for her work, including Portrait of the Year from WPPI in 2007. (Think Oscars for wedding and portrait photographers.) Her unique photography style has been featured in many magazines, including Rangefinder and Professional Photographer. She is also the creative mind behind the popular website Flourish Emporium which provides resources for photographers.

All that said, Nichole has always been a writer at heart. With an MA in English, she taught technical writing at Brigham Young University for ten years and has written more technical manuals than she can quickly count. She decided in late 2013 to start writing fiction and has since become an Amazon #1 bestselling author. Additionally, she has won a RONE award, as well as been a Whitney Award Finalist several years running. Her late 2018 release, *Seeing Miss Heartstone*, won the Whitney Award Winner for Best Historical Romance.

In February 2017, Nichole, her husband and three crazy children moved from the Rocky Mountains in the USA to Scotland. They currently live near the coast of eastern Scotland in an eighteenth century country house. Nichole loves her pastoral country views while writing and enjoys long walks through fields and along beaches. She does not, however, have a fondness for haggis.

She is known as NicholeVan all over the web: Facebook, Instagram, Pinterest, etc. Visit http://www.NicholeVan.com to sign up for her author newsletter and be notified of new book releases.

If you enjoyed this book, please leave a short review on Amazon.com. Wonderful reviews are the elixir of life for authors. Even better than dark chocolate.

Made in the USA
Monee, IL
17 October 2024